THE BULL FROM THE SEA

Mary Renault

arrow books

Published by Arrow Books in 2004

5 7 9 10 8 6

First published in Great Britain in 1962 by
Longmans, Green and Co.
Random House, 20 Vauxhall Bridge Road,
London SW1V 2SA

www.rbooks.co.uk

Addresses for companies within The Random House Group Limited
can be found at: www.randomhouse.co.uk/offices.htm

The Random House Group Limited Reg. No. 954009

A CIP catalogue record for this book
is available from the British Library

ISBN 9780099463535

The Random House Group Limited supports The Forest Stewardship
Council (FSC), the leading international forest certification organisation.
All our titles that are printed on Greenpeace approved FSC certified paper
carry the FSC logo. Our paper procurement policy can be found at:
www.rbooks.co.uk/environment

Typeset by Palimpsest Book Production Limited,
Polmont, Stirlingshire
Printed and bound in Great Britain by
CPI Cox & Wyman, Reading, RG1 8EX

To J.M. as ever

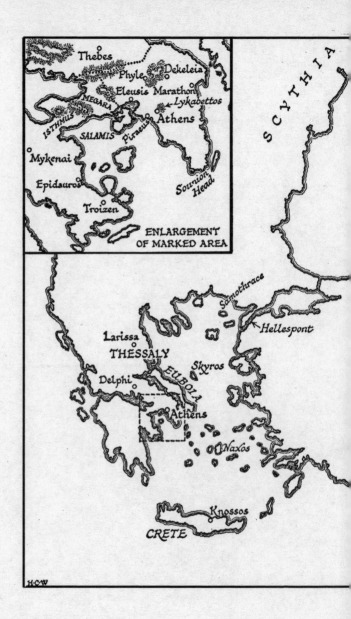

ENLARGEMENT
OF MARKED AREA

Thebes
Phyle   Dekeleia
Eleusis Marathon
MEGARA   Lykabettos
ISTHMUS   Athens
SALAMIS Piraeus
Mykenai
Epidauros
Troizen   Sounion
            Head

SCYTHIA

Samothrace
            Hellespont
Larissa
THESSALY
Delphi   Skyros
         EUBOIA
            Athens
               Naxos

Knossos
CRETE

H·C·W

Mary F⋯nd
St Hug⋯in
1937, sl⋯ee
novels ⋯ar.
In 194⋯It
was he⋯te,
Delos, ⋯nd
Marath⋯of
Ancien⋯

BOOKS BY MARY RENAULT

FICTION

The Alexander Trilogy
Fire From Heaven
The Persian Boy
Funeral Games

The Bull From the Sea
The King Must Die
The Praise Singer
The Last of the Wine
Promise of Love
Kind Are Her Answers
The Middle Mist
Return of Night
North Face
The Charioteer
The Mask of Apollo
The Lion in the Gateway

NONFICTION

The Nature of Alexander

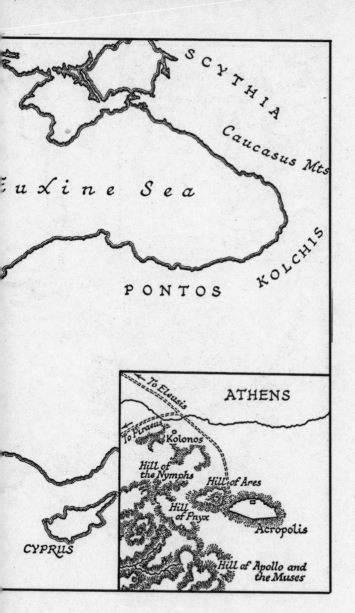

SCYTHIA

Caucasus Mts

Euxine Sea

PONTOS

KOLCHIS

To Eleusis

ATHENS

To Piraeus

Kolonos

Hill of
the Nymphs

Hill of Ares

Hill
of Pnyx

Acropolis

CYPRUS

Hill of Apollo and
the Muses

1

It was dolphin weather, when I sailed into Piraeus with my comrades of the Cretan bull-ring. Knossos had fallen, which time out of mind had ruled the seas. The smoke of the burning Labyrinth still clung to our clothes and hair.

I sprang ashore and grasped both hands full of Attic earth. It stuck to my palms as if it loved me. Then I saw the staring people, not greeting us, but calling each other to see the Cretan strangers.

I looked at my team, the boys and girls of Athens' tribute, carried to Crete to learn the bull-vault and dance for Minotauros on bloody sand. They showed me myself, as I must look to Attic eyes: a bull-dancer of Crete, smooth-shaven, fined down to a whiplash by the training: my waist in a gilded cinch-belt, my silk kilt stitched with peacock eyes, my lids still smudged with kohl; nothing Hellene about me, but my flaxen hair. My necklace and arm-rings were not grave jewels of a kingly house, but the costly gauds of the Bull Court, the gift of sport-loving lords and man-loving ladies to a bull-boy who will go in with the music and fly up with the horns.

Small wonder no one knew me. The bull-ring is a dye that seeps into one's soul. Even till my feet touched Attic soil, the greater part of me had been Theseus the Athenian, team-leader of the Cranes; the odds-on fancy, the back-somersault boy, the first of the bull-leapers. They had painted me on the walls of the Labyrinth, carved me in ivory; there had been little gold Theseuses on the women's bracelets. The ballad-makers had promised themselves and me a thousand years of singing. In these things my pride still lingered. Now it was time to be my father's son.

There were great shouts about us. The crowd had seen who we were. They thronged around calling the news along towards Athens and the Rock, and stretching their eyes at the King's son tricked out like a mountebank. Women screamed out for pity at the scars on my breast and sides from glancing bull-horns. All of us had them. They thought we had been flogged. I saw the faces of my team looking dashed a little, even in the rejoicing. In Crete, all the world had known these for our honours, the badges of fine-cut skill.

I thought of the solemn dirges when I sailed, the tears and rent hair, the keening for me, self-offered scapegoat of the god. All that could not be told broke from me in a laugh; and some old woman kissed me.

In the Bull Court, boys' and girls' voices had never ceased all day. I heard them still. 'Look, we are back! Yes, every one of us, look, there is your son. No, the Cretans will not chase us, there is no Minos now. The House of the Axe has fallen! We fought a great battle there, after the earthquake. Theseus killed the heir, the Minotauros. We are free! And there is no Cretan tribute any more!'

People stared and murmured. It was too great for joy. A world without Crete was a new thing under the sun. Then young men leaped and raised the paean.

I said smiling to the team, 'Suppers at home.' Yet my heart was thinking, 'Leave the tale so, dear comrades of our mystery. You have told them all they will understand; don't cry against the wind.' They chattered on; I could hear it now with an Attic ear, foreign as bird-song. 'We are the Cranes! The Cranes, the Cranes, the first team in the Bull Court. A whole year in the ring, and all alive; the first time in the annals and they go back six hundred years. Theseus did it, he trained us. Theseus is the greatest bull-leaper who ever was in Crete. Even here in Athens, you must have heard of the Cranes!'

The kinsfolk clasped their darlings, shook their heads and stared. Fathers were grabbing my hands and kissing them for bringing their children home. I made some answer. How we had prayed and plotted in the Bull Court to get away! And now, how hard to shed it from us, the doomed and fiery life, the trust stronger than love. It left a raw bleeding wound. A girl was saying to her betrothed, who had hardly known her, 'Rhion, I am a bull-leaper!

I can handstand on the horns. Once I did the back-spring. Look at this jewel; I won a great bet for a prince, and he gave it to me.' I saw his face of horror, and their eyes meeting at a loss. In the Bull Court, life and honour came before boy or girl. I felt it still; to me these slim athletes of my team were beautiful. I saw with the eyes of this fuller's son how free-moving and firm and brown she looked beside the milky maids of Athens. When I thought of all the Cranes had shared, I could have struck the fool and taken her in my arms. But the Bull Court was ashes and blackened stone; the Cranes were out of my hand, my rule was over.

'Find me a black bull-calf,' I told the people. 'I must sacrifice to Poseidon Earth-Shaker, for our safe return. And send a runner to the King my father.'

The calf came meekly, and bowed his head consenting; a good omen which pleased the people. Even at the stroke he scarcely struggled. Yet when he sank down his eyes reproached me like a man's. A strange thing, after his mildness. I dedicated him and poured the blood upon the earth. When I quenched the flames with wine, I prayed, 'Father Poseidon, Lord of Bulls, we have danced for you in your holy place and laid our lives in your hand. You brought us safe home; be good to us still, and hold fast our roof-posts. And for myself, now I am come again to Erechtheus' stronghold, let my arm not fail her. Prosper my father's house; and be it so according to our prayer.'

They cried Amen; but the sound wandered. There was a buzz of news behind. My runner was back, long before he could have reached the Citadel. He came to me slowly; and the people made way for him, drawing aside. I knew then he brought death-tidings. He stood silent before me, but not for long. No news so bad but an Athenian wants to be first with it.

They brought me a horse. Some of my father's barons came down to meet me. As we rode from Piraeus to the Rock, the sounds of joy fell back and I heard the wailing.

On the ramp of the gates where it is too steep to ride, the Palace people stumbled to kiss my hands and the fringe of my Cretan kilt. They had thought me dead, themselves masterless: beggars at best, slaves if they could not get away before the

Pallantids swarmed back to take the kingdom. I said, 'Show me my father.'

The eldest baron said, 'I will see, my lord, if the women have done washing him. He was bloody from the fall.'

He lay in his upper room, on his great bed of cedar, with the red cover lined with wolfskin; he had always felt the cold. They had wrapped him in blue with a gold border; very quiet he lay between the wailing women as they shook their hair and clawed their bosoms. One side of his face was white, the other blue from the rock's bruising. The skull-vault was stove in like a bowl; but they had wrapped a clean cloth round it and straightened his broken limbs.

I stood dry-eyed. I had known him less than half a year, before I went off to Crete. Before he knew who I was, he had tried to poison me in this very room. I bore no malice for it. A battered dead old man; a stranger. The old granddad who reared me, Pittheus of Troizen, was the father of my childhood and my heart. Him I could have wept for. But blood is blood; and you cannot wash out what is written in it.

The blue side of his face looked stern; the white had a little secret smile. At the bed's foot his white boarhound lay chin on paws, and stared at nothing.

I said, 'Who saw him die?'

The dog's ears pricked, and its tail struck the ground softly. The women peeped through their hair; then they screeched louder, and the youngest bared their breasts to pummel them. But old Mykale knelt by the bedpost silent. My father's grandfather had taken her in some ancient war; she was more than fourscore years old. Her monkey-creased black eyes met mine unblinking. I held them; but it was hard to do.

The baron said, 'He was seen by the guard of the northern wall, and by the watchman on the roof. Their witness agrees, that he was alone. They saw him come out on the balcony that stands above the cliff, and step straight up on the balustrade, and lift his arms. Then he sprang outward.'

I looked at the right side of his face, then at the left. But their witness did not agree. I asked, 'When was it?'

He looked away. 'A runner had come from Sounion, with news of a ship passing the headland. "What sail?" he asked. The man answered, "Cretan, my lord. Blue-black, with a bull upon it." He ordered the man to be fed, and then went in. That was our last sight of him living.'

I could tell he knew what he was saying. So I raised my voice for all to hear. 'This will be my grief for ever. Now I remember how he bade me whiten my sail, if I came safe home. I have been a year with the bulls since then, and through the great earthquake, and the burning of the Labyrinth, and war. My sorrow that I forgot.'

An old chamberlain, polished and white as silver, slid out from the press. Some pillars of kings' houses are earthquake-proof; it is their calling. 'My lord, never reproach yourself. He died the Erechthid death. So went King Pandion at his time, from that very place; and King Kekrops from the castle crag at Euboia. The sign of the god was sent him, you may be sure, and your memory slept by the will of heaven.' He gave me a grave silvery smile. 'The Immortals know the scent of the new vintage. They will not let a great wine wait past its best.' At this there was a buzzing, decent and low, but keen as the shouts of warriors at a breach that someone else has made. I saw my father's smile in his new-combed beard. He had ruled a troubled kingdom fifty years; he knew something of men. He looked smaller than when I went away, or perhaps I had grown a little. I said, 'Gentlemen, you have leave.'

They went. The women's eyes moved to me sidelong; I signed them away. But they forgot old Mykale, clutching at the bedpost to ease up from her stiff knees. I went and lifted her, and we looked at one another.

She bobbed, and made to go. I caught her arm, soft loose skin upon brittle bone, and said, 'Did you see it, Mykale?'

Her wrinkles puckered, and she wriggled like a child in trouble. The bone twisted while the slack flesh stayed in my hand. Her skull was pink as chicken-skin through the thin hair. 'Answer me,' I said. 'Did he speak to you?'

'Me?' she said blinking. 'Folks tell me nothing. In King Kekrops' day I was paid more heed to. He told me, when he was called. Whom else, when I was in his bed? "Listen again, Mykale, listen again. Lean down, girl; put your ear to my head. You will hear it like a sounding shell." So I leaned down to please him. But he put me by with the back of his arm, and walked out like a man in thought, straight from his naked bed to the northern rampart, and down without a cry.'

She had been telling this tale for sixty years. But I heard it out. 'So much for Kekrops. But here lies Aigeus dead. Come. What did he say?'

She peered at me: a wise-woman near her end; a withered baby with the ancient House Snake looking from its eyes. Then she blinked, and said she was only a poor old slave-girl whose memory would not hold.

'Mykale!' I said. 'Do you know who I am? Don't fool with me.'

She jumped a little. Then, like an old nurse to a child that stamps his foot at her, 'Oh, aye, I know you, outlandish as you've grown, like some rich lord's minion or a dancing mime. Young Theseus, that he got at Troizen on King Pittheus' girl; the quick lad with the meddling hand. You sent word from Crete by a mountebank, that he should put out his ships against King Minos, and bring you home. A fine taking it put him in. Not many knew what ailed him. But news comes to me.'

I said, 'He had better have sailed than grieved. Crete was falling-ripe and I knew it. I proved it too; so I am here.'

'Trust comes hard, when a man's own brothers have fought him for his birthright. Better he'd trusted Apollo's oracle, before he loosed your mother's girdle. Aye, he woke a fate too strong for his hands, poor man.'

I let her go. She stood rubbing her arm, and grumbling to herself. My eyes turned to my father. Under the cloth that wrapped his skull, a thread of blood was trickling.

I took a step back. I could have cried to her like a child to its nurse, 'Make this not to be!' But she had drawn away like the House Snake who at a footstep creeps towards his hole. Her eyes were like cores of onyx. She was of the ancient Shore Folk, and knew earth magic, and the speech of the dead in the house of darkness. I knew whose servant she was, and she was not mine. Where the dead are, the Mother is not far away.

No man will lie when the Daughters of Night are listening. I said, 'He feared me always. When I first came to him a victor from the Isthmus, he tried to kill me out of fear.'

She nodded. It was true that all news came her way.

'But when he knew I was his son, we both did what was proper. I fought his wars; he gave me honour. It seemed we loved as we ought. He would ask me here – you have seen us at evening, talking by the fire.'

I turned towards the bed. The blood had stopped flowing; but it lay wet still on his cheek.

'If I had meant him harm, would I have saved him on the battlefield? He would have been speared at Sounion, without my shield. Yet he feared me still. Would I have gone to Crete? Yet I felt his fear still waiting. Well, he might see cause now. He had failed me with the ships. That was to face between us. In his place I would have died of shame.'

When the words were out they shocked me. It was unfitting, before his face; and Night's Daughters hear such things. Something cold touched my hand. My flesh leaped on my bones; but it was the nose of the white boarhound, dropped into my palm. It leaned hard against my thigh; the warmth had comfort in it.

'When it came time to show the sail, I prayed Poseidon for a sign. I wanted to reach him before he knew of my coming: to prove I came in peace, that I bore him no ill-will for failing me, that I could wait in patience for the kingdom. I prayed; and the god sent me the sign I prayed for.'

The Guardians of the Dead received my words into their silence. Words do not wash out blood. There would be a reckoning. Yet I would like to have spoken with him, a man to a man. What I had been afraid he would do in fear, he had done in sorrow. There had been this kindness in him, beneath all his contrivance. And yet, was it so? He was the King. Sorrow or not, he should have named an heir, disposed the kingdom, not left chaos behind. That he knew. Perhaps it was true that the god had called him.

I looked at Mykale, and saw only an old slave-woman of the Shore Folk, and was sorry to have said so much.

She hobbled to the bier, and took a cloth left by the women

and wiped the face. Then she turned up the palm, which came stiffly – for the corpse was setting – and looked into it, and laid it down again and took up mine. Her hand seemed still cold from the touch of the dead. The dog pushed between, fussing and whining. She scolded it off, and brushed her robe.

'Yes, yes, a fate too strong for him.' A fading flame guttered in her watery eyes. 'Go with your fate, but not beyond. Beyond leads to dark places. Truth and death come from the north in a falling star . . .' She crossed her arms and rocked, and her voice keened as if for the dead. Then she straightened, and cried out strongly, 'Loose not the Bull from the Sea!'

I waited, but no more came. Her eyes had turned foolish again. I stepped towards her, but thought, 'What use? I shall get no sense.'

I turned away. Then I heard a sound of growling. It was the dog, his teeth bare, his tail wrapping his belly, the dark roots of his hackles showing. There was a shuffling of feet like old dry leaves, and she was gone.

The barons were waiting. I went out, with the dog's nose pressed against me. He was on my side; and I did not send him back again.

2

I buried my father richly, on the slope of the Hill of Ares with the other kings. His tomb was lined with dressed stone, the nail-heads wrought with flowers and gilded. His offerings of food and drink stood in fine painted ware on stands inlaid with ivory. I had a high and splendid death-car made, and wrapped him in a great hanging worked with lions. He had enamelled coffers, his richest dagger and sword, two great gold rings and his state necklace. When the mound was heaped above the dome, I offered eight bulls upon it, and a war-stallion for him to ride in the lands below. As the blood sank into the earth, the women keened his dirge and praised him. The boarhound Aktis followed me down; but when he whimpered at the blood, I had him led away, and two of the palace deerhounds killed instead. If he had mourned till the end, I would have sent him down to my father; but the beast had chosen me of his own will.

The people began to tread the grave-mound firm. Only the open door was left within its causeway, for the dead to witness his funeral Games. The chanting rose and fell, the people swayed and tramped to it, moving to the sound like blood to the heartbeat. I stood there spattered from the sacrifice, thinking about him, and what kind of man he was. He had got my message, that if he sailed against Crete the serfs would rise and we bull-dancers would seize the Labyrinth. Fame and victory I had offered him, and the treasure of a thousand years for spoil; but he would not throw for it. That is a thing I cannot understand, nor shall I ever, a man who wishes and will not do.

Howsoever, he was dead. The chiefs of Attica had been coming in all day, for the feast and for the Games tomorrow. From the Palace roof you could see the troops of spear-heads, threading the hills. On the plain the helmet-plumes towered behind the charioteers, and the dust went up from the footmen. But I had seen from the Labyrinth the great paved Cretan highways running coast to coast, with never a weapon but at the guardhouses. To me these bands were not the seemly sight they thought themselves to be.

They came armed to the teeth, and they had good cause. These Attic lords had never known a common law. Some were conquering Hellene stock like ours, chariot-folk from the north; you could tell those far off, because the other drivers gave them the road. But there were Shore Folk too, who had held some strong valley or mountain roost and patched a peace with the victors; pirates from headland holds with a few fields inland, who still kept up their trade; and men of my and my father's making, who had helped us in the Pallantid war and been given a carving from its spoils.

All these, if put to it, would own me as High King, so far at least that they would follow me to war, and not harbour my enemies. A few paid a rent of cattle or wine or slaves to the royal house or its gods. But they ruled their own lands by the custom of their forefathers, and looked to get no meddling. Since their neighbours' customs differed, and the stock, as like as not, had been at blood-feud for generations, these shields on the road were not for show.

I looked down at the great scarps of the Rock, the never-fallen stronghold. It was this, this only, had made a High King of my grandfather, of my father, and of me. But for the Rock, I should be like any one of those down there, leading a little band of spears, master of a few vines and olives, and of some cattle if I could keep my neighbours off at night. That and no more.

I went into the house, and looked at the Goddess of the Citadel in her new shrine. She had belonged upon the Rock time out of mind; but in my grandfather Pandion's day, when the brothers divided up the kingdom, Pallas had seized her and taken her to his hold at Sounion. When I stormed the castle in my father's war, I had brought her back again. I had shown her respect; in the sack I had looked after her priestesses as if they were my sisters, and kept her treasure sacred; but she had been at Sounion a good while, and to make sure of her we still had her lashed to her column with ropes of bull-hide, in case it came into her head to fly back there and leave us. She was very old. The wood of her face and of her round bare breasts was black as pitch with age and oiling. Her arms stretched stiffly forward; a gold snake was twisted round her spear-arm, and the shield in her left hand was real. She had always been armed; when I brought her back I had given her a new helmet, to make her love me. Under her shrine is the cavern of the House Snake, forbidden to men; but she herself is their friend. She likes shrewd war-leaders and princes good in battle, and strong houses that have stood in honour from ancient days. The priestess said that the House Snake gave good omens still; so it seemed her lodging pleased her. Lest we should omit any title she set store by, we called her in the votive hymns Pallas Athene.

Night came. The guests of the house were fed and bedded. But I owed my father some duty before the earth was closed on him for good. Most of the night I watched with the Guard about his barrow, and saw the wake-fire tended, and poured drink-offerings to the gods below. The fire leaped high; it shone down the long stone-lined cutting into the mound, showing the painted doorposts of the burial vault, the new bronze hasps of the open doors, and the Erechthid snake upon the lintel. But it did not pierce the dark beyond; sometimes when my back was turned I could feel him standing in the shadows beyond the doorway to watch his rites, as they show dead men in funeral pictures.

A half-moon rose late, to shine about the grove of tombs, the poplars and the cypresses like guardian spears, the ancient grave-mounds with their steles of lions and boars and chariot-fights, the poles of their mouldering trophies leaning earthward.

The fire's core crumbled; a drift of gold sparks flew up, and thin blue flames. The night grew cold, it was the ebbtide of living men. Faint through the dew the ghosts came creeping, to warm themselves at the flames and sip the offerings. At such times, when the fresh blood gives them strength, they can speak to men. I turned to the doorway in the deep of the mound; the firelight caught the great bronze door-ring, but all within was still.

'What would he say?' I thought. 'What is it like there, in the fields of Hades where sun does not rise or set, nor seasons alter? Nor do men change; for where change is, life is, and these, who are only shadows of lives past, must keep for ever the shape of their earthly selves, whatever they made of them when they walked in daylight. Need the gods judge us further? Surely that is sentence enough, to live with ourselves, and to remember. Oh Zeus, Apollo, not without glory let me go down into the land of twilight! And when I am there, let me hear my name spoken in the world of men. Death does not master us, while the bard sings and the child remembers.'

I took a turn round the mound, and rebuked two guards who were drinking behind a tree. My father should not say I had scrambled his rites, once I had got the kingdom. I had the fire built up again, and poured oil upon it, thinking, 'Some day I shall lie here, while my son does all this for me.'

At last the dawn-star rose. I called for a torch and climbed the long ramps to the Citadel, then up again through the dark echoing house, and flung myself down in my clothes to sleep. I must be up at sunrise, to start the Games in the early cool.

They passed off well. There were one or two disputes, as there were bound to be in Attica; but my judgements got the voices of the lookers-on, and the losers for shame accepted them. The prizes were handsome enough to satisfy everyone. I gave the best of all for the chariot race, to honour Poseidon of the Horses. First prize was a Hellene war-stallion, trained to the chariot. The second was a woman. She was the youngest of my father's handmaids, a blue-eyed bitch who had done her best to climb in my bed while he was still alive. Knowing what I knew of her, she was glad to get away to some man she could fool more easily, and be stared at by a hundred warriors on the way. She got herself up like a queen, and I won much praise for my liberality. The third prize was a sheep and a tripod.

My father had had his dues; now they closed the great bronze-bound doors and filled in the trench that led to them. His shade would have crossed the River now, to join the troops of the dead. Soon grass would clothe the barrow and goats would graze there. The young men trooped back from the river meadow to bathe and dress, their voices lifting freely; the elders, who had not warmed their blood with contests and still felt the chill of death, clustered together. But soon there came from them too a cheerful buzz like that of grasshoppers in a fine autumn, when the frost seems far away.

I went to dress for the feast. It was a warm evening; the royal robes felt thick and smelled stale. I thought of Crete, where only old men and low ones cover up their bodies, and a prince goes nearly as naked as a god. Not to seem too foreign, I put on Hellene short-drawers of scarlet leather, and a thick belt studded with lapis; above it, only the royal necklace, and rings for the upper arm. So I was half king and half bull-leaper, and the outside matched the man within. It made me surer of myself.

The young men were all eyes. Since I was first a wrestler, I had clipped short the hair across my brows, so as not to be grabbed by the forelock; they had taken that up (the cut is still called a Theseus) and I saw this would be next. But my mind was on the guests, to see who was missing. It was time to count my enemies. I found that all the great lords were there but one; and he the strongest. He was a man I had heard much of. It was a heavy matter.

Next morning I called them all to the council chamber. For the first time I sat upon Erechtheus' throne. Along the painted walls, on benches draped with fine patterned rugs, sat the lords of Attica. I tried to forget that many of them had sons older than I, and came to business quickly. Minos was dead; also his heir, the Minotauros; Crete was in turmoil with a score of masters, which is to say with none. 'This news will run like fire through the Achaean kingdoms. If we want to be lords of the Isles, and not some new Minos' vassals, we must put to sea.'

Crete is a land of gold; it was not hard to get a hearing. One man stood up and said it was a great land to conquer, we should need allies in such a war. This was sense and I had an answer. But there was a stir at the outer door; a ripple ran along the guests, half fear, half expectation. A few changed secret smiles, like men who wait for a show.

There was a sound outside of a troop piling its arms. A man came in. It was he who had failed the feast; he had come, late, to the council.

His excuse was cool, mere insolence; I heard it in silence, while I studied him. I had never seen him till now. He came down seldom from his castle on Kithairon, where he preyed on the travellers of the Theban road. I had pictured him black-browed; but he was round, smooth and smiling.

I said, 'You were missed, Prokrustes. But you come from rough country, and I daresay the ways were foul.'

He smiled. I told him the business shortly. My father had let him be for twenty years, sooner than risk a war with him. Every man here knew it. Since he came in not an eye was on me, and, I guessed, hardly an ear. It was plain they feared him more than me, and it chilled my heart.

While I was still talking, I heard a yelp from near his seat; my dog Aktis limped out, holding up a forepaw, and lay down by me trembling. I had seen nothing done. As I stroked the beast's ears, the man smiled sleekly. And I thought of a sudden, 'By Zeus! He is trying to frighten *me*.'

All these fawning faces had cast a damp upon me. Now I was as warm as a man can need. I have seldom been so angry and sat still in a chair. But I kept it within, and waited.

This man and that had spoken, when he rose and took the speaker's staff. You could tell he had been reared in a princely house. 'I vote for war,' he said. 'Men who will risk no battles will never leave to their sons a household rich in gold and home-born slaves.' He bowed about him as if this time-worn speech had been his own. No one dared smile. For myself, I was past joking.

'And so,' he said, 'before we talk of ships and men, we ought to follow custom and choose a war-leader, seeing the king is under age.'

There was a hush full of hidden whispers. Not a man spoke up for me. A little while before, it would have weighed upon my soul. But that had lightened, as the spark does in the updraught of the fire.

'We have heard you, Prokrustes,' I said. 'And now hear me. I am leading the ships to Crete, and these lords who sail with me will not be losers. For I know the Labyrinth, as well as you do the passes of Kithairon, you carrion jackal with your den of stinking bones.'

His smile had stiffened. He had really thought I would not defy him, in my own hall. He had come to smile at my shame. I wondered what my father could have swallowed from him, to bring things to this.

'You missed our feast,' I said. 'A man who is host to many travellers should have hearth-friends everywhere. I hear your guest-room bed is such a masterpiece that no man will leave it, unless he is carried away. I must come and see it. Don't put yourself out for me. You have given it up too long to strangers. When I visit you, by the head of Poseidon you shall lie on it yourself.'

He stood a moment staring, from face to face. But the Attic lords sat eased, as if their itch had been scratched for them. Suddenly someone gave a shrill laugh; then all joined in loudly, as men do who have been at stretch. The sound rose to the rafters.

He swelled like a snake full of poison, waiting to spit. His mouth opened; but I had had enough of him. 'You came under my roof,' I said. 'Get out and you can go alive. If you are here when I have told my ten fingers over, I will throw you off the Rock.'

He gave me one last hangman's smile, and went. And none too soon. There were old javelins on the wall behind me, and I had feared I would forget myself.

So I had that war on my hands, before the great one. But it paid me well. The chiefs had long hated themselves for putting up with him; if I had given ground, they would have shifted off their hate to me.

As it was, most of them followed me. He knew I would be coming, but not so soon; he had not even burned the cover about his cliffside hold, when we stormed the walls. What we found in his guest-room would do no one good to hear, nor me to remember. We saw his famous bed, and in the prison guests who had lain on it, waiting their next turn. Some clasped our feet and prayed for a quick sword-thrust. Indeed it was the best thing left for them, so we bound their eyes if they still had any, and set them free. The rest, who could get about, begged another gift from us. They wanted their host, to return his kindness. We had got him bound, and by then I was feeling sick; so I left them together and closed the doors. After some hours he died, and they asked me if I would like to see the body; but I had heard enough as it was, and told them to drop it down the gorge. His sons had been thrown off the walls already. It was a stock to be rooted out.

So died Prokrustes, the last of the mountain bandits, the greatest and the worst. I had known, before he opened his mouth in council, that he would be a bad man to have with me in Crete, and a worse to leave behind in Attica. He was in my way, and had let me see it; it was foolish of him to make me angry as well. But he was a slave to his pleasures, such as they were; he did not know me, nor consider how much I had to gain by putting him down. As it was, he came like the vulture who brings a lucky omen. My barons were all behind me now, and ready to follow me overseas.

3

While my fleet was getting ready news began to come in that Crete had a new Minos. I knew his name, Deukalion, and, from what I had heard, guessed him for a man of straw, put up by those lords whose strongholds had withstood the risings. But he came of the royal kin, and his army, scambled up from masterless spearmen of fallen houses, had seized back the Labyrinth from the rebel serfs. Something like this had been sure to happen; but it meant there was no time to lose.

For all that, I did not go at it like a charging bull. I knew Cretans, and made my plans remembering their subtlety. What I had forgotten was their insolence. They sent me an envoy.

He came into my hall, his love-locks sleeking his bare shoulders, his willow waist gold-belted. Before him black pages carried gifts of courtesy: a gold necklace with crystal pendants, painted vases of sweet oils, a rare rose-bush in flower streaked with blood and amber. Nothing was said, this time, about a tribute of boys and girls from Attica.

As we went through the courtesies, I thought, 'Have I seen you before, little peacock? Well, you will have seen me. You have smoothed your mouth with oil since you yelled at me from the ringside.' He met my eye unblinking, proclaimed his master, and asked for my allegiance. I did not laugh. To deal with Cretans like Hellene chiefs would be taking a boarspear after foxes. They had made me live a year among them, when I should have been learning kingcraft. Instead I had learned the Bull Dance, and their minds.

I asked where was Minos' body (which they would not find) and the royal seal, which I had brought away myself though I did not say so. All I needed was a little time. I said, 'Your ship is at Piraeus?' knowing he would have seen nothing there;

to hide my plans I was mustering my ships at Troizen, across the gulf.

He answered smoothly, but with some eagerness below: 'No, my lord, at Marathon. I beached out of the city, because I have another gift from my master still aboard, something more worthy of your fame. It would not do in the streets; it might scare the people. King Theseus; since the bull-dancers are scattered and the dance is over, my master has sent you as a gift of honour Podargos, King Bull of the sacred herd sprung from the sun. He is yours; do as you think fit with him.'

'Podargos!' I could not keep my face from lighting. Every bull-dancer in the Labyrinth had known Old Snowy, that great white portent among the piebald herds of Crete. He had been the bull of the Dolphins, and as tricky as he was beautiful; the Dolphins were a short-lived team. He would give good sport, charge straight forward, was a fine bull for the leap; but when he killed, all we trained watchers would argue how he did it and not agree. If our team had had him, I doubt if I could have got them all safe home. But I had always had an itch to tackle him myself; and even now I quickened at his name.

I came back from my dream, to find the Cretan smiling. 'A kingly gift,' I said. 'But for a god, not a man. Such bulls are sacred; Apollo would be angry if I put him in my herd.'

'He would be troublesome,' said the Cretan, looking put out, 'to carry again to Knossos.' I nearly laughed out loud. I could believe it. I would have liked to ask him how they had got him here; but I was not a bull-boy any more.

'There is no need,' I said. 'The Sun Herd is Apollo's. We will give him back to the god.' In any case I could not take such a gift from a man I meant to make war on. This way would save my honour, though it would go to my heart to do it. At least I would mate him first with some of my cows. He was the last of the Bull Court; he would hand on a spark of that strange year's life. The roar of the ring under the Cretan sun; it lingers long in the ear.

The Cretan bowed himself off. I sat remembering, then shook myself and took up my daily business. Later, I saw a runner come in from westward. I could see Amyntor, the captain of my Guard, tearing, himself, up the ramps like a man possessed. He was the best of the lads who had been with me in Crete; a little young for his place, but then so was I. He scratched at my door; then fell inside, and panted out as if we were still in the Bull Court, 'Theseus! Theseus! Podargos has got loose!'

'Get your breath,' I said. 'He will have to be caught, then.'

'He is running wild. Those Cretan ninnies let him go, and he is running amok in Marathon. Three men killed outright; four more and a woman dying. And a young child.'

'Old Snowy?' I said. 'But he never was a rogue. He never charged before the Dolphins had played him.'

'He has had the sea-trip. And been played too for that matter, by the men of Marathon trying to catch him. Three horses he has had besides the people; and the mules and dogs, no one has counted.'

I cried out, 'Dogs! The ignorant fools! Don't they know what he is?'

'I doubt they do. We got used to these great beasts in Crete, but the home breed must look like calves beside them. They take him for a monster.'

'Why did they meddle, the stupid oafs, before they sent for me?'

'They have done meddling now and started praying. They say he's been sent by Poseidon to destroy them; they call him the Bull from the Sea.'

The words rang like a gong. I stood there silent. Then I began to strip my clothes. When I was naked, I went to the chest where my bull-leaper's things were laid away. The ornaments I did not trouble with, but strapped on the loin-piece of tooled and gilded hide. One gets used in the ring to playing about with death; but no one wants to be gelded.

Amyntor was talking. But the words in my ears were the words of old Mykale. I had known at my father's bierside that she spoke with the Power. It had hung in my mind, a secret shadow; a waiting fate, moving to me slowly with its meeting stars. Now so soon it was here, while I had my strength and swiftness still, the fire of youth and my bull-boy's strength of arm. Within the day I would be free of it or dead.

Amyntor grabbed my arm, then remembered and let go again. 'Sir! Theseus! What are you doing? You can't tackle him now, a bull that has been baited!'

'We shall see,' I said. I was rummaging the chest for my lucky piece, a crystal bull on a neck-chain; I had never been in the ring without it. I spat on it for luck, put it on, and shouted for my chamber-groom.

'Send a herald post-haste to Marathon. He must cry the people to let the bull be, to go indoors and stay there till I send them word. Have Thunderbolt saddled for me. I want a bull-net tied to the pommel, and the strongest bull-tether they use at the sacrifices. Make haste. And no guard, Amyntor. I shall go alone.'

The groom opened and shut his mouth, and went. Amyntor struck his hand upon his thigh, and cried out, 'Holy Mother! Where is the sense? After a whole year in the ring, to throw your life away? I'll swear the Cretans played for this! I swear they had orders to loose the bull! This is what they hoped for. They knew your pride.'

'I should be sorry,' I said, 'to disappoint the Cretans, after a year in the ring. However, Amyntor, this is not the Bull Court. Do not shout in my ear.'

None the less he followed me down all the stairs, begging to call out the Eleusinian Guard and kill the bull with spears. Maybe he could be killed that way, by those who were left at the end. But the god had not sent this fate to me, for me to meet it with the lives of other men.

In Athens word had got about. People stood on housetops to see me pass, and some tried to follow. I had my riders turn them back and stop at the gates themselves. So presently the road grew quiet; and when I came down into Marathon between the olive groves all blooming with green barley, there was no one; only a hoopoe calling in the silent noonday, and the gulls upon the shore.

There was a road between tall black cypresses, leading to the sea, and by it a little wine-shop, such as peasants seek at evening when they unyoke their teams, a mulberry-tree above the benches, hens scratching, a couple of goats and one young heifer; and a little house of daub-and-wattle, old and tottering, all drowsy in the quiet sun. Beyond was the flat sour sea-meadow, the long harsh plain between bay and mountains. The blue sea lapped on a beach piled high with wrack and driftwood; slow shadows of clouds, grape-purple, swept the sunny heights. A thin poor grass, with yellow coltsfoot, stretched from the shore to the olive trees. Among the flowers, like a great white block of quarried marble, stood the Cretan bull.

I hitched my horse to a cypress and went softly forward. It was Old Snowy, sure enough. I could even see the paint of the bull-ring still upon his horns. The gilt stripes caught the sun, but the tips were dirty. It was turned noon, the hour of the Bull Dance.

You could see he was on edge, if you knew bulls, by the way he looked about him as he grazed. Far off as I was, he saw me, and his forefoot raked the ground. I went off to think. There was no sense in stirring him up before I was ready.

I mounted again; my horse slowed before the little wine-shop. There was the heifer, honey-coloured, with a soft brown eye. I thought how bulls are caught in Crete, and laughed at my own slowness. So I tied my horse to the mulberry-tree and went and knocked at the door.

A slow step shuffled, the door opened a crack, and an old eye peeped out. 'Let me in, Mother,' I said. 'I want a word with your husband.'

'You'll be a stranger here,' she said, and opened. Inside it was like a wren's nest, so spare and neat; she must have been widow longer far than wife. She was shrunk so small, she looked to be near a hundred. Her eyes were still bright and blue, but it seemed as if a breath would blow her away; so I waited, not to give her a start.

'Young man,' she said, 'you've no business walking abroad. Didn't you hear the crier? The High King of Athens sent for everyone to keep within doors, till he brings his army. There's a mad bull loose in the fields; they say it came from the sea. Well, poor lad, come in, come in, the guest of the land is holy. I can tell by your speech you're from foreign parts.' I went humbly inside. She was the first to tell me I had picked up a Cretan accent in the Bull Court.

She shuffled about, dipping a measure of wine into a clay cup, and filling from the water-crock. She sat me on a three-legged stool and gave me barley bread with goat-cheese. It was time in courtesy to account for myself; but I did not want to flutter her. I said, 'The Good Goddess bless you, Mother; I shall work better for that. I am the bull-catcher from Athens, come to take the bull.'

'Mercy!' she cried. 'What can the King be thinking of? One young lad alone, for a great bull in his rage? You should go back to him, and tell him it won't do. He won't know the ways of cattle, he hires others for that.'

'The King knows me. I learned my trade in Crete, where that bull comes from. And that's what brings me here, Mother; can I borrow your cow?'

The poor soul quivered all over, and her mouth opened like an empty purse. 'Take my poor Saffron for that wicked beast to murder? And the High King with a thousand of his own?'

'Murder?' I said. 'Not he. But she'll quiet him down; and if he serves her, she'll throw you the finest calf in Attica; you can sell it for a fortune.' She went to the little window, muttering and near tears. 'Be good to me, Grannie,' I said, 'for the sake of all the people.'

She turned round. 'Poor boy, poor boy. Braving the bull with your own flesh and bones; what's my cow to that? Take her, lad, and the All-Mother keep you.'

I kissed her cheek. The goodness green in the withered trunk came like a kindly omen, after old Mykale. 'I'll see you right with the King, Mother, I swear by my head, if I get safe home. Tell me your name and give me something to write on.' She brought me a worn wax tally from the shop; I smoothed out the old scores, and wrote, 'The King owes Hekaline three cows, a hundred jars of sweet wine, and a strong good slave-girl. If I die, let the Athenians send to Delphi, and ask Apollo how to choose a king. Theseus.' She peered at it nodding; of course she could not read. 'Keep that safe, and give me your blessing, Mother. I must go.' As I walked off leading the heifer, I saw her bright little eye at the shutter's chink.

Podargos had gone further off. I was going after, when I saw something on the beach, too white for driftwood. It was a body, almost bare. Then I went running; for it wore the dress of the Bull Court.

It was a girl from my team in Crete, one of the tribute-maids from Athens. She had set out to the bull with more pride than I had; as well as the loin-guard, she had put on her gilded boots, her handstraps, and all her jewels, and painted her face for the ring. There was a great tear in her side that must have gone through her liver. She was dying; but she knew me, and spoke my name.

I knelt beside her, saying, 'Thebe! What is this? Why didn't you wait for me? You must have known I would be coming.'

Her eyes were bright and wandering, and she gasped for air as the dark blood flowed away. 'Theseus!' she said. 'Is Pylia dead?'

I looked about, finding first a bull-net, then the second girl, lying half in the sea where the horns had tossed her. I came back and said, 'Yes, she is. She must have died quickly.' They had been lovers in Crete, after the custom of the Bull Court.

She put up her hand and felt the wound in her side. 'I need the axe; can you do it?'

They use it in the ring to dispatch the victims. I said, 'No, my dear, I have nothing; but it won't be long. Keep hold of my hand.' I thought how I had watched over them in the Labyrinth, trained them, heartened them, and jumped the bull for them on their bad days, only for this.

'We have done what is best.' You will see sometimes with a warrior going before his wounds are cold, that he will talk and talk, then snuff out like a dead lamp. 'We came back too proud, and our kinsfolk hate us.'

She paused, gasping. I stroked her brow and felt the clammy sweat.

'My father called me a brazen trull, for vaulting our old ox to show the boys. And Pylia, they found her a clerk to marry. Soft as a pig. In Crete we'd have thrown him to the bull. They said she was lucky to get him, having lived a mountebank and a public show.'

I said softly, 'They should have spoken those words to me.' But there was no one to be angry with, only the dying and the dead.

'They call us haters of men. Oh Theseus! There is nothing left like the Bull Court. No honour . . . so we tried . . .' Her head sank back, and her eyes were setting, when she opened them again and clenched her hand on mine and said, 'He gores to the right.' Then her soul went out in the death-gasp.

Her hand slipped from mine, and it left me lonely. The Bull Court was gone indeed. But as I got to my feet I saw along the mudflats a great white shape, wicked and noble, smelling the wind. There was still the bull.

I walked along the trees till I found a thick old olive, the last before the sea. I tethered the cow there, and tied the great hide bull-rope, with its running hobble, strongly round the tree. Then I climbed up with the net and hung it between two branches, lying easily. There was nothing left but to call upon the gods. I chose Apollo, since the Cretan bulls are bred from his sacred herd, and promised him this one if he would help me take it. Then I went to work.

Podargos had his back to me, switching his tail at flies. I licked my finger to feel the wind, hoping the heifer's scent might draw him. But the breeze blew from the sea.

Out on the sea-meadow I stepped, a pace at a time. The soil was caked and sun-dried, not good to run on. I did not want to get too far from the tree. I pitched a stone or two, but they fell far short of him. So I went further out, alone with my short noon shadow among dry yellow flowers, and threw again. The stone just hit him, though nearly spent, and he looked over his shoulder. I waved, to draw him. He would be fast as a war-chariot, once he charged. He swung down his head, and gave me a hard look, as if to say, 'I am resting now; be thankful, and do not tempt me.' And he moved a little away.

The slap of the waves on the shore-line sounded in my ears; and with them the voice of old Mykale. 'Loose not the Bull from the Sea!' And I thought, 'He has been loosed, and I must bind him; the luck of my reign is in it. Why do I wait?'

I ran straight out, half-way to him. He was watching me, one foot stirring the dust. I put two fingers in my mouth, and whistled hard the fanfare of the Bull Court, which they play when the bull is loosed into the ring.

He pricked his ears. Then he planted his forefeet squarely and lowered his head; but he did not charge. He was saying, as clearly as speech, 'Oho, a bull-dancer. Why so far off, if you know the game? Come up, little bull-boy, come up and dance with me. Take the bull by the horns.'

He had the wisdom of god-filled things. I should have known he would draw me back to the Bull Dance, which was sacred when the first earth-men fought each other with axes and knives of stone. I lifted my arm, as so often in the ring at Knossos, and gave the team-leader's salute.

It was strange to hear no shouting from the benches. 'Well,' I thought, 'it will be stranger to have no team.' That made me laugh. One would do nothing in the ring, without the madness of the god.

His hoof raked once. Then, quick as I remembered him, he charged head-on.

Most precious in the ring is the counsel of the dying. Knowing he gored right-ways, I feinted left to straighten him; then grasped at the stained and painted horns. My fingers and palms had lost the leather hardness of the Bull Court, but kept their strength. I swung upward with him, feet over head, feeling him steady to my weight as a familiar thing. A knowledge passed between us. And I felt a welcome. He was in a strange land, far from home, where men and dogs had baited him, the sacred sun-child used to the homage of a king. The touch and the weight, the grip of a bull-boy, cheered his slow in-bred wits. He felt more like himself.

Only with the Bull Dance would I coax him to come my way. So I made myself a whole team in one. That was the last and greatest dance of Theseus the Athenian, leader of the Cranes, which I danced alone at Marathon for the gods and for the dead.

When I came down from the vault there was no one there to catch me, or to play the bull away. But he was as unused to this state of things as I was, and his mind was slower; it was that which saved me. I would dodge when he turned, and come round to meet him, and leap again, always working nearer to the tree, till my hands were skinned from the horns and my arms began to shake with weariness. I stood to leap again, thinking, 'This time he will feel me flagging; then he will strike.' But he looked past me, snuffing the air, and ran on to the tree. The heifer lowed softly, and lifted her yellow tail.

I stood panting, aching and raw, till I saw he had forgotten me. Then I crept up, and fixed the hobble to his hind-leg, and scrambled into the boughs.

He did not feel it just at first, having pleasanter business. Then he lugged and tugged till the whole tree quivered. The trunk was two men thick and must have stood a hundred years, but I thought he would heave it up. If I had not clung like an ape, he would have shaken me out with the twigs and birds'-nests. The scared cow added her bawl to the bull's great bellow. But the stout rope held, and at last he tired. He had been caught before in the Cretan pastures, and no great harm had come of it. He stood; and I dropped the bull-net over him.

And now I was alone no longer. It was as if I had sown the furrows to bring forth men. They swarmed about me; they must have been creeping up while I was in the tree. The net's edge was hardly wide enough for the grasping hands. I climbed down and showed them how to catch his feet in it so that a pull would trip him. They would have killed him then with spears and cleavers, working off their fear, as small men do. I was glad I could tell them he had been vowed to Apollo; he did not deserve so base a death.

I made them all wait, and went on alone, leading the heifer. I had a debt to pay. She was so frail, I did not want her to learn who I was from anyone but me. So I knocked, but got no answer, and went inside. She was lying below the window; when I picked her up, she had no more weight than a dead bird. She had spent her last breath in care for me, watching my struggle; I hoped she had lived to see me win.

I sacrifice for her every year, at the tomb I built for her where the cottage stood, and the servant I promised her has grown grey serving her shrine. The folk of Marathon offer too, for they think she makes their cattle fruitful; so she will not be forgotten after my death.

The bull-girls lie close by; I ordered them a warriors' barrow and buried them on one bier. The kinsfolk murmured, till I lost patience and gave them some of my mind. They held their peace after that.

I went back to the bull. The people were still in mortal dread of him, and I said I would stay with him till he was offered to the god. I saw him stoutly haltered either side, then mounted his neck and rode him into Athens. He did not mind the shouting and thrown flowers; he was used to those in Crete; so he went consenting to the god who owned him, looking to the last for the bull-field and the good old days. It was I who knew they would never come again.

But when he had breathed his strong soul upward, and I heard the paean, my soul lifted with eagles' wings. I had met and mastered the evil of my fate; I was king indeed.

4

We fought the war in Crete before the summer broke, and the streams washed down the mountains into the rich plains. I led there two fleets of warriors; the second came from King Pittheus of Troizen, my mother's father, who had reared me as a boy before my father owned me. He was too old to go himself, but he sent a troop of his sons and grandsons, and good men I found them, well worth their share of the spoils. I knew the Cretan country hardly better than they, having lived out my year a captive of the Labyrinth; but the native serfs I knew, the land's first children, and they knew me; first as the bull-leaper they used to bet on, then as the man who led them when they rose. They thought I would give them more justice than their half-Greek lords, so they helped me every way. And if you go even now to Crete, you will hear them say that I kept faith with them.

Before the half-fallen, patched-up Labyrinth, stained black with fire, still stood the porch of the Bull Court with its crimson columns and its great red bull charging across the wall. In sight of it we fought the clinching battle for the Knossos plain. In the mountain lands to the east they are wild as foxes; it is freedom they want, not power. Minos ruled them lightly and so do I. But that Crete which had been lord of the seas and islands was in my hand; and it was not a bloody war. They were sick for a master, having been governed from the Labyrinth a thousand years. Fallen to petty chiefdoms, they had thought chaos come again. It was a lesson I took to heart; it would shame me, not to make my own land as civil as the one I had conquered.

I spared even Deukalion himself, when he asked for mercy. I found him what I had guessed, a puppet who would dance to my tune too: vain, not proud; content to be vassal king and subject ally, in return for the empty show. His wife was like him, lazy and fine, or in Crete she might have been dangerous. As it was, when I heard they were bringing up the little Phaedra, King Minos' youngest daughter saved when the Palace burned, I thought no harm to leave her there. I had meant to see her before I left, for she had been a taking child, who had made a hero of me when I was a bull-boy, in the way of such small girls. But there was always too much to do; at the harbour as I was sailing, I bought from a Nubian a cage of little bright birds from Africa, and sent it to her from me.

On the way home, I put in at Troizen with my uncles and my cousins, to greet my grandfather for the first time since I left his house. He was at the harbour mole waiting to meet me; a tall stooped old warrior, in his state robes. Last time I had seen him so, it was to receive the King of Pylos; and while we waited for the guest, he had sent me off again to comb my hair. That had been four years back, when I was fifteen.

The youths unyoked the horses and pulled the chariot up through the Eagle Gate, with rose-leaves and myrtles falling, and paeans sung. On the Palace steps stood my mother waiting. When we had parted, she had come straight from taking the omens for me at the Mother's altar; her flounces had clashed with gold, and about her diadem had clung the smell of incense. Now there were ribbons and violets in her hair and her skirts were stitched with flowers; she held in her hand a garland to crown me. Her beauty dazzled me; and then, when I came close to kiss her, I saw the last bloom of her youth was gone.

After the feast in Hall, my grandfather took me to his upper room. The stool was gone where I used to sit at his feet, and the chair brought in which he kept for kings.

'So, Theseus,' he said. 'High King of Attica, High King of Crete. What now?'

'High King of Crete, Grandfather, and King of Athens. High King of Attica is a word, no more. That comes next.'

'The Attic team will be hard to yoke together; ill-matched and rough. As they are now, they will pay your tithes and fight your enemies. That is much, in Attica.'

'Too little. The house of Minos stood for a thousand years, because Crete had one law.'

'Yet it has fallen.'

'For want of law enough. It stopped with the serfs and the slaves. Men are dangerous who have nothing left to lose.'

He raised his brows. It was the look of a grandfather at a boy; but he said no more.

I said, 'The King should have looked after them. Not only to quiet them; they were his charge. Don't we say all helpless folk – the orphan, the stranger, the suppliant, who have nothing to bargain with and can only pray – are sacred to Zeus the Saviour? The King must answer for them; he is next the god. For the serfs, the landless hirelings, the captives of the spear; even the slaves.'

He was slow to speak. Then he said, 'You are your own master now, Theseus, and many men's beside. But I have lived longer, and this I tell you: nothing is stronger in men than the will to possess their own. Touch it, and you will make enemies who will bide their time. And are you a king to sit quiet at home five years together? Beware of malice at your back.'

'I will, sir,' I said. 'I don't want to work anyone against the grain. All those customs they brought from their first lands; the little old goddess at the fourways, the village sacrifice, are a home roof to them against the naked wind. I have known exile, too. But they live in fear, from chief to pig-boy: of the raider from over the hill, the grinding master whose hired hands sweat all day for the scrapings of the pot, the brawling neighbour who kills the straying sheep and beats the shepherd. I will give them justice between chief and chief, craftsman and craftsman, if they will come to me for it. I killed Prokrustes, to show I can make it good. I think they will come.'

He nodded, thinking. He was old; but like every man good at his trade, he was ready to hear of something new.

'Men could be more than they are,' I said. 'I learned that in the Bull Court, when I trained my team. There is a faith, there is a pride, which has to be acted first and grows by doing.'

I saw his forehead wrinkle. He was trying to see me, his grandson and a king, in a life he only knew from songs and wall-pictures:

a jewelled mountebank vaulting bulls before base-born crowds, eating and sleeping and training with people from everywhere, sons of hanged pirates, barbarous Scythians, wild Amazon girls taken in war. It shocked him past talking of, that I had been a slave. He was wiser than the bull-girls' kindred, and much better; but he did not understand. There was no life like that glory in the dust.

So I talked to him of his sons' deeds in battle, praising the best as they deserved, for I knew he had not yet chosen out his heir. They were all sons of his palace women; of his queen's children only my mother had lived past childhood. As a boy, before I knew my own getting, I had thought he would choose me; but you could not expect him to leave the land to an absent lord, and I wanted him to know I had no more thought of it.

After this I went to look for my mother. They told me she had gone to sacrifice. I asked if nobody knew where she was, for night was falling; but they said I should find her at sun-up in the woods of Zeus. So I looked out a girl who showed me she had not forgotten me, and went to bed.

At morning I went up through the hillside woods, by the path above the stream. At first the woods were open, the clearings loud with birds; then the ancient forest grew high and met above. Grass-blades were thin and pale, and wet black oak-leaves lay in the falls of years, roots arched among them like stiffened serpents. I threaded the winding path that is never trodden clear but never quite grows over, till I came to the holy place where Zeus struck down the oak tree. It had spread wide, before its death, and still there was open sky there. Between its roots was the stone where my father had left his tokens for me, when I came to manhood. My mother stood beside it.

I stepped forward smiling; then my arms fell down. She had on her priestly robes and her tall diadem worked with gold snakes; I saw she was purified for some holy rite, and not to be touched by the hand of man. Before I could speak, she motioned with her eyes. There were two priestesses standing in the grove, an old woman and a maid of thirteen or fourteen years. They had a covered basket such as sacred things are carried in; the crone was whispering to the maiden, who stared past her with great eyes at me.

My mother said, 'Come, Theseus. This place belongs to Zeus, and is for men: we must go to another shrine.'

She turned towards a path that ran deep into the thicket. A night-bird's feather seemed to brush me coldly. I said, 'What is it, Mother?' although I knew. She answered, 'This is not the place to speak in. Come.'

I followed her into the green shades; out of sight behind I heard the old woman and the girl murmuring, or stepping on twigs and leaves. Presently we came to a tall grey rock. There was a carving on it, old and worn, of a great open eye. I stood still, knowing that this was a place of the Goddess, forbidden to men. The path bent round beyond; but I turned my eyes from it and waited. The priestesses had sat down, just out of hearing, on a mossy stone. Even now my mother did not speak.

'Mother,' I said, 'why are you bringing me before Her? Have I not toiled in Her lands and suffered, and lived with my life on my fingers' ends? Is it not enough?'

'Hush,' she said. 'You know what you have done.' She looked sidelong at the stone and the path beyond it, and drew me a little away from them into the wood, whispering, and moving softly. When she stood near, I saw I had grown an inch while I was in Crete. But I felt no bigger for it.

'In Eleusis, when you had wrestled with the Year King and he was dead, you married the sacred queen. But before your year was out you overthrew her, and set up the rule of men. In Athens, Medea the High Priestess fled for her life from you . . .'

'She tried to murder me!' I did not speak very loud, but in the quiet I seemed to be shouting. 'The Queen of Eleusis plotted with her, that I should die by my own father's hand. Did you send me to him for that? You are my mother!'

She pressed her hand to her head a moment, then said, 'I am a servant here. I speak as I am bidden.' She sighed deeply, with all her body. It was this great heaviness, more than her words, that chilled my blood. 'And in Crete,' she said, 'you took away Thrice-Holy Ariadne, Goddess-on-Earth, from the Mother's sanctuary. Where is she now?'

'I left her on Naxos, at the island shrine. Do you know the

rite there, Mother? Do you know how the Wine King dies? She took to it like a fish to the sea, though she had been reared softly, knowing nothing of such things. There is rotten blood in the House of Minos. I will leave my kingdom better stock, when I come to breed.'

I felt the great carved eye upon the rock boring my back, and turned to face it. It stared back, a dry eye of stone. Then I heard a sound, and saw the eyes of my mother weeping.

I stretched out my hands; but she stepped back, one arm waving me off, the other hiding her face.

After a while I said, 'You taught me a kinder Goddess, when I was a child.'

'You were hers then,' she said. The eye stared out beyond me. I turned, and saw the two priestesses watching. All the wood seemed eyes.

She turned to the stone, and made a curving sign. Then she leaned down and searched the earth, and rose with both hands full. One held a spouting acorn, the other dead leaves that were going back to mould again. She set them down, and took my arm, signing for silence, and led me off a little way. Peering through the trees I saw fox-cubs playing, soft pretty things. Near them on the ground, half-eaten, was a young dead hare. My mother turned back towards the stone. The hairs on my arms rose up with gooseflesh, and stirred in the faint airs of the wood.

I said, 'Then what must I offer her?'

'Her altar is within her children. She takes her due.'

'Poseidon is my birth-god,' I said; 'Apollo made me a man, and Zeus a king. There is not much woman in me.'

She answered, 'Apollo, who understands all mysteries, says also, "Nothing too much." He is knowledge, Theseus; but she is what he knows.'

'If prayers cannot move her, why have you brought me here?'

She sighed and said, 'All gods are moved by the appointed sacrifice.' She pointed to the path that led beyond the rock. 'The Shore Folk say that before the gods made their fathers from sown pebbles, this was a shrine of the earth-born Titans, who ran upon their hands, and fought with the trunks of trees.'

I would have spoken, though I had nothing to say, only to call her back to what I knew; she had gone into deep waters, while I was away. But the seer and the priestess wrapped her round; she went on to the staring rock, and I followed dumbly. The two priestesses had risen and came after.

At the rock she said, 'When we have passed the Gate, say nothing whatever you hear or see. No man may speak here. A sacrifice will be given you. Offer it in silence. Above all, that which is hidden do not uncover. The Dark Mother does not show herself to men.'

Beyond the rock the path went down into a gully, the deep bed of an old stream. Above the steep sides, trees met; the shadows were green and watery; the stones seemed dry till one trod in a hidden pool or heard a secret trickle. The rocks narrowed; there was a rope across, tied in a curious knot. My mother pulled it somewhere, and it fell apart. As we passed it, she pressed a finger to her lips.

Our feet slipped ankle-deep in water, the cleft sides stood three-man-high above our heads. Then they opened; there was a round rock-walled space, with trees growing in its sides. In the far wall, a little way up, there was a cave. The stream ran out from it, murmuring and chuckling; and mossy, low steps ran up, towards the dark within.

My mother pointed away, to a space between two boulders. I went there, my backbone feeling cold; but there was only a wild pig tethered. I dragged him out; by a slab below the steps the old priestess stood with a cleaver. There was black blood upon the stone. The boar snorted and tugged; the thought of his screaming froze me. I used all my strength, and clove his neck to the windpipe. His breath hissed, mingled with blood which ran into the earth. He died, and I saw in the mouth of the cave the three faces waiting: the green maiden, the woman, the crone. My mother beckoned.

It was dark in the cave. Further on, it sloped downwards into blackness. The stream, scouring one side, had smoothed itself a channel stained yellow and red. Baskets stood on the floor, of grain, of shrivelled roots and leaves; some were covered over. On the shadowy walls dim things were hanging; cloths or robes, or sacks of worked leather. On the other side of the stream, behind a jutting rock which cut off the light, was a curtain of kidskin hung over a wooden frame. A stone slab showed under it, like the foot of an altar.

They began the rites of appeasement. I was marked with the dead boar's blood, then washed with water from the stream; my head by the crone, my right hand by my mother. Then the maid came to wash my left. She was dark and slight, a girl of the Shore Folk with eyes like forest water, shy and unguarded. They gazed at me as she came up, gangling as a hound-pup and as tenderly made. In this awesome place I had forgotten my deeds and my fame. But this girl remembered.

I let my hand fall. She paused; then took it timidly in hers to hold it for the washing. Her brow flushed, then her face and her breast. But she kept her eyes down, and put away her pitcher neatly.

The rites were long. The women passed and re-passed the screened-off altar. Things were brought out and censed and sprinkled, taken back and hidden. I watched my mother, thinking how I had seen her year after year since boyhood, splendidly robed, her jewelled skirts clashing and swinging, making the harvest sacrifice upon the threshing floor in the bright sunlight; and all the while these secrets in her heart.

Fire crackled behind the curtain; there was a smell of burning gums and leaves. The pungent smoke itched my nose and throat. Where I had been in awe, I began to weary. The maiden passed behind the screen and I watched for her returning, thinking of her young coltish thighs and soft breasts. She came; and by chance or because she could not help it, her eyes met mine. My mother was not looking; I smiled, and moved my lips in a kiss. She looked down confused; and not watching where she went brushed the screen with her shoulder. It tottered and fell down.

In the bull-ring and out, I had lived hard that last year, with my life hanging on a quick eye. I had looked before I knew.

The Goddess sat on the altar, in a little throne of painted wood. But she herself was stone. She was round and dimpled, both a woman and a stone. Your two hands could have spanned her round. Waist she had none, being great with child; her small arms were folded between her great belly and heavy breasts, her huge thighs tapered to tiny feet. She was unpainted, unclothed, unjewelled; a small round grey stone. There was no face to see; it was bowed upon her breasts, showing only rough-carved curls. Yet I shivered and sweated; she was so old, so old. Zeus' oak-grove seemed like spring shoots beside her. Earth might have fashioned her from itself, before man's hands could carve.

My mother and the crone had run at the screen and put it up again. The old woman stood making the signs against evil. The girl was pressed against the far wall of the cave, her eyes fixed and staring, her knuckles against her mouth, standing in the stream. The red mud of its channel stained her feet like blood. I dared not speak in the holy place. I looked my pity. But she stood stiffly and did not see.

At last my mother came out from behind the curtain, white in the face, with stains of ashes on her forehead. She beckoned me, and walked down the steps below. I followed silently. Over my shoulder I saw the two priestesses were together no longer. The old woman was near, keeping close for comfort. The girl was alone, a long way behind.

We passed the rock with the eye, and came out into unhallowed ground. My mother sat upon a rock, and bowed down her face in her hands. I thought she wept; but she said, 'It is nothing, it will pass,' and I saw it was a faintness on her. Presently she sat up. While I waited I had looked out for the girl. 'Where is she, Mother?' I asked. 'What will become of her?'

She answered with half her mind, being still weak and sick, 'Nothing; she will die.'

'She is young,' I said, 'to lay hands upon herself.'

My mother pressed her hand on her head as if it ached. 'She will die, that is all. She comes of the Shore Folk; when they see their death they die. That is finished; it was her fate.'

I felt her hand; it was warmer, and her face had some colour back. So I said, 'And what is mine?'

She drew her brows together, and laid her fingers flat on her closed eyes. Then she put her hands in her lap and sat up straight. Her breathing grew deep and heavy, her eyes as marble were dead to mine. I waited alone.

At last came a great sigh, such as the sick give sometimes, or men bleeding upon the field. Her eyes opened and knew me. But she moved her head as if its weight were too great to bear, and all she said was, 'Go home and leave me. I must sleep.' I could not tell if the Sight had come to her, or if she could remember it. She lay just where she was, in the dry leaves of the wood, like a warrior after a long day's battle or a slave all-in. I paused beside her, not liking to leave her in the wilds alone; but the old woman came up, and spread her mantle over her, and turned and looked at me. So then I went.

As I walked down through the forest, I looked through the trees if I could see the maiden going. But I never saw her again.

5

It took me five years to bring all Attica under one rule of law. I have seldom worked so hard. In war the battle-rage and the hope of glory sweep one on; in the bull-ring there are the cheers and wagers, and the life of the team. This work was lonesome and slow, and patient as carving a statue from a flawed block one must humour, yet keep the shape of the god.

Tribe by tribe and clan by clan I went to them, eating with their chiefs, hunting with their lordlings, hearing their assemblies. Sometimes, to draw a voice from the silent, I would go alone like a strayed traveller, and ask shelter from a fisherman, or at some stony mountain farm, sharing goat-cheese and hard bread and milling with them the small chaff of their day's troubles, the skinflint landlord and the sick cow.

Always, before I made myself known and worked my little wonder, I would ask for the altar of the ancestral god or goddess, and make an offering. It pleased my hosts and served my turn. These simple folk, shut in their fold of the hills, did not know the gods' first names, nor that they were worshipped everywhere, but used some outlandish title from the old homeland; they seemed often to think, even, that their Zeus was theirs alone, and Zeus in the next valley was his enemy. And the mischief of all this was, it turned the local chief into a king. Of course he was the god's high priest, or the Goddess's husband; how could he swear fealty to the servant of another god?

With a hard question, one cannot do better than bring it to Apollo; and that very night he sent me guidance. I dreamed of playing my lyre, which lately I had neglected, and of singing something wonderful. On waking I forgot the song; but I saw what the dream meant, and how the god would help me.

I tried it out first myself, dressed as a poor men's bard who sings for his supper and a bed. Coming to a valley farm at evening, I gave them a lay of Peleia Aphrodite, whom they worshipped there as something else. But of course they knew her in the lay, the Foam-Born with her doves and magic girdle; and I put in the song how the King had made her a shrine at Athens for helping him home from Crete. This time I went away without telling my name; it had pleased me to have my music praised by men who had no hope of favour. They gave me wine and a good cut off the saddle; and what is more, a pretty girl I had been playing eyes with while I sang, came slipping to my bed when the house was quiet. Clearly, my plan had Apollo's blessing.

So then I got the bards together. I paid them well, since their work would bring them to places below their standing. But if I could do it, so could they. Besides, they could see glory waiting for them in Athens, once it had the chief shrines there of all the gods. They agreed with me that no service could be more pleasing to the Immortals; and very well they did it.

As for me, I had to go about in my own person among the chiefs, and it was often tedious. One must remember their fathers' deeds, right back to whichever god they sprang from; remark the heirloom in the hall; sit through the plodding lay strummed by a hanger-on. And never a look at the women; I had got a name for liking them, and where someone else could lead out the horse, as the saying goes, I could not glance at the bridle without putting the family in a panic. One could soon have enough of this. Often I wished for someone to share my mind with; but their hearts were in little things, they would have thought me a dreamer, and I had to plan alone.

One summer day, I drove down to my great pasture on the plain of Marathon. It was royal land; my father had not stocked it for fear of raiders, it being much open to the sea. But I had had it cleared and the stone folds mended; and there I had reared the bull-calf got on old Hekaline's heifer by the Cretan bull. He was three years old now, running true to the strain; last year's calves were coming on, and a score of cows were carrying. For his dark-red muzzle, I had named him Oinops.

I was coming along through the olive groves, when I saw the smoke of bale-fires rising above the trees, and heard the horns. My charioteer pulled up the team and the riders stopped behind us. He said, 'Pirates, my lord.'

I smelled the air for smoke. This was a new thing on the seas, since Crete had fallen; or rather, an old thing had gathered strength. The Cretan captains, when they came to the mainland to take our tribute, had claimed it went to keep pirates down. There had been something in it.

My charioteer gave me a righteous eye. It said, 'Why will you ride so ill-attended? I told you your father would have brought the Guard, if he went so far.'

'Come, hurry,' I said, 'and let us see.'

We cantered along, and presently met a young lad running; the son of a small chief near. He knuckled the flaxen hair on his damp brow – he was about thirteen – and said out of breath, 'Sir, my lord King, we saw you from the tower. My father says be quick, I mean be pleased to honour the house, sir, the pirates are landing.'

I leaned down an arm and heaved him into the chariot. 'What sails do they carry? What device?'

One always asked this. Some sea-raiders were just a cut-throat rabble, content to burn the nearest peasant farm, steal the winter stores and sell the folk to slavery. But there were men of lineage too, younger sons, and warriors out to better their estates, who would make a war of it, and scorn a common prize. So we might see deeds today.

Boys of that age know everything. 'Three ships, my lord, with a winged horse, red. That is Pirithoos the Lapith.'

I said, 'This fellow has a name, then?'

'Oh, yes, sir. He is the King's heir of Thessaly. They say he is a great horse-raider up north, but sometimes he goes to sea. Roving Pirithoos they call him. My father says he fights for the love of trouble, he won't wait till he needs meat.'

'He can have his wish,' I said. 'We must get to your father's place before him.' I set down the charioteer, who was the heaviest, and touched up the horses. As we got up speed, the boy said, 'He is after your cattle, sir. He has a bet on it.'

When I asked him how he knew, he quoted me a fisher-lad from over at Euboia, where the ships had watered. Often I wonder where such boys go later, when I look at the fool-ishness of men. 'This is a bold dog,' I said, 'to count his spoils beforehand.'

He had been clutching the rail, with rattling teeth, for the road was rough; but now he looked straight up at me. 'He wants to try you for the sake of his standing, sir, because you are the best warrior in the world.'

It would have been nothing from some place-seeker at Athens; but here it was good, as when they called out 'Sing again!' at the valley farm. I answered, 'Well, it seems that is for proving.'

As we neared the village, the beacon-smoke rose higher, and the sound of the horns; people were beating too on basins and pots and anything they could find of metal, as they do to ease their feelings when an alarm is on. At the chief's steading, the top of the tower was full of craning women. Further on were shouts, and the bawling of cattle.

The chief met me at the gate. He had seen from afar I had few men with me; he was afraid I would strip him of his, lose them in battle, and leave him naked. I took none, but sent a horseman to scout. He came back, having been no further than the pastures. Two wounded men were there; the rest of the cow-wards had run away. The gate of the fold was broken and the sun-herd gone; and the pirate band had turned towards their ships again. The boy had been right.

'Time is short,' I said. 'Have you two fresh horses?'

He gave me two, the only chariot-horses he had. I saw the riders would not keep up far with me; the great Thessalian breed were rare then in the southlands, and none of theirs would carry a man for long. But one could not sit doing nothing.

As we went down along the olive-slopes towards the plain, I saw the chief's son running down a path and waving. 'Sir, sir! I have seen them, I climbed the pine tree. Take me up, my lord, and I'll show you where.'

'This is war now,' I said. 'Have you your father's leave?'

He swallowed, and said strongly, 'Yes, my lord.' At his age I would have said the same. Seeing me pause, he said, 'Someone must hold your horses, sir, while you are fighting.'

I laughed, and pulled him up. It is better to learn war early from friends, than late from enemies.

I drove on, and when the riders flagged, waved them back before their ponies foundered. Presently from an open place on the slope one could see the plain. The boy pointed.

On the curved shore of the bay were three long snake-headed pentekonters, riding as pirates do, close in with a stone anchor, which they cut to get quickly away. They had left a strong ship-guard. Pirates do not carry oarsmen who are not spearmen too, and about half their strength must have been there, some eighty men. The rest must have planned an inland foray, to need this care. Mostly they go for what they can see from off-shore.

The sound of bawling reached me. I drove to the next turn, and then I could see the raiders. They were driving the herd, like men who know how. While I watched there was a check; they clustered, heaving to and fro; then one went flying. It was the bull, living up to his forefathers. But the odds were against him; presently they got more halters on, and pricked him along with spears. Counting the horns, I saw they had taken only the Cretan stock, and the cream of that. They could be well away, before the footmen could catch them.

I shaded my eyes. There was a man apart, waving his arm, giving orders. His helmet gave off a flash of silver. 'That's Pirithoos,' I thought. 'The man who is off to range the Hellene coast-lands, boasting of how he pulled Theseus' nose.'

I turned to the boy and said, 'You can get down now. I am going after him.'

He cried, 'Oh, my lord, no.'

'Why not?' I said. 'A man must fight when he is challenged. I daresay the fellow hasn't reckoned on my coming alone; but if he is a warrior and cares about his standing, he must meet me, not set on me with his band. If he is no gentleman, I am out of luck. But it only comes once to us.'

'But sir!' he said. 'I only meant don't put me down.'

'This loses time,' I told him. 'You have heard me. Out!'

'But I am your man now,' he said, grabbing at the rail and going red as if he would cry. 'You took me for the horses. I have to go into battle with you, or lose my honour.'

'Well, you have a fair case there.' I had to admit it. 'This is no way to go on, to make old bones. Very well, then, let us go with our fate. Hold tight.'

We clattered down the slope on to the flat plain. Then we could go. The light car hopped and bounced over the salty clods. The sun shone brightly. Marathon always has the feel of luck for me. The horse-hoofs pounded; my arms rattled about me; my shield tugged in the wind and I slid it off for the boy to hold. He clutched it with one hand and held on with the other, drinking with open mouth the air-wash of our speed.

The pirates had turned to stare. They were big hairy men, with the bow legs Lapiths have from getting off their mother's back straight on to a horse's. They pointed, shouting, at my team; I remembered they are famous horse-thieves, and thought it would be a comedown if they killed me just for these. Their words were half lost in hair; at sea they do not shave their upper lips like Hellenes, nor their cheeks, but let it grow down like bears before and behind. Some had it to their middles.

The herd milled about, the Lapiths hailed each other in their bastard speech, antique Hellene and pirate slang. With all the noise, the leader had not seen me; the herd was between. It was odds-on one of these ruffians would have me with a javelin first. Remembering the bull knew his own name, I yelled out 'Oinops!' and for a moment he stopped dead.

The bright-helmed leader came running; just in time, too; one of the pirates was an archer, and had an arrow fitted to his string. The chief shoved him toppling backwards, and beckoned his armour-bearer, who brought his spear and shield.

He was about four-and-twenty; taller than the rest, and barbered like a Hellene, with a black rakish short-clipped beard and the rest shaved clean. He had dark brows just like the wings of a hawk, with that upward curve at the outer tips; and his eyes were light-green, almost golden: wild, bright and watchful as a leopard's, only beasts do not laugh. He balanced his spear and called, in true Greek but with a broad up-country lilt to it, 'Hoy, get back there. Who are you?'

His clothes were rich, but with something antique about them: great studs of worked bronze, a helmet of burnished silver, a lion-skin cloak with the teeth and claws. Round his right arm a long blue snake was twisted, stained into the skin as the Thracians do it. But the Lapith kings have married often into Hellene houses; they know the right names of the gods, and the famous battle-lays, and the rules of war.

I called out, 'I am Theseus, the man you have come to see.'

He grinned, and the corners of his brows shot higher. 'Well met, King Theseus. Don't you feel lonely, so far from home?'

'Why should I,' I said, 'if I can find good company? I have come to fetch back my cattle. Leave them where they are. As you are strangers, I will remit the fine.'

The pirates bellowed, and started forward. But he barked at them, and they pulled up like well-trained hounds.

'Your bull knows you, it seems. Have you missed each other?' He added a joke so rustic that it shocked the boy. I could tell from his men's laughter that they loved him dearly.

I said, 'What are you, Pirithoos? A lord of men, or just a cattle-lifter? I have come to see.' And I reached for my shield.

'Call me a cattle-lifter,' he said, 'who likes to pick and choose.' His bright eyes were insolent as a cat's are; without malice, and lazy, until it springs.

'Good,' I said. 'That goes with what I heard of you. Well then, there is a matter of standing for us two to settle.' I gave the reins to the boy, who grasped them as if his life were in them. Then I leaped from the chariot with all my arms.

We stood there face to face. Now I had got what I wanted, I found myself thinking I had never seen a man I should be sorrier to kill.

He had paused too, idling on his spear. 'You seem in love with trouble,' he said. 'Well, you want it, I have got it to give. I will make dogs' delight of you or any man who comes to me asking civilly. And what a squealing of women over your body! Oh, I have heard.'

'Don't be concerned,' I answered him. 'No woman hereabouts will squeal under yours. Not girls but birds will be getting their fill of you, when our business is done.'

'Birds?' he said, raising his brows. 'Don't you mean to eat me yourself, then? You are not the man they told me of.'

'You should come down oftener from the hills,' I said, 'and learn the ways of folk who live in houses.'

He laughed, standing with a loose shield and half his right side bare to me; he knew I would not take him off guard. I could not make him lose his head, nor get really angry myself. But it was no use to dawdle and wish we had met some other way. 'Listen, Pirithoos; this boy brought me your challenge. He is a sacred herald: if I fall, don't chance your luck. And now let us stop calling names, like a couple of women yattering over a cracked jar at the well-head. Come on, stand up to me, and let us try each other's bronze.'

I threw my shield before me. He stood a moment, looking straight at me with his big green cat-eyes. Then he shrugged his shoulder out of the shield-sling, so that the tall shield fell clattering, and tossed away his spear.

'No, by Apollo! Are we mad dogs or men? If I kill you, you will be gone, and I shall never know you. Thunder of Zeus! You came alone to me, with a child for shield-bearer, trusting in my honour. And I your enemy. What would you be for a friend?'

When I heard these words, it was as if a watching god had stepped down between us. My heart lightened; my spear fell from me; my foot stepped forward and I held out my hand. His with the blue snake round the wrist came out to meet it; the grip seemed one I had always known.

'Try me,' I said, 'and see.'

We clasped hands, while the Lapiths rumbled through their hair. 'Come,' he said, 'let us start clear. I will pay your fine for the cattle-lifting. I have done well this trip, my holds are full, meeting my debts won't break me. You're the King; you make the judgement. If you weren't to be trusted, you'd never have trusted me.'

I laughed and said, 'I saw old Oinops squaring his own score. Feast me one day and we'll call it quits.'

'Done,' he cried. 'I'll ask you to my wedding.'

After that we exchanged our daggers as a pledge of friendship. Mine had a gold inlay of a king in a chariot, hunting lions. His was Lapith work, and very good, not what you would expect from looking at Lapiths; the hilt was covered with fine gold grains, and the blade had running horses done in silver. As we embraced to seal the pledge, I remembered the boy had come to see a battle. But he did not look downcast: even the Lapiths, when their slow thoughts had come abreast of us, cheered and waved their shields.

I knew, as one sometimes may, that I had met a daimon of my fate. Whether he came for good or ill to me, I could not tell; nor, it may be, could a god have told me plainly. But good in himself he was, as a lion is good for beauty and for valour though he eats one's herds. He roars at the spears upon the dyke-top, while the torchlight strikes forth fire from his golden eyes; and one's heart must love him, whether one will or no.

6

When we had sacrificed and feasted, I took it without saying he
would stay as my guest at Athens. He said, 'Gladly; but not till after
the hunt at Kalydon. I have come south ahead of the news, it seems.
They have one of those giant boars there, that Bendis sends for a
curse.' That is an up-country name for the Moon Mistress; there
was a good deal of Lapith in him, as well as Hellene.

'What?' I said. 'I killed a big sow once in Megara; I thought she
was the only one.'

'If you hearken to Kentaurs' tales, there used to be a mort of
them.' His Greek was partly stiff and stilted, the work of his
boyhood's tutor where even the court did not speak it daily; the
rest was the coastwise jargon that pirates talk, and only better than
his men's because his mind was quicker. 'They say their forefathers
killed them off with poisoned arrows. Kentaurs don't hunt like
gentlemen; they are too wild.' I thought of his Lapith band, and
wondered what folk were like who seemed wild to these. 'They
eat meat raw,' he said, 'and never come down off the tops except
for mischief. If the pigs had killed their forefathers, it would have
been all one to me. Or if their fathers had made a right end to the
pigs, that would have been something. Kentaurs are curse enough;
and once in a while there are the pigs as well.'

I had been offended with him for refusing to be my guest; but
he had always some odd yarn to turn one's anger.

'In Kalydon,' he said, 'they sacrificed some virgins to Artemis.'
He had remembered her Hellene name this time. 'Three they
burned, and three they shipped up north to that shrine of hers,
where the maidens sacrifice men. But she sent them omens that
what she wanted was the boar. How they angered her I don't know,
but she is a goddess needs watching out for. Even Kentaurs look out

for *her*. So the King has a hunt on, and open house for warriors. This, Theseus, forgive me, I cannot miss. Friendship is dear where honour is dearest.' (I could see the tutor, beating the old lays into him.) 'Well, no need to part company. We'll go together.'

I opened my mouth to say, 'I have work to do.' But it seemed I had been working harder than a ploughboy for months and years. I thought of a footloose journey north, with Pirithoos and his Lapiths. It tempted me like a sweet look from someone else's wife.

He said laughing, 'You can stretch your legs aboard; I left deckroom enough for your cattle.'

I was still young. Not far behind me was the Isthmus journey, not knowing at dawn what the day would bring; Crete, and the Bull Dance. I had had the sign of Poseidon; I was born to be a king; and while I moved to it, everything within me worked the one way. Now I had got it. The King had enough to do. But there was another Theseus fretting idle; and this man knew him, too well.

'Why not?' I said.

So I put my business by, and went to Kalydon. I saw ships rolled over the peaceful Isthmus, the gulf of Corinth blue between mountains, and Kalydon by its mouth. And a fine boar-hunt we had there; great deeds, good company and a rich feast. It was good only while it lasted; for it started a blood-feud in the royal house there, and, as happens often, the best man died. Still, it was a great victory feast, for young Meleager and the long-legged huntress he shared the prize with; the grief was all to come. But the faces round the board grow dim to me, and I see, when I look back, Pirithoos everywhere.

I have been the lover of many women, never of a man. It was the same with him, and our friendship did not change it. Yet if I picked up a spear or a lyre, mounted a chariot, whistled a dog or caught a woman's eye, it was his eye I thought of. There was emulation mixed in our friendship, and even in our faith a kind of fear. From the day I met him, I would have trusted him with the woman of my heart, or my back in battle; and so would he have trusted me. But what he loved best in me, I myself had doubts of; and he could charm it like a bird out of the wood.

I went out of my way home from Kalydon, westward to Thessaly, to be his father's guest. We travelled light, cross-country, with the men he could spare from working home his ships; for speed, he said, but from the love of trouble as I could see. We had enough of it, from wolves and robbers and leopards and the mountain cold. Once, where the track clung to a steep gorge-side, a gale tore through it that made it sing like a great flute of stone; our shields were plucked and tugged by the hands of the wind-god, and would have sailed us off the face if we had not laid them down and filled them up with stones. One Lapith was lost that way.

At last we were looking down upon the plains of Thessaly, where the rich land lies in broken stretches between long arms and shoulders of wooded hills. The Lapiths encamped beside a spring, and prayed to the god of its river; then they washed and combed themselves, shaved their upper lips, and trimmed their beards. They came out likely and proper men, and three parts Hellene. When they had signalled with smoke, the Palace Guard came out to meet us. Then first I saw the real Lapith wealth: not growing in the ground but running on it, with the thunder dear to Poseidon. This is the home of the great horses, that can carry a man.

They were bloomed like new-shelled chestnuts, with manes as long as girls'; so fast and strong, I almost believed Pirithoos when he said that at their mating time the black north wind of Thrace came rutting down through the passes to leap the mares.

We rode them down the river valley. There the stream flows brown under poplars and silver birches; the stark mountains are only glimpsed far off, through tender leaves. Dark forests furred all the footslopes; Pirithoos called them the Kentaur woods.

Lapiths are great shipbuilders, being so rich in timber; they make the houses of it too, with carved lintels painted red. The palace of Larissa stood on a hill by the river, in the midst of the greatest plain. There Pirithoos' father met us at the gate. He greeted me most courteously, but was short and harsh with his son. Every time he went off roving, the old man saw him dead; when the fear was laid, the memory rankled. Above, in Pirithoos' room, I saw the fresh bed and rich hangings, and everything kept sweet while he was gone.

While I was there, Pirithoos showed me the Lapith riding-tricks; spearing a trophy at full gallop, snatching a ring from the ground; standing in the saddle, or shooting from it with the short bow they use. He could ride two horses standing, with a foot on each. His people swore that Zeus had taken on the likeness of a stallion to beget him. He had been riding great horses at an age when I was still standing on tiptoe to give them salt. I never had his style; but before I left, I could keep along with him more or less. A horse is not so hard to stay on, after the bulls; and sooner than give him the best of it, I would have broken my neck.

Once his father took me aside, and talked to me of kingcraft. We spoke of our laws and judgements and such things; and presently he asked me if I could not make Pirithoos put his mind to them; 'For he is a boy no more; yet he acts as if I would live for ever.' I had seen that he moved slowly always; his flesh was sunk, and his skin too sallow for a man not yet turned sixty. Afterwards I said to Pirithoos, 'Your father is sick; and he knows it too.'

He drew his brows together. 'Aye, so do I. After being away, I saw the change. I spoke with the doctor again this morning. Talk, talk; it's the empty jar that clinks so loud. There's nothing for it, I must take him up the mountain.'

I asked if Paian Apollo had a healing shrine there. He looked a little sheepish, then said, 'No, there's an old horse-doctor we go to when the rest give up. Come too if you like; you were wanting to see a Kentaur.'

I must have stared, after his talk. He whittled away at a bulrush (we were sunning by the river, after a swim) and said, 'Well, they have earth magic, if you can find a good one.'

'Where I come from,' I said, 'that is women's business.'

'Not among horse-folk. You southerners took that up from the Shore People you conquered. We keep the ways of our wandering forebears. Oh, yes, my father knows why I go roving; it's in all our blood; it's only his sickness makes him fret. Well, with horse-folk, women count as baggage, like the cattle. What else can they be while the people move: unless you want to have them take up arms, like the wild-cat Amazons?'

I opened my mouth; but I had talked enough of
and feared I might grow tedious.

'And Kentaurs,' he said, 'are horse-folk too, after t
hunted these hills all my life, and barely seen the rump
woman. At the first smell of you, they're off into the
when I was at school up there –'

He broke off short and I said, '*What?*'

He hemmed awhile, then said, 'Oh, it comes before our rite of
manhood hereabouts, among the royal kin. Other kings' houses
do it too; at Phthia they do, and at Iolkos. It's our dedication to
Poseidon of the Horses. He made the Kentaurs; they claim he
made them before Zeus made proper men. Or some say they were
got on horse-stock by earth-born Titans. We are horse-masters, we
Lapiths; but they are horse-kin, they live with them wild. Aye,
and shameless with the mares as noonday. Full of horse-magic, the
Kentaurs are; and that's worth more than any woman's corn-spell,
here in Thessaly.'

'But how did you live up there?'

'On the naked hills, and in the rock-holes. A lad should be hard,
before he calls himself a man. When you take arrow-poison, you
lie up in the sacred cave. No one forgets that night, by Zeus!
The dreams . . .' He covered his mouth, to show that telling was
forbidden.

'Arrow-poison?' I asked.

'Old Handy makes you sick with it; it can't kill you after, or not
for seven years. Then you must have another dose; but it's nothing
to the first. Well, you will see him for yourself.'

Next morning we started out at cocklight; we two on horseback,
the King on an ambling mule. We threaded groves of bay and
arbutus where the dew of the mountain mists brushed our bare
knees in the grey daybreak; then up the ilex slopes where it sparked
in sunrise; then through thick pinewoods that brought back night
again, with our mounts' feet soundless on the needle-pad, and
hamadryads pressing so thick and silent we almost hushed our
breath. Always the track was clear, not thickly trodden but never
quite grown over; there were horse-droppings, and the prints of
little hooves.

Even Pirithoos was quietened. When I asked him if Old Handy lived much higher, he half-looked over his shoulder, saying, 'Don't call him that up here. That's only what we boys called him.'

The sick King followed us, picking his way by the easy turns. He had the face of a man returning. His head had been sunk forward, when we set out; but now he looked and listened, and once I saw him smile.

The high air grew keen and sweet; we were among small fir-scrub, grey rocks and heather, blue space all around us, cold peaks beyond. In such a place you might come upon the Moon Mistress blazing like a still flame in her awful purity, staring out a lion.

Pirithoos reined in his horse. 'We must wait for the groom with the pack-mule. He has got the gifts.' So we waited, hearing new-waked birds, and the lark arising, and deep quiet behind. After a while, I felt someone was watching us. I would look round, and find nothing; and the hair would creep upon my neck. Then I looked again; and clear on a boulder a boy was lying, loose and easy as a basking cat, chin upon hands. When he saw my eye, he rose and touched his brow in greeting. He was dressed in goatskins, like a herd-boy; barefoot, with matted hair; but he gave the King and Pirithoos the royal salutation as it is done in princely houses.

Pirithoos beckoned him, and asked if the Kentaur priest was in the cave. He did not call him Old Handy, but by his Kentaur name. That tongue is so ancient and uncouth it is hard for a Hellene to shape his mouth to it; full of strange clicks, and grunts like bears'. The boy said in good Greek that he would see; he went springing over the rocky ground as light as a young buck, while we rode softly after. Presently my horse snuffed the air and whinnied. At the next turn, I saw a sight made me nearly jump from the saddle: a beast with four legs and two arms, for all the world like a rough-coated pony, with a shock-haired boy growing up from its shoulders. So it seemed, first seen. Coming near, I saw how the pony grazed head down, and the child sitting up bareback had tucked his brown dirty feet into the shaggy pelt.

He greeted us, making with his grimy hand the sign of homage you see in a royal guard. Then he turned his scrubby mount with his knee, and trotted the way of the first boy, quick as a goat over the stones. Presently as we followed, back came the first on just such another pony, some twelve hands high. He spoke the Kentaur's name again, and said he was in the cave.

As we rode, I asked Pirithoos whose son that was. He said, 'Who knows? The High King's of Mykenai, as like as not. They come from everywhere. The Old Man knows who they are; no one else does, till their fathers fetch them home again.'

I looked down at his feet; he sat his long-maned stallion the same way. I could see him then, with wild black hair falling into his green eyes, living like a mountain fox-cub by what was in him. It seemed there were other schools for that, besides the Bull Court. It was what had drawn us together.

The trail went round a shoulder. Beyond was a slope of rough grass, whin and bramble, stretching to a tall grey cliff-face; and in the face was a cave.

Pirithoos dismounted, and helped his father down; the pack was lifted from the mule and the beasts led away. I looked about me, and heard the piping of a reed. Sitting on a flat stone under a thorn-tree, a boy was playing; when he took the pipe from his mouth, a strange singing answered him. A lyre hung in the tree, which the wind was sounding softly. And coming nearer, I saw twined in the branches a great lean polished snake, swaying its head with the tune. I was going to warn him of his danger; but he shook his head, and looked at the serpent smiling, and waved me very courteously to be still.

Pirithoos and his servant were unpacking the gifts, when I looked at the cliff again. Two men were riding along its foot, towards the cave. I stared, and went up softly between the boulders. These were not princes living rough, these were the Kentaurs.

They were naked except for a clout of goatskin; but I thought at first they were clothed all over, so thick was their hair. On their necks and shoulders it did not hang, but grew down, in a thick ridge like a mane, tapering off over the backbone. The backs of their long arms and their bandy legs were thatched as thick as the bellies of their wild stocky ponies in whose fur they had tucked their toes, seeming to grasp with them like fingers. Little beasts the ponies were, like the boys' but cobbier, with strong hairy fetlocks, and an air hard to put a name to: disrespectful, you might say. If they were servants, it was only as the jackal serves the lion; they had struck their own bargain, this for me, that for you. Even as I watched the men slid off them, leaving them naked as they were foaled, to wander as they chose.

The men shambled along, with burdens in their arms. Their brows were as low and heavy as lintels, their noses short and wide; and as if their beards had all been spent upon their shoulders, a mere scrub bristled their shallow chins. Wild as the woods they were; and yet, they knew respect for a sacred place. They ceased their grunts and clucks to one another, and trod to the cave as softly as hunt-dogs at heel. There they bent and set what they carried close to the threshold. I saw each pick up a handful of its earth, and rub it on his forehead, before they went away.

Pirithoos had been busy with his own gifts: a sheepskin dyed scarlet, a painted crock of honey, and a netted bag for herbs. He beckoned me to come up the slope with them. The sick man was weary now, and his son laden, so I gave him my shoulder over the stones. As we neared the cave mouth, I heard a weak keening cry, and saw what the Kentaurs had left there: a comb of wild honey, and a child. It was a Kentaur baby, staring with old wrinkled eyes. They had wrapped it in a bit of catskin; its knees were drawn into its belly, as if it ached there.

Pirithoos spread his gifts upon the rocks, beside the honeycomb. The old King went forward, nodding to us, as if to say, 'You have leave to go.' Then he lay down on the bare warm grass at the cave mouth, near to the child.

We waited, Pirithoos and I, among the boulders. The servant had crept further off. Time passed. The King stretched out in the cool sunshine, as if he would sleep. There was no sound but the whining child, the mountain bees in the heather, and the boy who piped to the wind's harping and the snake's ear.

The shadows stirred in the cave, and a man came forth from it, a Kentaur. I had thought, from what I had been told, he must have some Hellene blood. But he was Kentaur all over, grizzled and old. He paused at the cave's mouth, and I saw his wide nostrils snuff the air like a dog's that has been indoors, his eyes following his nose. He went first to the child; picked it up, smelled at its head and rump, and spread his hand on its belly. Its crying quietened, and he laid it down on its side.

I gazed long at his face. Whatever wild shape his guardian god had put on to beget him, some god was there. You could see it in his eyes. Dark and sad they were, and looked back a long way into the ancient days of the earth, before Zeus ruled in heaven.

The sick King on the grass lifted his hand in greeting. He did not beckon, but, as one priest with another, waited the Kentaur's time. He nodded gravely; he was scratching as he did it, yet his dignity seemed no less. Just then a few notes from the boy made him prick his ear; he went and took the flute and piped a phrase. I heard a bird answer from the thicket. The boy said something, and he replied. I could not hear what tongue they spoke together, but the lad seemed easy and at home. And I knew the old Kentaur's sadness. He had come further up from the earth than all his people, who feared his wisdom and did not know his mind; so these were all his company, children who went down the mountain and turned to men, and forgot his counsel or were ashamed of it. 'An old horse-doctor,' they would say, 'who charmed us against arrow-poison.' But when the fear of sickness or death caught them back to childhood, then they remembered him.

He went to the King on his short bent legs, and squatted down by him, and heard what he had to say. Then he got on hands and knees and smelt him all over, and laid his little round ear to his breast, and felt his belly, first kneading it deep, then, when he started, gentling him like a horse. Presently he went off into the cave, with the Kentaur baby on his arm.

After a while he came back, with a draught in a cup of clay. When the King had drunk it, he sat down by him, and for a long time sang softly. What Kentaur god he was invoking, I do not know; it was a slow deep drone, burring in his great chest. The boy's piping, the wind in the lyre, and the chirr of crickets, all mingled with it; it was like the voice of the mountain. At last it ceased; the King touched hands with him, and came away. His step was no stronger than before, and yet there was a change. He looked like a man who has made peace with his fate.

Pirithoos looked at him awhile, then ran up the slope towards the cave. The Kentaur met him there, and they talked together. I saw Old Handy peer at him, perhaps to trace the boy he still remembered. When they parted, Pirithoos lifted his hand, as men do who make a pledge. All the way home he was very quiet; but in the evening, when we were alone and the wine had loosened us, I asked what promise he had given. He looked at me straight, and said, 'He asked me to be good to his people, when I am King.'

7

The Athenians welcomed me home; seeming indeed, like women, to love me more for my unfaithfulness; but they had saved up all their tricky disputes and tangled judgements for me to settle. Having dealt with these, and found them still content with me, I grew bold to push my plans. I proclaimed a great all-Attic festival, in the month of harvest home. The priests of the Goddess from every shrine, no matter what name they called her by, were bidden to the sacrifice; there were Games in her honour, where the young men could meet under sacred truce, and forget their feuds. And the tribal chiefs who were shepherds of their folk before the gods, I asked as guest-friends into my house.

Till that time, I had never found it weigh on me to be priest as well as king. Poseidon had been good to me, giving me the earthquake warning that the dogs and birds have, but, among men, only the blood of Pelops' line. Him I listened to, and did for the other deities such duties as are prescribed. But now, to reconcile the rites of all these jealous goddesses was like a judgement where a wrong verdict may start a ten years' war. One night I dreamed that they all appeared to me, threw off their sacred robes, and stood there mother-naked; it was my fate to give a prize to the fairest, and be cursed by all the rest.

This dream so shook me that I got up in the night and poured oil and wine before Athene. Her shrine was dark. In the hand of the priestess I had roused from sleep, as she shivered in the midnight chill, the lamp-flame trembled. The face of the Mistress, in the helmet's shadow, seemed to move like a proud shy girl's who says without words, 'Perhaps.' When I lay down in bed again, I slept sweetly; and next day when I met the priests and kings to plan the feast day, I got them easily to agree.

It seemed she liked her offerings. The feast and Games went through as if her hand were leading us all the way. The old men said that in all the tales of their own grandfathers, there had been no such splendour in the land. Luck touched us everywhere; fair weather and good crops; no new feuds starting; good omens at the sacrifice; at the Games, clean wins by men with few enemies. The people glowed, the youths and girls had a gloss of beauty, the singing was sweet and true. When I stood up to give the prize for wrestling, a great paean rose up from the people, so that one might have thought that they saw a god, and I said to my heart, 'Remember you are mortal.'

I threw with my luck, and at that same feast made all Attica and Eleusis into one kingdom with one rule of law. Lords, craftsmen and peasants all agreed to have their causes tried in Athens; the priests acknowledged their gods in ours, adding, if they liked, the name they used at home. At last they understood that this was the end of war in Attica; that any man, unless he had killed with his own hand and paid no blood-price, could pass through his neighbour's deme unarmed.

It was not long after this, that I rode out to Kolonos, to take the omens of Poseidon.

It is a pretty place, not far from the City, good for grapes and olives; young men in love go there to hear the nightingales. But the top is sacred to Poseidon Hippios; and even in those days, people let it alone. There was nothing to see, except broken boulders with a clump of fir-trees; but if you stood at the top, below you was a round flattish dip, as if a great horse-hoof had struck the ground; about as wide as a young boy can throw a stone.

It was a thousand years, I daresay, since the god had stamped there; scrub and thorn had grown over, the shrine was small, the priest sleepy and fat. But it had made me angry, last time I went, to see the place neglected, for the god was certainly present; when I stood on the crest, my nape shivered, and a ripple like a cat's ran down me. I asked the priest if he could not feel it, and he said he could; I knew he lied but could not prove it. Earth-Shaker himself did that within the year. The shock was nothing much; but the priest's house fell down, and killed him in his bed. The people of the deme were half dead with fright, and sent post-haste to me, begging me to make their peace with the god.

I drove out there in a three-horse chariot with a mounted guard. We had made our beasts fine, to honour the Horse-Father; my team with red-plumed headstalls and braided tails, and all the rest beribboned. We brought the finest stallion of my herd, wreathed for the sacrifice. But the god had chosen otherwise.

As we drew near, I looked out for the people who had so besought my presence. The road was empty. The feel of the god's wrath was heavy on the ground; I was on edge, and wondered if he had struck again. Amyntor was riding on to see, but I waved him back. I could hear over the slope voices shouting, and a woman's wail. I was angry now, and wanted to see for myself what they were up to. So I stopped the column and walked up on foot, with only a Guard of four.

As I got near, I heard the woman's voice begging for pity, rising and falling with broken catches as she beat her breast. There were curses, and the thud of stones. Mounting the rise, I could see the village people stoning a man. He was crouching down, guarding his head with his hands; there was blood on his white hair. The woman, who was still young, was struggling to go to him, begging them to spare her father who had suffered enough. When they thrust her back, she gave a great cry, calling upon Poseidon. At that I stepped forth with a shout, and they turned round gaping, dropping their stones.

The woman came running to me, sobbing and stumbling over the broken clods between the vine-rows; her clothes were torn, and bloody from her scratching her breast as she wailed. She looked old before her time, as peasants do, and yet not like a peasant; the lines had been drawn by other cares. She hurled herself down and clasped my knees and kissed them. I could feel her tears.

I turned up her dust-smeared face, whose bones were noble, and asked what they accused her father of. But the village headman spoke first. This outlaw, he said, unclean before all gods, had touched Poseidon's altar, trying when Earth-Shaker was already angry to bring death to them all. Meanwhile, hearing us speak the man had risen to his knees. He held out his hands before him, seeking something, I suppose the girl. I saw that he was blind.

'You can go to him,' I told her, and held my hand up to keep the others back. She went over and raised him, and put his stick into his hand and led him up to me. He was bleeding, but had no bones broken yet; and I could see by the way he got himself along that he had been blind a good while. She muttered in his ear, telling him who I was. He turned his head my way; and a shiver went all through me; for that old man had a face like Fate itself. Beyond sorrow, beyond despair; with hope and fear forgotten as we forget the milk of infancy.

He came up prodding his stick at the ground before him, and leaning on the girl. He wore a short tunic, as for a journey; it was torn and bloody, and had been soiled and worn before; but the wool was fine and the borders patterned, the sort of work that takes a skilled woman a long time on the loom. His belt was soft tooled leather, and had been studded once with gold; you could see the holes. From there I looked to his sandals; but I did not see them. For I saw his feet. They were strong and knotted and had carried him many miles; but they were warped like the wood of a tree which has been spiked as a sapling, and grown about the scar. Then I knew who he was.

A cold gooseflesh stood up on all my limbs. My hand came up of itself, to make the sign against evil. His sunk and shrivelled eyelids moved a little, as if he saw.

I said to him, 'You are Oedipus, who once was King of Thebes.'

He went down on one knee; there was a stiffness in his bending which was not of his joints alone. And for a moment I let him kneel, because I knew it would be courteous not to bid him rise but to touch and raise him; and I could not make my hands obey me.

When the people of Kolonos saw I did not move to him, it was as if I had opened a farm-gate to a pack of curs. Barking and baying they ran forward, picking up their stones again. You would have thought they danced upon their hind-legs, for me to pick the old man up like a skinned carcass and throw him to their jaws.

I shouted, 'Back!' My gorge rose at them, more than at what

knelt before me. So I took him between my hands, and felt his lean flesh and old bones like any other's, only a man in grief.

The woman had ceased her wailing and begun to weep, stifling it in her hands. He stood before me, his face tilted up a little, as if his mind's eye saw a taller man. Now it was quiet, I could hear the growling of the people, muttering to each other that even the King should not tempt the gods.

Kolonos of the Horses is always an uneasy place to me, for all its prettiness; and that day, as I have said, there was a lour about it, a brooding in the ground. Suddenly my anger swelled so that my body felt quite light with it. I turned to the snarling crowd and shouted, 'Silence! What are you; men? Or boars, wolves, rock-jackals? I tell you it is the law of Zeus to spare the suppliant. And if you will not do it for fear of heaven, by the head of my father Poseidon, you shall do it for fear of me!'

There was a hush then, and the headman came forward whining something. What with my anger and the awe of the place, I felt strange, as if the god's finger brushed my neck. 'I stand here for this man,' I said. 'Lay hand or stone to him, and you may well fear Poseidon's anger. For I will curse you in his name.' And it was as if a shudder flowed up into me from the earth beneath my feet; I felt I had the Power.

Now there was really silence. Only a bird cheeped somewhere, and even he spoke softly. 'Stand further off,' I said, 'and in good time I will ask his mercy for you. Now leave this man and woman for me to deal.'

They drew away. I could not look yet at the girl. I had been going to say, 'This man and his daughter,' when I remembered she was his sister too, out of the one womb.

She took her head-scarf and wiped his face where a stone had grazed it; I saw she was daughter in her heart, keeping faith with her childhood. It was time to greet him in some words fitting to his birth. But one could not well say, 'Oedipus son of Laios,' when he had killed Laios with his own hand.

So I said to him, 'Be welcome, guest of the land. Men should walk softly, where the gods have struck before them. Forgive me for these people, that I have not taught them better. I will make

amends. But first I must make sacrifice, for the omen will not wait.'
I was thinking I should have to bath beforehand, to take off the
pollution.

Now for the first time he spoke. His voice was deep, stronger
and younger than his body. 'I feel the touch of the god-begotten,
the promised guide.'

'Rest first and eat,' I said. 'Then we will lead you on your way,
and see you safe through Attica.'

'Rest is here,' he said.

I looked at him, and snapped my fingers at the men who carried
the wine for sacrifice. He had turned as pale as clay; I thought that
he was dying. My cupbearer fumbled and held back so long, I had to
snatch the cup from his hand. After the wine, the old man looked a
little better, but I had to hold him up. Some of my men offered to
help; but their faces were pinched as if they must touch a snake or a
spider, so I waved them off. There was a big slab of stone hard by,
some boundary of old-time men, and I set him there beside me.

He fetched a great sigh, and sat up straighter. 'A fine, full wine.
Thebes cannot match the wine of Attica.' It was the speech of feasting kings. I had been too awed for tears till then. 'God-begotten,'
he said, 'let me know your face.'

When he raised his hand, he felt the blood and dust upon it,
and wiped it on his tunic-hem before he reached it out to me.
'The tamer of bulls, the slayer of the Minotaur. And the shape of
a young dancer. Truly the gods are here.' His hand traced upwards
to my face, and touched my eyelids. 'The god's child weeps,' he
said. I did not answer. My men were near and I had to keep some
seemliness.

'Son of Poseidon, no grief is here, but a blessing. The sign long
waited has come at last. I am here to give you my death.'

It found me silent. How could one wish him longer life, or a
better fortune? Done was done. And though I pitied him, as any
man must not made of stone, I did not want his bones in Attica.
The Furies follow such men in a travelling swarm, like flies after
bleeding meat.

Just as if he had seen me look over my shoulder, he said, 'They
are here. But they come in peace with me.'

Certainly the air was gentle there; you could smell the ripening grapes. It was from the earth the tingling came, and I knew that of old; at Kolonos, Earth-Shaker seems always close beneath the ground. Without doubt he was angry, and might lose patience any time. It seemed to me this was no gift to please him.

'Why speak of death?' I said. 'In spite of what these oafs have done to you, you have no mortal hurt. Is it a sickness; or have you had it foretold; or do you mean to call it to you? Truly, you out of all men have the right. But such blood puts bad luck into a place, not good. Come, let your heart endure; it has borne worse things.'

He shook his head, and paused as if thinking, 'Will he understand?' I thought of his great sorrows, and waited humbly, as a boy before a man.

At last he said, 'To you I can speak. You went to the bulls of Crete for the Athenians. Surely, you had the sign of sacrifice?'

I nodded, then remembered and said, 'Yes.'

He put his hand to his grazed brow, and held up the wet fingers. 'This blood comes down from Kadmos and Harmonia: the line of Zeus, the line of Aphrodite. I too know the virtue of the given death. When the plague struck Thebes, I waited only for the omen. I sent envoys to Delphi, sure in my heart the oracle would say, "The King must die." But Apollo's word came back to seek the unclean thing. So I began to seek step after step into the darkness, on the path that led me to myself.'

He was still, as a well without bottom when you drop a stone. 'Past is past,' I said. 'Do not grieve in vain.'

He laid his hand on mine and leaned forward, as if he would tell a secret. 'When I had wealth and fortune, I would have died consenting. Yet after, I lived on. I have been hunted with dogs from villages. I have smelled on the dews of night the dog-fox running to his earth, and lain down with a stone for pillow, where Night's Daughters hounded me from dream to dream. Yet I, who would have died for the Thebans, would not do it for myself. Why, Theseus, why?'

I did not say that beggars often love life more than kings. 'All things pass; and patience brings a better day.'

'I know why now. I waited for the Gentle Ones. When the

score is paid, they take no more. The rest they hold in trust for you. All this last year, the sorrow has been like water caught in a deep cistern; not the beating rain that leaves you dry. I thought I should die at last like a winter sparrow, that falls in darkness from the bough and is nothing, save to the ants that pick it clean. But the store has grown. The kingly power is here again. I have a death to give.'

The girl, meanwhile, had been straightening her dress and hair; now coming nearer she sat upon the ground. I knew she wanted to overhear him; but he had dropped his voice, so I did not beckon her.

'Did you know, Theseus, that in dreams the blind can see? Oh, yes, yes; never forget it; it is a thing the young don't know. Remember, when you take up the brooch-pin, that at night your eyes will see again, and neither fire nor bronze will serve you then. There is a place the Solemn Ones would bring me to, where I saw what I must see. I came again to it; but all was stillness. They swept the floor with brooms of alder; then they sat down, like grey cobwebbed stones. First there was mist; then a clear darkness, with a little prick of windless flame. It burned up bright and tall; and in it stood the Lord Apollo, naked as a core of light, looking down at me with his great blue eyes like the sky that looks upon the sea. I thought, being unclean, I should avoid his presence; but pure in his fire he showed no anger, and I felt no fear. He raised his hand; the Solemn Ones slept fast, as ancient rocks do though the sun streams into their cave. And then he spoke, saying, "Oedipus, know thyself, and tell me what you are."

'I stood in thought. It came to me that I had stood just so, puzzling a hard question, in the Place of Ordeal sacred to the Sphinx. And then remembering, I knew the answer was the same. I said, "My lord – only a man."

'The Slayer of Darkness smiled at me. His light went through me, as if I had turned to crystal. "Come then," he said. "Since you have come at last to manhood, do what is fit, and make the offering."

'There was a stone altar in the cave, which I knew of old; but now it was washed of blood and strewn with laurel. I went up to it, and the first of the Solemn Ones came up with shears, like an old priestess with a kindly face. She cut my forelock and laid it on the altar; and I saw the hair fire-red again, as at my dedication when I was a boy.'

His hands were folded in his lap, and his face saw. I kept quiet, lest I bring the darkness back again. But presently he stood up straight, and called 'Antigone!' like a man used to be obeyed.

The girl came up. She looked as a dog does, when the house is stirring for some change it does not know; one not very quick, but trusty, the kind that will lie on a grave until it dies.

She held out her arm for his hand – it seemed that the long use must have worn a hollow there – and they talked together. I could have heard their words, but did not. For as soon as I had a moment by myself, I knew why it was my brow felt tight and my belly sinking, and the cluck of hens pierced my head like needles. If a child had clapped its hands behind me, I should have jumped a foot. A cold snake seemed coiling along my bowels. I looked at the olive trees of sweet Kolonos; already scared birds were flustered and chittering. It was the wrath of Poseidon Earth-Shaker, coming to a head at last and ready to burst the ground.

I looked about; at the old man talking to the girl, my guard yawning at ease, the gawping peasants beyond the vine-rows. When my warning comes, I get enraged with the people round me, all so unmoved while I, who have faced things most of them would run a mile from, am sweating cold. But the gift and the burden is from the gods; and one must bear it so. I kept quiet, and beckoned the Kolonians. They came hopefully, picking up their stones again.

'Be still,' I said. 'I have the warning of Poseidon. He will strike here before long. What do you expect, when you stone the suppliants at his altar?' At this they did not drop their stones, but bent and laid them like eggs upon the ground. I pointed them down the hill, and they went off, trying to run tiptoe. I could have laughed if I had not felt so sick.

Amyntor, who understood, said quietly, 'I have seen to everything, the horses and the Guard. Come away and rest.'

'Yes,' I said, 'but we must look after our guests first.' I turned to Oedipus, saying, 'Come. It is time.' So it was and more; I had trouble to keep my voice steady.

He kissed the girl's brow; she walked off down the hill, like a good dog sent home, and reaching out for me he laid on my arm his light strong fingers, with their seeing touch. 'Child of Poseidon, if your father is ready, so am I. Bring me to where his door will open, and give me to the god.'

I stared at his empty eyes. When I took his meaning, I could have run like a horse from a forest fire. All my life, when the earthquake-sickness took me, I had schooled myself to give my warning before I got away, and that took all my steadfastness. My hair, which was already prickling, began to rise upon my head. He could not know what he asked of me. And then I thought, 'But the god – he knows.'

Surely it was a Sending, this fearful thing; it could not have come from man. If I failed from fear, for certain his power would leave me. I said to Amyntor, 'Take the men down the hill, and wait.' He stared at me. I looked sickly, I daresay. 'Go,' I said, reminding myself what a good man he was, or else I might have struck him. 'I must do this for the god.'

He grabbed up my hand and pressed it to his forehead, then quietly fell in the Guard and took them off. I was alone with Oedipus the Accursed, while the still air lay like lead on the moveless treetops, the bees were silent, and the birds cowered among the leaves.

He tightened his fingers, asking where we should go. 'Hush,' I said; the least sound made me retch and shiver. 'Wait, I must see.' But all I could feel was the longing to flee in time. So I thought, 'Where do I want to run?' and then, slowly as an ox to the altar, I walked the other way. I saw where this was leading me, to the broken ground with the fir-trees. Then such a horror squeezed my heart, that I knew it was the place.

The blind man came with me quite easily, tapping with his stick before him. I steered him through the vine-rows, and up the slope to the gate. At every step my bursting head grew tighter, my heart beat harder, the gooseflesh rose on my neck and arms. That was my only guide, to go smelling like a dog after the scent of fear.

As we came up into the stony wasteland, he slid his fingers down my wrist to my hand. His felt quite warm and dry. 'What is it?' he said gently, but still too loud for me. 'You are sick, or in pain.'

One does not put face on, with a god breathing down one's neck. I said, 'I am afraid. We are getting near.' He pressed my hand kindly. I saw no fear in him; he had passed beyond it long ago. 'It is only my warning,' I said. 'When the god has spoken it will pass.'

The boulders with the fir-trees were close ahead. I could have looked more quietly at my own grave. I have never been much scared of dying; I was brought up to be ready any time, for who can tell when the god will want his sacrifice? This was not fear of anything, or I could have met it. It was just fear, like a burning fever that makes you shake with cold. And yet, his voice no longer grated on me. There was even comfort in it.

'You are the heir of my death. I cannot give it to my people. Our line was sent as the curse of Thebes; God grant that my sons are childless.' His voice had hate in it; for a moment I glimpsed him in his prime, a red man with pale fierce eyes. But the flame died quickly. 'To you, Theseus, and your land, I give my death and my blessing.'

'But,' I whispered, 'they stoned you at the altar.'

'Why not?' He was calm and reasoning. 'I killed my father.'

We were among the boulders. He threaded them without much help, seeming to feel them before the touch. My fear was sinking from my head to gripe my belly; I slipped away from him and voided it, and felt light and cold, but a little better. Coming back I steered him to clearer ground, and said, 'Fate was your master. You did these things unknowing. Men have done worse at less cost.'

He smiled. Even as I was, it awed me. 'So I said always, till I became a man.'

We had come to the edge of the horse-shoe dip, and the fear in me was saying, 'Be anywhere but here.' My head felt so empty it must float away; women say it is so before they swoon. So I thought, 'I can no more. The god will take me or leave me, I am in his hand.' And I leaned upon a boulder, as limp as a wrung-out rag. But he still talked on.

'I was reared Polybios' son. But I never favoured him; it was talked of, and I heard. And when I asked the god at Delphi, his only answer was a warning. "You will kill the planter of your seed and sow the field you grew in." So. Did I not know that every man or woman past forty must be my father or mother now, before the god? I knew. When the redbeard cursed me from his chariot's road and poked me with his spear, and the woman laughed beside him, did I not remember? Oh, yes. But my wrath was sweet to me. All my life, I could never forgo my anger. "Only this once," I thought. "The gods will wait for one day." So I killed him and his foot-runners, for my battle-fury made me as strong as three. The woman was in the chariot, fumbling with the reins. I remembered her laughter. So I dragged her down, and threw her across her husband's corpse.'

His words roosted in my mind like crows in a dead tree. I was so spent, I hardly shuddered.

'And later, when I rode as a victor into Thebes, shaven and washed and garlanded, she met my eyes and said nothing. She had only seen me in my anger; blood and rage and the grime of the dusty road will change a man. She was not sure. And the soft bright look of the wolf-bitch at the new leader of the pack . . . It is Theban law, that the King rules by right of marriage. To be a king, to be a king . . . I gave her a stranger's greeting. I never told, she asked no questions. Never, until the end.'

I heard these dreadful words; but they came to me like children weeping. For the presence of the god was pressing on my skull, and up the soles of my feet and through my loins from the tingling rock. I stood upright, as if his arm had thrust me forward. My fear was quenched in solemn awe. I was out of myself, only a string for his sounding; I knew what it is to be priest as well as king.

The blind man stood where I had guided him, a little below me in the trough of the holy hoof-print, his face looking to the earth. I said, 'Be free of it. Go in peace to the house of Hades. Father Poseidon, Earth-Holder, accept the offering!'

Even while I spoke, the birds flew upward screaming, and the dogs howled. I saw him stretch out his hands in prayer to the gods below; and then I saw no more. Deep down under, the hill's core gave a great grinding jar. I lost my footing, and slipped among falling stones and shale, till I fetched up against the roots of a fir-tree, sticking up naked from the earth. Close by I heard a mighty, bounding thud, another, and a heavy settling. At once the earthquake-sickness left me; my heart stilled, and my head was clear. It was like waking from a nightmare; so that I called out briskly, 'Where are you? Are you hurt?'

None answered. I pulled myself up by the fir-tree. The shape of the rocks had changed. The hoof-print's groove had opened in a cleft, and great boulders filled it. I made the sign of reverence to the god, and crept to the edge upon my knees; but the depths were still.

Far off, the people of Kolonos were calling the god by name and blowing bull-horns; and a lone ass hurled up his bray to heaven, as if all things that suffer had made him their spokesman to accuse the gods.

8

It was a year and more since I had seen Pirithoos, for he had buried his father and was King in Thessaly. It stopped his roving for a while. But when he did come, it was by sea again; salt-stained, storm-beaten, as hairy as his men, and clinking with gold. He had swept down on Samos while the King's men there were away fighting a war, and sacked the royal palace. He had brought a Samian girl, and even kept her a virgin, as a gift for me.

I had not been idle either; for I had conquered Megara.

The war concerned the tolls of the Isthmus road. Nisos the old King, whom I had had a treaty of free trade with, had died with no son surviving. He had been my kinsman; the heir was neither kin nor kind. He taxed all traffic from Attica, making excuse that when the treaty was drawn up, I was only King of Eleusis; as if any man of honour would not have stretched the point for me, who had cleared the road of bandits. At first, when I sent word to him, he gave civil answers and amends, then civil answers and excuses; then the answers shortened. This was foolish. It made me think, as any king would who cared to leave a name behind him, that with Megara in my hand I could push the bounds of Attica right up to the Isthmus neck.

So I came down on him before the weather broke. I dressed my men as merchants; their arms were stowed in their bales, and I had myself carried in a covered litter, such as well-born women use. We surprised the gate-tower, let in the army which had been waiting behind a hill, and were almost at the Citadel before the land was roused. We could have made as great a sacking as Pirithoos' at Samos; but I forbade it on pain of death. I had never yet ruled folk who hated me.

Pirithoos grieved to have missed the war, and sailed on home. I was busy with Megara all that year. Like the peoples of Attica, these had their ways, which I would not plough under; but that work had taught me something, and my hand was surer here. I was resolved to build a strong house that would stand after me, not a shoddy make-shift to fall on my son's head. So I was thinking, all the while I settled Megara and the Isthmus, built the great altar of Poseidon to mark my new-made boundary, and founded his sacred Games. And once every few days, I remembered I was rising five-and-twenty, without a wife.

Chance, mostly, had made it so. My father could not betroth me as a boy, since he had kept me hidden; soon after he acknowledged me, I had gone to Crete. When I came back I had great things in hand, and grudged the time.

My house had women enough, there when I wanted them, out of the way when I was busy; I had taken some more girls in the war, and could suit my mood; or if I found one tiresome, I could pack her off. What I should be doing, I knew full well; but I thought of all the tedious business: embassies; visits from kinsfolk and back to them; treaties and portions, with days full of paper and old men; the women's rooms to be brought in order, the tears and screams and threats to jump off the walls; the mess of girls and gear the bride would bring along with her, the quarrels and the jealousies, the tedium of the same face each morning on the pillow. It would do next season. Then an arrow would pass me near in battle, or a summer fever touch me, and I would think, 'I have no heir but my enemies; tomorrow I will see to it.' But tomorrow was another day.

And then, the year after the Megarian war, a big ship stood off Piraeus, flying the royal pennant of Mykenai and a red sail with the guarding lions. I made ready for a guest of honour, wondering what it meant. Soon came ashore a herald from Echelaos, the King's heir. He had taken the omens of the winds, before passing Sounion Head, and had got a bad one; could he be my guest for the night?

I met him at the port, and found him what I had heard: a big man of about my years, personable and proud, but able to be easy when he wished to please.

Since we met, as he said, by luck and weather, he put on the lightness of men at the hunt or at the Games: told battle-tales and jokes, admired my horses. At evening, over wine in my upper room, he loosened further, gossiping about his father's health and his mother's strictness; she was too hard, he said, on his younger sister who would soon be a woman. 'A girl who is shooting up like wheat, and coming into beauty, one cannot keep her a child for ever.' He looked down at his long brown hand, and turned his signet.

I kept a pleasant face, though my mind was buzzing. This was what had come of putting off. I thought how it would have rejoiced my father, when Attica was a rock in a little plain. To me it was a baited trap. My power was too new to come under the great shadow of Mykenai; they would suck me in, and my heir would be their vassal in all but name. A few years more, and it might have been a match of equals. So they thought too, it seemed.

Well, this would teach me to delay! It was now or never. To pause, and consider, and withdraw, would be a mortal insult; and the Lion House does not stomach insults much better than the gods.

Haste would be improper. He had managed his part well, and so must I. So I sent for a Cretan girl who played the Egyptian harp, and bade her sing. I was glad to see he fancied her, for he might need sweetening. She saw it too, and made the best of herself, her mind on a jewel from the golden town. I had kept her for her music, and never slept with her; even the scent she used brought back the Labyrinth, the secret midnights, the dreadful farewell on Naxos. But Echelaos' eyes were busier than his ears.

When the song was over, he looked like a child who sees the honey-pot being put away. So I motioned the girl to stay for another song, and said to him, 'Yes, it's a pretty air. I heard it sung by the girl I am betrothed to, while she was still a child – King Minos' daughter Phaedra. Ah yes; it is time I sailed to Crete again.'

He took it well, clearly believing me, and saying, even, that he had heard as much. He had come, as now I guessed, to sound me and make sure. Soon he went to bed, and I sent the girl to him. That would leave him no time to brood. As for me, I stood late upon the balcony, thinking how quickly fate had settled this over my head.

It was the only marriage, as I had long since known. I had thought I could take my time, since they could not betroth her without my leave. Of course they had not asked; they had been waiting for me. Well, there could be no more trifling, after today.

I had not seen the child since I was a bull-boy. She had been seven or eight years old. Before the Bull Dance, they would bring in the little ones of the princely houses, just to see the procession of the dancers into the ring, and be shown the first in fame. Before the bull-gate opened and there could be blood, their nurses took them away. Thus she had come, one of a crowd of piping children I would sometimes wave to, as I passed by. One day, when a rumour ran round that the bull had killed me, she had screamed herself so nearly into a fit that her scared nurse had fetched me up to her, to prove I was still alive. That was how I remembered her; a naked tear-drenched child on a painted bed, curled up in tumbled linen, clutching my hand.

Then I had met her sister, and came into the ring with my mind on other things; but now and then, lest my face wore my thoughts too clearly, I would turn to the children's balcony and smile and wave. By my counting, now, she must be about fourteen.

Like a winding thread, my thoughts passed and re-passed about the Labyrinth, and came at last to Naxos.

I had never set foot there, since that midnight sailing. But my ships, when they passed that way, had had orders to bring word if ever Ariadne the Thrice-Holy should leave the shrine. So much was needful; to hold her could bring great power to an enemy. But she had grown too sacred; years passed and she was still there, in the sanctuary of Dionysos on its off-shore island. Each vintage moon, she led the maenads up the mountain; at nightfall they came down swaying with wine and weariness, their hands wrist-deep in blood; and last year's Vine King was no more seen.

For a long while after that Naxos feast, my tongue had been sealed with horror. But kings cannot sit hand on mouth, like frightened children. She had to be accounted for. In Crete, when I freed the Labyrinth, I had told the people she would be my wife. So when I went back there, and had put the land in order, I told this story to the princes: that I had had a dreadful dream at Naxos in the Isle of Dia, Dionysos appearing to me in his shape of terror and warning me off his chosen bride. Which was true enough, after its kind.

So I had put her off with a show of honour. In time, having passed through the Islands mouth to mouth, my own tale came back full of marvels. She was so dear, it seemed, to Dionysos, that his vine-grown ship would glide by starlight to the water-stairs, and he would come to her in the shape of a black-haired man. I hoped it was true she had found a lover. She was a girl it would come hard on, to sleep alone.

And then, after a few years more, news came that she was dead in childbirth by the god. Whether the child had lived I could not learn; Dionysos' shrines have many secrets. I should lie, if I said I grieved. It was a burden lifted. And it left young Phaedra clear heir of the House of Minos, last of the Children of the Sun.

When Echelaos left next morning, I gave him for his guest-gift the Cretan singer. It made him my friend for a long time after; and as he shortly became King, the present was well spent.

I had thoughts of going to Crete for the betrothal, to see the girl for myself. Then there was a blood-feud at Eleusis, which no one else could deal with. So I sent an embassy instead, with a great gold bowl as a pledge to the kinsfolk. For the maiden I ordered something prettier; she had been a delicate child, small-boned and silken-haired; the palace goldsmith made her a wreath of lapis hyacinths, with sprays for the ears. But my mind's eye still saw her in the nursery with monkeys painted on the wall. So I sent her one in a little scarlet coat, and wondered if she would remember.

The ship came back bringing the kin's consent, and the gifts of compliment. One was a likeness of the maiden, painted on ivory; but it was just like any Cretan picture of a girl or goddess. Even her hair had been done black, which I knew was fair light brown.

I had given my envoy leave to go, when he lingered and caught my eye. He was a white-haired baron I had chosen for his gentle manners. When I had sent the rest away he said, 'My lord, I have something in trust for you.' He brought out a packet of embroidered stuff. 'The princess sent it herself, by an old nurse of hers. I was to tell no one but you, for her aunt would scold her, but you would understand.'

Inside was a wreath of plaited hair. There were two colours in it. I stared; then it came back to me. That day in Crete after the Bull Dance she had begged a lock of my hair, saying, as little children do who know nothing of the matter, that one day she would marry me.

The old man said, 'She has been kept much alone; it is only innocence. Ah, but the bird is knocking there within the eggshell; and a lovely bird it will be.'

I told him the tale, being happy and glad to share it. Now the thought of the maid began to take hold of me, and I grew her in my mind from child to woman. Beside this picture the Palace girls looked coarse and stale, and most nights I lay alone. The lands were quiet; once more the fancy took me to sail for Crete.

I sent no word before me, meaning to do it from some port near by. I had not told even my pilot yet where I was going, keeping my secret like a lad. When I ordered my ship fresh painted, a new awning, a fanciful gryphon beak from the bronzesmith, I saw smiles sometimes, but did not care. As the news of the match went round, I saw that it pleased everyone. Even the lords who had hoped I would choose a daughter of their house, were glad their rivals had been passed over. Everyone would have feared the tie with Mykenai, as they would have feared one with Minos in the great days of his power. But now Crete was down, they saw a bond that would hold the great land safe in vassalage. The men praised my wisdom; the women had heard about the keepsake and thought it pretty as a minstrel's tale.

I was at the harbour seeing the new beak fitted, when there came a shout from the watch-tower that a pirate fleet was in sight.

A great outcry began, people driving the livestock inland and carrying off the bales. Sea-rovers had been getting bolder; there had been flying raids all along the coasts to the Isthmus. Soon we saw longships, coming in under oar and sail. But the foremost signalled with a polished mirror, three times three. I laughed, and sent to disband the warriors and make the guest room ready.

The people looked rather askance at Pirithoos, having been

afraid to the last that he meant to sack the harbour. For myself, I was overjoyed; I needed a friend to talk with freely.

This time he was fresh and barbered, his ships in trim. He was outward bound though it was high summer, for the kingdom's business had held him. I did not wait for his story, being full of my own. Upstairs after dinner, the wine at our elbow and the servants gone, I poured it out to him. He was all for the marriage, till I said I was off to Crete; then he stared and laughed, and said, 'Have you lost your wits?'

I had got used to prettier phrases; even the Palace girls had kept their thoughts to themselves. Before I could answer, he went on, 'Can't you see it is the way to spoil your marriage, to see her now? A little giggler with the puppy-fat not fined off her yet, and spots as like as not. All idle Palace-bred girls go through it; it's only peasants who work it off that are pretty at fourteen. Oh, no doubt she's a good girl, and will be beautiful. So wait for it, don't start with downcast hopes and a dismal bedding. Mark my words, if you wed now you'll be stale for her when she comes to her best, and she will have a roving eye.'

This dashed me a little. I said, 'I need not marry yet. When I see her I can decide.'

'Don't see her at all, if you want to love her after. And when you bed with the pretty bride you dreamed of, don't forget to thank me. Meantime we have sailing weather, and deeds to do.'

I had guessed all along he had been pleading his own cause. Yet there had been something in it.

He said, 'And your ship is ready. A lucky omen! Listen, and see why I've sailed a week out of my way to fetch you.'

He told me the venture he had in hand: to sail north to the Hellespont, and force the straits, and on into the unknown Euxine, searching for gold. 'There is a river comes down in the sand; they tie rams' fleeces to strain the stream, and haul them up full of gold-dust. I talked with a captain of Iolkos who brought one home with him. He didn't get it without trouble; but what are we, women? Why flog along old sea-roads, when one can see the world?'

I began to say, 'We could sail on after Crete,' but I knew there would not be time. All my life I had wanted to see the country beyond the straits, at the back of the north wind. Reading it in my eyes, he gave me a long tale of marvels, earth-born warriors spawned from dragon-teeth, witches who could make old men young in a magic bath, and such sailors' yarns. I laughed. And then he said, 'Oh, yes, and we shall hug the Pontos coast. That's where those Amazon girls come from, that you thought so much of in the bull-ring. Don't you want to see how they live at home?'

'Why should I?' I said. 'Bull-dancers never talk of home. It's like belly-ache, it takes your mind off the bull.'

So he went back to the Kolchian gold and dragons, while I stared into the lamp-flame in its bowl of streaked green malachite, seeing pictures in the grain.

'Well,' he said at last, 'but they are waiting for you in Crete. You don't want to offend them.'

I answered, 'I've not sent word yet.' It was all he got that day from me. But he knew that he had won.

9

Half Athens saw us off at Piraeus, when we had sacrificed to the Lady of the Winds. I thought, when I heard the cheers, how times had changed. In the great days of Minos, pirates were no better thought of than brigands on the land. But now there was no fleet strong enough to guard all the sea-roads. Kings fought for their own shores, and sometimes sailed out to take vengeance; and where there is war there's spoil. From this it was not far to roving on adventure. Young men could set themselves up in life; kings could grow rich without hard taxes, which pleased their people; warriors could show what they were made of, and see the wonders of the earth. Only the greybeards murmured, when I put to sea with Roving Pirithoos and manned the benches of my ships with spearmen. Chiefs' sons, whose fathers would have had blood from anyone who offered them an oar to pull, were nearly fighting in my presence chamber to get their names in first.

They had time to work their hands in. We got a steady south wind all the way to the straits; dolphins curvetted in our bow-wave, and blew glittering spray from so blue a sea that one looked to see it dye the oars. Once or twice we saw smoke on shore, and longships beached there; men on our business very likely; but they let us be. It could be seen from our strength and blazons that we were a royal fleet; and wolves make way for the lion.

I could have dived in and swum with the dolphins for joy to be alive. For a long time the rover in me had been a slave and captive of the king; and now he was on holiday. My eye was as fresh as a boy's, and my heart as light.

If we had been sailing to plunder Hellene lands, I should have felt less easy. To me all Hellenes are kindred of a sort; which is why, in the Hellene lands I have conquered, I have treated all men as my own people and made no serfs. Some kings know nothing beyond the neighbour they are at feud with; for them, you are foreign if you come from ten miles off. But I have been a prisoner where strange gods were served, and what was dear to us was nothing to our masters. It draws one to one's own kind.

We coasted north to the mouth of Peneus, where Pirithoos' people lit a smoke-fire for him, to let him know that his lands were quiet. So we went on, and rounded Mount Athos safely, and sighted Thasos where they mine the gold of Troy. A Trojan fleet was there, loading, and must have had a king's ransom aboard. But one does not bite the gryphon's tail, where the head can reach so quickly. So we passed Thasos by.

Ahead was Samothrace, where great dark cliffs and wooded steeps stand straight up from the sea. It has no ship-harbour, which has kept it wild. But it is sacred; Pirithoos and I had ourselves rowed ashore in their boats of hide, taking our stern-pennants to be charmed against shipwreck and defeat by the dwarf gods of the mountain.

We climbed steep winding paths that tacked about the crags, up through mist-swathes that danked the fir-woods; past rocky slopes where the hamlets of the Sai, the oldest Shore Folk, are perched like the nests of storks, and on their roofs nest the storks themselves. At the very top, above the cloud-wet woods, are high stony uplands. The dwarf gods' rough-hewn altar is there, and the holy cave. Having come so far, Pirithoos and I asked to be charmed against defeat and shipwreck ourselves. The rites are secret, so I will only say that they are brutish and nasty, and foul one's clothes. I left mine on the beach below and, to feel clean again, swam all the way to my ship. However, we were neither wrecked nor defeated, so one must say of the dwarf gods that they kept their word.

While we were in the cave, a hunchback priest with the legs of a bandy child asked us each apart in a vile coarse Greek if we had done any crime beyond the common run. The dwarf gods, he said, had had to be cleansed for murdering their brother; so the man in need of cleansing wins favour there. I told him how I had not changed my sail coming home from Crete, and what had come of it; and he said it would be much to the dwarf gods' mind. They seemed pleased too with Pirithoos; but he never told me why, and, wishing to keep my own counsel, I did not ask. As we clambered down the mossed craggy paths, the wooden rhomboi, that they dance to in the cave, boomed and roared in our ears; and when we had rowed out of the long shadow of the mountain into sunlit water, it was like being born again. But it is true that I never dreamed again about my father, after that day.

Then the straits of Helle were there before us, like the mouth of a great river. We hove-to, to wait for night. In summer the north-east wind blows down head-on all day there, but drops at sunset. We put ashore for water with all hands armed; for the people there are great ship-robbers and wreckers. Pirithoos showed me a chart the captain from Iolkos had made for him, showing which shores to hug where the eddies would run our way. This man, he said, had been a king's heir whose father had been put aside by a powerful kinsman. The sailor son had not wealth enough to raise an army and get back his heritage; but in this voyage he got enough fleeces full of gold-dust to hire all the spearmen he needed. He had given his chart to Pirithoos because they had been boys together at Old Handy's school; and because, as he said, he would not live to make another voyage to the Euxine. He was King in Iolkos; but he suffered a good deal from a curse that a northern witch had put on him. 'So give them a wide berth,' said Pirithoos, 'even if they offer to do you favours. He told this one he'd marry her if she showed him how to get the gold from Kolchis. Now the curse is eating his bones, and by his looks he won't last long.'

'Kolchis?' I said. 'Did he tell her name?'

'The crafty one, he called her. Aye, and that was her name. Medea.'

I told him how she had been my father's mistress and had tried to poison me. As to his share in it, he had been frightened for the kingdom; and the least I could do was to respect his memory.

Five nights we nosed along the straits, catching the inshore eddies; first through the narrows, then by Propontis where you lose the further shore. By day we lay up watch and watch; for the Hellespont is by water what the Isthmus used to be by land. We rigged up bulwarks of shields and hides to keep off arrows, as the

Kolchian captain, Jason, had warned Pirithoos to do. Even so one man was pinned by the arm and died of it. And we had only the chiefs to deal with, being too strong to tempt the lesser bands; so this Jason must have been a good man, to have forced the straits with a single ship.

On the sixth night the water got so narrow we could hear jackals barking on the far side, and see men move around their watch-fires. Just towards dawn, a new breeze struck our faces, open and salt. The two shores fell away; our prows pitched in a sea-swell. So we hove-to till light, and it showed us a wide grey ocean. It was the Euxine, the Traveller's Joy. So they call it; for its gods are the sort one had best to be civil to.

We steered to the east; and when the sun had risen the sea was blue, dark-blue as lapis. First the land was low; then it rose in high mountains, cleft with gorges carved by the winter rains, and hung with deep forests or sunny woods. When we put in for water, we found it splashing down boulders gleaming like black marble, into pools of mossy stone under the shade of myrtles. Birds sang sweetly, and the woods were full of game. We longed to camp ashore, eat fresh-cooked meat and wake to the sun through green leaves. But Jason had said the forest folk were fierce hunters, who would pick you off with poisoned arrows before you had seen one move. So we posted watches and slept on board; and the night guard got with javelins two men who were sneaking up to throw fire into the ships.

Next day, still pushing eastward, we had flat calm; but by now the rowers' hands were hardened, and a good singer had worked them in. Towards evening, we saw cloud on the mountain-tops. At once Pirithoos called out to pull for shore. Before we made it, down came a black, wicked north-east squall. We were driven out beyond sight of land; great green-black seas tossed us as we ran before the wind, and we needed more men baling than rowing. At fall of night, the storm dropped as swiftly as it had come, and left us in calm under a sky of clearing stars. We rocked about in the swell till daybreak; while I thanked Blue-Haired Poseidon, who had never yet forsaken me on land or water.

The sun rose out of a jagged skyline. Great heaven-spearing

mountains reared, tipped with snow, above the nearer hills which had hidden them while we hugged the shore. As we set course, Pirithoos conned the chart and shouted from his ship that we must be near Kolchis, and should beach soon for a war-talk.

Presently we sighted a dip in the hills, and a river mouth. When we came nearer, there was a little plain beside a river, with a city of wooden houses thatched with brush, and a king's house of stone. We steered away, and put in at a creek beyond the headland, to make them think we had sailed on.

Our weapons had suffered from the storm; the hide shields were wet and heavy, and all the bowstrings were spoiled. But we had our spears and swords and javelins; and we agreed together that whereas Jason with a single ship had had to get his gold by stealth and bribe a sorceress, we need not be so modest. We would lie up till dark, and sack the town.

And this we did. The Kolchians kept a good watch and saw us landing, though there was no moon; but it did not give them long to get their goods up to the Citadel, and they left a good deal behind. We fought in the streets by the light of the burning houses; and the men of Kolchis giving way before us, we caught up in the mountain road with the mule-train that had the gold. There were rich townsmen too, who had slowed their flight with too much gear. But mothers carrying children I let go free. Some of the men, who had been some time at sea and wanted women, were displeased by this, especially Pirithoos' Lapiths. But he took my part from friendship, and told them that if they wasted time they would miss gold enough to buy them girls for a year.

We threatened the men of the gold-train, to make them tell us where the fleeces were: promising more, indeed, than we could have performed. Neither Pirithoos nor I could stomach torture; it was one of the things on which we both agreed. However, they showed us the fleeces in the stream; they had not very much gold in them, having been lately changed. But they made good trophies, and I never washed the gold from mine, but hung it as it was in my Great Hall.

What with the gold, the loot from the houses of the King and headmen, the goblets and brooches, worked swords and daggers and fine-woven clothes, we were well content, and ready to turn for home with what the gods had given. But first we scuttled all the Kolchian ships, which Jason had had no chance to do; and that, as he had said to Pirithoos, was the root of all his troubles after.

The day dawned calm. Though we were weary, we rowed hard to shake off the Kolchian shore, lest the King might have allies near. Soon after sun-up we got a breeze, and let the rowers sleep at the thwarts. The pilot's watch, who had caught a doze while the ships were beached, saw to the sailing. Pirithoos and I, each in his own ship, lay down on our pallets aft to rest. I looked at the blue sky up above, with the great serpent-painted sail straining at the yard; its creaking soothed me, and the thought of the good work done.

I woke up knowing that something was afoot. It was past noon; the sea was as dark as wine, the sunshine like pale honey. We were close inshore, under hills with green woodlands gilded by the westering light. The ship was rocking and listing, as the men craned and scrambled to the landward side. I jumped up swearing, and made them trim her; then I went to see. Right up in the beak was a ledge for the pilot to stand on and con a tricky passage. I clambered into it, and grasped the bronze gryphon by its comb.

I soon saw what the riot was about. Rounding a point close in, we had come right on a troop of girls bathing. Not dabbling either, like women washing their clothes, but swimming in the open sea. Now of course they had made for land; the steersmen without orders had put their helms hard over, and the warriors were at the oars.

This was madness, for the woods might cover anything, and came right down to the shore. I opened my mouth to curse them and order them back on course; but the words delayed. I too had been weeks at sea; I had to pause for a look.

The ones in the water were going so fast, with clean flashing arm-strokes, that I might have taken them for boys if some had not got ashore. They were running for the covert, going over the pebbles lightly, as if their feet were hardened; yet they had not the look of peasants. They moved too proudly. Their thighs were taut and sleek, the legs long and slender; their shallow breasts were as perfect as wine-cups turned on the wheel. All over they were gold with sun, not skewbald from wearing clothes; and on the brown their pale fair hair shone like silver. They all wore it alike, not very long, and drawn into one thick plait behind, which bounced between their shoulders as they ran.

The quickest had reached the woods; where the groves were thin I could see the sun-dappled gold limbs moving. And I thought, 'If these are the women, what are the men like? Surely, a race of heroes. If they come it will be a battle for bards to sing about, and some of us will feed the kites. Well, if they come, they come.'

I waved to the boatswain, and shouted, 'Faster!'

The warriors leaned laughing on the oars. We were coming in so fast, the girls who had been furthest out were still in the water. One was a short javelin-cast ahead. There was a splash alongside. Young Pylenor, a famous swimmer who had won many prizes, was out to get another. He shook the water from his eyes and shot off like a spear. The men cheered him; it brought back Crete to me, and the roar of the ring.

All the rest of the girls had got ashore and into cover. 'No matter,' I thought. 'The slope will slow them; trust a hungry dog to find the hare.' Young Pylenor was gaining fast. I made someone stand ready with an oar to throw him. There would be a struggle for sure, and both might drown.

The beach was all empty sand and kicked-up footprints, when the thicket parted. Out came a girl again, and came running like a deer straight down to the sea. The men yelled with joy, and called out the greetings of their choice. I did not add mine. For one thing, I saw why she had wasted no time on dressing. She had slung on her quiver, and got her bow.

It was the Scythian kind, short and strong. She waded in nearly to the knee, before she tossed the rope of silver back from her shoulder, and nocked the arrow to her string. By then, I was hit already. The lift of her breast to her back-bent arm, the curve of her neck with its strong and tender cord drawn like the bowstring, shot me clean through with a shaft of flame. She stood to aim, all gold and silver touched with rose; her brows pulled together, her eyes level and clear, and the bawdy clamour passing her by as rain runs off crystal. Her glance raked us over like a hunter's who from some bellowing herd chooses a beast for the pot. I never saw a face of such flawless pride.

She was ready; but instead of shooting she called, 'Molpadia!' Her voice was cold, wild and pure like a boy's or a bird's. She signed with her head; I saw what she was up to. The swimming girl, coming head-on, was between her and the man.

I shouted 'Pylenor!' loud as a war-cry. The girl had swerved in the sea. But, deaf with water and the fury of the chase, he neither saw nor heard. He turned in her wake, giving his side to the shore. The 'Paff!' of the arrow was like the sound of a rising dolphin; it was the end of his dolphin days. It took him under his forward arm; like a speared fish he jerked up gaping, thrashed about, and sank.

My men were shouting with anger. I felt the ship rock as the archers sprang on the benches, heard the dull pluck of the sea-spoiled strings, the arrows puttering and splashing. The ship drove on. I felt as if my eyes were pulling it.

She stood laughing in the water. Her laughter made my backbone ripple. It had neither shame nor shamelessness; she laughed alone, pleased with her victory over strange monstrous things. She was like the Moon Goddess, deadly and innocent; gentle and fierce like the lion. She waited to cover the swimmer coming to land.

The light off-shore breeze bucked the bronze beak; I seemed to ride it like a stallion. My blood was all wine and fire. I watched her hand dip to her quiver, and heard with half an ear voices behind me: 'My lord, get down, my lord, take care; sir, sir, you are right in bowshot.' The bow rose and her eyes followed the arrow – nearer, nearer to mine.

To meet them I swung out from the gryphon, holding by one hand. That opened them wide. They were grey; grey as spring rain. Next moment they narrowed, and her arrow vanished behind its point.

Men were telling each other to pull me down off the prow. I knew none of them would dare. I had to speak. But what would reach her? Only the speech of mating lions; he sheaths his claws when she growls. Let her know me by it, now or never. I leaned out from the beak, and raised my arm in greeting.

For the moment all three were still: her steady eyes and the arrowhead. Then all three shifted just a trace; she loosed the bow, and skewered the padding of some man's war-helm. She waded further to grasp the wrist of the swimming girl, and ran into the thicket with her, never looking back.

The rowers backed water, the ship hove-to. I stared at the check, no thought in my mind but to follow and find her. The pilot said, 'It was about here he went down, my lord.'

He was a man I had valued; I had forgotten him as if he had never been. There was the dark blur of his body. I stripped and dived in myself to raise it. It was partly to do him honour; but I thought, too, I should be quicker than the others.

Even while I was about it, I was thinking, 'Does she watch us among the leaves? What will she say to her mother? "Some men saw me bathing"? Or "I saw a man"?'

Someone was hailing me. It was Pirithoos, leaning from his poop. 'Ahoy, Theseus! How's that for an Amazon?'

I had not thought of it. I, who had been in Crete; who had seen tossing in the Bull Dance such silver hair. She had seemed only herself, without kind or peer. Slowly the truth came home. There would be no men of her tribe to fight for her. No; I had met the warrior I must win her from. She with her weapons and her lion's pride, and I disarmed.

Then I thought, 'She came down alone to the water; but the rest were never held back by fear. So they had her orders. She is one who is obeyed.'

Aloud I said, 'They owe us something. Let us see what they will give us, to clear the debt.'

The men gave a cheer; but their voices had less heat in them than before. They looked at the shore, a gift to hidden archers, and thought of their spoiled bowstrings. Their zest was for something softer. If I did not take care they would be for going.

I called to Pirithoos, 'One of my men is dead, and we must make him a decent funeral. Let us coast to the first clear place. There we can share the loot as well.'

This carried everyone. I advise any chief who leads warriors on adventure never to put off sharing the spoil. If it lies about too long, men take a fancy to this or that and set their hearts on it. Then you will have trouble.

A little way on there was a rocky point with a beach beside it. I gave orders for Pylenor's grave and cairn. Then I took Pirithoos aside, and told him what I meant to do. He did not answer, but looked at me. At last I said, 'Well?'

'Shall I tell you then?' He stood with hands on hips and head cocked sideways, and his glinting look. 'No, I've had time to swallow what I had to say. We should quarrel, and all the same you would go; then when you were dead I should be sorry. Get gone, fool, and I'll pray for you. If I can I'll bring home your body. And if you get her, be easy; she's safe from *me*.'

After this we shared the spoils. I took care that the men were satisfied. Then I said, 'This sword and bracelet I am giving from my own portion, as prizes in the funeral Games. Let the dead be honoured; as well as grave-gifts we owe him vengeance. This is the only chance we have, while their lookouts think we are busy over the rites. Who will come with me?'

About a score stepped out, who were ready to miss the Games for love of Pylenor, or of me, or of adventure. The day stood midway between noon and the summer sunset. Up there it comes later than at home.

While they cleared the track for the foot-race, we slipped up into the woods; then skirted the hillside till we struck the footpath the girls had used to the beach. It led us up through the open glades, by the winds and falls of a stream. There were hoof-prints, and once a ribbon wet from the sea. Before long we sighted a village clearing. But when we crept up, we heard men's voices and the cry of children; it was a peasant hamlet like any other.

There was no doubt about the path or the bay below. 'So,' I thought, 'this is not a land of women, such as the tales tell of. They are something else, a people within a people.'

The path passed the stream's source – and here they had paused to drink – through the woods of myrtle and oak and walnut; the trees thinned, there were brambles ripening. The sky showed oftener, then opened wide; arbutus grew and birch and the little flowers of the mountain. I heard the singing of a lark, and something mixed with it. When the lark broke off, it was the laughter of a girl.

My heart stopped, then leapt till it nearly choked me. I signed for silence; but the lark would not hush, and I must wait his careless pleasure. At last he sank to earth, and I caught, far off, the sound again.

In the open ground before us there were slender aspens growing from short fine grass. The path threaded the trees; and a tuft of blue wool was tied to one of them. I thought, 'This place is holy and forbidden,' and my neck shuddered. But I could no more have turned back than one can from birth.

Ahead, jutting from the mountain, was a buttress of huge piled boulders as great as barns. The path led round them. Beyond were voices; there would be a guard for sure. I signalled the men to wait, and climbed a little way down the slope where some whins were growing. Through these I crept till I reached the ridge. Then I looked down.

Below and beyond was a broad shelf with a shallow dip to it. It was like the lap of the seated mountain, whose arms of rock rested either side upon her knees. Above was her tall head; her stony breast leaned over; and below, down from her knees, fell a great sheer crag. Nothing showed past its edge but wide air and distant sea, with eagles sailing. At the very rim was an altar of rough-hewn rock, with a thick pillar by it, and on the pillar a thing shaped like the boat of the waxing moon. Its crust was strange: glassy and rough, like pitted clinker. I had seen such a thing, once, at another shrine; but that was smaller than a fist, and this was as thick as a man. It was a mighty thunder-stone. You could see it smelted and fired by the heat of the lightning; its strange ores glittered moltenly in the slanted sun. Smoke rose from the altar by it, and there was a smell of sweet resin in the air. Then I knew it was a sanctuary of Her whom men must not look on. And sitting on the grass in the hollow's shelter were the guardians of the shrine.

They were dressed now. Their clothes were of soft worked leather; tunic bordered or fringed, and Scythian trousers shaped to the leg. The dyes were bright and deep, as of berries and jewels; buckles of gold and silver twinkled. They looked like slender princes in the flower of youth, who meet after the hunt to drink wine and hear the bard.

They were talking, or lying at ease in the late sun, or mending their gear. One was feathering arrows, with bundles of reeds and plumes beside her; some oiled their bows and javelins; another, bare to the waist, stitched at her tunic, while the girl beside her, as one could see from her speaking hands, was telling a tale. Behind them, backed to the mountain, were low stone houses roofed with thatch, and a wooden stable. There was a stone cooking-hearth with a fire in it, and some peasant girls in the dress of women fixing a spit. All this my eye passed over, as it sought in vain.

Nothing stirred in the open doorways. She was not there. Yet I did not think, 'What now?' My fate had grasped me with death-strong fingers. It had not brought me so far to let me go.

I waved back to my men, that they must be ready to wait awhile. Then I lay down behind the ridge, looking through the whin-bush, with my breast to the breast of the mountain, breathing the air of her home, hearing its murmurs and its breeze. One of the girls played a lyre and sang. It was an ancient lay I had heard at home, sung by the harpers of the Shore Folk. It is a tongue I know well; some of my people have it. 'If she knows it too,' I thought, 'we can speak.'

There was a sentry up on a rock, black against a white cloud, with two javelins in her hand and a crescent shield. She raised it, saluting someone beyond; and I heard a hunting horn. I waited. The cry of every bird, the edges of leaves, cut into me like bronze. I heard horse-hoofs strike stone, then drum on grass. I was praying, though to what god I do not know.

Over the far ridge came streaming a pack of deerhounds, plumy and as white as curd. They flung themselves on the girls, who made much of them or laughed and cuffed them down; then jumped to their feet among the leaping dogs, like a household that expects the master.

Down the gap of the far ridge came hunters riding, and she was first.

I knew her by everything, though her face was too far to see: by her seat on her mountain pony, the set of her shoulders, the tilt of her light spear. Under her little cap, the bright hair on her temples had come loose, and flicked in the evening breeze. There was a dead buck across her horse's shoulders; the bridle and headstall were hung with disks of silver that rang and glanced as she rode. On the easy ground the horse seeing its stable came at a hand-gallop; she was borne to me like a bird in flight. The girls ran to take the quarry; I saw her clear flashing face, while the riders came up after her and called the tale of the hunt.

She swung down from the barebacked horse and stroked him before they led him away. The girls began to break and skin the deer, setting the sacred haunch aside. They worked briskly, like strong young men, not flinching at the bloody entrails; and the fighting sense in me warned me that they were warriors. But I could have looked for ever, careless of life or death.

They flung the offal to the dogs, and washed their arms at a spring, then, while the cook-girls spitted the meat to roast, they took the haunch to the altar. It was she who offered it. She was their leader, as I had known.

The smoke rose thickly. She went to the very edge of the great cliff and prayed, lifting her arms to the sky. As I looked at her, the strength of my limbs was turned to water, and my throat swelled as if with tears. She was so young; yet some god had touched her. I saw her alone with the holy one that she must answer to, and not to man or woman walking under the sun. And I thought, 'She is more than queen. She understands the sacrifice that goes consenting. There is a king's fate in her eyes.'

Like the shadow of a dream was all my life gone by to me; like the womb's dark threshold which the child forgets as he breathes and sees the day. I said to my heart, 'Why did I come here? To kill her people and seize her with their blood upon me, like a common prize of war? Peleia of the Doves must have sent me mad; but this face has brought back my soul again. I will send my men home; I shall never avenge their comrade. If two or three will follow me for love, so be it; or if not, so. Here in these hills I will live by my spear and by the chase; and some day I shall meet her as she rides alone. Then she must come to me, since a god wills it. For I am consumed as the fire from heaven consumes a forest; how can I suffer this but from a god?'

She had left her prayer, and turned her face from the light of the low sun that sank towards the sea. One of the huntresses came up and walked with her. They talked like friends; it seemed to me this was the girl she had saved from Pylenor. I had heard in Crete that the Amazons are bound in love to one another; some said they took vows, and chose for life. Yet I felt no trouble at it; I thought only, 'Our fate is joined; as I am born again for her, so will she be for me.'

The light grew red as burnished copper; down in the valley it was already dusk. The fire looked brighter, and its glow leaped on the rocks. Someone brought to the altar touchwood soaked in resin, and it burned with a clear flame.

I heard the soft tinkle of a sistrum. Five or six girls had come with instruments, and sat upon the ground. They had little drums, and flutes and cymbals. Softly at first, feeling their way into the time together, they began to sing and play. The rest stood round in a wide ring.

The beat and the song grew stronger. It was music for a dance; a fierce pulsing tune that turned itself in an endless round, each time gathering fire. It pounded in my head; I felt that sacred, forbidden things were coming. But I lay on the rocks and looked, clasped by my fate.

One of the girls leaped up. She pulled off her tunic of yellow kidskin, and stood half-bare in the red light of the sunset and the fire. She was young; the tender curve of her half-ripe breasts was like polished gold. Her face was intent, almost to sternness, and yet serene. She held out her hands, and they put in them two sharp daggers, whose new-honed edges rippled with brightness. She lifted her armed hands towards the thunder-stone, and began to dance.

She moved slowly at first, weaving her arms across each other in subtle curves and signs. Then she spun faster; suddenly she flung out her hands, and bringing them inward sank the dagger-points in her breast.

My breath hissed in my throat. But the maiden's face had hardly changed. She had frowned a little as the points went in, then her stern calm returned. She drew out the daggers; I waited for the gush of blood. But her flesh was clear and smooth. In time to the beat she raised her hands again and again, pricking her waist, her throat and shoulders. Shudders of awe ran through me; my knuckles were pressed upon my mouth. Her skin was as whole as polished ivory before the carver scratches it. The drums throbbed, and the song soared higher.

Another girl stripped and leaped in beside her, tossing a hunting spear. She danced forward lightly, and leaned herself upon it, over the heart, again and again. But when she bent away the skin closed bloodless and white.

'Theseus son of Aigeus,' I was thinking, 'what have you done? You have seen the mystery which is death for men to look at. Run, hide in the woods, sacrifice to Apollo who frees men from curses. Why are you waiting?' But I answered, 'For my life.'

The sun was down; the bellies of the clouds were like glowing embers floating in a cool clear green. Two more girls were dancing, one with hunting-knives, another with a sword. I looked into the ring of watchers. She stood silent, her hands at rest while the others beat the time. Her eyes were still. I thought I saw trouble there. Would she dance too? I was shaking, and could not tell if it was horror or desire.

The girl Molpadia was dancing already; it was she who had the sword. She whirled it round her and pricked her bloodless throat; then she stretched out her hand, and called, and pointed upward. In the fading depths of the sky, like a ghostly sickle, the new moon had appeared. The cymbals crashed and a great cry rose from the singers. The music spun like a fiery wheel, the blades glittered and stabbed, the watchers were leaping into the dance, calling their leader. Her eyes as she lifted them to the crescent grew wide and dreaming. Suddenly she threw her cap away, and shook out her loosened hair, like a thick sheet of moonlight. The song shrilled like eagles' screams.

And then mixed with it came a sound that dashed me awake like icy water. It was the bay of a watch-dog that cries out 'Thieves!'

I had not thought of the dogs since they were fed. They had been tied or shut up, as we do our dogs when there is dancing.

One must have slipped out and come our way. At his cry, someone loosed the pack.

In the gloaming I saw the rush of whiteness. I leaped to my feet, fighting them off with shield and spear. Then I understood; for my men were fighting all round me. They had grown tired of waiting in ignorance, and guessed I had forgotten them; they wanted to see the dancing. But the dog had smelt them first.

I cursed both men and dogs; we beat off the pack before they could tear us piecemeal, and wounded some, so that they bayed us from a distance, jumping to and fro. Over their noise I heard the music stop in a broken jangle; and then the war-horn.

That sound made me myself again. I shouted to the men, 'Take care! They are Moon Maids of Artemis. I saw the shrine. Let no one fight who can hide or run. Don't force them; it is death-cursed. The Queen . . .' But there was no more time. The dancers came skimming over the edge, as swift as stooping falcons, bare to the waist, with their weapons of the dance. They seemed to be dancing still; their eyes fixed in the sacred ecstasy.

I cried out to them I don't know what, as one might to the sea when it bursts the sea-wall. Then the girl with the two daggers was upon me. I tried to hurl her off with my shield; but she squirmed under it like a mountain cat, her fists reaching their blades at me like claws. The love of life we are born with did its work for me; I shortened my spear and thrust. She died pinned through the heart; but there was scarcely a trickle from her death-wound, and her face set in a smile.

The fight was scattered on the hillside, lost in the twilight among the rocks. The dogs fought too. It was like a fever-dream one cannot wake from. Then I heard horse-hoofs clatter, and saw her come.

These were the Amazons who had heard the call with waking ears. They rode, or ran with the mounts of the riders. On their arms were their crescent shields, in their hands their war-spears.

In the dimming west a last cloud burned; a deep russet tinged the mountain. Through this glimmer she rode, her red clothes deepened to crimson, her pale hood of hair loosened and free, her throat bare, as she had made ready for the dance. In her hands was the sacred axe, with the crescent blade of the Moon Maids. Its silver inlay glittered as she swung its slender shaft above her head. Her cold pure young voice sang out the war-call.

I thought, 'If this is my death a god has sent it.' But even then, I could not forget that my fate was my people's and their gods'. 'Very well then,' I thought, 'I will live. But I will have her. With my whole life I will it. This I will do.'

As I offered myself to the daimon of my fate, my soul grew steady; my mind was a clear stream, full of quick-darting fish. I stepped forth, and in the speech of the Shore Folk gave the herald's cry. It is sacred all the known world over, and even at the ends of the earth it was worth trying.

She reined her horse. Her head tilted back against the sky was a thing to stop your heart. With a motion of her shield-arm she halted the troop behind her. In the pause, I heard the yammer of a furious dog choked with a spear-thrust, and the sound of a man's death-grunt. Then there was quiet on the mountain.

I came towards her. She was delicate and strong as the creatures of the wilderness, the panther, the hawk, the roe. She looked at the fallen dancer gravely and proudly; she had seen such sights before. My heart said to me, 'No sighs, no pleading. She is not for cowards.'

She spoke, slowly, in the tongue of the Shore Folk. 'We have no herald.'

'Nor we,' I said. 'Let Herald Hermes stand between us. I am Theseus the Athenian, son of Aigeus son of Pandion. I am the King.'

She looked again then. It seemed my name had come even here. Harpers will hear of harpers, and so do warriors of their peers. She spoke over her shoulder to the troop, telling them the news it seemed; for they craned to see, and chattered together. But she turned back to me, knitting her clear brows as she felt for words. She knew the language less well than I, and pieced it together slowly. 'No men here, no man-gods.' She swept her arm, and spoke a strange-sounding name, as if that told everything. Then she thought, and said, 'This is Maiden Crag.'

I said, 'And you?'

She touched her own breast and answered, 'Hippolyta of the Maidens.' Her head went up. 'The King.'

My heart leapt out to her. But I said only, 'Good. Then we can speak, we two. I come in peace here.'

She shook her head with an angry jerk. What she meant was 'Liar!' I saw her fingers snap impatiently, because she had not the word. She pointed to us and said 'Pirates!' and the troop behind her shouted it in their own tongue. Yes, I thought, and she remembers me.

'In peace,' I said. 'While I live I shall never lie to you.' I tried to speak to her eyes. 'We are pirates, yes; but it is my pleasure, not my trade. I am King of Athens, and of Eleusis, and of Megara to the Isthmus' end; and Crete pays me tribute. I am sorry we were insolent by the shore; we are strangers, and the men have been long at sea. But you have taken blood-price enough. Make it peace now, and friendship.'

'Friend-ship?' she said, drawing it out, as if asking was I a madman. One of the girls laughed wildly in the troop behind. She rested her axe on her horse's shoulder while she got the foreign speech together, and pushed at her shining hair, which fell down over her fingers. 'This place,' she said, putting down word on word, 'is holy.' Her hand made the word greater. 'No man must come. And you – you have seen the mystery. For that – death, always. We kill you, the Maidens of the Maiden. That is our law.' Her eyes met mine; grey water, grey clouds; yet there was speech in them, beyond the words. 'We must die too maybe.' She turned on her horse, pointing to the shrine. 'We are all in her hand.'

She drew her breath for the war-cry. I cried out, 'Stay!'

'No! She is angry.' But she stilled her horse with her hand, and paused.

'Hippolyta.' It tasted of wine and honey. 'My men, there, have not angered Her. It was I who saw; I, alone, up there. They were beyond. They did nothing.' I spoke slowly, watching that she took my meaning. 'So, I will answer for myself. Do you understand me? It is you and I; hand to hand, King to King. I call you to single combat, King of the Maidens. That is our debt to the folk who honour us.'

She had understood. It was King to King, indeed. It had touched her soul, even though, as I guessed, they had no such custom. There was no fear in her face, only strangeness and doubt. Her mount tossed its head, and the silver disks clinked softly. I thought, 'She hears the voice of her fate.'

A girl came up the hillside holding a sword. It was the one she had saved, the swimmer, Molpadia; tall and strong, with blue sullen eyes still clouded from the trance which must have lifted now, for a wound in her arm was bleeding. Hippolyta leaned down and looked at it, and they spoke together. The tall girl frowned.

'Meet me, Hippolyta,' I said, 'and let the gods decide. A king cannot refuse a king.'

The dusk was deepening; but I saw her face by its own light. She was young, with a young warrior's pride and honour. Honour called to her, and pride, and she knew not what. 'If I die,' she said, 'you will spare the holy place, the Maidens? You will go away?'

My heart raced in my breast. 'I swear it. So will my warriors.' They had come up to listen, the wounded leaning on the whole; but some were missing. They growled the Assent; they had had enough. 'No vengeance,' I said, 'whichever falls. Our peoples shall part in peace. If I die, bury me on this mountain, by the path you take to the sea. And if I win – you are mine.'

She stared, and said slowly, 'What is that? Yours?'

I nodded; and, to be sure she understood me, chose out the simplest words. 'If I win, and you live, you shall take me for King, and follow me. Your word for mine. By my life I swear it, by the Sacred River, the vow gods dare not break, I will never shame you, nor force you against your will. You shall be my friend, my guest. May your Goddess eat my heart, if I am false to this. Do you accept my terms?'

She frowned in a kind of wonder. Then she made a wide sweep with her hand, which meant, 'All this is nothing.' She touched the blade of her axe, with the silver signs inlaid on it. 'I fight to the death,' she said.

'Life and death are with the gods. Do you agree, then?'

The girl beside her broke in, in their own tongue. I saw she was against it, and said quickly, 'The choice of weapon is yours.'

The girl grasped at her arm. She turned and seemed to tell her something; then dismounting put into her hands the sacred axe, and kissed her, and spoke her name to the troop behind. They assented grievingly; I guessed she had named her heir. Then she stepped forward; her eyes looked wide, as they had when the new moon rose. A fear came to me, that she could fall into the sacred trance at will, and turn into a fighting maenad, wild as a leopard, who knows no law but to kill or die. But the mystery had been broken; her face was only grave. I thought, 'She is offering herself in sacrifice. She looks for a royal death.'

'Theseus, I will fight,' she said. 'With javelins, and then the sword.'

The name was hard to her tongue, and she stumbled on it. But the sound was sweet to me. 'Agreed,' I said. 'Let us stretch out our hands to the gods, to witness our given word.'

She paused a moment; then slowly her hand came out. It seemed it would have been a little thing, as we stood so, for me to reach out and take it. So may the other shore look near, before you swim the strait.

I armed myself with two sharp throwers from the men behind me. She did the same, then looked about her. 'It gets dark,' she said. 'I know this ground. We need torches. I will fight you equal.'

I said in my heart, 'This love may be death but it is not folly. I have seldom met a man with such pride as that.'

'There is light enough,' I said. I walked to a level place, and motioned my men to clear the field. They fell back and I said, 'It will do as it is. I could see you without my eyes.'

We were alone now, no one within two spear-casts of us. It is the time when warriors whip up their blood by hurling insults to and fro. I saw her frown, as if she were angry with herself, and blamed the lack of language. 'Say nothing,' I said. 'That is not for you and me.'

She raised her brows. She had put on her cap of Phrygian leather lined with bronze. The scarlet flaps fell on her neck and cheeks, bright as a pheasant, but left her face clear to see. I said to her, 'This is all – I love you. You are my life's love. I came here for you, to win you or to die. Do as you must, as your law commands you; I will not have you disgraced for me. If I die it was my fate, and I ran to meet it. Be free of my blood. May sorrow never come near you. My shade will love you, even in the house of Hades under the earth.'

She stood with gleaming arms under the fading sky and the little moon, straight, slight and strong; and I saw in the eyes of the king and warrior a startled maiden, who since childhood had not spoken with a man. She looked at me dumbly. Then grasping at the thing she knew, she cried, 'I must kill you! You saw the Mystery!'

'Yes, you must try. Come to me with your honour, for in yours is mine now. Come, begin.'

We drew apart, and began to circle each other, crouching behind our shields. I wished she had not chosen javelins; I had hoped it would be hand to hand at once, with the axe or spear. Now I had two sharp throwers to get rid of without hurting anyone; also two to avoid. The sooner done the better.

I twisted the throwing-thong, watching her do the same. She was so quick and light-footed, any throw was chancy. I aimed slowly, to show her where it was coming; but as I would have done myself, she took it for a feint, and jumped towards it, away from where she thought the real throw would be. I was only just in time to miss her. I have never been so frightened in any battle; and it spoilt my eye. Next moment there was a smart on my thigh that set my teeth on edge. Her javelin-side had glanced it; the gash was not deep, but wide open, and I felt warm blood on me in the evening cool. The leg was sound, and would not hurt much till it stiffened; but I made a limping step as I cast my second javelin, to fool her and bungle the throw. It fell flat half-way between us. She still had one more. I turned my shield side to her, and drew my sword.

The Amazons had cheered the hit, and called her to throw again. She stood balanced like a dancer. It was too dark to see the weapon's path. I could only watch her aim. I caught the javelin on my shield, and it was no mean cast, for it pierced the hide, just missing my arm and jarring it to the shoulder. I sprang back watching her while I trod on the haft and wrenched free my shield. Then I stepped forward sword in hand, and she came to meet me.

It was deep dusk now, but one could just see one's foothold. So far so good. I had risked the javelin-duel in the bad light, to have its advantage later. I did not want her to see what I was about. Wrestling was born in Egypt and taught in Crete. I had brought it myself to the Isle of Pelops, and then to Attica. It was still hearsay in Thessaly, barely rumoured in Thrace. And this was Pontos. When she had thought I could not take her alive, it had told me all I needed.

She prowled around me, as lithe and quiet as a leopard. Through the inner curve of the crescent shield came her curving sword-blade, slicing the air like silk as she watched my point. It was a weapon I had not dealt with much, and I did not like it. Once under a Hellene longsword, and you are in; but this looked fit anywhere to take your hand off. Both my arm and blade were longer; it would have been simple, if I had been out to kill my man. I thought, 'I am glad I have not this to do every day,' and it made me laugh.

She laughed back at me, her white teeth flashing in the twilight. She was a warrior, and the battle-light was coming into her eyes. She took my laughter for defiance, and it freed her from the trouble my love had laid on her. She would fight better now. And yet, as we thrust and foined, we felt one another's mind as dancers do who dance often together, or lovers who can speak with a touch of their fingertips. 'Surely,' I thought, 'she must know it now as I do.' But she had been given in childhood to the Goddess, and kept from men. How should she know? If she felt a strangeness in the blood, a wildness she could not name, she took it for the call of glory. She could kill me in this innocence, and wither after, not understanding her grief.

Most of this time I was simply parrying, or taking her cuts on my shield; but now and again I would thrust or feint, to deceive her while I watched my chance. For she had felt I was up to some trick or other; that I could tell. I wanted to get the sword off her, before I went in. She knew that much, and was too good for me.

'Well, then!' I said to myself. 'Did I think she would be got for nothing?' With a quick jump backwards, I threw my shield away. I made it look as if the sling had broken, helped by the darkness. She had never thought of that, and it took her in. So then I did what is natural in a man who has lost his shield: made a reckless lunge at her. When I missed, she was inside my guard. I had to be quick then. As she lifted her sword for a down-cut, I let mine go and grabbed her arm, spinning her round as I pulled it over my shoulder. She was so astonished that as she flew up, I got her fingers off the sword. It was too late to check the throw; so over she went, in a perfect flying mare, and fell clean but hard with all the breath knocked out of her. I threw myself down by her on the mountain grass.

Her arm was still in her shield. I lay upon it, and reached over to pin the other. She lay half stunned, face upwards to the sky, all stilled. I was still too, dizzy with the fight and with being all at once so near to her, her mountain-scented pale hair beside my mouth, feeling under my arm the embroidered leather and the tender breasts.

The warrior in my head, still wakeful, warned me she was quick as a whip, and had not yielded yet. I turned my mouth to her ear, and said, 'Hippolyta.'

Her head turned, and her eyes met mine, as wild as a netted deer's. I did not dare let go of her. So I talked awhile. What I said I don't remember; it is no matter, for I spoke in Greek. I only wanted to let her know, as she came to herself, that she was not with an enemy. She began to look around her; then I said in the tongue she knew, 'The fight is over, Hippolyta, and you are not dead. Will you keep your vow?'

It was much darker. But I saw her eyes seeking the sky, as if for counsel. None came; a cloud had come down from the mountain crest, and the new moon's sickle was gone behind it. The warriors muttered together; quick whispers came from the Amazons, and long silences. Suddenly she started up; not in anger, but as if she might find it was all a dream. I pressed her back and said, 'Well?'

She said, under her breath, 'So be it.' Then I let her go, and stood up and leaned to raise her, slipping the shield from her arm. When she was on her feet, she swayed from dizziness; so I gathered her up, my arm under her knees and her head upon my shoulder. She lay quiet, as I carried her off the field, fitting my arms as if they had been made for her, feeling her fate and her home.

10

They gave me her horse to set her on, and bring her down the mountain. As I walked at its bridle, I heard behind me on Maiden Crag the sound of wailing, with flutes and muffled drums. It was the lament for the fallen, and the lost King. I looked at her face; but she stared straight before her, still-eyed, into the night.

We came to the hamlet we had passed before, and found it empty. All the folk had fled at the sound of the battle, to some fastness in the hills. So we rested there till daybreak, to save our necks on the mountain track. I told the men to take enough for their meal, no more; we were not Isthmus bandits, to rob the poor. Even the headman's house had only one room and bed. I sat her down there, and lit the lamp. She looked dead tired, and dark under the eyes; small wonder, after the swim, and the hunt, and the fight.

I brought her what supper I could find; some rough wine and cheese, and barley bread with honey. She looked at the food like an untamed colt at a piece of salt, watching for the halter in the other hand. But I stood there quietly, as one does in the corral; and presently she took it with a nod of thanks. She had not spoken since we left the sanctuary.

She could not eat much, but she drank the wine. Meantime I had looked at the servant's lean-to, and found a bed of straw which I dragged inside. I did not want my men to see it; they would think me bewitched, or laugh at me. When I had thrown it down by the door, I looked round and saw her watchful eyes. I felt her mind, as I had in battle. For her it was life at stake. She would never outlive dishonour; she would find some way. And yet, I could feel her judging me for the truth's sake, not just from fear, concerned with the man

I was, the good and the evil. A king, truly, lived in this white-haired girl.

'What is she?' I thought. 'Where was she a child? For she was not born on this mountain, like a fox or a bird. These savage rites, this fierceness, how deep are they in her soul? The lioness is noble, but only a madman walks into her lair. She made me a vow before the battle; but do her customs bind her? Did she even understand it clearly, in a tongue that was not her own? She is proud; she offered torches to light the ground. She is faithful; she stood naked before the warriors, to save her friend. But the lioness fights for her kind, yet is death to men. Have the gods sent her to me to fill my life or end it? It is the one or the other, that is sure.'

'So, then,' I thought; 'if one accepts one's fate, one must go to meet it. Come, let us see.'

She sat on the side of the bed, with the cup and trencher by her. Her eyes never left me, as I took the things away; though she sat unflinching, I could feel her all sparks like a cornered cat. I spoke to her gently, giving her time to follow. 'I must go for a while, to see the camp in order and set the watches. No one will come in. But it is not good to be among strangers weaponless. Have this to keep by you.' And I unslung my sword and put it in her hands.

She took it from me, staring at it and then at me. I did not stir. I thought of the Mystery, the girl with the daggers leaping forward. In the lamplight, gazing at the sword with wide strange eyes, she was beautiful as deadly things are, lynxes, or wolves, or the mountain spirits who lure men to the cliff. I stood with my empty hands before her. Presently she slid the blade half out, and touched the edge with her fingers, and stroked the inlaid pattern to feel the work. 'It was my father's and my grandfather's,' I said. 'But my Cretan swordsmith shall make you one as good.'

She had twisted back her hair into its thick braid; they only loosen it for the Dance; but it was soft and wild as a child's about the brows. Her pigtail had fallen forward, as she bent over the sword. She gave it a tug – the first time I ever saw that trick of hers – and peered at me, her eyes bright with danger, fearing some trick. 'What is it?' I said. 'I am only doing as I promised. As for why, I have told you why.'

I left her with the sword across her knees, her head on one side, looking at the inlay and pulling at her hair.

As I was posting the guards, my servant came up and asked if the girl would fetch the water and wash me, as though she were some common prize of the spear. I told him to mend his manners, and take hot water to her instead. For myself I washed at the fountain. But I saw my men staring and glancing. If I did not spend the night in there, they would think I was off my head, or else afraid.

After a while I scratched on the door and opened it. She had left the lamp burning; I saw her bare arm slide from the bed to the floor and grasp the sword. She had a linen shift on; her outer things hung on the bedpost. She had trusted me. But she could not have understood I was coming back. Her limbs had grown taut and still, her eyes had narrowed. If she had got to die, she was going down the River with her enemy, as a warrior ought. The more honour to her, I thought.

'It's only I,' I said. 'Why don't you sleep? You have had work enough. I shall lie here at the door, to keep it; that is best, among roving warriors.' I looked at the shadows round her bright open eyes; her fate had moved too fast for her. Torn from her kind and all she knew, she had no one but me to look to. 'Take care of the sword till morning,' I said. 'I have got my spear.'

I took off my leather corselet. As I bent to put out the lamp, I heard her speak; a low half-muffled growl, not like her clear voice before the fight. I came towards her, but her eyes were like a wildcat's holed up in a rock, so I stopped again. 'What is it, then?' I said. 'I cannot hear you.' She slid her arm out of bed, and pointed to the wound on my leg, which I had had no time to see to. 'Wash!' she said, and jerked her thumb towards the ground, growling, 'Bad, bad.'

I told her it had dried, and would do in the sea tomorrow; but she pointed at the wine-flask, saying, 'Good!' She was forgetting the language, with all that she had been through. Poor girl, I thought; everyone knows what a captive's lot is like, when the man who took her dies. So to give her some peace I washed it, though it smarted from the wine, and fresh blood came.

'Look,' I said. 'All clean.' She raised her head from the home-spun pillow, and muttered something. 'Goodnight, Hippolyta. You are my honoured guest-friend, sacred to the gods. A blessing on your sleep.'

I stood a moment, wishing only to put my hand upon her head; it would feel like a child's, I thought, through the fine hair. But it might scare her; so I smiled, and went to the lamp again. I heard her voice, under the blanket, growl out 'Goodnight' as I drew away.

Between my heart's happiness, and the fleas in my pallet, I could not sleep. I dreamed, of course, of love to come; but even this time as it was seemed precious. Some god must have warned me that there was none to waste.

Outside was the village square of beaten earth; the sentries had got a watch-fire going there, which they fed all night. Its light came through the door-chinks and the little window, nearly as bright as the lamp had been. She turned on her side, and saw me looking at her; then she turned again, and faced away. But presently she dozed, and at last slept deeply. She was weary, and young. Little by little her even breathing lulled me, till I grew drowsy myself. It had been a long climb, round through the woods and up the mountain.

I woke to a scratching on the wall. It was only thin daub-and-wattle. Rats I loathe; they come on battlefields for what the kites and dogs have left. The first sound of their gnawing always wakes me. The watch-fires had burned down dull and red; it must be half-way to morning. I was sleepy still, and thought, 'Let it go, since my dog's in Athens.' Then a flake of plaster fell from the wall beside her bed. There was a hole; and a hand came through it.

I thought at first that one of my men had had the impudence to make a peephole, and reached softly for my spear. But as the hand came in, I saw it was finer than a man's, and had a sleeve of embroidered leather. It reached down, and touched her shoulder. Then I lay quiet, and looked under my eyelids.

She woke with a start and gasp, having forgotten where she was. Then she saw, and turned to look if I did. But I had foxed in time. She took the hand in both hers, and laid it against her cheek. She looked young, wild and lost, crouched by the wall in the faint firelight with the dip of shadow under her throat. And yet, it seemed she was offering comfort more than taking it.

The hand clenched hard on hers, then slipped back into the wall. When it came again, there was a dagger in it.

She gazed, unmoving; and so did I. It was like the daggers of the Mystery; short, thin and needle-pointed. There was a moment's waiting, then a scratch upon the wall; I guessed there was a guard not far off, and there could be no whispers. At the sound she took the knife, and stroked the hand and kissed it. Then it went away.

She kneeled on the bed and put her eye to the hole; but too late it seemed, for she soon left it, and sat with her feet curled under her, the weapon in her hands. The light flickered on it, as she shivered in the cold before the dawn. Her little shift left bare her arms and her long slim legs, with a fine silk upon their brown like the silk of beech-nuts. Presently she tried the point upon her fingertip, and laid it down on the blanket, and sat some time with her arms wrapped round her breast. She was looking down at the floor beside the bed; I remembered, though I could not move to see, that it was where she had put the sword.

At last she lifted her hands in prayer, and turned up her face to where no moon was, but only the dusty rafters. She took the dagger in her hand, and slid to her feet, and came towards me softly.

She would see now if I looked, so I closed my eyes. I could hear her light breathing, smell her warm shift and her hair. With any other woman in the world, I would have jumped up laughing and closed with her. But like a man bound by a god, I could not do it. Even though I could not tell what bidding had been put on her, stronger than her vow to me – for she was King no longer, and under who knew what laws – yet I could not do it. I lay hearing my heartbeats and her breath; remembering how her javelin had pierced my shield, I thought, 'If it comes, it will be quickly done.' The wait seemed endless; my heart drummed over and over, 'I must know, I must know.'

She drew a short sharp breath, leaning close above me. Her breathing paused. I thought, 'Is she getting ready?' Then something touched me; but it was neither hand nor bronze. It was a drop of warm water falling on my face.

She was gone. I heard her soft flying footfalls. With the grunt of a man half-wakened, I turned over and lay still again, where I could see from the side of my eye.

The fire outside had been raked together, and put up a spurt of flame. It glittered on her tears, as she stood fighting for silence. The back of her hand with the knife still clenched in it was pressed against her teeth, and her breasts moved shudderingly under the thin white shift. When she lifted the hem to wipe her eyes, it hardly roused me, I felt such pity for her. I longed then to speak; but I feared to shame her, remembering her pride.

She grew quiet after a while. Her arms fell to her sides; she stood spear-straight, looking before her. Then slowly she lifted the dagger up, as if offering it to heaven. Her lips moved, and her arms passed to and fro, weaving a subtle pattern. I watched her, wondering; then I remembered. It was the ritual of the dance. Again she raised up the knife; her knuckles were white upon the hilt, and the point hung over her breast.

In the Cretan bull-ring I had lived by swiftness; but in all my life I have never moved so fast. I was there before the sight of my eyes caught up with me, one arm about her, the other grasping her wrist.

I took the knife and tossed it into a corner, and held her away with her shoulders between my hands, in case I should forget myself. She stood shaking like a plucked harp-string, and choking back her tears as if they were something against nature. 'Come, child,' I said. 'It is over. Be at peace.'

All the Shore Folk speech had been driven out of her. Her eyes searched my face, asking the questions she would have been too proud to put her tongue to, if she had known the words. 'Come,' I said, 'you are catching cold.' I sat her on the side of the bed and wrapped the blanket round her, and called through the window to the man on guard, 'Bring me a crock of fire.'

He answered startled; I could hear them outside muttering. I turned back to her and said, 'You know, who are a warrior, that one often stakes one's life on a little thing. So why not on a great one? That was what I thought.'

'You won the fight.' She had looked down, and I could hardly hear her. 'You fought fair, so . . .' Her fingers twisted in a fold of the blanket.

The guard scratched and coughed outside; he had brought the fire in a clay mixing-bowl. I took it at the door from him, and set it by her feet on the earthen floor. She sat staring into it, and did not turn when I sat beside her.

'I shall watch with you now till light, in case anyone comes to trouble you again. Sleep if you like.' She was silent, gazing into the embers. 'Don't grieve,' I said. 'You were a faithful hearth-friend, and true to your warrior's vow.'

She shook her head, and murmured something. I could tell what it meant; 'But I broke another.'

'We are mortal,' I said to her. 'One can only do so much. It would be a bad business, if the gods were less just than men.'

She did not answer; and being so near, I saw well enough she could not. There was no doubt what she was needing, warrior or not; so I put my arm about her, and said, 'What is it?' softly.

This brought the rain from the sky. She had been taught it was shameful to weep, and at first it hurt her, breaking through; but presently as it eased her heart she lay in my arms with the strain and stretch all loosened, as trusting as a child. But she was not that; she was a woman eighteen years old, strong, with warm blood in her; and when man and woman are born to love as we were, they will find it by any road. We felt one another's mind, as we had felt it fighting; love came to us as birth does, knowing its own time better than those who wait for it. Though she knew less than any maid who has heard the women chatter, yet she knew more, knowing only me. My own life left me to live in her; with all women before I had been myself alone. And though what I had learned with them, which I had thought was much, went all for nothing, yet I learned again from her trust, and it was enough.

By daybreak, we had forgotten the need of words, or that we had never spoken together at all in our own tongues. When the guard outside argued together if they should dare to wake me, she knew by my smiling what they said; we pulled the blanket over our heads till they had looked through the key-hole and gone away. Not till I heard the voice of a runner from the ships, sent up by Pirithoos to learn if I was dead, did I come back like a stranger to the world of mortal men.

11

The Straits of Helle passed like a dream. Even its wars were dreamlike. All things else were a sleep we woke from to one another. I did not care what my men made of it, and they knew better than to tell me. As long as they showed her respect, it was all I asked.

As for Pirithoos, when I brought her down to the camp he rolled his eyes to heaven; but having given me up he was glad to see me, and kept the right side of a quarrel. She was proud, and had cause to be shy, and at first she took against his roughness. But valour won him always, even in women; and when he found she knew the war-customs all along the coast as far as the mouth of Hellespont, he changed his tune. In council of war they got a respect for one another which turned to liking. She was never his notion of a girl; if she had been a youth, indeed, he would have settled to it more easily, and half the time in those early days he treated her like a boy of some kingly house over whom I had lost my head. But, knowing nothing of such customs, she only felt his goodwill; before long, he was teaching her pirates' Greek.

She warned us, among other things, that the tribes who had let us through on the voyage out, would attack us when we came back laden. So we were ready. These wars, when I remember them now, come back to me shining like harpers' tales. I could not put hand or foot wrong with her there beside me. Lovers of boys may say it is the same; but I should think it is easy to be looked up to by a lad not come to his full strength, whom you are teaching all he knows and helping out when he is overmatched. We two fought like one. We were still finding one another; and war, to those who understand it, shows forth a man. We learned as much of each other in battle as we did in bed. It is good to be loved for the truth struck out of one in the eye of death, by a lover who has no fear to make her judgement humble. Her face was pure in battle, as it had been when she offered to the Goddess. Yet it was not blood she offered, nor the death of the enemy, but faith and valour, and the victory over fear and pain. There is no cruelty in the face of the lioness.

We fought among the longships that came forth to meet us; and at the springs of fresh water on the slopes; and in the creek where we beached to caulk the hulls, and the dark blue-painted Thracians charged us naked, creeping up behind the sandhills and scrubby tamarisks. By night we waked from each other's arms to take up shield and spear; and sometimes even by day, when the fight was over, we would go off with its blood and dust still on us, to lie down in love among the bracken or the dunes; and if there was nowhere to go it was a grief to us.

My men found this strange, which was enough to make them mistrust it. It is the mark of little men to like only what they know; one step beyond, and they feel the black cold of chaos. They had taken for granted that I meant to break her in, and till I had made a house-woman of her like any other, would feel myself half a man. As for my manhood, I reckoned it was proved by now and I could leave such cares to others; for the rest, one does not clip one's hawk and put it in the hen-yard. For her I was man enough.

Pirithoos, who had more sense than this, still wondered aloud that mad for her as I was, I would risk her in war. I could only tell him it was as it was. Besides, I had beaten her hand to hand, her first defeat since she took up arms; and as our bodies knew each other's needs without asking, so with our souls. It was a joy to feel her get back her pride. He would not have understood, however; and still less did my fools of spearmen. If I had torn some screaming girl-child from the household altar, and forced her before her mother, it would have been all in the day's work to most of them. But now, I started to find the evil-eye sign chalked upon the benches. They thought she had bewitched me. Pirithoos said it was because when we fought together we never got a scratch, and the Amazons were said to have a charm against it. At this I said no more; if one of them after all had seen the Mystery, I did not want to be told.

We came out into the Hellene seas and fair blue weather. All day we would sit handfast on the poop, watching the shores and islands, and learning to talk with words. What with her tongue and mine and the Shore Folk speech stringing it together, it was a patched-up business at first; but it served our turn.

'When I told you my name,' I said, 'you knew it.'

'Oh, yes. The harpers came to us every year.'

'Did I look as you had thought?' I know what harpers are, and wondered if she had expected a man seven feet high. There was barely an inch between us.

'Yes,' she said. 'Like the bull-dancers in the pictures, light and quick. But you had put up your hair under your helmet. I missed your long hair.' She touched it as it lay over her shoulder. Then she said, 'On New Moon's Eve I saw an omen, a falling star. And I thought when you came, "It fell for me. I must die; but with honour, by this great warrior; and they will put my name in the Winter Song." I felt – oh a change, an end.'

'And then?' I said.

'When you threw me and got my sword, that was a death to me. I woke all empty. I thought, "She has given me out of her hand, though I kept her laws. Now I am nothing."'

'That is the way of it, when you hold out your hand to fate. I felt the same on the ship going to Crete.'

She made me tell her about the bull-ring; we did not speak of the dagger in the wall. I knew she had been torn in two, and the wound not healed yet. But a little while after, she said to me, 'On Maiden Crag, if a Moon Maid goes with a man she must leap down the cliffside. That is the law.'

I answered, 'Maiden Crag is far away, but the man is near.'

'Come nearer.' We leaned our shoulders together, and wished the light away; there is not much chance, in a war-fleet, to be alone.

It was still like this with us when the ships reached Thessaly. As we rode along the river path towards Pirithoos' palace, he edged up his horse to mine. 'Well, Theseus. This seems a good dream you're having, though it never troubled sleep of mine. You will have to wake up when you get back to Athens; so you had better borrow my hunting-lodge, and dream a little longer. Look, you can see the roof, below that shoulder of the mountain.'

So I shipped home my men, all but my body-servant and a Guard of eight. Half a month we stayed where the forest thins and the high woods are open, in a Lapith house of logs with a painted doorway. There was a table of pinewood, sleeked with hand-rubbing; a round stone hearth with a bronze fire-basket, for the cold upland nights; and a carved red bed, whose bearskins we would throw down at evening before the fire. Pirithoos sent up a groom and huntsman, and an old woman to cook. We would find errands for all these people, to be alone.

We slept as much as nightingales. We would be up at the dark of dawn to eat bread dipped in wine, and ride into the hills as the stars were paling. Sometimes on the lonely tops we would see startled Kentaurs shambling away from us; we would make them the sign of peace we had learned from Pirithoos, and they would pause to stare under their low heavy brows, or point us where there was game; then we would leave them a hunk of meat in payment. When we had fed our household we killed no more, but would give the gods their portion, mine to Apollo and hers to Artemis; that is how the custom of the double offering started, which you will find now in all my kingdoms. After this, we would sit on a rock or in an open glade as the sun grew warm, learning each other's language, or hushing to make the little birds and beasts come near us; watching the horse-herds like swarms of ants on the plain below; sleeping sometimes, to make up for the night; or locked in love, knowing nothing beyond ourselves but some leaf or snail-shell on the ground next to our eyes.

She liked the great Thessalian horses, which she had only known by hearsay, and was soon as bold on them as a Lapith boy; but up in the high hills we used the little Kentaur ponies with eyes in their feet, such as she had known at home. She had been only nine years old, when they offered her to the Goddess. Her father was the chief of a tribe inland from Kolchis, a mountain people; as long as she could remember, she had known her parents had vowed to dedicate her, if they should be given a son. Since they had paid their pledge she had never seen them, and they were growing dim to her; she remembered best about her father how he darkened the doorway as he stooped to come in. But her mother she saw always lying in bed with the new-born boy, while she herself watched silent, seeing the joy and knowing they did not grudge the price. They had sent her to the precinct in the foothills, where the little girls were trained and toughened like boys, till they were of age to bear arms. 'Once,' she said, 'the Warrior Priestess found me crying. I thought she would beat me; she used to beat the cowards. But she took me laughing in her arms, and said I should live to be a better man than my brother. That was the last time I cried, till the other day.'

Once I asked her what became of the Maidens when they grew old. She said that some became seers and gave oracles; the rest could serve if they liked at the shrine of Artemis down in the plain; but often they chose to die. Sometimes they leaped from the Crag; but mostly they killed themselves in the sacred trance, as they danced the Mystery. 'So would I have done. I had made up my mind I would never live to wither and stiffen and be dead alive. But I don't dread it now, because we shall be together.' She did not ask, like other women, if I would love her still.

Once a Kentaur came to us with a gift of wild honey – that is all they have to give – and begged us with signs to kill a beast that was taking their children. While we beat the coverts for a wolf, I heard a furious snarling; running over I found her with a full-grown leopard on her spear. Before I could help her, she cried out, 'No! He is mine!' as fierce as the beast itself. It was a hard thing, to let her be; she knew it after, and was sorry, but full of her triumph all the same. Yet she could whistle birds to her hand, and would bring all manner of creatures into the house; a pecked pigeon, and a fox-cub she fed till the vixen came for it. It bit me, but she could handle it like a pup.

She was always after me to teach her wrestling. To tease her I said for some time it was my mystery. But at last I laughed and said, 'Well, then, find somewhere to fall soft. For I won't have you grazed and bruised all over, and that, my girl, is the price of taking a man.'

We found a dip in the pinewood, drifted full of needles, and went at it properly, stripped to the waist. She was as quick as I, and as strong as it needs if you are quick enough. Neither of us could surprise the other, we knew each other's minds too well; but she learned quickly, and liked the sport, saying it was like the play of lions.

She had given me a fall, but I had brought her down with me; we rolled on the springy pine-mat, in no haste to rise again, when she stopped laughing and pulled away and said, 'A man is watching.'

I looked up. There coughing and stroking his beard was a baron of Athens, whom I had left as a judge when I sailed away.

I got up and went over, wondering what bad news could have made him come so far himself, instead of sending a courier. A rising in Megara? The Pallantids landing by sea? As he greeted me, I saw him fidgeting and looking down his nose. I knew then, and said, 'Well?'

He brought out some tale, rehearsed beforehand, of this and that; matters a few spearmen could have settled, or he himself in judgement. He said some ship or other had brought a rumour I was sick. But I could see through his shuffling well enough. The warriors had been talking. Oh, yes; Theseus had been himself on the voyage out; he had sacked Kolchis, and filled their hands with spoil; all had been well till the Amazon had worked her Scythian magic on him, stealing the soul from his breast in return for her charm against weapons; then he had left the fleet as a hound-pack leader goes off on the trail of a wolf-bitch at full moon, to run mad with her in the forest.

It was beneath me to read his thoughts aloud to him. I said that since no one in Athens could deal even with trifles while I was gone, I would come myself and see to them. I saw there was no choice; playtime was over. If hearsay got about and crossed the borders, some enemy might see his chance; then these fools would have bred the thing they feared.

I turned to speak to her; but she was gone, without my hearing a footfall. So it was then, and often after; if she thought herself a hindrance to me, she would be off like a deer in covert. She would come back as quietly, saying nothing of it, from love and pride.

My dry-nurse had not come alone. Up at the house were three

more like him, waiting to see what I had turned into since I was bewitched. The best of them – I think he had really had some fear for me – gave me a tablet tied with cord. It was from Amyntor, whom I had left in command of the army when I sailed off. So he could do as he chose; and had chosen to write his message in Old Cretan. It is used in the rites of the Bull Dance, and by the native serfs; you must go to Crete to learn it. I saw by the glum faces they had all had a look inside. After the greetings, the message said, 'There is nothing here your spearmen cannot take care of, till you wish to come. I saw your heart, sir, in the Bull Court, but fate was not ready. We, who remember, will have a welcome for the fair and brave.'

After we got back he had married Chryse, the best of the bull-girls; so he understood. But things must have gone far enough, if he thought this message needed.

I called the servant to bring wine. I suppose they had thought to stay the night in my house, before they saw it. Their eyes crept round all four walls, lingering on the bed. I was growing weary of them. 'I will not keep you now,' I said. 'The track is dangerous in the evening mists. I want a message taken to the Head Steward at Athens; send a runner if no ship is leaving. I want the Queen's rooms opened up, which were closed in my father's day; cleaned, painted and made handsome. I want to find them ready.'

There was a pause. They did not look at one another; I saw to it that they did not dare. But their thoughts spun between them like cobwebs in a breeze.

'You came by ship,' I said. 'Is it fit for me to sail in?' Indeed, they said, it was well prepared. 'The Lady Hippolyta is coming with me. She was a royal priestess in her land, and will be treated as befits her. You have leave to go.'

They laid fist on breast, and started backing out. In the doorway they took root, blinking; and the lesser ones edged behind the greater. The chief of them, who had found us in the wood, seemed to have words stuck in his throat like a fishbone. I waited, tapping my fingers on my belt. At last it came. 'By your favour, my lord. The ship for the Cretan tribute is at Piraeus, waiting to sail. Have you any commands? Some message?'

He had not the face to hold my eye. I was getting angry.

'You have got already,' I said, 'my message for the runner. There is nothing in Crete that will not wait.'

12

All peoples have their time-marks. In Athens they will say, 'It was while we still paid Minos tribute,' or 'In the year of the bull'. But sometimes in my presence they check and pause, and count by the feasts of Athene or the Isthmian Games. They do not say, 'In the time of the Amazon,' though all Athens says it. Do they think I shall forget?

It was ripe autumn, the turning of the grapes, when I brought her home. We would stand on the Palace roof, while I showed her the villages and great estates; then she would point to some peak of Parnes or Hymettos, and say, 'Let us go *there*!' I took her, whenever I could. She was not used to sitting indoors, and would get into mischief, meaning no harm; running up to me in the council chamber with two couple of great wolfhounds, which knocked the old men over and trod in the clerks' wet clay; getting some rich baron's daughter to strip and wrestle with her, so that the mother, finding them at it, screamed and swooned; clambering in the beams of the Great Hall to get her hawk; and so on. I once overheard my chief steward call her a young savage. But he was so frightened when he saw me, that I was content and did no more to him. I was too happy to be cruel.

They had made the Queen's rooms fine again; but she only used them to dress and bathe. It was in mine she liked to be, even when I was not there. Our arms hung up together on one wall, our spears stood in one corner. Even the deerhound I gave her, a tall bitch from Sparta, mated with my Aktis as soon as it was grown.

Against her coming they had laid out a treasure of jewels and clothes, embroidered bodices and gold-hung flounces. She walked up to them softly, like a deer smelling a trap, wrinkled her brows, drew back, and looked at me. I laughed, and gave her the jewels to play with – she loved clear bright things – and let go the clothes to the Palace women. Hers I had made by my own craftsman, in her own style, but richer. The kidskin was Sidonian dyed, the laces were plaited gold tagged with agate or crystal, the buttons lapis, or Hyperborean amber. For her caps, I got the one thing fine enough to put against her hair: the silk that comes a year's journey before it reaches Babylon, woven with flying serpents and unknown flowers.

As I had promised, I gave her arms; a shield with her leopard crest, a cheek-flap helm plated with silver and plumed with sheet-gold ribbons that glittered when she moved. I had brought her a Scythian bow from the Hellespont; and she used to come with me to the smithy to watch the making of her sword. It was the best one made in my time in Athens. The centre rib had a line of ships let into blue enamel, in memory of our meeting; the pommel was made of a green stone from the silk country, like clouded water, carved with magic signs; the golden hand-grip of the hilt was beaten into lilies. I taught her myself to use it. She used to say it handled like a living limb. Often at evening I would see her lay it across her knee, and run her fingers over the work to feel its fineness. Her hands lie on it still.

The Cretan ship had sailed, with no message from me. Sometimes I was sorry, as one would be for forgetting a child's name-day. But Phaedra was leaving childhood, and it would be crueller still, I thought, to let her think I would soon be coming. 'There is time enough,' I would say to myself; though for what, I did not know.

As the people saw it, there was one more woman in my house, a captive of my spear, who had caught my fancy above the rest. Kings marry notwithstanding, and get an heir. Only I knew, and she who never thought to question it, that I could never watch another woman walk in front of her.

The Palace girls guessed, however, finding me so changed, who had never before kept to one alone. I had brought them all gifts from Kolchis, and gave them leave, if they were lonely, to go with my guests of honour. Those with growing children of mine for whom they still hoped favour, took it well; but I saw some looks that I did not like. A great house must have women, who are as much its wealth as corn and cattle; there must be proper service; besides, they are the signs of victory. But I told Hippolyta, if she had any trouble, to bring it straight to me.

She said nothing, so I thought no harm, till one evening I came in as she dressed, and she said to me, 'Theseus, must I undo my hair?'

'What need?' I said, smiling and catching her eye across the maid; I used to undo it in bed. She answered, 'This gift of yours will need it.'

She lifted it in her hands; a heavy golden diadem, crusted with gold flowers, with a shower of gold chains on either side to mingle with the hair. She was going to put it on, when I jumped forward and caught her wrist, and called out, 'Stop!'

She put it down jingling, and looked at me surprised. I said, 'I did not send this. Let me see it.' I put out my hand; but it drew back as if from a snake. There was no doubt what it was. Someone had brought out the crown of the witch Medea. She had worn it when I had seen her first, sitting by my father in the Hall.

Hippolyta, too, sat there at my right hand; perhaps in the very chair. She would have worn this for my sake before all the barons, if I had not come in time. It broke my night's sleep; I would reach over to feel if she was breathing. In the morning, I sifted the matter out.

The treasurer owned to me, since there was no help for it, who had coaxed him for a peep inside the strongroom. He was no worse than a doting fool, and had served my father, so I only took his office from him. Then I sent for the woman.

While I walked up and down, Hippolyta came in. I heard her behind me, but would not turn. I was angry with her for keeping her mouth shut. Any woman can tell when another hates her; she might have been poisoned, instead of this. The truth was, of course, that she had felt herself a victor; it was beneath her to trample on the fallen. I heard her breathe hard behind me, and a clink of bronze. Trying to harden my heart, and keep a rebuking back to her, I could not help a quick look over my shoulder. She was dressed for battle, down to her shield.

Our eyes met. She was as angry as I.

'They say you have sent for her here.' I nodded. 'Her, without me?'

'What is this?' I asked. 'Have you not seen enough of her? If you had done as I said, it would have been better every way.'

'Ah! You own it! And what did you mean to do, then, fighting my quarrel? Tell me that.'

'Fighting? You forget I am the King. I shall do judgement. Go now; we will talk afterwards.'

She came up in two strides, and looked at me eye to eye. 'You meant to kill her!' she said.

'It is a quick death, off the Rock,' I said, 'and better than she has earned. Now go as I asked, and let me deal.'

'You would have killed her!' Her eyes flashed, and narrowed like a lynx's. Even when we were hand to hand at Maiden Crag, I had not seen her like this. 'What am I? A peasant wife, one of your bath-girls? It was the same when I killed my leopard! Oh, yes, I remember; I had to shout or you would have had that too. And you swore not to dishonour me!'

'Dishonour you? Not to stand by and see you wronged, is that dishonour? I warned you against letting things come to this. You would not heed; and who is the better for your pride?'

'I am, if you are not! Did you think I would come creeping to you like a slave-girl, telling tales? Have I never been taught honour, or the law of arms? I know what calls for a challenge, as well as you do. Yes, and if you had been any other, I would have had your blood too, for this.'

I nearly laughed; but some voice said danger. If she lost her head and defied me, she was too proud to draw back; and who could tell the end of it? But, I thought, if I give in first will she not despise me? We stood at stretch, fizzing like cats upon a wall. I don't know what would have come next, if we had not heard outside the Guard bringing the woman. That brought back my wits.

'Very well,' I said. 'I give her to you. But remember, after, it was you who asked.'

I went and sat apart, in the window. But the woman, when they brought her in, ran straight past Hippolyta, fell down clasping my knees, and wailed excuses. She blamed it all on the treasurer; who had loved her, poor fool.

'Get up,' I said. 'I have nothing to do here. The Lady Hippolyta can right her wrongs without help from me. Attend to her; there she is.'

I looked across. She was sickened already by this grovelling; she could not meet my eye. But she stood her ground, showed the weapons (axe, spear and javelin, as I remember) and offered her enemy first choice.

There was no answer, but a squeal of fear. When it sank to sobbing, Hoppolyta said quietly, 'I have never fought with a knife. I will take one against your spear. Will you fight now?'

Yelling as she ran, the girl came back to me, and fell upon the ground clawing her hair, begging me not to have her butchered by the Amazon, who had bewitched me for sure, else what could I see in such a freak of nature? Then before I could think to stop her (one does not think of such things) out came the bile such women hide from men till hate or fear makes them careless. I got six months' siltings, thrown in one drench; thrice-chewed, spat-out backbitings of the closet and the bath. I gasped in the stream, then stood up, letting her fall. She lay on the floor between us, looking from face to face, gulping and moaning. She found she had meddled with something outside her ken, and did not like it. 'What now?' I said, speaking across her. 'She is yours.'

We exchanged silent glances. We could not talk with the woman there. At last Hippolyta said quietly, 'I never yet killed a suppliant. If she is mine, send her away.'

I had her taken out, still grizzling to whoever had ears to hear. When we were alone together, I said, 'I would have spared you that, with your leave or without it, if I had known.'

She turned slowly. I wondered, if she struck me, what I would do. But she said, 'I am ashamed,' and covered her face.

'You?' I said. 'Of what? The shame is mine. With that I made do, before you came.' Then we were reconciled, and more in love than ever, if that could be. As for the girl, keeping my word I sold her to some Sidonian trader at Piraeus.

That was enough for me. I made a clean sweep of every girl

I had doubts of. Since still she would tell no tales, no one was punished; I gave them to my barons, or with dowries to marry decent craftsmen. That left a quiet house, but short service. Though lack of company was better than what she had had, the dose of poison had left a sickness on her spirit. I could not bear to see her dimmed.

And then one day she said to me, 'I have been talking to Amyntor.'

She spoke as simply as a boy. She had still much innocence. After what had happened, I was pleased to see it. I smiled and said, 'You could do worse. He was my best lad in the Bull Court.'

'He tells me his wife was there too, and better than he. I should like to see her. But he says he must have your leave.'

'He has it,' I said, thinking how times had changed, when men wanted to bring their wives under my roof. It was clear he had planned for this. When I sent for him he almost owned it. 'She has settled down, sir, since she had the boy. I think she is happy most of the day, and perfection is for the gods. She knows that I understand; but no one forgets the Bull Court.'

'No wonder. Nor will I forget that back-spring she used to do, off her finger-ends. She went like a song.'

'There was a song,' said Amyntor. We hummed the air.

'She would have grown too tall,' I said. 'We were just in time, there.'

'I once found her crying over that. But not since the child.'

'She can bring him; would she be willing to come?'

'Willing? She has been on at me, sir, board and bed. But you've surely seen, since your Lady came, every bull-dancer that is left would die for her.'

So Chryse came from Eleusis. She had grown a tall full-breasted Hellene beauty; all but she herself, I suppose, had forgotten the fearless golden child of the Cretan songs. She loved Amyntor. Yet princes had staked on her a chariot-team or a country villa; young nobles had risked their necks and bribed the guard, to send her as the custom was their verses of hopeless love; she had heard ten thousand voices shout for her as she grasped the horns. Something she must have missed among the house-bred women with their talk of nurses and children, scandal and clothes and men.

She and Hippolyta were friends at the first glance, neither having a mean thought to hide. I would find them in the evening telling tales of Crete or Pontos, or laughing while the little boy played at bull-leaping with a footstool. Peace and order came to the women's quarters, which had stood in some need of it; and people began to say that the Amazon, for all her strangeness, had made King Theseus steady.

But the barons, as I knew, thought more than they said when they saw her sitting by me in the hall. They knew it meant I would not marry yet, feared it would lay up strife for the day when I did, and wanted the bond with Crete tied firmly. Nor had they forgotten Medea, who had been, besides a sorceress, a priestess of the Mother, scheming to bring back the old religion and end the rule of men. Now here was another priestess of a Goddess; one who knew magic, as they had heard. It did not move them, or quiet their fears, that she wanted nothing but to be free in the woods and mountains, or else with me.

So winter passed. We had a great wolf-hunt on Mount Lykabettos, following the tracks in new-fallen snow to their den in the high rocks above the pines. It was a fierce fight and a good killing; we laughed to see her bitch and my dog fight side by side, as we did. In her jacket of russet lambskin with her scarlet boots and cap, her eyes and her cheeks all glowing, she shone in the white cold like a warm bird. She loved the snow.

I asked to this hunt, and the feast after, all the young men who had gone to Crete with me, and as many of the girls as chose to come. Chryse, who had fined-down and toughened with riding and running, was the first of these; there were two more who were serving Artemis in a shrine above Eleusis. For Thebe and Pylia it was too late.

After this, the word went round that those who had known the Bull Court would be welcome in my hall. They had always been so; but I had been much away, at war or about the kingdoms, and had not had time to seek them out. Now I began to see not only those who had sailed with me from Athens, but those who had been levied from all the old tribute-lands of Minos, lads and girls I had led to freedom when the Labyrinth was destroyed. They came from the Cyclades; from the Twelve Isles of Asia; from Phoenicia and Rhodes and Cyprus; and from Crete itself. Some came for what they could make out of it; some to give thanks for life and freedom; some, whom I remembered among the best in skill and daring, out of mere restlessness, because the mark of the Bull Court was on them yet.

They were still young, for the tribute-ships had taken them from thirteen upwards; and though they were mostly men who made so long a journey, they had known the fellowship where maids and men had lived by what was in them. Some had stayed on in Crete, and were horse-tamers or charioteers; they came in the fringed kilt of Knossos, with shaven faces and curled hair, wearing the jewels of the Bull Court; for though the House of the Axe had fallen, the glory of the bull-ring was slow to die. Some had gone roving, and were spearmen in pirate ships, or had set themselves up by it with steadings in the islands. And some, who had known no trade or a poor one, or had been slaves at home before, had turned to the life of tumblers, roaming from town to town; the best keeping their pride, dancing with swords or fire instead of bulls, the worst content to please the ignorant, and sunk to petty tricksters or common thieves. Even these, for the sake of all we had endured together, I would not send off without a meal, a night's lodging and a guest-gift; and the Palace people who had lived softly all their lives could make of it what they chose. None grumbled openly, knowing their own sons and daughters might have seen the Bull Court, but for them and me. It is true that some of them looked odd in a king's hall. The quiet and steady, who had taken up their old lives among their kindred, had business and did not come. The footloose came, who loved adventure, and had the taste for gaiety and splendour that one learned in Crete.

There were many of the best I found places for, not only in my chariot-stables but around the court. Gently born or not, they had picked up behaviour in the Labyrinth, from eating at lords' tables there; only quick learners lived long among the bulls. Often their manners were nicer than those of my home-bred barons. They honoured Hippolyta from the heart, for what she was, not with the lips from fear of me. They gave a polish to the household; and whatever they brought of the ways of Crete they did not bring its softness, but what was skilful, quick and bright; so it did no harm.

Before long, with such a market ready, came the battle-bards and harpers, the master chariot-builders, the swordsmiths and famous jewellers, the carvers of gems and rings. All these Hippolyta delighted in. She loved all fine things, but still more the talk of the craftsmen, their tales of travel, their thinking and their skills. She had no greed of show, no wish to put other women down or prove herself regarded. She would keep one perfect thing with her all day, to feel and understand it. Bards loved to sing for her, for, as one told me, she never asked a foolish question, and saw straight through to the core.

The barons' wives and honest matrons, who talked of the same things year by year, felt their minds as far outpaced as their legs would have been, if they had raced with her on the hills. I would see them look down their noses when she talked with men, and then peep to see if I was jealous. They were full of the arts she knew nothing of, to keep their men in doubt of them and cloud the clear truth of love. If she had changed to me, I would have known it as soon as dust blown in my eye.

Yet she could keep her counsel for others' good. There were some young men of my Guard whose cult it was to worship her, and honour Artemis for her sake. It started as a pretty fancy, but one had kindled a fire to burn him. At last, being out of his head with love he importuned her in secret. From pity for him, she dealt with it all without a word to me, till in despair he drowned himself; then she brought me her grief to comfort. I too was sorry, feeling in my own joy the measure of his want; and I named one of my new towns after him, because he had no sons.

But it gave me a thought; and to bring a good thing out of trouble, I gave her her own Guard. I chose these same young men to lead it; they wore her badge of a leaping leopard, and she trained them herself for war. Thus I showed the world my trust in her; and something that might have grown dangerous was brought into the open, where it turned to pride and honour. There were no more dark deaths, but good clean rivalries. It was the same when they teamed against my Guard at the Games, for bad feeling would have slighted us both alike. Those who understood such things, we liked to have about us; the rest could make the best of it.

Of course there was some muttering in corners. It was a time for the young. The world had changed and could not be put back again; it was no place for men whose minds were stiffening. All their long lives, they had been fretting under the power of Minos; now they thought it could be broken, and nothing would move that it had held. If I had not ridden the change, I could not have steered the kingdom through its dangers; but once they had built their houses and married off their sons, they wanted the ride to stop. As for me, I had the reins in my hands and the wind in my hair, and love beside me in the chariot; and it seemed to me I would never weary.

The Hellene lands were all in ferment, now there was no Cretan fleet to keep down upstart greatness. The kingdoms were finding their own level, learning to live by what was in them. In these years, both weakness and overweening brought their reckoning quickly. One needed a feel for it, when to give and when to take, such as wrestlers learn.

It was the time of the Theban war. Oedipus' curse had flown back home, and his brother-sons were battling for the kingship. I watched, biding my time. It tempted me, to snatch the bone while the dogs were fighting. But the son in Thebes had the people with him; the one outside had Argive chiefs for allies, with whom I wanted no blood-feuds. Both sides sent me envoys; I parleyed, and took the omens, which were bad for both. Within a month they were dead by each other's hands; the Argives went home, and uncle Kreon was King.

But I doubted the curse was laid yet. I had taken Kreon's measure while the war was on, and did not doubt he had pricked his nephews into hatred, hoping for what had come to him. During the siege, the gods had called for a royal sacrifice, and he had left his son to step forth and die. He was getting old, and trying to make fear do the work of strength. For terror's sake, he left the dead chiefs to rot in the sun unburied. So the poor girl Antigone, chained to her pieties like a patient ox, crept out at night to strew earth on her worthless brother. Her indeed King Kreon gave a tomb to; but he walled her in alive. It outraged his own people, and all the Hellene lands. The kin of the riteless dead came to me suppliant, with ashes on their heads. And then I moved.

The Thebans were sure by now I would not meddle; surprise was easy. We slipped down at fall of night from the Kithairon foothills, and by moonrise had scaled the walls. There was hardly a fight; the people were sick of war and Kreon. I put him in prison only, wanting no part in that poisoned blood-guilt; but his sins sat heavy on him, and he shortly died. By then I ruled Thebes in all but name.

Better than the assault, I remember the tail-end of the night in the taken Kadmeion, when Hippolyta and I went to unarm and rest. We had not considered, till we were there, that they would bring us to the royal bedchamber. The heavy roof-beams were painted red and purple, and carved with knots of snakes; on a hanging that filled one wall crouched a huge black Sphinx, the ancient Theban goddess, with dead warriors in her paws. We could not sleep, for the creaks and whispers that filled the dark, like the swing of a weighted rope; nor could we join in love – not in that bed. We lay there clasping each other like cold children, and presently lit the lamp.

But one good came of it; we spent the hours till light in council. To talk with her always cleared my mind. I saw that to sit on the throne of Kadmos would be that one thing more that sinks the ship. The greater kings would have taken fright, and joined to bring me down. Besides, half a night in that room told me no luck could come of it. So when morning came, I proclaimed the elder brother's son, who was still a child, and promised him my safeguard, choosing his council from some of the men who had called me in. Then I went home. Everyone praised my justice and moderation; and Thebes was safer in my hand than if I had been King.

We had a great homecoming. The people sang me as judge and lawgiver of Hellas, and shared the pride of it. And indeed, from that time on wronged folk from all the clans of Attica would come to sit on my threshold: slaves with cruel masters, widows oppressed or orphans disinherited; and not even the chiefs dared murmur when I saw right done. It was called the glory of Athens; for myself, I saw it as an offering to the gods. They had used me well.

Often I thought how, if I had been roving off with Pirithoos, I should have missed my chance at Thebes. The times moved quickly. Besides, what should I rove for? It would never bring me such a prize again. I was content, and stayed at home.

And then, as we got up one morning early for a ride, Hippolyta sat down on the bed again and said, 'Oh, Theseus, I am sick.'

Her face looked green and her hand was cold; soon she threw up. While they fetched the doctor, I felt sick myself from fear; my mind ran upon poison. He came, and asked for her women, and waited for me to go. I was still too slow to understand, till he came out smiling, and said he must not steal the midwife's trade.

When I got her alone, she was brisk and light, as if she had got a scratch in battle that she did not mean to make a song of. But when I took her in my arms she said softly, 'You told me true, Theseus. Maiden Crag is far away.'

At the fifth month, she put on woman's dress. I found her in it, alone, standing hands on hips and feet apart, staring down at her skirts and her growing belly. When she heard me, she kept her back turned and said in a sulky growl, 'I must be mad, or I would be killing you.'

'Then so must I,' I answered. 'For when I can't have you, there's no one I can fancy; and that never happened to me all my life.'

She wore the clothes well, from pride lest she should be laughed at; seeing her sweep by, I could have laughed, or cried. But soon after, when I stood on the balcony looking out across the Attic plain, I heard her feet behind me in their old swift stride. She put her hand over mine on the balustrade, and said, 'He will be a boy.'

Later on, as she grew heavy and idle, she would send for the bards to sing. She chose the songs with care; no blood-feuds, or curses coming home, but lays of victory, or the birth of heroes from the loves of the gods. 'Who can be sure,' she would say, 'that he does not hear?' At night she would take my hand and lay it over where the child was, to feel it move. 'He sits high. They say it is the sign of a man.'

Her pains began when I was over in Acharnai, dealing with a lord who had beaten a serf to death. I got home to find she had been three hours in labour. Strong as she was, always in the open and never ill, I had thought she would bring forth quickly. But she was travailing all night, with long hard pains. The midwife said it was often so with girls who had followed the life of Artemis; either the Goddess grudged it, or their sinews were too strongly knit to stretch. I went to and fro outside the door, hearing voices murmuring and the sputter of torches, but no sound from her. In the cold low hours, I was seized by a notion she was dead, and they dared not tell me. I pushed through the gaggle of sleepy women on the threshold, and went inside. She was lying quiet between the pains, pale, with sweat on her forehead. But when she saw me she smiled and held out her hand. 'He is a fighter, this lad of yours. But I am winning.' I held her hand awhile, till I felt it tighten; then she snatched it back saying, 'Now go away.'

As the earliest sunlight touched the Rock, while the plain was still in shadow, for the first time I heard her cry aloud; but there was triumph in it as much as pain. The midwives chattered; then came the voice of the child.

I was so near the door, I heard what the midwife told her; but when I went in, I let her be first with the news. She did not look sick now, only dead-tired as if after a day in the hills or a long night's love. Her limbs lay slack, but her grey eyes glowed. She threw the bedclothes back and cried, 'What did I say?'

The midwife nodded, and said no wonder my lady had had to work all night, with this great boy. I took him up; he felt heavier than my other children I had handled, yet neither big nor small, just what was right. Nor was he red, or wizened, but bloomed and glowed as if the sun had ripened him in a good year. And though his eyes were the dim misty blue one always sees at birth, wandering and squinting, yet they were already hers.

I gave him back, and kissed her, and put my fingers into his hand, to feel his grip. As I played with it, I set his palm upon the royal ring of Athens, and his grasp closed on the bezel. My eyes met hers. We were silent, for there were others within hearing; but it never needed speech between us, to share our thought.

13

He flourished like spring flowers, and grew like a young poplar planted by a stream.

We found him a good wet-nurse; his mother had not much milk, and fretted for the wild hills and me. But she would come running in from the hunt, to pick him up and toss him upon her shoulder; he loved her strong hands, and would squeal for joy. Before he could walk, she would ride full gallop holding him astride before her; he had no more fear of a horse than of his nurse's lap. But by the evening fire she would take him on her knee like any mother, and sing long northland songs to him in her own tongue.

I have fathered a good many sons, and there is no child of my body I have known of that I have not cared for. There were six or seven in the Palace. But it seemed in the nature of things that when I came to look at them their mothers said, 'Quiet now and behave; here comes the King.' The people were not long in seeing that this one had taken my heart.

But the brighter the light, the further seen. It shone too clearly: her love and mine, his excellence, and the hope of my heart. I had ruled now nine years in Athens, and I knew the people; I felt, as a pilot feels the set of the tide, that here they were not with me.

When I had loved here and there, they had taken it lightly; indeed it was their boast. I could have peopled, myself, another Attica, if all the tales had been true. It had made a good one, that I had bedded even the Lady of the Amazons and got her with child. But when time passed, and she lived my queen in all but name; when they saw that by my choice she would have had that too; then their face altered.

It was not in the small man's fear of change and newness, that the danger lay. The real fear was old, deep-rooted in every Hellene.

She had served the Goddess; and I had not tamed her. They too remembered Medea. They thought, and maybe rightly, that if I had not come she would have edged my father off his throne, and sacrificed him at the year's end as was done in the days of the Shore Folk who had the land before us, and brought the old religion back again.

It was close to the ground, among the peasants, that this rumour spread like bindweed. If I had foreseen it, I daresay I would not have named the boy Hippolytos; it is a Shore Folk custom, for the son to take his mother's name. But it would have been a public slight on her to change it; nor could I think of him by any other.

The barons, if they had chosen, could have done much to check such tales. They knew her life, and could see the truth for themselves. But they had their own grudges. They were jealous of her power with me; of her friends, and the new blood in the Palace; they thought she taught their daughters hoyden ways; above all, the nearest to the bone, they were set on the Cretan marriage.

The fate I waited for had not stepped in to free me. The girl was Minos' child; and Crete is too full of the old religion to set aside the female line. If I gave her to another man high-born enough not to disgrace her, he would have Crete in his hand; if I gave her to a peasant as once was done in Argos, I should be disgraced myself, and the Cretans would not bear my rule; if I kept her unwed, she would be a lure for every ambitious king in Hellas and every lord in Crete. Even this I might have risked, for my girl's sake and her son's; but there was more yet, there was Mykenai. Echelaos was king there now. He had long since married off his sister; but if he learned that what I would not do for the Lion House, I had done for a captive of my spear, he would not rest till he had washed out the slight in blood. Nor would he believe that for so slight a cause I would refuse their match; he would think me his enemy already. Then Mykenai and Crete would make two millstones, and Athens would be the grain.

As time ran out, I saw there had been only one hope for Fate to bring me. It was Phaedra's death that I had hoped for in my heart. I thought about it, as one must think when one sees the certain means to the end desired. Every king has men about him to whom he need only look a wish. But there is evil beyond one's reach, as there is good.

When all this was pressing close on me, I got a message from Pirithoos, bidding us both to his wedding. We went gladly, hoping the people of Attica would turn their minds to other things, once we were out of sight. But it turned out the most unlucky feast in Hellas, worse than that one in Kalydon after the boar-hunt.

All began well. Pirithoos had found himself just the right girl; some great lord's daughter, and a Lapith of the Lapiths, one who like her mother before her would put up with a roving man. The palace was crammed to the doors with food and wine and guests. The Lapiths are great hosts. As well as the hall for the kings and lords and warriors, the whole courtyard was set out with tables for the grooms, tenants and peasants; and beyond, under the trees, were more tables still. Pirithoos told me these were for the Kentaurs.

When I stared, he said, 'Why not? I promised Old Handy I'd do my best for them, and I've kept my word. I let no one hunt them for sport, nor steal their ponies, nor burn their honey-heath; if they're caught sneaking a lamb or kid, I give them a proper trial – the farmers used to nail them up on trees, to scare the rest. And they've done their part, better than I ever looked for. They're like horses, they feel a friend. Last month, they gave me warning of a cattle-raid; came right down into the plain to do it! Such a thing was never known in Thessaly. I owe them a dinner; and they'll have a good one, for I know their likes; I should. Meat; an extra cartload of raw bones, which they like cracking for the marrow; and mare's milk fermented with honey. I've stored that over there, for the smell makes most people vomit. Out here, there'll be no fear of the wine going their way. Wine sends them mad.'

On the wedding day, I rode with Pirithoos as his groomsman in the bridal car, bringing home the bride, a great train of mounted Lapiths following. It was a fine sight, winding down from her father's castle and through the plain. The peasants cheered; the Kentaurs joined in with a tuneless howl that would have made the horses bolt, if any but Lapiths had had hold of them. Then we settled down to the feasting. Doing my groomsman's duty, I went about to see that all was going well, and found the Kentaur feast flourishing under the shady trees, though, as Pirithoos had said, a queasy sight. Only one corner had decorum. There Old Handy sat, served by his boys. I daresay they had taught him something, but he had taught them more. I would not have known them, washed and combed and gold-decked as they were, but they were all at the wedding, and there were never less than two or three about him, leaving their kindred to do him courtesy in the stink of the Kentaur feast.

In Thessaly the women sit apart at festivals; but I could see Hippolyta by the bride. She had put on women's dress, knowing Pirithoos would like it, and none could match her beauty. But so it always seemed to me.

Besides my servants, I had brought as my body-page a youth called Menestheus. He came of the royal kin, a son of my father's cousin Peteus, who had died in exile during the wars of the kingdom. I saw no need to visit these old troubles on the lad, especially as there had been no love lost between him and his father, by all accounts an overbearing man. So I gave Menestheus a place at court, and found him useful; he was quick-minded, and did not need telling twice. If he had a fault, it was to run ahead of what was wanted; he had been overmuch corrected, and was fond of showing where others had fallen short. But officiousness always looks easier to train than dullness.

Just now he was serving tables, with the other youths of good blood. But when I sat down to my meat, a boy came to my shoulder, and bent down and said quietly, 'Did you know, my lord, that your page is giving Old Handy wine?'

For all his sleek hair and embroidered short-drawers, he was brown as old wood, and he had used the clucking Kentaur name; so I went out quickly. Sure enough, Menestheus with his jug was standing before Old Handy. One of the boys who was serving him with meat had got behind his shoulder to signal 'No'; but Menestheus missed it, or did not heed.

Old Handy's head came forward; I saw his nostrils twitch at the sweet strange scent. But his wisdom stayed him, or else he trusted his boys. He turned his head aside, and pushed the jug from him; a gesture as simple as a beast's, yet, as he made it, somehow kingly.

One of the boys grabbed Menestheus' arm, and showed him I was beckoning. But he had to pass the Kentaur benches, and they had smelled the wine. Presently one made a long arm and snatched the jug; then two were scuffling, pulling it to and fro and swigging by turns.

Menestheus came up, still not much put out. I was angry by now, remembering I had given him Pirithoos' warning, and asked him what he meant by it. He looked righteous, and said, 'I thought, sir, they were failing in respect to him. First he is put outside; then they keep the wine from him, which all the Palace clerks are getting. He is their tutor, even if he is a Kentaur.'

'Tutor?' I said. 'He is a king. And he was never under a roof since he was born. His boys know what he is, and love him. That is love. You are in love with your own notions, which is only with yourself. When you are ready to learn before you teach, you will be a man.'

By now the Kentaurs were licking the jug for lees. They had spilled a good part, so, I thought, there could not be much harm done; and I said nothing to Pirithoos, who was whispering to his bride. The meal was ending, and it would soon be time for the dances.

The women were getting up. It is a Lapith custom for the bride to make a progress with her train among the guests, who throw flowers and blessings, before the men's dancing that ends with carrying her away. Evening was coming on, and indoors they were lighting the torches. Hippolyta and I changed smiles as she slipped off; our bridal had not been much like this.

The music struck up. The women swept round the hall, with pretty children bearing torches, and the bride on her father's arm. They went out through the doors, and we heard the cheering and songs in the courtyard, going further off. Then the noise changed. It grew loud and ragged; an old man far off shouted in anger, and Pirithoos jumped to his feet. As I followed, I heard a clear voice yell, 'Theseus!' It was Hippolyta's, pitched to carry above a battle.

The men jumped up in turmoil, and raced for the door. 'Wait!' I shouted. 'Get yourselves armed!' There were old war-trophies on the walls, and some men who had come a journey had stacked their arms by the door. I took a Lapith battle-axe, and a sword. As we were arming, three or four children came pelting in, their bridal clothes dusty and torn, their screams of terror pulsing as they ran. We had no time to comfort them, but dashed out into the dusk.

The courtyard was empty, the peasants' benches overturned. The noise came from beyond the gates. Outside was a scene like the sack of a city; shrieking clawing women thrown down upon the tables among spilled meat and curds, with Kentaurs grabbing and gobbling over them, or growling at one another; the peasants, who had run to help, yelling for help themselves as loud as the women. No shame to them, for Kentaurs have Titan blood, and when they are maddened have two or three men's strength; one had torn a poor wretch's arm off. Through all this I ran, shouting my war-cry and Hippolyta's name; when she answered, it was like black night lifting. Running over bodies writhing or dead, over food and crocks and torches, I found her fighting with a knife from the carver's table, guarding the bride. The old lord, her father, lay trampled and bloody on the ground before them. Just as a Kentaur got the knife away, I got there in time to split his head. It was so thick, it nearly turned the axe in my hand, and I had trouble to wrench it free. I gave it to Hippolyta, and drew my sword, and we fell to it side by side. Pirithoos set the bride behind him against a tree, and got to work with his long spear. The women's screams grew less; the war-cries rose, and the great bellows of the Kentaurs.

I have been in some bloody fights; but this was the bloodiest, and the ghastliest too, for it was neither war nor beast-killing, yet the worst of both. I have forgotten most of it and am glad. But I remember barking my shins on the huge wine-jar which the Kentaurs had sneaked out from the courtyard, smelling their way to it as they do when they raid the folds. And I remember seeing Old Handy. His table was overturned, and he stood before his chair of honour, with a boy in either arm. He had them clasped to his sides, like his own young; his old yellow teeth were bared, defying the rest to touch them, and the hair had lifted on his back. He was roaring to his people in the Kentaur tongue, trying to make them stop. But they were too mad to hear; and as I watched, the boys writhed in his arms, and twisted free, and drawing the little gold daggers from their jewelled belts flew screeching like hawks into the battle. I was busy then for some time; but near the end I looked that way again. Old Handy was standing alone, his hairy arms hanging by his bent knees so that the knuckles almost swept the ground, his head sunk in his shoulders, looking before him. I have heard it said that Kentaurs are too near the earth to weep as men do. But I saw it then.

At last it was over. The Kentaurs ran howling to the hills, whence later the Lapiths hunted them like wolves. Those that were left fled to the wild back-country, and there are none in Thessaly today.

As the sound of the chase grew less, we who were guests of the land did what we could for the wounded, and carried in the dead. Those of mankind, I mean; the Lapiths no longer counted Kentaurs as men, and burned them the next day without rites, like murrained cattle. Yet I have thought that in time they might have grown more manlike, from being friends with men, but for this unlucky feast that roused the beast and quenched the man in them. Maybe Old Handy had bred some sons; and no doubt we killed them. He went off with the remnant of his people, to take up the burden of his priesthood on some other mountain; so I cannot tell.

Hippolyta all bruised was inside helping the women, and I was making for the courtyard fountain to get clean, when I met in my way the youth Menestheus, white in the face. There was plenty to do, but he stood there looking sick. I was mired and bloody and ploughed with Kentaur claws; I thought of the dead, of the young bride crying on her virgin bed, for her father was unburied, and who would get children on such a luckless night? My wounds smarted at the sight of him. I said, 'This is your work, you meddling, smug young know-all. Does it please you still?' And I gave him a clout on the head.

He gave me one look, and went. I daresay he saw his father once again. Sometimes I have wondered how much good was mixed with his self-conceit, and whether, like the Kentaurs, with a little more trying he might have been changed. I doubt it; it was his nature to believe anything, before he would believe he could be wrong. In any case, I was out of patience. He went off to think his own thoughts, which he ceased to tell me; and when next I knew them, it was too late.

14

We got home to find the boy thriving in Chryse's care; even in that short time he had been growing. The barons and the commons had not, as I had hoped, forgotten Crete; but that was little, beside some news Pirithoos had given me in Thessaly, which I had to carry alone.

Far to the north, beyond the Euxine and the Ister, there was a great movement of the peoples. The Endless Plain, at the back of the north wind, is so far from the sea that if you bring an oar there, the folk take it for a winnowing fan; but storms were blowing there, and nations foundering like ships on a lee shore. The southern Thracians had heard it from the northern ones, who had it from southern Scyths, and they from the Scythians northward, that a people called the Black Cloaks were coming out of the great north-east wastes, and eating the plains before them. What kind of people they were, he could not tell, only that they worshipped no gods but the night and day, and that the fear of them ran before their tufted spears like the cold wind before the rain.

Pirithoos did not think they would come to the Hellene lands; they were too far, and having great herds moved slowly. 'But,' he said, 'if they come south-westward, they will push the Scythians south, and those will come down, landless and hungry, as they say our own fathers did. Let's hope we can hold harder than the Shore Folk who were here before us. If the Black Cloaks move some other way, it may never come. But, Theseus, look; if it does I shall have my hands full. If you want good friends in the bad time, you had better think again of this Cretan marriage. You know I don't mean to slight your lady; she has more sense than any woman I know, and I swear she never had a wish that could do you harm. She must see it as well as I.'

Those were his words to me. If he had any with her, I do not know. But one night in Athens, when I was lying awake in bed and thinking of these things, she laid her arm across my breast and said, 'Theseus, we are what we are. But you must marry the Cretan.'

I answered, 'We are what we are. And if I give her what you ought to have, you will never have it.'

'I am a warrior,' she said, 'who took you for my King; my honour is in serving yours. Nothing undoes that vow; it is the truth of my heart. So don't make me a traitor.'

'And the boy? There is bad blood in the House of Minos. Must I graft on that stock, to pass him by?'

She lay silent awhile, then said, 'He is in the hand of some god, Theseus. I felt it while I was bearing him; he seemed stronger than I. I think he feels it too. Sometimes I see him listening.'

So we talked about the child; but she broke off, and said again, 'Marry the Cretan, Theseus. Since you were betrothed to her, you have not been there once. Can you trust your governors and the Cretan lords for ever? Of course not; and it has been upon your mind.' She always knew my thoughts without telling.

She slept at last, but I lay waking. When the first birds called and the sky lightened, I knew what I would do.

I called the barons, and told them that having considered their counsel and the kingdom's good, I would sail to Crete and take to wife Minos' daughter. But to hold the land in peace, I would honour its ancient law which came down from the Old Religion there; that inheritance is through the mother, and a woman who marries with a foreigner will lose it if she goes from her land to his. So I would leave her in Crete, with fitting state and proper guardians, and visit her when I went there on the kingdom's business. Thus both realms would be well secured.

They were overjoyed. I had done well to put them in mind that this queen too might serve the Goddess. Almost they thanked me for not bringing her home.

That year I remitted the Cretan tribute, and asked only that they build a house for the bride, and for me when I was with her. I chose the old fort by the southern river, by the shrine of the Sacred Three. I had meant to have it strengthened in any case; it was easy to have it made handsome too. Not for all the world would I have raised up again the Labyrinth, in whose very dust you could smell the wrath of the gods. Deukalion had patched up the western wing; and he was welcome to it, for me.

So that year passed, while the house was building. The child still grew and grew. As soon as the first mist had cleared out of his eyes, they had been like his mother's, grey as a cloudless dawn; and the silvery hair he was born with hardly darkened. She loved the light on it, and would not have it curled. His skin, like his hair, was fine; but with a little sun it would glow like golden fruit. He was quick and strong, and would scramble everywhere. When he was three, he was found in a brood-mare's straw, his arms and legs round the new foal; he had tried to ride it, and when the two babes tumbled, the mare leaned down and licked them both. You could see, as his mother said, that he had the blood of Poseidon. It was a hard parting, when I set out next spring for Crete.

Life had been picked up again in the great island, as it always is while men live on. If you kept away from the ruined strongholds (I had burned some myself, during the war) there was little amiss to see. The fields were tilled, the vine-stocks greening; the almond tree blossomed by the fallen wall. New houses were going up, less fine than those before but snug and bright. The potters were at work again, those that were left, and had started one more new fashion, this time for birds.

The native Cretans welcomed me as loudly as on the day when I had led them against the Labyrinth. It pleased them that I would hold my wedding-feast among them like their own king, and not a conqueror. Some of the Hellene barons who held from me, and had grown oppressive in my absence, were not so pleased. The best and greatest had been trustworthy; but it would not have done to stay away much longer. When I had dealt with what was pressing, I drove to Deukalion's house to meet my betrothed.

Whatever he thought, he greeted me very civilly. Once I was married, his throne hung on my favour more than before. He had been king only in name, and now would be barely that; but the shadow was precious to him, or perhaps to his lady wife. She came swimming up to me with a chatter of jewelled skirts and a cloud of scent from Egypt, languished awhile, and with a great play of eyes withdrew to bring the Princess.

All this long while, I had seen in my mind's eye the child who loved the bull-boy, smiling through tears in the nursery painted with apes and flowers. Now I saw led in by the hand a little Cretan lady, just like the portrait I had been sent. Her hair had darkened, and was crimped in long serpent ringlets, before and behind. Her lashes and brows were blackened with kohl, her eyelids painted with lapis paste, her breasts with powdered coral. Her open bodice was clipped in trimly above her tight gold belt; the skirt with its seven flounces showed only her hennaed toes. She cast down her eyes, and touched her forehead with small tapered fingers which, when I took them, never moved in mine. I kissed her closed lips, as one may in Crete; they were fresh and warm under the rouge, and as still as her hand.

Later came the day-long pomps of the wedding, the offerings at the shrines, the sprinklings by the priestesses, the gifts to the kindred; the sunset drive in the gilded car, and the feast as hot and bright as noonday with the scented oil of a thousand lamps on painted stands. Singing the women led her to the bridal room, and did whatever takes women an hour to do; and the youths with torches, singing, led me in to her. Then the crowds were gone, the doors were shut, the lamp was low; there was a sudden stillness, only the softly plucked harps of the night-music beyond the door.

I lay down by her, and took her chin in my hand, and turned her face towards me. She looked up with dark silent eyes. They had taken off her day-paint and put on paint for the night; the colours were softer, but it hid her still. 'Look, Phaedra,' I said, and showed her the old scar across my breast, 'I am still marked with the Bull Court. Do you remember when they told you I was dead?'

She answered stiffly, as if we were in a hall of audience, 'No, son of Aigeus.' She meant her eyes to tell nothing, but she was young. They told me, among the rest, that she was Minos' daughter; and there was no doubt that she knew everything.

'I am Theseus still,' I said to her. 'I told you if the bulls did not kill me I would be a king, and come back to marry you. And here I am. But fate never comes in the shape men look for. See what has passed over us between then and now; war and earthquake and change, and all those chances that living brings to men under the sun. Yet I have never forgotten how you wept for me.'

She said nothing. But I would have thought worse of myself for ever, if I had lain till morning with a woman I could not warm. There was never yet a son or dauther of the House of Minos, but had in them some of the fire of Helios from whose seed they sprung. I was there to serve my kingdom. Perhaps if I had gone about my duty briskly, without trying to make it better than it was, and left the fire unwakened, the shape of future things might have been changed. But I pitied her, for fate had been her master, as it had mine. Also it is my nature to want victory, in this as in other things. No man can outrun the destined end, from the day he is born.

My days were full of business, which I had left too long. When I met her then, she was quiet and soft-spoken, with the pretty airs and graces high-born ladies are taught in Crete, which are for any man. She seldom raised her eyes to mine. By daylight we did not speak about the night, nor make the secret signs of lovers. But the night had its own laws; and indeed when the time came I might have grieved to leave her, if I had been going anywhere but home.

15

The Hellene lands were quiet; and because the people had missed the wedding, I made a great feast of the Isthmian Games, which were due that year. I dedicated the festival to Poseidon with a hekatomb of black oxen, and proclaimed they should be held each second year henceforth for ever. Thus I gave them a show, without linking it to the wedding, which would have slighted Hippolyta and our son.

As he began to get about, even his mother and I, whose pride it had been that he feared nothing, found him too daring for our peace. At five, he was slipping off to scramble on the great rocks below the Citadel. At six he stole a lynx-kitten from its lair between the crags, and then, hearing the mother yowling and crying, would have climbed down to give it back again, if someone had not caught him and saved his life. When the creature died he wept for it, though he could knock himself black and blue without a tear.

A little after this he was missed at bedtime. His nurse tried at first to keep it from his mother, and she at first from me. When it grew late, I turned out the Guard and made them search the Rock. The moon was as bright as day, but they could not find hide or hair of him. Hippolyta paced about, her arms across her breast and one hand tugging her pigtail, muttering moon-charms from Pontos. Suddenly as she gazed upwards, she grasped my arm and pointed. There was the boy on the Palace roof, sitting between two teeth of the battlements, his feet hung over the drop, his face turned skyward, quiet as a stone. We ran up, then stood tiptoe, in dread to make him start. His mother signed me not to speak, and whistled softly. At that he swung himself in, and came to us walking lightly, as if he had no more weight than one has in dreams. I had been angry after the fright; but in the silence, with his still face and wide eyes, I could not raise my voice to him. He looked at us both, and said, 'What is it? I was quite safe. I was with the Lady.'

I let his mother lead him away, for she best understood him. But some of the Palace people had followed us up and heard; and it began to be gossiped that the boy was being taught to set the Goddess above the gods.

It was a bad time for such rumours; for a child had been born to Phaedra.

I had been to Crete to see him, a small lively babe with a fuzz of black hair which, the nurses told me, was the kind that falls away. Meantime it made him look very Cretan. Phaedra was pleased with him and with herself, and seemed more content. But it had given me much to think of. We had called him Akamas, which was an old royal name there; for it was certain that he must succeed in Crete. But the mainland kingdoms I had given to Hippolytos in my heart, even if it meant dividing the empire.

I was sure the people would come to choose him, rather than a foreigner, if he took any care at all to please them. He looked through and through a Hellene; his courage was already talked of; he could stick on the back of his little Kentaur pony like one of Old Handy's boys. Of affairs he knew nothing and cared less; but he had a feel of his own for what matters in men, and could tell a liar though he did not understand the lie. Anyone he took against, I had learned to watch out for. Yet always, coming and going like a cloud, was this secret strangeness.

I spoke of it one night to his mother, as we talked in bed. 'Of course,' I said, 'he must honour Artemis. For your sake I would be angry if he did not. But before the people, we must see he gives her just what is proper, and shows respect to the Olympians. You know what hangs on it.'

'Theseus,' she said, 'I know what people say, that I have taught him some secret worship. But you know better; you know the Mystery is not for men. Whatever he has, it is his own.'

'All children tell themselves tales. I suppose he will outgrow it. Yet it troubles me.'

'When I was a child,' she said, 'I made believe a playmate. But I was lonely. He, when he is alone, will sing for joy. And he makes friends everywhere. Yet this will come, and everything falls away from him. I have seen it begin with long looking at something; a flower, or a bird, or a burning flame. As if his soul were being called out of his body.'

I made in the darkness the sign against the evil eye. 'Is it witchcraft? Should we seek it out?'

'But then he would surely pine. He is stronger and taller for his age than all the others. I have told you; a god is with him.'

'He said, "The Lady." You were a priestess; can you get an omen, or any sign?'

She said quietly, 'I was a maiden, Theseus. She will not speak to me. Sometimes, during the Dance, the Sight would come. But I left it at Maiden Crag.'

Not long after this, I heard a commotion outside the Palace, but muted, as if people were keeping their voices down; so I sent to see. In came one of the Palace elders, bringing in the priests' servant from Zeus' sanctuary, with a bleeding cut on his arm. With a long face and well-pleased eyes, the house baron said my son had done it. The boy, it seems, had found a kid tied up for sacrifice, and started petting it. When the man came to fetch it to the altar, the boy defied him. He got on with his duty, as he was bound to do, whereat Hippolytos in a fury drew his toy dagger, and set upon him. How fortunate, said the baron (relishing it like good wine), it had been the servant and not the priest.

That was something, certainly; but it was still sacrilege, and all the Palace knew it. Apart from the bad luck it might bring, he could hardly have done worse than insult King Zeus. For his mother's safety, as well as the honour of the god, I must do justice before the people.

He came all flushed and tumbled, the tears of rage still in his eyes, but sobered at being brought before me. He should be ashamed, I said, to strike a servant who could do nothing back. I suppose I should have begun with Zeus the King; but he, after all, prefers kings to be gentlemen. It went home to the boy, as I could see. He said, 'Yes, Father, I know. But the kid could do nothing either; what about him?'

'But,' I said, 'this was a beast, without sense or knowledge of death. For that would you rob the King of Heaven?' He stared me in the face with his mother's eyes, and said, 'He did know. He looked at me.'

For his own sake, it was no time to be soft with him. 'Hippolytos,' I said, 'you have lived seven years, and in all that time I have never raised my hand to you. That is because I love you. And because I love you, I am going to beat you now.' He did not look scared, but studied my face, trying to understand. 'You have angered the god,' I said. 'Someone must suffer for it. Is it to be you, who did the wrong; or would you rather go free, and let him curse the people?'

'If it has got to be someone,' he said, 'let it be me.' I nodded and said, 'Good boy.' 'But,' he said, looking up at me, 'why should Zeus curse the people, when they did no harm? *You* would not do that.'

Just as if a man had spoken, I found myself saying, 'I do not know. It is the nature of Necessity. I have seen Poseidon Earth-Shaker throw down the Labyrinth, crushing the evil and the good. The laws of the gods are beyond our knowing. Men are only men. Come, let us have it over.'

It was hard to do as I knew I must. I had got to mark him, for justice to be seen. He never whimpered. Afterwards I said, 'That was kingly borne, and King Zeus will like it. Now don't let it be for nothing, but respect the gods.'

He swallowed, and said, 'Then he won't curse the people now; so can I have the kid?'

I kept my patience, and sent him to his mother. Of course the thing was talked about for a month, and never quite forgotten. She was a servant of Artemis, who loves young beasts; so it was a gift to her enemies, who, for the most part, had first been mine. She was only their weapon. They were the elder lords, whose power I had curbed over their serfs and slaves; who hated change, and envied the newcomers from the Bull Court, with their youth and gaiety and foreign ways. And these, for their part, not being fools, soon felt it, and let it be seen that they were on the side of the Amazon. So, where there had only been rivalry between man and man, there grew up two factions in the Palace.

Often, I knew, Hippolyta met with such pinpricks as can be done in the dark by those who would not dare an open enmity. This time they were not bondwomen who could be sent away. And this time she did not keep it from me. She was a wild girl no longer, but had an understanding as good as a man's; she was concerned for my sake, and for our son's.

Angry as I was, yet I was doubly careful when I gave judgement to hold the balance true, and give them no case against her. I believe they sent spies after her when she rode into the hills, to find if she had secret rites there. And I know they tried to use the boy; for, knowing no contrivance, he would tell us how he had been questioned, not understanding what it meant. Though his mother had nothing to hide, yet there was danger in his innocence; her friends, who loved laughter, might say in joke what would not sound well in earnest, and his own fancies be twisted by subtler minds. I did not warn him; he was clear as water, it would appear and breed more suspicion. I put more faith in his own nature, not to talk freely to those he did not like.

It is my way to bring things into daylight, and fight them out. It irked me to take such care. But rumour still drifted from the north; garbled and foolish mostly, yet with a feel of truth behind. The ship must be whole, if the storm was coming.

And soon I knew it was; for I heard from Pirithoos. He sent me his own wife's brother, with a letter under his royal seal, to give me when we were alone. It said, 'The Black Cloaks turned due south. It is the tribes east of Euxine who are on the move. They are coming down towards Hellespont, and I do not think the straits will stop them. If not they will reach Thrace this year. Don't count on winter to slow them down, for hunger and cold may drive them faster. The rest, Kaunos will tell you.'

I turned to the Lapith, who was waiting for it. He said, 'There is a message Pirithoos thought better not to write. It is this: "Warn your lady that the fighting women of Sarmatia, who serve the Goddess, are riding with their men; and the Moon Maids are leading them."'

16

I did not tell her, thinking there would be time enough for trouble. I made out, to her like all the rest, that Kaunos had called in friendship as he travelled by. But as soon as we were in bed that night, she said, 'Come, what is it?' and had it out of me. She could feel my thoughts through my breast.

When she heard she was long silent, lying in my arms. Then she said, 'Perhaps the long-haired star has come again.'

'What?' I asked her. 'Have the Moon Maids left their shrines before?'

'They say so. They say that as long ago as an oak tree takes to grow and die, the people of Pontos lived beyond the mountains, by the shores of another sea. Then this star came, with fiery hair that streamed all across heaven; and it drew the peoples like a tide. The priestesses of that time read the omens, and saw the land could not be held against the hordes of the Kimmerians; so they went with the people fighting in the vanguard. When they reached Pontos, part of the star fell down upon the earth. So they took that land, and held it.'

I remembered the thunder-stone. But she did not like to talk with a man on these sacred things.

'It is no joke,' I said, 'for a whole people to cross Hellespont. Then there is Thrace, a wild country full of fierce warriors. Somewhere north of Olympos they will be stayed; we shall never see them.'

She lay quiet, but too lightly to be sleeping. I felt the thought of her heart, as she felt mine.

'What is it, little leopard? What do you fear? I love your honour like my own. Never would I ask you to fight sworn comrades, not even if they stormed the Rock. If it does come, it is your time to be a woman; sick, or with child. Or you shall have omens not to fight on either side. Leave everything to me.'

She clung to me, saying, 'Do you think I could watch you from the walls, and not leap down to you? You know we are what we are.' In the light from the starry sky I saw her eyes as bright as fever. I stroked her and told her to be at peace, it would never come to pass. At last we slept; but she woke me tossing and sighing, and half-choked with sleep she gave the Moon Maids' war-cry, as I had heard it at Maiden Crag. I woke her, and made love till she slept again. But next day I sent without telling her to Delphi, to ask the god what to do.

Meanwhile the Palace people were still at odds, and the boy grew stronger. He would ride into the hills and lose his groom, and be found on a hilltop or by a stream, talking to himself, or with his eyes fixed on nothing. Yet there was no sign of madness in him; he was quick-minded and, to tell the truth, could write and figure better than I. Nor did he do anything outrageous, after the theft of the kid, but was gentle to those about him. But one day a baron came to me and, pretending to let it fall by chance, told me the boy had made himself a shrine of the Goddess, in a cave among the rocks.

I answered lightly; but at fall of dusk I climbed down myself to see. The path was steep and dangerous, fit for wild goats. At last I came to a little ledge that looked towards the sea, and a cave-mouth blocked by boulders. There was carving at its mouth; it was very ancient and flaked away, but I saw it was an eye. The shrine had been long abandoned; but on the rocky slab before it there were flowers and shells and coloured stones.

I said nothing to the boy, but asked his mother if she knew. She shook her head. Later, when she had coaxed him to speak, she said to me, 'Theseus, he had not even seen the sign; you say that it is worn. And I find he does not know its meaning. How should he? It is women's business. And yet, he says that the Lady comes there.'

My backbone shivered. But I smiled, and said, 'He sees the gods in your likeness, that is all; and who am I to blame him?' With the barons' envy and the peasants' ignorance, she had troubles enough.

Presently came news from the north that beyond Hellespont there were great wars, and the folk were fighting from their citadels. It was said they had burned their harvests, choosing to live like the birds all winter, if it drove the horde from their fathers' lands. It needed no divination to see where this would lead.

It was soon after this that my envoy came back from Delphi, crowned with the garland of good news. The god had said that the Rock would not fall before the coming generations equalled those that were gone; a storm would break on it, but would ebb after the appointed sacrifice. The envoy had asked what must be offered; and the oracle had replied that the deity who required it would choose it also.

I thought about this. Next day I had brought up to the Citadel some of all the beasts the gods are pleased with, and had lots cast among them. The lot fell on a she-goat, which I sacrificed to Artemis. Thus the oracle had been fulfilled. The beast backed from the altar, and fought against her death. It is never good, when the sacrifice does not go consenting. But I had done what was decreed.

Autumn came cold that year, and early. I sent to Argos for three ships of grain, and stored it in the vaults under the Rock, and warned all the people to make no great feasts at harvest time, but save their food. Rumour was everywhere; it was too late for silence, which would only make fear grow. And in the month after the longest night, word came that the horde had crossed the Hellespont. They had done it without ships; winter itself had made a bridge for them. In the great cold, huge blocks of ice had drifted down from the Euxine and jammed the narrows, and the strait had frozen round them. They had crossed over dry-shod, in a night and a day. Now they were over-running Thrace like starving wolves.

I knew now in my heart that they would come to Attica. I called the chiefs in council, and ordered all the strongholds to be stored with food and weapons. By luck the harvests had been good. Over in Euboia, where the straits would protect them, I had a camp built for the women and children and old men, with a great stockade for the cattle. The frosts were over; the first hard buds were on the fig-trees; there would be no ice this time. Those who had gold I gave leave to store it in the Rock, and saw just tallies given. Then I sacrificed to Poseidon and Athene, the City's gods, and gave offerings to the dead kings at their tombs. Remembering Oedipus and his blessing, I went out to Kolonos and made gifts to him also.

All winter the horde worked down southward, picking clean the hamlets and the farms. Some small strongholds fell, but the great ones held, where the people had fled with their stock and stores. So the horde lived leanly on the gleanings of the fields, on roots, and wild game; on old horses and sick cattle not worth saving, and the sack of lonely farmsteads, which they burned behind them. Pirithoos sent me word when they reached Thessaly, before the gates of the forts were closed. I knew then that it would not be long.

So the herds of Attica were rafted over to Euboia, and after them all the people who could not fight. It was a day of weeping; I held a sacrifice to Hera of the Hearth, to give them hope. But Hippolytos I did not send there. I did not trust him out of my keeping where his mother's enemies could seize their chance. I sent him oversea the other way, to Troizen and to Pittheus my grandfather. He and my mother would understand him, if anyone could; and he would be safe there as I had been in childhood when my father was fighting for his kingdom. When he had taken leave of his mother, I said goodbye to him. He looked white and still; but he did not ask to stay; I guessed he had begged that of her already. At the last he roused himself to smile, remembering one must do so to warriors before battle. I saw there the makings of a king. He was too young yet for me to say to him, 'If I die, I leave you this realm, but you will have to fight for it.' The old man at Troizen knew my mind, but he must be growing frail, and could not be much longer above the earth. To the gods I commended him, and saw his pale bright hair in pale bright sunlight grow faint as he sailed away.

Now fresh news came to us every day, as fugitives came over Parnes through the passes, half dead from the mountain cold, with babes on their backs and blackened toes that died from off their feet. I shipped them to Euboia or sent them down to Sounion. And I set watch-posts above the passes, with great beacons piled up to light for warning. In my mind was the thought that Attica is Land's End. Till now they had only had to fight for the day's food; down here they must fight for being.

The fugitives told their tales, and the people listened with fear-sharp ears. And each tale had some word of the warrior women, the Sarmatians who must each bring as her bride-dower the head of an enemy killed by her hand in battle; and the bright-clad Moon Maids charmed against fear and weapons, who led the vanguard. All this I learned from the suppliants when I questioned them. My own folk never spoke of it in my hearing. We both knew what that meant.

One morning Hippolyta got up from my side, and went over to the arms upon the wall, and put on the dress she wore when she drilled her Guard.

I jumped up and put my hand on hers to stay her. She shook her head, saying, 'Indeed it is time.'

'Steady, little leopard,' I said to her. She looked thinner, and too clear, as if burning with an inward flame. 'I told you to let me deal. I am taking those lads back into the Palace Guard; you need answer for them no longer.'

She searched my face. 'They have not told you. I must then, since they are all afraid. The barons have been putting it about that the Maidens are coming for my sake, to avenge the slight to me, because you married the Cretan. They are saying I sent them word.'

Without thinking what I did, I took one of the javelins from her; then I found I had broken it in my hands.

She said to me, 'Dear love, you have made there your own omen. With such broken arms you will go to battle, if in anger you divide your chiefs and warriors. You can do nothing, Theseus. The Athenians will believe what they can see. I must answer for myself; no one else can do it.'

'When we first met,' I said to her, 'you called me pirate. And what better have I been to you, if it comes to this?'

'Hush,' she said, 'these are words,' and kissed me. 'Fate and Necessity are here; and like us, they are what they are.'

Then she went out and called her Guard, and spoke to them

of the trial to come, urging them on to honour, before she put them to throwing at the mark. The youths sang out her paean; the barons' faction looked downcast. It was true enough that she had done what I could not. Afterwards she went about laughing and gay. It deceived everyone but me.

That night our love burned up as bright as it had beside the Euxine. But in the quiet after, when the heart tells all it knows, she said, 'Is it certain they have wronged me? What if I have really brought this on the land?'

I tried to hush her. There are some things best not spoken of, lest you give them power. But she whispered, 'What I gave you, Theseus, I had vowed before to the Maiden. Did you guess?'

I answered, 'Yes. But there was some god within us. What could we do?'

'Nothing, perhaps. If two gods do battle for us, it is our fate. But the loser will be angry, and is still a god.'

'So is the winner. Let us trust the stronger.'

'Let us keep faith. One does not change sides upon the field . . . We said that Maiden Crag was far away, but now it has come to find us.'

'Sleep, little leopard. There is work tomorrow.'

In that I was right. Before the stars had paled, the light of the beacons leaped on Parnes; and at daybreak there was war-smoke on the hills.

It took them two days to come down through the passes. The watch I had set there harried them by rolling boulders down, and shooting from the heights. I could not spare men for more. Soon we saw from the walls the dark tide creeping on the plain, like waters that have cracked the dam. I did not go out to meet them. We were too few. The men of Eleusis had to hold their own strongholds, and the men of Megara to close the Isthmus. And if all of us had come out into the plain together, we would still have been swept away.

I trusted in the Rock, as my fathers had for longer than men remember. It would be a siege, but one done backwards; it was we who must sit down and starve them out. In these early months, the fields were bare of everything; they could not close us round and wait in quiet. To get a living at all, they would have to straggle. The farms were stripped bare, the strongholds well stocked and manned. I reckoned to let them waste themselves little by little, with want and vain assaults; then when they were most dispersed and weakened, to choose my time.

As they came near I saw they had cattle with them. But they were lean with winter grazing, and when they were gone there would be no more. As for us, men can live long and keep their strength up on barley and cheese and raisins, olive oil and wine.

The Eleusinians had sent their cattle and the useless mouths across to Salamis; and there also I sent my ships. We had signals agreed on, smoke by day and fire by night. They knew my plan for them, when the time came.

The moving mass came over the level plain; the cattle slowly, the warriors at the front and flanks, with horses and in chariots, going about the horde. I remembered old tales of how our own fathers had come down like this from the north; just so they must have looked to the Shore Folk, gazing from this Rock that they could not hold. I wondered how it had fallen, by treachery or assault. Then I called the herald, and said, 'Sound for the fire.'

He blew; and from the houses down below, outside the walls, came the first thin smoke. Soon flames leaped through it, for brush-wood was stacked inside. I had left this till the enemy was in sight, to daunt them. Before long there was a heat like summer on the Rock; we coughed in the smoke, and the warriors whose homes were burning smiled grimly. The men who had set the torches came clambering back; then the gates were closed, and great millstones rolled behind them. The Rock was sealed.

Now after so much haste and toil there was a pause. The fire had devoured the smoke; the distant hills seemed to dance and ripple in the rising air; one heard no sound but the roar of flames and the loud crack of timber. All night it spurted and crumbled and flared again, so bright that the watchmen could not see beyond it. But at dawn, the horde was on the move, and by noon the vanguard was before the Citadel.

Soon all the plain between us and the harbour seemed filled as if by swarming ants. It was well to be seen that they were led by warriors; they took the low hills that faced the Rock, and began to throw up walls.

On the Palace roof Hippolyta watched beside me. Her eyes were good, as mine are. The clothes of the Scythians seem dark from far away, when you do not see their ornaments. Even from here, you could not mistake the bright spots of colour moving about in front, the scarlet and saffron and purple of the Moon Maids. I remembered how she had told me the chief of them had their own colours, which they were known by. I turned to her, and found her looking at my face. So she stood awhile, then said, 'I have seen nothing there but your enemies. Come, let us go in.'

Thus the siege began. They took all the hills: the Pnyx where I called the people to Assembly, the Hill of Apollo and the Muses, the Hill of Nymphs; all but the Hill of Ares, which faces the great gate. That is in bowshot, and my Cretan archers covered it. One night when the moon was dark the enemy crept up there and built a bulwark; from that time on, stray arrows fell within the walls, but we shooting down did better, and they never came there in strength.

The nights were worst. There seemed as many watch-fires on the plain as the sky had stars. But, as I would tell the men on the walls when I did my night-round, many were cook-fires at which they were eating up their stores, and they had all their folk there, while we were warriors only. In rain or snow, rested or weary, I always went round the walls in the dead hours of night. It was partly to see good watch kept, but partly lest the married men grew envious; for, except the priestesses, mine was the only woman on the Rock. Often she would divide the round with me. She knew each man's name as well as I did. Now the old men who hated her the most were gone with the women to Euboia, factions grew faint, and the danger that pressed us round drew us together. Valour and steadfastness and high-hearted laughter were the riches of our state; no one could show them forth as she did, and not be loved.

And then one morning, at the light of day an arrow was found shot from the Hill of Ares. It had a sickle head, which is for witchcraft, and a letter wrapped round the shaft. No one could read the language, and they brought it to me. Hippolyta, who was by me, took it from my hand, saying, 'I can read it.'

She read with a steady countenance; but I saw her face grow drawn, as if it had drunk her blood. At the end she paused, but not for long. Then she said aloud, in hearing of the warriors round us, 'This is for me. They ask me, because I was once a Moon Maid, to let them in by the postern.' Only I, who was near enough to touch her, could tell that she was trembling. 'If more of these come,' she said, 'I will not see them. Give them to the King.'

They murmured together, but I could hear they were praising her. Then Menestheus said, as eagerly as if he feared someone would be before him, 'Did they fix a signal? Or name a night?'

It was then I wished for the first time I had put him to death with the rest of his clan. He had no feeling, but for himself, and saw that everywhere. Such men turn even the good they seek to evil.

I took the letter from her hand and shredded it, and scattered it on the wind. 'Her honour is mine,' I said. 'Do you think it fit for a warrior, to play decoy and lure old comrades into ambush? If any man here would do it, I would not trust my back to him in battle.' Then I looked at him straight. He turned red and went away.

When we were alone, she said, 'They would have guessed. To tell them outright was better.' 'Yes, little leopard,' I said; 'but now tell all. What threat did they put on you if you said no?'

'Oh, they reproached me for living on when I had lost my maidenhood. Then they said the Goddess would forgive me if I betrayed the Citadel, because you took me against my will.' She smiled. But when I had her in my arms I felt on my cheek her tears, trickling like blood in silence. I knew then that they had cursed her. And the curse had not far to fly.

My own body seemed to chill and sink, as if I felt it with her. But I forced a cheerful face, for curses feed on fear, as I have often seen. 'Apollo will take it off,' I said. 'He can cleanse a man even from his mother's blood; this will be nothing to him. He is Artemis' brother, and she must obey him. Once he himself took a huntress from her, and got her with child, and their son founded a city. You will see, he will be your friend. Get ready, we will go to the shrine together.'

She said she would; but some of the captains had to speak with me, and while I was busy she slipped off there alone. When she came back she looked clear and calm, and said the god had given omens of consent to turn the curse aside. So I was glad and put it from me.

For two nights all was quiet. I guessed they had waited till then for a sign from her. The third night, they tried to scale the walls.

Some time before, I had picked out the men who saw best in the dark, and had one or two on every night-watch, walking round and round. But for that, the attack might have succeeded; it was led by skilful climbers, who had blackened their faces and their limbs. At the alarm, we threw down torches and fired the brush below; by that light we aimed our spears and arrows, and the slingers shot. Hippolyta with her strong, short Cretan bow stood by my side, aiming steadily as if at the mark. She had changed since the letter came; I felt her no longer pulled two ways. When the dead were carried off below she stood quiet and calm. She sang with our men the paean of victory, and came away with me and was gentle, saying little. Her face in the torchlight put me in mind of her son's.

As the days passed, we saw the cattle dwindling upon the plain; and bands of Scythians would go off into the country round. They seldom brought cattle back with them, mostly poor herds of goats; and often the men looked fewer. Then a smoke would go up from some castle that its lord still held, on Hymettos or towards Eleusis, signalling that they had beaten off a raid, or, with an extra puff, that they had made a good killing. But one day over on Kithairon, instead of the signal-smoke came a great cloud, and we saw no more from them. It was the hold that had been Prokrustes'; with so many angry ghosts in it, one could not expect much luck. That time the band returned well laden, and we heard the rejoicing from the walls. Still the fort had been stocked for a garrison, not a tribe. Soon they were ranging further and further off.

Twice more they tried a night assault upon the Rock. On the seventh dawn after, we saw the horde thickening and working, like dough with leaven in it, and knew they meant to try by day.

They swarmed upon us from the south and west at once, clambering on over the bodies of the fallen, with ladders and notched pine-trunks to scale the walls. As they came on, I shouted to the warriors, 'Hold on through this and we shall win! This is high tide! They are desperate now; they will not have heart to try again. Blue-Haired Poseidon; Pallas Athene, Mistress of the Citadel; save your own altars! Help us in our hour!'

Against this time I had had stones piled thick along all the ramparts: pebbles for slings, hand-sized stones for hurling, and great boulders with crowbars and levers under them, all ready to roll down. We held our hands till the slopes were thick with men, and then began. Our weapons we saved for close quarters.

In this battle for the first time we could see the warriors clearly: the Scythians in their sheepskin coats, and loose trousers tied at the ankle, with leather helmets long behind; the Sarmatians who fought in pairs, a man with a youth one would have said, if we had not known the beardless ones for women by their screeching war-calls. They looked savage, and dirty, and unkempt; yet when I saw one sink, and the other bend over the fallen, I was glad to look another way. But wherever one looked, out in the vanguard with bow and javelin, slender and swift and bright as fighting-cocks, were the girls of the Goddess, light on their feet in the trance of battle, feeling neither fear nor prick of weapon until they died.

Beyond the scrimmage, the folk stood watching from the hills. Now one could tell out the fighting strength from the useless mouths; from where I stood, I reckoned them half and half. Most of the weak, and old, and the babes in arms, must have perished in that winter wandering, over the mountains and on the march. The watchers were mostly women – the Amazons and Sarmatians were the only ones in battle – but I saw herdsmen among the cattle, and wondered it had not been left that day to the young boys. But Hippolyta said, 'Oh, those will be slaves who have lost their eyes. The Scythians do it to captives they take in war. They can milk the cows and make cheese as well without them, and they cannot run away.'

'Then we had better win,' I said. 'Let Zeus the Merciful bear witness, I have given the people better laws than that.' And I told the news to the men upon the walls, to make them stubborn. The second wave of attack was coming; if we broke it, I knew we were past the worst.

The Rock had weathered many sieges. Down in the caves I had found the great bronze-shod pikes from my father's wars, to fling down ladders and climbing men. All round the walls I saw them bristling, then dipping to their work. War-yells and death-yells rose again, stones crashed and rumbled, cutting swathes through screaming men; arrows pattered on earth or sank in flesh; the battle rose up the Rock like a stormy sea. Hippolyta stood beside me on the western wall, where the ramps slope to the gates and the Citadel is weakest. There I had posted the little dark Cretan archers, in their quilted jerkins, and the Hellene spear-throwers, the tall young men who had won prizes at the Games. I threw well myself that day. The press down there was seething below the ramp. They were going to charge.

We heard a wolf-like paean. A thick swarm thrust out from the mass upon the zigzag causeway, like an angry snake writhing upwards; and, like a snake, marked brightly at the head. For in the van were the Amazons; and out before them strode a Moon Maid dressed in purple, tossing in her hand the sickle axe of the King.

The arrows whistled, the javelins flew, bodies fell from the ramp's edge to the rocks below. But the girl ran onward, as lightly as at a hunt, and sprang on an outcrop beside the path, and gave a loud high call. The tongue was not so strange to me as it once had been. 'Hippolyta! Hippolyta! Where is your faith?'

She stepped out from beside me, while I called to her to take care and held my shield before her. She hollowed her hand to her mouth and cried, 'It is here! With my man and my King! These are my people.' She added more, which I could not follow word for word. But her voice was saying, 'Do not hate me. I can do no other.'

The girl stood fixed for a moment. Hippolyta was still too, waiting; I felt it was only to hear her say, 'What must be, must; it was our fate,' and that would have brought her peace. But the Amazon below screamed out, as shrill as a wheeling eagle, 'Treacherous whore! Your man shall feed the dogs and your people the ravens, and when you have seen it we will throw you off the Rock!'

Hippolyta gasped and shuddered. Then her mouth set; she pushed my shield aside from her, and fitted an arrow to her string. But I could see her anguish, and her hand moved slowly; the Maiden King leaped down unhurt into the press. I did not see where she went, there was too much to do.

Almost to the gates they pressed their charge; but in the end we turned them. Little by little they lost their thrust, and wavered, and sank like turbid water back on to the plain, leaving a silt of corpses and stones. Our joy was too deep to cheer. Old warriors hugged the comrades next to them; men stood singing alone a hymn to their guardian gods, and vowing offerings. Hippolyta and I walked round the ramparts hand in hand, like children at a festival, praising and greeting those we passed. We were too tired to talk that night, but sank to sleep in each other's arms as we fell to bed. But I had myself called at midnight, just as usual, lest victory make us careless. It was they, not we, who I meant should be taken off guard.

I reckoned three days. The first they would lick their wounds, and look out for us to follow up our victory; if we did, it would cost us dear. The second they would settle to think what next, and count their stores. The third, unless I was far out, half of them would go foraging. They would have no choice. And since they had stripped the land for miles, I doubted they would be back by nightfall.

Just so it proved. On the third night I gave orders to light the signal fires, having done already what else was needful. To hide our purpose, we sang loud hymns about the beacon, as if at some god's festival. They did not know our customs; and indeed we had need to pray. The wine and oil we poured – for drink-offerings were all we had to give – made the flames leap higher. I asked the priest of Apollo which god to choose as patron of the battle; and looking into the smoke he said I should pray to Terror, son of Ares. As I lifted my hands, I saw a point of light on the peak of Salamis; a single beacon, signalling 'Yes'.

Athene gave us a dark sky. That was her second favour; the first I had asked already. For, since even in darkness an army coming down the ramps would have been spied, we must go another way. It was sacred, secret, and forbidden to men; I had heard of it from my father, but never seen it, till the night before when I went alone with the priestess, to ask for leave.

It was always night there. It went down through the cavern of the House Snake, in the very core of the Rock. Its mouth, my father had told me, was in the western scarp below the sheer of the walls; but it was closed with raw stone, so that even I who knew of it had never found the place. It could only be opened from within.

The priestess was old. She had served the shrine before we brought Athene back from Sounion. But beside the House Snake, she was a little child. Some said he was Erechtheus himself, the ancient snake-king, the founder of our line. Neither my father nor my grandfather had ever been into his presence; and as the old woman with her lamp went down before me, my palms were cold with awe. The way was steep, the steps little and shallow; often I, who am not tall, had to bow my head. But when we reached the cave, the roof over the narrow walls was lost in shadow. It was a split in the living rock, going up into the stones the Palace stood on. Though only the naked feet of each single priestess had trodden the floor-flags, they were worn in a channel a hand-span deep.

On the steep rough wall, going far up into the dimness, were pictures like the work of children; little men with bows and spears, hunting beasts no one has seen. In the flickering light they seemed to leap and run. At last she stayed me with her hand, and pointed; there was a narrow hole by the wall, a cleft within a cleft. She lifted the lamp, and stood finger on lip. Deep down I saw thick folded coils, as big as a man's calf, heaving and squirming. I covered my mouth, and the hair rose on my nape.

She took from a ledge a painted crock of milk, and set it beside the hole. The coils worked and furled among themselves; I saw the gleam of an eye. The head rose up, as pale as bone, marked with strange faded signs; the eyes were blue and milky, and did not see me; they looked only at fate. The mouth was shut; but a forked tongue flickered from it, dipped in the milk, and drank. The priestess stretched out her withered hands. For all the clammy sweat upon me, I saw thanksgiving in her eyes.

Since he had given consent, she led me to the closed end of the passage, and showed me the old signs carved there, where to put crowbars in. So, when she had concealed the sacred things, I had led my masons there, and now the way was open. It would be our path to battle.

In the dark before cocklight, we went to arm. As I reached for my gear, Hippolyta stayed my hand. 'This once,' she said, 'I will do like other women.' She belted my sword on, and when I had slung my shield upon my shoulder, gave me my helm. I said smiling that no other woman would be half so neat, and swung back the shield to take her in my arms. We stood together in the great curved shell of bull-hide; as she pressed her face to mine and stroked it with her fingers, some sorrow reached me from her silence, and I whispered, 'What is it, little leopard?' But she answered lightly, and drew away and put her helmet on.

I looked at the crest of glittering sheet-gold ribbons, that danced and caught the lamplight. 'It will soon be day,' I said, 'and out there you have enemies. Wear something less showy.' She laughed, and tossed it to make it flash. 'Will you do so?' she said; for I was plumed with scarlet, so that my men could see me. 'Or shall I stay back from your side, in case they know where to find me? We are what we are, love. Let us keep our pride.'

So we went out together and joined the warriors.

Every man before he entered the holy precinct had cleansed himself and prayed. They crept down soft-footed, hand on mouth; not even the enemy near could have hushed them like the dread of the cave. A torch smoked in an ancient socket; if a man coughed, or clinked his bronze, echoes went back and forth, and died like the chitter of watching shades.

I went through first, in case the men feared ill-luck from it. No light must show from the mouth; so after the last black grope, the cloudy night seemed clear. Waiting while the spies marked out the path before us, I felt that I knew this place. As I looked about, I saw marks on the rock, and peering closely found a carved eye, rubbed with time. My foot crunched on a shell; on the threshold-slab there were withered flowers. Secretly in the dark I made the sign against evil. Time out of mind, the place had not been opened. How had he known?

Once marked, the path was easy. The men filed out, catching at each other, stumbling and saying Hush. It seemed to take half a night, and I wondered if we had left time enough. But all were through before the first fading of the stars. Last came Hippolyta, who had stayed to see good order and reverence in the shrine. When her hand touched me, I gave the word to go. Man passed it to man, with a sound like rustling reeds.

We crept over the level ground, towards the Hill of Apollo. It is the highest of the ridge, and commands the rest. Already the cocks were crowing; skylines looked black against less than blackness. We reached the footslopes and slipped upwards among the trees.

We did not give them time to see us. As we reached the open with day's first grey, we gave a great war-yell, and charged the camp. The omens were faithful; Terror was our friend. Watching the ramp and the northern postern, their sentries had not looked where the walls were sheer. The first sound of their outcry told us we had them. Before dawn had kindled the tops of Parnes, we were masters of the hill.

It had been manned with fighters only; the horde was in the plain beyond. Among the dead we found some Sarmatian women; but no Moon Maids were there. If any had been, they had got away to ready the other strongholds. I did not mean to give them leisure for it. My heralds blew their horns; and the horns of Amyntor answered from the Rock. He had been at work behind me; the great gates were unbarred. Now with the force that I had left for him, he came charging down on the Hill of Ares, covered by the Cretan bowmen, to take them from the flank.

Day came, clear and cold. It shone upon the Rock, and on the strong house of Erechtheus with its crimson columns, its chequer-work of white and blue; the house of my fathers, which I had staked on a single throw. Across the dip it looked near enough to toss a stone at; but if we lost, I should never come within its gates again. I turned to the plain of Piraeus and the sea; for my men were pointing, and breaking into cheers.

The bands of plunderers were returning, streaming from the south. No good news there. But out beyond them, the beaches of Phaleron Bay were bright with ships. They were the ships from Salamis, the fleets of Athens and of Eleusis, the fleet of the Salaminians, coming to join the battle.

Before us on the ridge of hills, seething and swarming, were the Scythian warriors. They covered the top of Pnyx, the next hill north beyond the saddle. We were above them now; but we must storm them from below, with no surprise to help us. I heard the shouts of the horde beyond. Yet further off, Amyntor blew the call of victory; he had taken the Hill of Ares. Now was the time. I raised my hands to Zeus. Somewhere above the sky he sat with his great scales in his hand, weighing our fate. I threw up my prayers into his balance. But it would need more than prayers, to tip the pan.

Hippolyta touched my arm. 'Listen,' she said. 'A lark is singing.'

He hung above us bubbling music, soaring and lapsing in blue air. She said, 'He brings us victory,' and smiled at me, her grey eyes clear as the song. The fresh breeze fluttered her glittering plume, and the flag of fair hair that beat her cheek still flushed with battle. She was all gold and fire.

I gave back her smile, and spoke. I do not know what I said to her. A strange lightness was in my head, and everything echoed there, as if in a hollow shell. The hills, the battle, the sea with its coloured sails, the Palace and the warriors, glowed bright and flat and far, like pictures painted by a skilful Cretan on the walls of some great room where I stood alone. Only my fate was with me, sent from the god. My soul waited for the word.

The sea was far, the ships like toys on it. Yet it seemed to me that I heard it roar. Distant at first, then nearer, the surge grew in my ears. I knew it was the voice of no mortal waves.

I had heard this sound before: when I lifted the stone at Troizen and got my father's sword; when I offered myself to the god, to go to Crete. It is the token of the Erechthids, time out of mind. At the great turns of fate it comes so, and, when the deed has answered it, it dies away. But now it grew, as if the flood that made it surged round my soul, to wash it from its moorings and drift it out on a shoreless ocean. And I knew its meaning. A great solemnity closed me round, a great grief of loneliness, a great exaltation. It was the voice of Moira, the voice that calls the King.

The tide would sweep to the Rock, Apollo had said at Delphi, and would be turned by the appointed sacrifice, which the god would choose. Why had I not seen then that in such great peril there would be only one? I should have married sooner, I thought; I leave children for heirs and a realm divided; Crete will break away. But that too was fated. The god of my birth, Blue-Haired Poseidon, has it in his hand as he has me. He has told me my part, to make the offering for the people; that is enough for a god to tell a man. I shall die on this field; to this all my life has led me; but I have saved my kingdom and made it great, and the bards will not leave my name to perish. So be it, then; I prayed always for glory before length of days. Father Poseidon, I consent; accept the offering.

So I said, praying within in silence; for warriors going into battle must hear of victory, not of death. And the surge of the sea grew steady and strong all round me, a great voice of triumph, bearing me up and making my body light. I turned to Hippolyta, standing by me in her valour and her beauty. She, even she, the nearest to my heart of all things mortal, seemed out beyond this wall of crystal in which I stood alone with the singing god. If I had felt the coming of a common death, I should have said farewell to her, and given her counsel what to do for herself and our son. But I walked with fate, who says that what will be, will be.

This is our last deed, I said in my heart; our last fight together. Let us go with the gods, in pride and battle-joy. She will have time to weep.

She was looking steadfastly at me with her clear eyes. I did not know what time had passed, since I heard the voice of Poseidon. No one seemed impatient; it could not have been long. She said to me, 'I see you clothed with victory, as if a light shone through you.' 'You too,' I answered; for some solemn presence seemed to have touched her also. 'In the gods' name, then. Come, it is time.'

And I gave the herald word to sound the onset.

We ran down into the dip between the hills then threw our shields before us against arrows, and climbed towards the Pnyx. Up there was the man who would send my life to the god; or the woman maybe, for the Moon Maids were there shouting their high war-calls, bright as cock-pheasants in the morning sun. The hill was steep, but my feet were light on it, as the tide of fate bore me along. Yet something hindered me; it was my heavy shield of dappled bull-hide. It made me laugh, that being given to death I should lug along, from habit, this burden which had no use but to keep me safe. I loosed the buckle of the sling, and tossed it from me and ran onward. It was not my business, to choose when I should fall.

I was glad when the shield was gone. It made me freer, given altogether into the hand of the god. This is a mystery, which I tell only to kings, since it concerns them: consent and fear nothing, for the god will enter you and take away your grief. I give you this counsel, which no other man has lived to give. Surely it must be good for something, to some leader of the people in time to come. Or why did I live?

The warriors came with me, singing the paean and cheering, till the hill's steepness caught their breath. No one cried out on me for going shieldless; they saw that the god inspired me, and thought I had omens that I could not fall. It gave them a feel of luck. Even Hippolyta did not reproach me. She kept close at my side, except when she paused to shoot. The Moon Maids above had seen her; they screamed their war-yells at her, and shook clenched fists. But her face was rapt and tranquil. Even when we saw upon the rampart the Maiden King, Molpadia, lifting the sacred axe and calling on the Goddess, it did not change.

The crest was near. Arrows and stones and javelins flew round me, and passed me by as if the god enclosed me in his hollowed hands. When I fall, I thought, this strength I feel will flow into my people; they will not lose heart at my death. I felt love for them, not hatred of the enemy, who were doing as they must, as our own folk had done before them. Their fate was between them and the gods, and so was ours.

The King of the Maidens put down her axe, and reached her hand to her bow. As she took aim, I felt the music of the god rise like a thousand sweet-toned horns. It sang to me that I should not leave my people nor the Rock, that my shade would come back here on great days of joy and peril, called by their paeans and prayers. As the bent bow straightened, I thought, 'It is now.'

But no arrow pierced me. Only the music ceased, in a moment, cut off and quenched so that my head was giddy at the silence; and in its place I heard a cry.

The gold plume was falling, that had tossed so lightly; going down with a sinking flutter, like a shot bird's. Closed in with the god, sure of my death, I had not seen her leap before me. She dropped to her knees, with outstretched hands; before I could reach her she pitched forward, and then heeled sideways, turned by the arrow fixed in her breast.

I kneeled on the sharp rocks, and took her in my arms. The voice of the god, the wind-borne lightness, had gone like the dream one wakes from to a cruel day. Her eyes were wandering, blind with death already; only her hand groped here and there. When I took it in mine her fingers tightened, and her lips moved in a smile.

They parted to speak; but only the death-gasp came from them. Her soul paused for a moment, hung on her flickering breath. She gave a great jerk and shudder, as if a strong cord had broken. Then she grew heavy, and I knew that she was gone.

I crouched above her, the battle all about me. If they had passed on and left me, I would not have known. So stoops the wolf whose mate has fallen to the hunters, dumb, without understanding, and as she stirs from his licking, looks to see her move with life again.

Yet the knowledge of a man was in me. I saw how she had slipped off in secret to trick me with Apollo, conjuring him who had loved a huntress to let her take my death.

I raised my eyes to the hilltop, drawn by noise. Molpadia had lifted up her axe to heaven; there was a shout of triumph from the Amazons, like a wild laugh.

I got then to my feet. Standing about me I saw the lads of her Guard. They were weeping, though my eyes were dry; it was many days before that comfort came to me. 'Stay with her till I come,' I said to those who were nearest. Beyond them were the warriors; the whole host had its eyes on me. They were ready; they had known me before I knew myself. But I felt it now, as the dog-wolf feels it; that for the pain of loss there is no cure, but anger eats and is filled.

I leaped up on a rock, where I could be seen, and gave my war-yell.

Three times I shouted; and at each the roar of the host rose
higher, as if I called up the sea. On the hill I saw the hands of
the archers and slingers sink, and faces turn to one another. Then
I ran forward.

The climbing of the slope and of the earthwork, I remember
that. I scrambled up the walls with my hands and feet and spear-butt.
Then I was among them. But not much of that day comes back to
me, after I began to kill.

I know I did not draw my sword, for it came back bright in its
scabbard. Soon after I scaled the heights, there was an axe in my
hands. The axe was good; as it bit and smashed about me, I felt
it matched to my desire. I did not look to see if my men were
following; I felt them there, like red sparks streaming behind my
rage. I might have outpaced them if I had gone straight onward;
but I was thorough, and killed also on either side.

I could not quench the thirst that drove me. Men who could die
I struck; their blood ran down the lifted axe and made my knuckles
sticky. But I could not kill the pain within; I could not kill fate, nor
the gods, nor the knowledge that tore my heart, that I was angry also
with her. Why had she meddled, when all was well? She had taken
too much upon her. We were equal war-comrades, but only one
was King. I had joined hands with my fate, and seen my finished
days as a harper's song. There need have been no parting, since she
held her life so light. Hand in hand we could have crossed the River
to the house of Hades. But she had left me alone, with my people
about my neck and no god to guide me, to be King, and live.

My soul cried vengeance, and took it where I could. Soon no
one was left to kill on the Hill of Pnyx; I led on over the saddle,
towards the Hill of the Nymphs. They were there on the top, and
I shouted out to them. A few arrows came down. But they broke
quickly before us, and I knew by their squealing they were on the
run. Men were shouting behind me that we had saved the City.
But I only felt too many would get away. In the pursuit I fell;
a man of my Guard helped me to my feet again; I gazed round
blinking, to find the Scythians streaming down the slopes towards
the plain, and the men from the ships awaiting them. But beyond,
on the hill ahead, I saw armed warriors; and shouting that these

should not escape us, I charged towards them. Their leader ran before; I gave my war-call; but he cried to me, 'Sir, it is I! Will someone look to the King; he cannot see. It is Amyntor, Theseus! The field is ours. How is it with you, sir; what is it?'

I lowered the axe, and the men who had held me stood away. My eyes cleared slowly, and I saw the army from the Citadel, meeting mine and cheering, with men weeping for joy. I stood there, dreading to awaken, while they talked across me softly, as men do about the dying. One said, 'He must have taken a head-blow.' But another answered, 'No. Where is the Amazon?'

That I understood; and I answered, 'On the Hill of Pnyx. I will bring her home.'

I started to walk back there, then stopped, and said, 'First bring me Molpadia, King of the Maidens. She has a debt to pay.'

A captain of Athens who had fought along with me said she was dead. It did not please me, and I asked who killed her. 'Why, sir,' he answered, 'you yourself with her own axe, as soon as you scaled the heights. There it is in your hand; you used it all through the battle.'

I wiped it on the grass, and looked. It had a slender shaft, and a blade like a crescent moon, with signs upon it of silver laid into the bronze. When first she rode to me on the heights of Maiden Crag, this had been in her hands. All along, it had gone with me as if it felt my thought.

Since that day I have gone into battle with no other weapon. Even years after, it seemed still to have the feel of her. But all things fade. It has forgotten her hand, and knows only mine.

She lay on the hillside, with the young men round her. They had straightened her, and laid her upon a shield. Not daring to touch the arrow, they had sent the youngest to the Citadel, to fetch the priest of Apollo. He had pronounced her dead, and drawn it out, and covered her with a pall of scarlet lined with blue; and the lads had laid her hands upon her sword. The priest said to me, 'The Lord Paian sent her the omen. But she asked if it was his command to keep it secret; and he answered according to her wish.'

'Sir,' said the youths, 'a bier is coming for her. Shall we carry her down the hill?'

I answered, 'You have done well, but it is enough now. Leave her to me.'

I took off the pall, and picked her up in my arms. Her body was cold, the limbs beginning to stiffen. I had been gone too long; her shade was far off already. I held a corpse with her face. She had felt like sleep, when I went away.

At the foot of the hill they met us with the bier, and I laid her on it; the battle had been long, and I was tired. As we came nearer to the Rock, I heard the paeans of victory. It stirred my anger; yet it was what she would have wished to hear.

Soon I too must give thanks, standing before the gods for the Athenians; that was my work. The City had been saved for a thousand years. This day, I thought, will be sung of; and I seemed to hear the song. 'Thus fell King Theseus, giving his life for the people; in the flower of his age, with his love beside him, honoured by gods and men.'

The sweat of battle had cooled upon me; I felt a sharp wind from the sea. The Palace stood on its rock and waited. It was not long past noon. I could not tell what I should fill even this one day with; and there were years ahead. She had taken my death, lover for lover; she had been a woman at the last. She who was once a king should have known that only a king can offer for the people. The gods are just; but one cannot mock them.

She had saved her man alive to weep for her. But the King had been called; and the King had died.

17

I have sailed all the seas since then, and sacked many cities. Unless there was war, I went roving with Pirithoos every year. To see new things, and live from day to day, is better than wine or poppy, and fitter for a man. I have passed between Scylla and Charybdis by the smoking snows; and off the Siren Rocks, where the wreckers send their girls to sing you over, I have caught a siren and lived to tell. Women I have had in plenty, though none for long. A face glimpsed over foreign walls, not to be had without guile and danger; till she is won, it can hold your mind from before and after, and you can believe she will not be like all the rest.

My people forgave me many years of this, because I had saved the City. Winter was long enough to bring the realm in order; if I found oppression growing up behind my back, I brought down a heavy hand. But by spring I would have wearied of it all, and of the royal rooms where my arms hung alone upon the wall; I would shut the door and be off to sea again.

If I had stayed in Attica all the year, I could have sent for young Hippolytos, and tried to get him accepted as my heir. Each spring I had half a mind to it. But the sea would call, and new places free from memories. I would leave him in Troizen one year more; he was happy there, with old Pittheus and my mother. When I heard he was known for three kingdoms round as Kouros of the Maiden, I thought of calling at Troizen as I passed; but the wind was contrary, and I let it go. I remembered those stubborn silences. The lad in Crete, who was gay and easy, would sit at my knee by the hour for sailor's tales; him I could have talked to; though you would not look at him and say, 'There goes a king.'

One year at the winter's end, a courier brought a royal letter from old Pittheus, sealed with the eagle. It was the first I had had since the Cretan war. It said he was feeling the touch of age (the hand was a scribe's, and the signature looked as if a spider had fallen in the inkwell). It was time to name his heir; and he had chosen Hippolytos.

I had never thought of this. He had got sons without number. It was true, however, that only my mother was left of his lawful children. He might have chosen me; but seeing how I lived now, I could not blame him; and with Troizen added to my kingdoms, I should have had to give up the sea. I thought the old man had done well and justly by us; it would give the boy standing if he came to Athens, the people might be more ready to accept him there also, and he could still join the kingdoms when I was gone. It reminded me that it was four years since I had last put in at Troizen. The boy must be seventeen.

In the sailing month I made my way there. As the ship rowed in, I saw the waiting people part to let through a three-horse chariot. A man stood in it. He was the child I had seen last time.

He bowled neatly down to the wharfside. The people knuckled their brows before his eye had reached them, and did it smiling. So far, good. As he jumped down, and young men ran to hold his horses, I saw he topped the tallest by half a head.

He ran aboard to greet me, and went straight down on his knee. As he rose, he took my kiss upon his cheek and gave one; then he went on rising, up and up. He had been too civil to stoop.

Commanding warriors, I am used to tall men about me. I have met plenty in battle, too, and come off best. I could not tell why this shocked me so, as if it were I who had lessened, or shrunk with age.

Then my eye took in his beauty. That shocked me too. He was like the image of a god; there seemed a kind of hubris in it; yet it was not that. As he greeted me with the grave reverence proper to some foreign deity, I met his grey eyes, as clear as snow-water; shaped by long gazing, as a sailor's are, but more still. They seemed to speak to me simply and frankly, in a language I did not know. They were her eyes no longer.

Tall trees grew on her grave-mound. The pups of our hounds' last mating had grown grey-nosed and died. Her young Guard had sons who were learning arms. As for me, she would hardly have known the face the mirrors showed me now, grey-bearded, darkened with salt and sun. She had seemed to die again in all these passings. But just now, far off in the chariot, I had seen the hair pale as electrum, the springing stance, the joy in the swift horses, and for a moment she had lived again. She was gone now, and for ever.

He led me to the chariot, mounted, and lashed the reins about him, holding the horses still as bronze for me to get up. The people cheered; he bent over the team as if he were a hired driver, leaving all the cheers to me, but turned with a shy smile to see that I was pleased. He was only a boy still. What I had felt seemed strange and foolish. This was my son and hers; and if I was not proud I must be hard to satisfy.

I praised his horses and his driving, and asked how long he had handled three. Not long, he said; he had had a pair since he was fourteen, but the third was for great days and festivals. He smiled again. So the sun stirs among the moving barley, though it has been shining all along. I had left him a long time in this little kingdom, when there was a great one in Athens. I had not looked to find him so well content.

We trotted out through the harbour town, the horses moving like one to his big light hands. He was careful even of the village pye-dogs, leaning out to give them a warning flick. He left me all the greetings, except when the children called to him, at whom he smiled. His bare shoulders shone before me, brown and broad, rippling like the horses' glossy flanks; his own in their leather short-drawers were lean and strong. With his big-boned hands and feet, he would be taller yet. When I had been a child here, before my father owned me, trying to believe I was the son of a god, this was what I had prayed to grow into; but I had to make do with what I was given. Men have done worse with more.

As we left the town he pointed things out to me, telling the kingdom's news, as keen as a young farmer, yet not thinking as yokels do that it filled the world. His sense seemed sound. I wondered what he found to do here. It all seemed like a small-holding, after Attica and Crete.

He had just touched up the horses for the open road, when a

woman rushed out of a hut with a screaming child in her arms, and stood in the way. Instead of shouting to her to look out, he brought the team to a dead stop, took an extra hitch of the reins round his waist, and held out his arms without a word. The mother gave him the child, black in the face and jerking all over. He held and stroked it; presently it got its breath and colour back and quieted down, and he handed it back again, saying, 'You know you could do that too, and better than I.' She seemed to understand this, blessed him, and said it seldom happened nowadays. As we drove on he said, 'Do forgive me, sir. It looked half-dead this time, or I'd not have made you wait.'

'Quite right,' I answered. 'I am glad to see you care for all your children, even those who were lightly got.'

He turned his head, his grey eyes wide open; then he laughed. 'Oh, it's not mine, sir; it is the woodcutter's.' He went on smiling to himself; then turned serious, and looked as if he would speak, but changed his mind and bent to his driving.

At the Palace my mother greeted me. While I was a lad in Crete she seemed to age five years in one; since then in this quiet place she had grown no older, and might have been the lad's mother instead of mine. Some of her half-brothers were there to bid me welcome, men still in their prime, and I watched how they looked at him; he, after all, was a bastard as well as they. But they seemed to accept him, just as the people did. Perhaps it was this gift of healing. No one had sent me word of it; but then I had not sent for news.

Inside, my mother said to me, 'I will see if Father is ready. I told him you were coming, Theseus, but he forgets again. Now at the last he calls the women to wash and comb him. Hippolytos, don't stand dreaming; look after your father and see he has some wine.'

He served me himself, sending off the steward. When I bade him sit, he took a low stool, and sat with his arms folded lightly upon his knees. Looking at their muscles and remembering them at the reins, I thought, 'What arms for a woman!' It was time he thought about marriage; if Pittheus was too old to see to it, I had better take it in hand.

But when I asked him if he had a girl in mind, he looked amazed, and answered, 'Oh, no, sir. It's too late to think of that.'

'Too late?' I said staring. But to laugh would hurt him, and do no good. 'Come, lad; whatever happened, everything passes. A girl was it, or a boy?'

'I thought, sir, that you knew.' He had now got very serious; it made him look older, not younger as often with the young. 'I have made an offering of all that. It's settled and done.'

Since I had met him at the harbour, some unease had dogged me. Now it was as if a door creaked open to show me the ancient enemy. But I would not look. 'You are a man now,' I said, 'heir to a kingdom. You must put your toys away.'

His brows, which were strong and darker than his hair, slanted and drew together. I saw his quiet did not come from meekness. 'Well, sir, call it that if you wish; but how shall we talk then? It will be hard enough if both of us are trying; words don't say much, in any case.'

In my heart, his patience angered me. It was like the patience of a great dog, that lets the small one snap. 'What is this? Let me know it, then. You are your mother's only son. Don't you think her blood worth passing on; do you hold it so lightly?'

He did not speak for a while. His quiet stare seemed to say, 'What will the man think of next? There is no knowing.' That too made me angry. At last he said, 'She would not think so.'

'Well?' I said. 'Come, get it over; have you taken some vow, or what?'

'Vow?' he said. 'I don't know. Yes, I suppose so; but it makes no odds.'

'You do not *know?*'

He said, trying hard with me (he was so young, he hardly expected anyone of my age to follow him), 'Vows are to bind you if you change your mind. I shall take one if I am asked to; it makes no odds.'

'To what god?' I asked him. It was better to have it done.

'If I take a vow,' he answered, 'that will be to Asklepios, when I am ready.'

This was something new. There were things behind, which he would not talk about, as there had always been. But this he had said quite briskly. He had been a riddle, I thought, since he was born.

I questioned him, expecting some high-flown words. But he said, 'It started with the horses,' and then paused, thinking. 'I used to doctor them. I always had a feel for it. Perhaps it comes from Poseidon.' He had a sweet smile. A woman would have melted. 'Then at a push I had to give a hand with men, and that took hold of me. I started to wonder: what are men for?'

I had never heard such a question. It made me shrink back; if a man began asking such questions, where would be the end of it? It was like peering into a dark whirlpool with a deep spinning centre, going down and down. I looked at the boy. He did not seem sick, nor frightened; only a little way out of himself, as another boy might if a girl he was crazy for had just passed the window. 'That,' I said, 'is the business of the gods, who made us.'

'Yes, but for what? We ought to be good for it, whatever it is. How can we live until we know?' I gazed at him; such desperate words, yet he looked all lit up from within. He saw I was paying attention; that was enough to draw him on.

'I was driving my chariot once, going to Epidauros. Let me take you, sir, we can go tomorrow, then you will see . . . Well, never mind that, we were going well along the sea-road, there was a wind at our backs . . .'

'We?' I asked him, expecting to learn something of use.

'Oh, it seems like that with a team, when you are all going like one.' I had put him off; it took him a moment or two to get back again. 'The road was good, and clear, nothing to hold back for. I let them go and they went like thunder. And I felt it then; I felt God going down into the horses, down through me. Like a steady lightning that does not burn. It lifted my hair upon my head. And I thought, "It is this, it is this, we are for this, to bring down the gods as the oak leads down the lightning, to lead down God into the earth. For what?" The chariot was racing beside the sea, everything blue and shining, our manes all streamed in the wind, they were running for joy as they do wild on the plains. And I knew what it was for; but one cannot tell it, the life goes out with words.' He jumped to his feet as if he had no weight in him, and strode across to the window, walking on air. There he stood looking out, with the sun upon him, blazing without heat in stillness. Then he came to himself again and said, quite shyly, 'Well, but one can feel all that with a sick pup in one's hands.'

As if she had heard, a nursing bitch came in heavy with milk, a wolfhound, and reared up with her paws against his chest. He stood rubbing her ears. Just so I had seen his mother stand, soon after I brought her home, eighteen years old. He was our living love, and through him we could live for ever. Without him we died.

'If you have the healing from some god,' I said, 'all the more need to get sons and pass it on. The Immortals won't thank you to waste it, that is sure.'

He came down slowly from his lightness, finding he would need words after all. I could see him turning them over; like a racehorse hauling logs.

'But that is it,' he said. 'Not to waste it, that is the thing. This power takes all of a man; go off after this or that, and it wastes away. Girls, now; if I once made a start, whether I married or just had one at the Dionysia, I daresay I couldn't do without them after. They look so pretty and soft, like little foxes. Likely enough one could never have enough of them, once one had begun. Much better not to begin.'

I stared at him dumbly. I could hardly believe I had understood him. At last I said, 'Are you joking, or trying to make a fool of me? Do you mean that you are still a virgin? At seventeen?'

He flushed. It was not modesty, I perceived; he was man enough to feel an insult. A warrior was there; but a warrior under orders. He answered quite quietly, 'Well, sir, it's part of what I mean.'

So there was not even a wild crop on the hills of Troizen or in the farms, to carry the strain on; nothing. I thought how she had showed me him in the morning, after the long night's travail. Now he flung our hope back in my face. If he had been a woman, he could have been made to obey; but no one can force a man to breed. He was the master; and he did not care.

All I could find to say was, 'At your age, I had children in Troizen old enough to run.'

The scowl sailed off his brow like a summer cloud. He was amused. 'I know that, sir,' he said. 'I should hope I know my own brothers.'

'You take it lightly,' I answered. Being angry, I added something more. It would have been nothing much on the deck of a longship. I knew it was not seemly for a son to hear from his father; but I was past minding.

He stared. Then looked sick. If it had been with me, I daresay I might have borne that better. But no; it was with himself, for having tried to tell me his heart. I felt that as the last injury; for the core of my anger was love and pride in him. If it had been young Akamas in Crete, he could have gelded himself in the rites of Attis, and I daresay I should have got over it. A good boy enough; but there were plenty more where he came from.

Breaking his silence, I seemed to hear a laughter that was not of men; from the Labyrinth, from the hills of Naxos, from Maiden Crag, from the cave beyond the Eye. They wove in a round dance three in one, and I heard their whispering laughter – the Mother, the Maiden, the Crone.

My anger burst from me. But I kept down my voice, as I have learned to do; there are better ways than shouting, to reach a taller man. I said, among other things, that it was infamous to accept the heirdom of Troizen, to cheat in his dotage a King who had been great, and had sons who would have done right by him; to mock his hopes in his last days. 'He has loved you,' I said. 'Have you no shame?'

He did not open his mouth; but his face answered for him. It turned red, and the muscles rose on the clenched jaw. He was not a man with much use for words, one way or another; from the grip of his hand upon the window-sill, I saw it was not speech that would do him good. Well, he might think I did not understand him; but at least I knew that anger, better than any other man.

Almost I could have told him so. But while we glared in silence like enemies in the field, in came my mother and said that the King was ready. She looked from face to face, but said nothing. I daresay we both avoided her eyes like boys.

They had propped my grandfather up in bed; he looked as clean as thistledown. His hands of bone and milk-skin lay on the blue wool spread which scarcely showed a body under. When he greeted me, he held his hand as low as if to a child, and I saw his eyes had a clouded film. I knelt by him; he stroked my hair and said in a voice like rustling reeds, 'Be faithful, boy, it is all we know to do. The gods know what to do with it.'

He drowsed again. But my youth came back to me. I remembered how I had had the call to go to the bulls of Crete; how the people had wept, and my father had cried to me that I was leaving him to his enemies in his failing years – yes, and it was true. Yet I had gone, and could do no other.

I heard horses, and looked from the window. Down on the road was the lad driving away. The dust from his wheels was pink with sunset. As he took the bend, I could picture his eyes devouring the ground before him till he came to the flat where he could go.

I ran out to the stables, calling for a chariot and a good fresh pair. The charioteer came hurrying, but I waved him off and took the reins. You do not roam from land to land without racing sometimes with borrowed horses, and these knew who was master. I turned them out of the Eagle Gate upon the road to the sea. The folk of Troizen, who had lately seen me drive by in state, stood staring in my dust, remembering courtesy when I was gone by.

I could see him at the turns; but he never looked back, only forward towards the hard mudflats of Limna; when he reached them he leaned forward over the team, and they raced away. But, I thought, though he had the start of me, he was a big lad; my beasts had less weight to carry. He had unhitched his third horse, the one for festivals, and was only driving the pair.

The ripples of the landlocked Psiphian Bay plashed upon shining stones. On this same road I had driven to seek my father, and try my manhood in the Isthmus, just at his age. And now I was galloping till my teeth rattled in my head, for all the world as if I were a boy again with a taller boy to beat. Which was not so; a man does not get wet year after year at sea, without finding a stiff joint here and there. Mine would ache tomorrow. All the same, I meant to win my race today.

I was gaining when a long turn hid him. He had not seen me. It was my will against his whim. I rounded the headland; there, quite near, was the chariot. But it stood empty beside the road. Without sense – for the pair stood quietly, the reins hitched to an olive tree

– my heart tripped and hit my throat. Then, seeing all was well, I tied my own horses near them, and took the path up the hill.

I thought he would give me a long scramble, knowing his ways. But he had not gone very far. There he was in an ilex-grove; and as I walk lightly, he did not see me for the trees. He stood still, panting deeply from the drive, and the climb, and, as I saw, from anger. His big hands closed and unclosed as they hung beside him, and he paced the clearing like a beast in a cage. Suddenly he reached upward, and, with a great sound of cracking, tore off a limb near as thick as my arm. He trod on it and broke the middle, then snapped all the lesser branches across his knee. Leaves and white splintered wood lay all about him. He stood over this mess, staring down. Then he knelt, and felt about it, and came up with something in his cupped hands. His touch had changed; stroking and delicate. But the thing was dead, whatever it was. He dropped it – some little thing, a bird or a squirrel's young – and put his hand to his forehead. When I saw his grief, I knew he had come to himself and was sorry for what had passed between us. That was enough for me. I came forth and held out my hands to him, saying, 'Come, boy, it is past. We shall know each other better.'

He looked at me as if I had dropped from heaven, then knelt and touched my hand with his brow. As he rose up I kissed him; and now, when he straightened after to his hero's height, I felt only pride.

We talked a little, and smiled together at our race, and then fell silent. Evening was far spent; the hilltops grew gold above the water drenched in their shadow; there were scents of sea-wrack and dewy dust and thyme, and a shrill of grasshoppers. I said, 'I took your mother from the Maiden, and she claims her debt. The gods are just, and one cannot mock them. Even though you serve one who has never loved me, be true and you will be my son. Truth is the measure of a man.'

'You will see, Father,' he said, calling me this for the first time since childhood, 'I will be true to you as well.' He paused, and seeing he had more to say but was shy, I answered, 'Yes?'

'When I was small,' he said, 'I asked you once why the guiltless suffer too, when the gods are angry. And you said to me, "I do not know." You who were my father, and the King. For that I have always loved you.'

I made him some kind answer, wondering if I should ever make him out. Well, trust must do instead. As we walked back to our chariots, I asked him where he had been going. He said, 'To Epidauros, to be cured of my old sickness which I thought was gone. But you came instead.' I saw that he meant his anger. Strange words for a young man in his strength, just of an age for war.

The sky grew bright with sunset; the earth glowed, and his face also with its own light. I drove home in peace, and that night's sleep was sweet to me. But it is given only to the gods, to live in joy for ever.

18

That summer I sailed with Pirithoos as far as Sicily, to sack the city of Thapos. It was a night assault, from the sea, and went so well we were on the walls before the alarm. I could hear the watchmen yelling. It was not 'Theseus of Athens!' as it used to be, but 'Theseus the Pirate! Theseus the Pirate!'

I was angry, and the Thapsians paid for it. All the same, it set me thinking. All I had to show at each year's end, these days, was a load of plunder, and a girl I would be weary of next year. Once it had been a hold of bandits cleared, the borders strengthened, laws broadened or fined-down to a better justice; some old blood-feud settled between two tribes; a suppliant freed from a bad master. It seemed, when I thought, that no one had been much the better for my life, this year, or last, or the year before.

As we coasted back past Italy, I thought of what had passed at Troizen. I could let things drift no longer. Hippolytos had chosen his own heritage, such as it was. Young Akamas, Phaedra's boy, must be the heir of all my kingdoms. He must come to Athens, and be seen.

There was no harm in the lad, and no little good. But he was too easy-going, and lived from day to day. Courage he did not lack, as I had often seen; but there seemed no thrust of ambition in him. He was the son of my wedded queen, with clear title, if I chose, to the mainland kingdoms; yet, as far as I could see, he waited for Crete to fall into his lap, and looked no further. It was true he was all Cretan, just like some graceful prince of the Older Kingdom painted in the Labyrinth, walking in a field of irises with the royal gryphon on a string; it was true, too, that I had made him so. I had only fetched him to Athens on a few short visits, all his life. He had been a delicate child, which was my excuse. The truth was I had wanted to keep him content with Crete. There had been enough brothers fighting over Attica, in my father's day. But he would have to be seen there now. The people would have forgotten him; and it was time he was taught his trade.

He still had the fecklessness of a child. He was too old never to have asked himself — as it seemed he had not — how long he could hold Crete without the mainland fleet to back him. It needed thinking of; for Deukalion was dead, and his son Idomeneus was quite another man. If he was not already conspiring to get the throne, it would not be fear that was stopping him, but a pride too high to risk disgrace. He had the blood of Minos, both the Cretan line and the Greek; and he was five-and-twenty, while I was past forty now and taking no great care of myself, as anyone could see. He would wait a while. But once I was gone, young Akamas would need both hands to hold on with.

Women in Crete have always understood affairs, so I wondered what his mother made of it, and how much she had tried to push him on. He had a truly Cretan reverence for her; yet last time, he had seemed more at ease with me.

She had never asked me to bring her to Athens, though neither her people nor mine would have quarrelled with it after so long. Often I had thought about it; then looking at the closed rooms that still had echoes, I had put it off for another year. So I had said nothing to her; and she was never one to tell all her mind. She was turned thirty, and that is late to start again among strangers. Also she was Minos' daughter; perhaps she did not care to step into the shoes of the dead, which would never have been hers while the living wore them; or to go where a bastard had been set above her son. Perhaps she had heard my house had too many girls and that, with my being away, they got out of hand. Like enough all these things had part in it.

The summer was far gone. If I thought too long I should put it off again. So I parted from Pirithoos at sea, and made straight for Crete.

The boy was there to meet me, full of spirits; asking where I had been, what I had brought him back, and how soon he could sail with me, though he was barely turned thirteen. He chattered like a starling all the way in the chariot. On the terrace of the royal house stood his mother waiting, small, neat and jewelled, her fine brown hair sleek in the sun, her bare breasts round and firm as the grapes down in the vineyard, whose scent the warm Cretan sun drew up to us.

When we were alone, I told her how matters stood, saying, 'It would not have been just to pass over Hippolytos, when his mother gave her life for me and Attica in the war. If I had died then, with both sons children, neither could have hoped for much. But he has offered himself to Artemis, to pay her debt. The gods know best, and we must do what is left to do.'

'Yes,' she said, 'that is true.' She sat silent, her tapered white hands folded in her lap. I almost said she need not come to Athens, unless she liked. I felt the words ask to be spoken, like a dog asking at a closed door. But I knew it would seem a slight to her. She had had a good deal to put up with; my calls had been short, between Athens and the sea. I had never, myself, flaunted my women at her, but the isles were full of tales and songs about the sea-raids I had got them in, and she must have heard. So I said she should be there to share in her son's honour; that she could trust me to put the house in order, and see she was well served.

'I should like to see Athens,' she said quite coolly, and paused in thought. 'But what a strange young man, to give away a kingdom. Will he hold to it? Youths of that age are full of whims, and next year it is all forgotten.'

'Not he. What his mind is set on, he does not give up lightly.' She raised her dark brows. 'Neither do you.'

'He has had his chance. He knows it. And horses will fly, before he learns to intrigue. Take my word for that.' So without much more said, she agreed to come, and I gave her some jewels I had found in Sicily. My mind had been more on Akamas, and how he would take the news.

He looked astonished, as if such a thing had never crossed his mind; worse still, I guessed it was true. When I had done, he said, 'Father, are you quite sure Hippolytos doesn't want it? I could not take it if he does; not from a friend.'

It might have been some boy's present, a chariot or a bow, to hear him talk. It brought back all my doubts of him. A light mind, I thought; no harm, no greatness. 'He is your brother,' I said. 'Don't you think I shall deal justly between my sons? As for friendship, you have never met.'

'Not met! Father, of course we have.' He opened his dark, slanted Cretan eyes, with the surprise of a child who finds his own matters have not filled the world. 'It was when I was going home from Athens, last time I stayed with you. You sent some letters to Troizen, and we were a week there, waiting for a wind. He drove down the moment he knew that I was there, and we spent the whole time together. He let me drive his chariot, once, on the straight; I had it all, he said so, he was scarcely touching the reins. My dog, Frosty, was his guest-gift. Didn't you know? His sire was one of the sacred dogs of Epidauros. Surely they told you it was Hippolytos who took me there, and got me cured?'

'Cured?' I said. 'You left Athens well enough.'

'Yes; but when I got there, I had one of those choking spells.' I had forgotten; in childhood he used to go quite blue with them. 'The priest at Epidauros knew all about it; he called it Asthma, which was just what Hippolytos had said. You do know, Father, don't you, he is almost a doctor? He would really be one, if he had not had to be a king. Well, I slept the night in the sacred grove, and had a true dream from the god.' His brown, sparkling face turned solemn, and he laid two fingers on his lips. 'I mustn't tell it; but it was true. Then Paian went away in music, and I was cured. Father, can't Hippolytos come to Athens, while I am there? Then he can see how Frosty has turned out. He is really my greatest friend; and we shall hardly know each other, if we don't meet soon.'

'Why not?' I said. 'We will see.' This unguessed love came like a gift of heaven. I felt ashamed to have kept the boys apart; yet who could have forgotten the Pallantid wars? Certainly, he must come. Yet there was another thought behind it all: that once in Athens, seeing his young brother's hands so slack upon the reins, the elder would reach out for them. Phaedra had been right; what my heart was set on, I did not give up lightly.

And then, of his own accord, he wrote to me from Troizen. He wanted to come to Eleusis, to be initiated in the Mystery, and asked my leave. 'Surely,' I thought, 'the luck is running my way.'

I had a lookout watching for his ship, and when it was sighted, went up on the Palace roof to see. I remember, as it stood in past Aegina, how the white sail caught the sun.

Driving down to meet him at Piraeus, I thought it was too soon to give him such consequence before the people; but I did not care. As he crossed the gangplank, I saw he had grown again. His face was stronger, the softness of youth fined out of it. 'Did I make this?' I thought. 'No, it was she.' It came back to me how all she remembered of her father was that he had darkened the doorway with his height.

We drove up through the sea-gate, and on into Athens. I felt their minds as a pilot feels the weather, through the cheers and songs. In boyhood he had been Son of the Amazon, no more. Now they were like children with a new toy; the women cooing, the men likening him to Apollo Helios. If they could, they would have said to me, 'Why have you kept this from us?'

In the Palace it was the same. The old men who had hated his mother were dead and gone. It was all getting forgotten. I had been long in knowing it, I who did not forget. Young folk, who had been little children when she died, admired what they called his Hellene fairness. One heard this 'Hellene' everywhere, and often it had meaning. Dark Akamas, with his slender waist and lithe Cretan walk and lilting accent, was the stranger now; it was his mother who had the shadow of the Goddess on her and needed watching. Why had I not foreseen it? If Hippolytos would stretch one hand out for his birthright, they would toss it him like a flower.

He was surer of himself; the habit of kingship was growing on him; he was not one to be pushed here and there by any man. So much the better; but I knew something of the business too, and we would see.

Akamas met us in the hall. He was awed at first by this tall brother; but soon, Hippolytos remembering some old joke between them, they were skylarking like any boys. As we came to the inner rooms, Akamas was asking if it was cold up there so high; Hippolytos shouted, and tossed him overhead to see. In the midst of the horseplay, the younger grew quiet, and the elder turned his head. Phaedra was there, waiting to be greeted. That morning, having slept badly, she had been out of temper with her women; her hair was ill-done, and she had not kept still while her mouth was painted. Seeing herself overlooked, she greeted him coldly and did not waste many words. He had come up with a smile to beg her pardon, but now grew grave with shyness; and having said what was proper, got away with his brother as soon as he well could.

I followed soon after. I was sorry she was offended; yet perhaps it was better she saw him first at disadvantage, than looking too much a king; the first sight sticks, they say. I was sorry, indeed, that I had ever brought her to Athens. She was bound to glimpse in him her rival's beauty, and that was bad. She might come to see, too, her son's supplanter; and that means danger anywhere. I had cause to know it; it was what Medea had seen in me.

So I got him out of the way at first, riding and hunting with his brother and me, to put him out of her mind. She only saw him with everyone else, dining in Hall. It was true he made a good show then. He went bare to the waist, in the fashion I had brought from Crete, with short-drawers of scarlet; and a great necklace which was the royal jewel of the heir of Troizen, made of golden eagles with outspread wings. His smooth brown skin showed off the gold, and the hair which he still wore uncurled as in his childhood, spilling over his shoulders like silver over bronze. I could always hear, when he took his place by me, a soft murmur among the women. Once it had sounded for me. But men must live with their seasons, or the gods will laugh at them.

Before long he went to Eleusis to be purified. It was early by half a month; but he said he had things to ask there. At first he would drive home at evening; then he moved to the precinct and was no more seen. Presently, I heard from the High Priest of Eleusis, priest to priest, that he had been chosen to hear the inner doctrine, which they had had from Orpheus before the maenads killed him, and which was scarcely ever taught outside the priesthood.

I missed his presence, but felt his absence for the best, since Phaedra seemed herself again. Indeed she looked better, not complaining as she had at first of the water and the air of Athens, and the people's ignorance; she dressed with more care, and was pleasant to the men of standing. She had seen, I thought, that her son might lose by her sullenness. When the rites came nearer, and the women were making their new clothes, she said she would be initiated.

I admired her prudence. It would please the Athenians who feared the Old Religion; for at Eleusis the rites have been tamed, as everybody knows. Before my time, a dead king was dug into the cornland every year. When it came to my turn, I had other notions. But I did honour to the Goddess, by marrying her to a god instead, and calling in the great bard to devise the ritual. Though it was secret, the initiates could say there was no more unseemliness, nor danger beyond what comes of bringing one's mortal soul before the Immortals. And after that darkness, there is light.

So I did not hinder her, even though I saw in it ambition for her son. She would make friends among the women, and had been too much alone. Besides, who could tell if Hippolytos would change his mind? Sometimes I wondered if the two lads would settle it themselves one day over a cook-fire in the hunting field, without a word to anyone. It is hard for the young, to break their minds to their elders. What could one do, but leave it with the gods? But I am forward-looking by nature, and would find myself planning still.

On the proper days, she went with the women to be taught the cleansings, and told what things to abstain from, one of which was our bed. It was her fast, not mine; there was a honey-dark girl I had brought from Sicily, skilled in the dances of Aphrodite Peleia. I had kept her out of the way for the sake of peace, but was glad to see her again.

Two days before the rites, the mystae came back to Athens so that the priests could order the procession. I had appointed Hippolytos to lead the youths, since his brother was not of age. They might have stretched a point for Akamas if I had asked; but no one could say he had been slighted. It is a strong wine, the people's praise on great days of festival. If Hippolytos got one good deep drink of it, it might show him his own soul.

He came among the last, when the Agora was full already. Though he had grown thinner, his eyes and his skin were clear;

he was washed and combed like a child who does it from duty when he would rather be at play, shining and unadorned. He seemed happy. I thought, 'I planted this seed of life, yet from it comes this mystery, a life where I am a stranger. The ways of the gods are dark.'

After this I was busy, as before all great festivals. When I came out in my chariot to lead the men of Athens to the shrine, the youths were gone on foot before, carrying the god-bridegroom's image and the holy things.

I thought, on the way, about my own initiation. I had been the last to enter the old Mystery, and the first into the new. Though I had known in part, from the priests and from the bard, what was to be done, yet there was great power in it, great dread and darkness, great light and bliss. Passing years and their deeds had worn the memory thin. But now I thought of it, and of the lad about to meet it. What would he have made of the old one; the wrestling to the death, with the throned Queen watching; the marriage bed in the dark cave, the shameless torchlight? Would he blush and run for the hills? 'Yet,' I thought, 'surely he has heard of it. She whom he serves is not a maiden always; and before all her faces she likes due incense burned. He is made more like a man than most men are. Some day the Bride will say to him, "Is my altar to be cold for ever?"'

It was a fine shining night. The mystae stripped themselves, men and women, and waded with their torches into the sea, the last rite of their cleansing. Once it had washed them of the dead king's blood. Even then, it was grave and seemly; how solemn it is now, all the world knows. For a long time the torch of the priest was leading; then another passed it, mirrored in the water, held by a taller man who could wade deeper in. Somewhere among all the wavering lights was Phaedra, safe with the Good Goddess, where she would take no harm.

The lights went out. There was a long pause, for the re-robing. Through the gloom I saw from the Citadel above only a stir of shadows; they were trooping into the sacred temenos, where all the rock-gaps had been closed to keep the Mystery secret. Into the deep hush rose a sound of chanting, sweet and full of grief. It was too far to hear the prayers. The night fell back into silence. Somewhere a dog howled, as dogs do when they feel solemnity; it broke off in a yelp, and all was still.

It is the time for dying (I say no more; the Twice-Born will understand) and my thoughts were with the dead. Once more my heart died with her. At last from within the earth the gong tolled out, the voice of darkness; even from far off one felt the awe. But for me it had no terror. No dread; and no promise either.

Then came the clear light shining; the silent wonder, the great cry of joy, the hymn. New-lit torches flickered forth like fireflies from a cave, and the dance began. I watched its measure, unwearying as the course of stars, till dawn broke on the mountain. Then I led the people down to meet the mystae and bring them home.

As the risen sun made a sparkling sea-path towards Athens, they met us by the shore, with their new white robes on, crowned with wheat-ears and flowers. The faces, I suppose, were what one sees each year: some still half-dazed after the fright and the glory; some, who had dreaded it long before, just happy to have it behind them; some joyful at having won a happy fate in the Land beyond the River. I looked at the youths, and the lad who led them, thinking to see him sleep-walking in a trance, still seeing his vision. But he gazed about him, all delight, as if his eyes could find nothing that was not precious and dear. His face held great peace, and wonder; but, also, the tenderness that goes with half a smile. Picture a grown man who has watched children stumble through some solemn game, seeing in it beauty they do not know of, and a meaning beyond their reach. He looked like that.

I spoke the ritual welcome; the priests made answer. It was time for the mystae to break their fast among their friends. As Hippolytos came towards me with a smile of greeting, there was a great dark swoop of wings across the sun. A raven, sailing from the high crags to scan the plain, had paused above us; hovering so low, one could see the purple sheen upon its breast, like the enamel-work on precious swords. The people pointed and called to one another, arguing the omen. But the lad just gazed upward, happy and still; you could tell he saw nothing but the beauty that hung outspread upon the breeze. As it stooped lower, he reached out his hand, as if to greet it; and it skimmed down almost to his fingertips, before it swept out towards Salamis and the sea.

I watched it, feeling troubled, till a fussing among the women drew my eyes away. It was Phaedra who was being held head-down, and given wine. What with the fasting and the standing, and the strong awe of the rites, one or two women always faint at the Mysteries. This year there were four, and I thought no more of it.

19

It was quite soon after this that Akamas looked pale one day, with circled eyes. When I asked him how he was, he said he had never felt better. But his mother told me he had had a choking fit in the night, the first for years.

'I will send the doctor,' I said. I was thinking it would be a bad business, if the next king turned out as brittle in body as in mind. 'But meanwhile, it might do him good to see his brother first. Hippolytos has a good deal to do today; he sails tomorrow; but it seems he helped the boy before.'

I sent to seek him. He had been bidding farewell to his friends, and their love came with him, like a scent of summer. It ran to waste off him, his power over men he could have turned into mastery. As the love came he bloomed in it; it was enough for the day. When the harvest ripened, he would give it away for nothing.

After being with Akamas some time, he came back thoughtful and sat down by my chair. He would have squatted like a page, if I had not pushed him the footstool. It was not humility, but the carelessness a man can afford who stands six feet and three fingers. He talked quite simply, like a good ploughboy speaking of his ox. 'Last time he had these turns, it was something on his mind. Nothing much, as Apollo showed him; all it wanted was the air let in. This time he won't talk, which is a pity; but by my guess it's not far different. His mother does not look so well as before the Eleusinia; do you think so, Father? Maybe she's homesick for Crete.'

'Maybe,' I said. 'I will ask her, at least. At this rate, I don't know how the boy will get on leading warriors in the field. He could do with some of your strength. Well, he will be sorry you must sail tomorrow.'

'Oh, I told him I would stay a day or two, if I have your leave, Father. May I send a runner to the ship?'

That evening I went over to Phaedra's room. She had kept to it since the Mysteries. That first night she had been tired; I had had the girl from Sicily; and so it had gone on, with nothing said on either side. When I came in, she looked up quickly and called for her shawl. She looked thinner, and higher-coloured, as if with fever; there was something about her taut and crackling, as if her hair would spark under the comb.

When the maids were gone, I asked after Akamas whom I had just seen sleeping easily, and then after herself. She said she was well enough; she had some headaches; it was nothing; yet it made her tired. I said Hippolytos had been concerned for her; on which she sat up, laughed at his fancying himself a doctor, and asked what he had said.

'They don't laugh in Troizen,' I answered, 'they think he has healing hands.'

'Why, then, the thought will heal them. What did he say?'

I told her. She stiffened in her chair; then jumped to her feet with the shawl clutched round her. What had I been about, she cried, to allow such insolence? Because this youth thought himself too good for anyone, would I let him command my household now? Where was my pride? Her voice grew shrill; she was shaking from head to foot; I had never seen her so angry. I thought it must be her moon-time, and answered calmly that the lad had spoken in kindness, meaning no harm.

'No harm? How do you know? Oh, there is something behind. Why does he want me sent away? He wants us forgotten, me and my son, to give him first place before the people.'

'You are much mistaken.' She was late with her fear; the irony made me want to laugh. But I held it back; she was Minos' daughter. 'As you know, he has made his choice.' But she still ran on about his pride and coldness. Such pettiness seemed unlike her. I feared that she guessed my wishes; it was a thousand pities I had brought her here, to make her ambitious for her son. Only a fool, however, will try to reason with women when they have their times. I went away and, the night being young, found other company.

Next day Hippolytos took young Akamas to Phaleron Bay to dive and swim; they came back brown from the salt and sun, all loosened and at ease. Seeing them together, I thought, 'He will lean on Hippolytos for everything, and it will be the same when he is King. The elder will rule here in all but name.' And then I thought, 'What life is that, for such a man as he will be? Sly old pandars can do as much, or whores. To stand for the people before the gods, that is kingship. Power by itself is the dross without the gold.'

It was about this time that Hippolytos said to me, 'Father, what sort of man is Menestheus? What does he want?'

'Want?' I said. 'To think well of himself. So he takes trouble and does not make mistakes. He is a useful man, and will make a good envoy, when he can be kept from meddling.'

'You are thinking of Halai,' he said. They had had a land-dispute there, and I had sent Menestheus to see the chiefs.

'Oh,' I answered, 'he had planned a great day for the tribes to come together and make speeches before each other and me. Of course they would have dragged up every old grudge for generations back; got to mortal insults by noon, threats before sundown; and first blood would have been spilled on the way home. Then we should have had ten years of it. And so I told him. When I got the story from him, I just drove down there alone, saw the headmen quietly, and got them to agree. Each gave up something; but it was all gain for the peasants, who would have starved when the crops were burned. Maybe Menestheus hoped for some consequence out of the meeting; but it was the Halaians we were supposed to be concerned with.'

'Was it consequence he missed?' Hippolytos said. 'I thought it was the anger. He seemed restless for it, I don't know why.'

I thought about it, for he never said such things lightly. 'It would not have brought him any gain.'

'Oh, no; not gain. He is very upright. Whatever he did, he would need to be pleased with first. Perhaps anger helps him. But have you noticed, Father, when a man has bad luck, no matter how he suffers, Menestheus doesn't notice it? He only pities him if he is wronged; he must begin with anger.'

'His father beat him,' I said. 'Like many another. Why it is only Menestheus who can't forget it, I cannot tell. Well, he is a lightweight when all is said, not worth making much of either way.'

So it was often, when we talked about affairs. He had learned no more shrewdness than in his childhood: yet he would cut clean through intrigue that would have tangled a shrewder man; he scarcely knew it was there, having nothing it could catch him by, no envy, spite or greed. Yes; but he was like the man who is made weapon-proof, save in that one place where the god who did it grasped him. One sees clearly, after.

A day or so later, word came to me that the Queen was sick.

I broke off my business, feeling concerned; but I was put out, too. She had had my leave to go, as Athens did not suit her; if she had stayed, no doubt it was because she would not leave Akamas with his brother and me. The boy had been too much at her petticoats, and needed men.

When I came to her room, the curtains were all closed; she lay in a dark-red gloom, with cloths upon her brow which the women changed continually, wringing them in cold water. The room smelled of Cretan essences, heavy and sweet.

I asked what the doctor thought of it. 'Oh, I can't bear him near me; he can do nothing for my headaches, yet he won't leave me in quiet, but talks till my head is splitting.' She tossed about, and smelled at a pomander a girl held out to her, and shut her eyes. I was going away when she opened them and said, 'And Akamas drives me mad with his "Send for Hippolytos" all day. Oh, let him come, let him come; I know it can't help me, but there will be no peace till you all see it for yourselves. Bring him, do, with those great healing hands of his, and let us have it over.'

'He will come,' I said, 'if you ask him. But I see no sense in it. It will only vex you more.' My guess was that she wanted to make a fool of him, to vent her fretfulness. She dragged the damp cloth off her brow and reached out for another, and said, 'Yes, yes; but I am so on edge with all this talk of it, I shall have no more rest till it is done. Do send him, though it is nonsense; then I can sleep.'

I found the lad. He was in the stables, talking horse-medicine with an old groom, their heads over a thrushy foot, the horse nosing his neck. When I had got him inside and told him, he said, 'Well, Father, if you like; but I think I'll have more luck here. The horse trusts me; and it needs that, to make a path for the god.'

'I know; she is tired and crotchety, and I don't suppose you will get much thanks. Come all the same; after all, it will not kill you.'

I remember that we smiled.

As we crossed the courtyard, I was thinking how often he spoke with reverence of Apollo now. Once it had been all The Lady. But he would have learned Paian's worship at Epidauros; they are brother and sister, after all.

Phaedra's women had opened the curtains just a crack. She had been combed and propped upon fresh pillows, and her eyes touched up with blue. I led up the boy and he stood at the bedside, looking, as I had never seen him, awkward and gawky; his big long hands hung at his sides, uncertain, seeming to think by themselves. He muttered something, to say he was sorry she was in pain.

I was pleased that she spoke pleasantly. 'Oh, it comes and goes. But it is bad today, and I have tried everything now but you; so do your best for me.'

He drew into himself, as I have seen healers do before, looking and thinking; then laid his hand across her brow and stood as if he listened. She shut her eyes. Presently he put both hands on her temples, pressing a little, with a half-frown and this listening look. After a while, he would have taken his hands away, but she pulled at his wrist, so he kept them there a little longer. At last he stood back and shook his head, saying, 'I am sorry. Elixir of willow-bark might help it.'

She opened her eyes and said, 'Why, it has gone!'

'Gone?' he said, and leaned over to study her. 'What a strange thing; I never felt it. I am glad you are better. You will sleep now, I hope. Goodbye.'

As we left I said to him, 'I will thank you for her, since she forgot.' He said smiling, 'The god did it by himself. I wish I knew how. Well, back to the horse; that's a simple case.'

In the next few days, she sent for him once or twice. The first time, I brought him to her, the next I was busy and sent him with her woman. The day after, she sent for him again; but he had gone driving, taking his young brother with him. After all, as I told her, it was to help the boy he had stayed on, and they would not have much more time together.

I had business still in Halai, sorting out the boundaries, which were in a muddle centuries old. Most days I went out there. I had let too much go, in the years of roving. The evening after, I found Phaedra had sent for Hippolytos again and, though he was in, he had not gone. When I asked him why, he said quite shortly, 'I sent her some physic. It will do her more good than I can.'

'Maybe,' I answered. 'But go in courtesy. It makes for a pleasant house.'

'Let us both go, then,' he said, 'and see how she is.'

'I have no time.' I daresay I was curt; it was not for him to tell me my duty. 'Go before it is too late.'

He went off with the maid. We had just eaten; he was dressed for the Hall, with his great gold necklace. It comes back to me clearly now, though then I did not heed it much; his belt of coral and lapis studs, his hair just washed, all bland and shining, and how he smelled of sweet herbs from the bath.

I went up early, with the girl from Sicily, and next morning was in council. It was not till noon I looked for him; when I learned from his page that he had been gone all night, and not returned.

It seemed nothing much, considering his ways; but I went to ask Phaedra if, before he left, he had obeyed me. She was still in bed. One of her girls ran by me weeping, with the marks of the rod upon her; she herself was haggard, as if she had not slept, and the whole place seemed to be by the ears. She looked at me as if she hated me – but it was plain no one could please her – and said, 'How should I know where your son is, or care? He might be anywhere, he was so strange and rude last night.'

'Rude?' I said. 'That is unlike him. What did he say?'

She scolded on, without amounting to any sense. He had no heart for suffering; healing was nothing to him, but to serve his pride; he had had some strange teaching, that was sure; he had left her worse, not better, she would be fit for nothing all day. He had better not come near her; yet he should come at least to beg her pardon. And so on. I thought of the beaten maid, and felt sure she was making much of little, but I said I would speak to the lad, when he could be found. At that she started up, and asked where he had gone. This showed me her face more clearly. She seemed feverish, and had lost flesh; but did not look older with it, as women mostly do. With her constant calm all gone, so wild and frail, she brought back to me for the first time since our marriage the wilful girl-child in the Labyrinth, with wet hair tousled on the pillow and tear-swollen eyes.

'He will come home,' I said, 'when he is tired, or hungry. You know what he is. When he does I will rebuke him. Now see a proper doctor who knows the tricks of his trade, and get something to make you sleep.'

Suddenly she clutched my arm, and clung to it weeping. I did not know what to say; but I stroked her hair. 'Oh, Theseus, Theseus!' she sobbed. 'Why did you bring me here from Crete?'

'Only for your own honour. But if it will ease you, you shall go back to Crete again.'

She shook all over, and clung to my arm till I felt her nails. 'No, no! Not now! I cannot leave you, Theseus, don't send me away or I shall die.' She gasped and swallowed and said, 'I am too sick, the sea would kill me.'

'Come, hush,' I said. 'Nothing shall be done that you do not wish. We will talk when you are better.' It was unseemly, with the women there. I went out, and sent for the doctor. But I was told he was with Prince Akamas, who was very ill. They had been looking for me to tell me.

I went to his room, and nearly choked in the doorway; it was full of drug-smelling steam the doctor's servant was making in a cauldron. The firewood smoked, and the slaves coughed as they knelt trying to clear it. I could hardly see the boy, who sat up in bed wheezing and blue, with the doctor blistering his chest. I shouted to them all to get out with their messes, before they stifled him. When I asked him how long he had been sick, he said just since last night, barely getting out the words. 'Well,' I said, 'by the look of you, these fools with their stinks haven't helped you much. I don't know what everyone is about today.' The house seemed full of sickness and megrims; it made me feel old. My mind went back to the years of the Amazon, the swift chariot-ride when I had known what I was for. 'I will find your brother. He can't be far, and he can surely do better than this.'

He shook his head, and tried to say something, but choked upon it. I knew, when the fit was on him, he did not like to be seen. As I got up to go, he reached to catch me back again; I called his old Cretan nurse to him, who had more sense than the rest, and went to seek Hippolytos. When there is sickness, I thought, the doctor should not go missing.

Only his page was in his room, staring at the window; a stocky, simple-looking youth of about fifteen. As soon as he saw me he said, 'I know where he is now, my lord. He went down the Rock.' And then, seeing my face, 'Oh, sir, he is quite safe; I have seen him sitting there.'

'Where?' I said. I was near the end of my patience.

'You can't see from above, my lord, but you can if you climb round under. I thought I would just look. I know most of his places.'

He was not a man of mine, so I said quite quietly, 'Then why not have fetched him?' He looked amazed. 'Oh, I never go after him, sir, unless he tells me first.'

I could see, as one knows when a dog will bite, that if I ordered him he would disobey me. So I asked where was the place. 'In that old cave-mouth, sir, on the western scarp, where the Lady's shrine is.'

It had been built there after the Scythian war, as a thanks for victory. I remembered the dedication, the blood and flowers, the raw stone where the boulders had been closed up again. I had not been there since. It was the last door she had passed through living. But by now I was so sick of people, that I went myself.

The way had grown over, and was nearly as rough as when the cave was opened. I was not quite so supple now as then; once or twice my foot slipped, and gave me a start. But I got down without much trouble.

He was sitting with his back against a rock, staring out to sea. By the look of him, he had not moved for hours. He did not turn till I was almost beside him. I knew his moodiness, from his first years. But I had never seen it work such a change as this. It seemed to have taken even his youth away, all the bloom and the charm. Here was a man, well-made; a face you would call handsome, if the joy of life had been in it, all drawn and sullen with care like a peasant's whose ox has died. I saw that first; a loss, and not knowing, after, which way to turn.

He got to his feet, not even looking surprised to see me. There were deep red prints upon his back, scored by the rock in his long stillness.

I said to him, 'I thought you stayed to look after your brother. He is half-dead, and I have been searching for you all day.'

He started. With a shocked face, striking his hand upon his thigh, he said, 'Holy Mother! I should have known.'

'It would have saved my shoes upon this goat-track. But I suppose you are your own master. Well, if you want to help the boy, you had better hurry. Go on ahead.'

We walked to the path, then stopped. I thought he was put out at being tracked to the shrine, and was making too much of it, whatever had taken him there. He paused, with drawn brows and harried eyes. I expect my impatience showed.

'I doubt,' he said at last, 'if I can help him any longer. Are you sure he asked for me?'

'He is past asking. Nearly past breathing, too. Will you go, or not?'

He stood still, with this shut-in, heavy look, not meeting my eyes. Then he said, 'Very well. I will try, then. But if he doesn't want me, I shall have to leave him be.'

He went straight upward, light as a cat for all his height, taking short cuts on the cliff where his long arm-reach helped him. I followed in my own time, and waited in my room.

He was gone so long, I wondered if he had strayed off again. At last came his voice at the door. But when it opened, Akamas walked in first. He was washed, combed and dressed; he looked worn to a thread, with dark-ringed eyes, but his breathing was quiet again. Hippolytos stood behind, with an arm about his shoulders.

He did not look much better than his patient, to my eye. Neither might have slept for nights.

'Father, I shall have to sail home tomorrow. Can Akamas come with me? I want to take him to Epidauros. We can put him right, there. He will do no good staying here.'

I stared at them. 'Tomorrow? Nonsense. Look at the boy.' I had hardly got over seeing him on his feet again. He cleared his throat, and told me hoarsely that he felt quite well. 'And hear him,' I said.

'It is only one day's sailing.' I knew that look. As well talk to a donkey that will not go.

'Princes cannot scramble off overnight,' I said, 'like cattle-raiders. It will make talk. Come back with all this next week.'

'He ought to go now. You asked me to help him, Father, and this is the only way.' The boy drew closer to his side; remembering however not to lean, lest I should think it weakly.

'What is all this haste?' Everyone seemed bewitched; I could make no sense of it. 'You had no great business yesterday, and there has been no message since. You can wait, I should think, to get off decently, and give your brother some rest.'

'Father, I have to go.' I saw again the driven look he had had upon the rock. 'I must . . . I have had an omen.'

I thought of that night-bird's roost, unsleeping, upon the crag. It made me feel the prickle of the uncannny; I did not like it. I asked him, 'From the Goddess?'

He paused, his mouth set and a deep furrow between his brows. Then he nodded.

I was dog-tired, what with the day's work, the climb and all this turmoil. 'Very well,' I said. 'It is no worse, I daresay, than choking the boy with smoke. And which of you will tell his mother?' They both gazed at me like sick deaf-mutes. 'Neither, of course; it will fall on me.'

I went at once, to have it over. Phaedra was still in bed; the doctor had given her poppy-syrup; but she was awake, looking dully at the door. I began with news which should please her, that Hippolytos was leaving, coming later to the boy. Though I saw that she had stiffened and clenched her hands, she was quiet when I had done, and I slipped away.

My sons sailed next morning. It was raining, and I sent Akamas under cover. Hippolytos said goodbye to me on the poop, a black cloak wrapped round him, his fair hair plastered to his cheek by the wind and rain. Sometimes, at the hunt, I had seen his mother's lie so. She had kept no secrets from me, deeper than a leaf's shadow on a stream. I had known where I was, with her.

At the last he looked at me, as if he would have spoken. This sudden haste had been strange; I had not harmed him, that he should be so close with me. It seemed to me that something strained in his eyes; but he had never been a man for words. The pilot called 'Cast off!' and the rowers' wet backs leaned over. I did not wait to watch them out into the open sea.

20

Autumn set in. I had less to do than in other years, having been at home all summer. The rooms seemed empty; I would come in with something to say which was not stuff for servants; but only servants were there. Amyntor was long dead, in some family bickering not worth his sword. I had learned to keep my own counsel, till these last weeks.

A ship from Troizen brought me a letter from Hippolytos. He said that Akamas was much better, going to the sanctuary only one night in three, to take his physic and sleep. 'So, Father, will you forgive me now for going? It was no wish of mine. No other man can teach me what I was learning from you. And I was happy.'

This letter was carved in wax, on a pair of tablets much worked over, as if it had cost him thought. I put it away, in the chest with his mother's things.

The house was so quiet, one might have hoped for peace. But as soon as her son had gone, Phaedra began to fret over him: first that he would have a seizure, and die without her near; and then, when the news was good, that he would forget her. She seemed always sick, yet the doctors could put no name to it, except this grieving for the boy. I tried to reason with her; was it love, I said, to want him back uncured? These fits could cripple his life, and the kingdom's with it. In a word, it could not be. I feared an outcry; but she said quite meekly, 'You are right, Theseus. Yet I can't rest night nor day, for fear he is in some danger and a god is warning me. Do only this for me: let me go myself to Troizen, to your mother, and stay awhile. I could see the doctors at Epidauros, too. Do let me go; surely it is not too much to ask.'

'It is a good deal,' I said. 'Crete would be well enough; but Troizen will make people think you are being sent out of the way. We can do without such talk.' It was too late now for Crete, the gales had started. I looked about her room: the mess of clothes and jewels hung up or thrown down when she would not choose; the phials and jars and mirrors, the pots of physic everywhere; the warm frowst of women in a closed-up place; and I remembered it long ago, curtains flung wide to the sun, clean polished wood smelling of beeswax and lemon thyme; a bow and a silk cap on the unused bed; a lyre propped against the window-column, and crumbs on the sill for birds.

The place looked hateful to me, spoiled and profaned. I wanted only to be gone; but the sailing months were over. So I said, 'Very well; we will both visit Troizen, and see the boy. Then no one can make mischief of it.'

She offered again to go alone, saying she would not be a burden. 'You will be none,' I answered, 'so long as you keep peace with Hippolytos. He is master of the house already, in all but name, and you will be his guest. Any complaint you have, you must bring to me.'

I sent a courier on over the Isthmus, to announce our coming. But the ways were foul; he fell down a gulley, was nursed by ignorant folk, and did not get his message on till we ourselves had started.

After Akamas' sickness, the priests at Athens had taken omens, and said it was a blood-curse for the Pallantids, killed all those years ago in my father's war. My guess was that the doctors were jealous of Epidauros. But to please everyone, and appease the Gentle Ones if they were really angry, I made it known I was taking my blood-guilt out of Athens, and would come back purified.

It was an autumn journey, tedious and slow. The road was slippery, or blocked with stone-slides from the hills; the leather curtains of the women's litters barely kept out the driving rain. It made me feel stiff, and I feared Phaedra might catch her death crossing the Isthmus; but she bore it cheerfully, ate well, and looked better, though all her women had colds.

We turned off the coast road, to stop at Epidauros. The sheltered valley was like a dish to catch the pelting rain. As the servant towelled me down in the guest-house smelling of pine and resin,

I looked out at the winding glade with its autumn-turning leaves and wet green bay. The sleeping-houses for the sick had their doors shut-to against the weather, the thatch streaming, damp stains on the wooden walls. The yellow beeches dripped and shed their leaves into the stream, whose stones chattered and ground in the whirl from the opened sluices. Pools lay in the grass, with tall seed-heads bending out of them. You will say, a dismal scene. And yet, there was a calm, an ease of soul, a feel of living in time with the seasons and the gods ... I would have liked to send off all my people, only to sit in one of those thatched huts watching the showers drive by, hearing the stream, waiting in no haste for a late sun to dapple the water through the boughs, for the sweet moist earth-scents of evening, the blackbird's whistle, and a wagtail stepping on the grass.

We had come with short warning; but doctors are used to haste. All was prompt and in order. If I had cried, 'Help! I am dying!' I could see it would be much the same. Soon came the Priest-King of the Asklepiads, kindly and brisk, yet with something withdrawn about him, from keeping the secrets of the sick, as the god's vow binds them to do, even from kings. He was younger than I, dressed simply, more priest than king, ready to work with his hands among the sick in the god's service. His kingdom has no need of war, being holy; nor of wealth, for the offerings keep it. When I asked for Akamas, he said the boy was there that day, and well; but it would not be good to wake him after his physic, and bring him through the rain. He spoke very courteously; but he spoke as King. I did not argue; there was too much calm in the place.

Since Phaedra had come so far to see the boy, I feared she would make a fuss; but she said impatiently that since there was nothing to stay for, we had better make haste, and get the journey over.

The rain cleared on the way. The air was soft and fresh; yet I thought at Epidauros it would be sweeter. Looking back from my chariot, at the turning of the road, I could hear far off the votive cocks all crowing; the birds of light, greeting the sun.

We reached the bounds of Troizen at evenfall. The shadow of the wooded mountain drowned the house in gloom; great folded sheets of blood-red light stretched over the sky and dyed the islands;

the sea was a thin pale blue. On the road ahead, gold glittered and burned like torchlight; plumes and manes tossed; above them was a paler shine. It was my son riding to meet me.

We met in twilight. He had come in state; his charioteer held the horses, while he jumped down on foot and came to stand by my wheels, putting his rank aside. His shadowed eyes looked almost black. As he handed me down, I met them: and a darkness touched me, as night's first finger had touched the Palace. This gaze of a warrior armed for a doomed battle; why should it hold compassion? It was a face of fate. And it was as though he had let me glimpse it against his will, like a mortal wound, in some last hope of help from me that he had known must fail.

I was tired from the drive, aching and cold; my mind on a hot bath, mulled wine, and a good warm bed. This strangeness chilled my spirits, the only part of me that had been at ease. I remembered his flight from Athens, the strange vigil before. This came, I thought, from meddling in women's mysteries. No good could come of it, only bad dreams and sick fancies. It was best made light of; and I greeted him briskly, with some joke about the journey.

The dread and sorrow left his face; he smiled, as one might draw a mantle to cover blood, ashamed of having shown it. Then he went over to Phaedra's litter. I saw him bow his head; but she opened her curtains a bare handsbreadth when she answered. I was displeased; she owed better manners, both to King Pittheus' heir and to my son. A bad beginning.

21

The pebble moves upon the mountain, shifted by a goat's foot or the scour of rain. For a while it tumbles and rolls, and a child's hand could stop it. But soon it takes great bounds, swift as a slingshot; at last it leaps out from the crag like Apollo's arrow, and can pierce through a war-helm into the skull of a man.

So swiftly came the end. Or it seems so now. Yet time passed at Troizen, days passed, there was time even for the year to move. Mists hung in the mountain oak-woods, and blew away; the drifted oak-leaves lay ankle-deep and crisp, warning the deer of the hunter; rain fell upon the drifts and they turned to leaf-pads, which clung to the earth, dark as old hides, smelling of smoke.

As some ancient ship settles evenly in a dead calm, so it was with Pittheus. His eyes had turned milk-white now, and saw only moving shadows; and his mind was much the same. He liked to have my mother by him; but half the time he took her for some long-dead handmaid he had carried off in war when he was young. He would tell her to sing, and to please him she asked all the old folk what songs this girl had known; but no one remembered even her name. It was sixty years since a king had died in Troizen; when we came to bury him, there would be no one living to tell us what the custom had been before. It must be this great life ending, I thought, which made the very light seem strange, as it is before the thunder, when far isles look near and clear.

My mother was all day in his upper room, coming out only for the household business, or the rites, or else to rest. So she did not watch us; and if she saw death-omens in the spinning of spiders or the cry of birds, that was nothing strange.

Akamas had come back from Epidauros, but still slept in the grove one night in three, the priests saying they could not get omens yet to pronounce him cured. The place seemed to have sobered him; from his quiet he might have been a priest himself. All his time indoors he spent with one of the Palace craftsmen, making a lyre; he had been told to do this, as an offering to Apollo. But whenever he could get his brother to take him along, he followed him like a shadow. I could see Phaedra did not like to see them slipping off. But what could I tell the boy? 'Hippolytos is four years your elder: years of the Amazon, when your mother, daughter of Minos and a thousand years of kings, waited in Crete till I had time to spare'? At his age, he might have seen it for himself.

Once I said to him, 'You ought to spend more time with your mother; she came all this way in the bad season for your sake.' He seemed to shrink into himself; then said quite steadily, 'She doesn't mind, sir; she knows I'm better now.' For a moment it might have been a grown man speaking, used to keeping his own counsel. But it was true enough she never asked for him, once he was out of sight.

From decency more than choice, I had brought no handmaid with me. It was high time in any case that our marriage was put in order. But at night there was always something; faintings, headaches, unlucky signs, or the moon. The time was long past when I would have turned her women from the room and had it out with her. But she had never been unwilling, until this year. I was not yet fifty, and no woman could ever say I had disappointed her; yet now I began to think, 'Am I getting old?' The mists of autumn damped my spirits; I grew restless, mewed indoors, kept even from hunting by the rain. I made up my mind to go back to Athens, leaving Phaedra behind; but on that same evening, there was a new pretty girl among the homely bath-women; the battle-prize of some house baron lately dead. It was clear her tears would never disturb his shade. King Pittheus, she said, bringing out her lesson pat, had sent her to wait on me. I had seen him that day; he hardly knew night from morning. This shy gift came from my son.

He is a good lad, I thought, and means well to me. Yet it seemed odd, unlike him. Though I kept the girl, who pleased me, yet it nagged my pride, to think it was common talk that I slept alone. I said nothing, thinking like him that it would not be seemly. For that matter, we seldom talked much now. The moodiness I had seen at meeting him had not lifted, but grown. It was more than his old day-dreams; something was wrong; the lad was brooding; I should have said he was sick, if I had not seen him climbing the crags like a mountain lion. The closed drawn look he had had in Athens at the shrine, was seldom off him now. He was losing flesh; in the morning his eyes were heavy; he would be gone by the day together, no one knew where. Hearing him asked for, I found he was neglecting even the kingdom's business; fixing times for it, forgetting and going away. Often from the walls I would see along the Epidauros road his chariot going as if it raced for a prize; he would come back mud-splashed from head to heel, plunged in deep thought, barely coming out of it to smile and greet me. Or he would be gone on foot; I would glimpse his bright hair on the path that led to Zeus' oak-wood, and beyond. My mind's eye followed him, past the rock with the eye of stone. What did he seek, what omen? Would he have more welcome there than I?

One day his slow young page came up to me, asking awkwardly if I had seen him; he had a note for him from the Queen. When I offered to see it he gave it me quite easily. Perhaps he was simple; perhaps less simple than he seemed.

The tablet said, 'Theseus misses you; do you forget he is your guest? Of myself, no matter. You offend and slight him. What is it that you fear?'

I told the page I would see to it, and went straight to her room. When I had her alone, I said to her, 'What is this? What have you been up to with Hippolytos? Is this your promise?'

I finished more quietly than I began, for I could see she was not well. She had sunk back, with her hand clasped to her throat. She had been full of vapours lately; yet she had refused to go to Epidauros, after all.

'Come, calm yourself,' I said. 'I am to blame; I should have known you two would never agree. Why, we both know; but what use to speak of it? What's done is done; but it was long ago, and she is dead. You came here to see Akamas; you know now he is well. Any day the old man may die; I will not have strife brought into the house, when my son is taking up his heritage.

Two days from now I am going back to Athens. You will come with me.'

She stared a moment; then she started to laugh. It was low at first; then it rose wild and screeching, peal on peal. I called her women, and left her. I knew, when I married her, that she came of old rotten stock, given to all extremes. But I had to think of the kingdom.

Hippolytos was out, as usual. It was not till dusk he came plodding home, limb-weary as a field hand, his clothes stained from the forests, green and brown. He greeted me with courtesy, which did not make up for his neglect; yet, remembering he had borne patiently, for my sake, his stepmother's scoldings, I told him without anger that we were going home.

He began to say something; stammered and broke off; then knelt and put my hand to his forehead. He was down there so long, that I told him to get up. Slowly he rose. His eyes were streaming. He stood still, taking deep breaths, while great silent tears ran down his cheeks. At last he muttered, 'I am sorry, Father. I don't know what it is . . . I am sorry you are going.' His voice choked and he said, 'Forgive me,' and hurried out. Turning I saw young Akamas, who had hung about for him (often lately he had shaken off the boy to go about alone), stare after him in horror, and run out another way. He thought too much of him, not to be ashamed at seeing him unmanned.

The day passed, and the night, and the next morning. I don't know how I spent the time, the memory has been swept away. But a little before noon, I went out to the stables, to see what shape the horses were in for the journey. The rain held off; but grey clouds covered the sky and the breeze was moist, blowing from the sea.

Suddenly I heard a woman's high yelling scream. For a moment, I only felt it go through my head; I had not noticed till then an ache beginning. Then the sound broke into shrill jerking spurts, as if the woman herself were shaking, and I thought, 'Her husband is knocking her about.' Then came a great shriek, 'A rape! A rape!' And I knew the voice. The eyes of my charioteer met mine. Like one man we started forward.

He unhitched two horses and we leaped up. The cries came

from the olive grove beyond the barns. It was sacred to Mother Dia, with a little altar where my mother used to sacrifice in spring, to bless the trees. We rode as near as we dared to the sacred precinct, dismounted and ran.

Between the trees, not far from the Altar-stone, sat Phaedra on the ground, wailing and sobbing, flinging her body to and fro, beating her clenched fists first on the earth and then upon her breast. Her hair hung wild, her bodice and skirt gaped open at every clasp; her shoulders and arms and throat were covered in great red finger-weals, whose shape could be clearly seen.

I ran up to her. She clutched and pawed at my arms, gabbling and gasping; I could not make out the words. When I tried to raise her, her clothes began falling off; she pulled away her hands to grab her belt about her, her breath heaving and shivering; then scrambled up, her skirt bunched in one hand, and pointed with the other through the grove. Her voice broke in a rough caw like a raven's. 'There! There!'

I heard men's voices, running footsteps, rattling arms. The outcry had brought the Guard. They were still coming up; but the foremost had heard her words and were off through the trees already, like hounds with the quarry in full sight. They called to one another; then their voices changed. And looking along the grove, I saw the man.

He was running out to the hill-slopes, clambering over the boulders, wild as a stag. The light caught his hair as the sea-wind lifted it. In all Troizen, there was not such another head.

I stood still. A great sickness swept down from my head into my body. There seemed room in me for nothing else.

All round me went the din of the hue-and-cry. My temples throbbed with it. Only the foremost understood, yet, whom they were after. But when the word spread back, they would all run on. There are laws bred into the very bones of men, older on earth than princes.

I sent someone to fetch the Queen's women. To the rest I said, 'Stand back. Leave us alone.'

She had fixed her skirt-clasp somehow. Now she stood wringing her hands, round and round each other, as if she were washing and could not get them clean. 'Quickly!' I said. 'No one can hear. In the name of Zeus, what happened? Speak.'

She stood panting; with each breath came a rattle from her chattering teeth, and nothing more. Still I kept hold of myself, from the habit of doing justice. 'Speak up, hurry, before they bring him here.' But she only rocked about, washing her hands. A sudden hot light flashed before my eyes; I came and stood over her and shouted, 'Speak, woman! Did he get it done, or not?'

'Yes!' she cried, and left her mouth open, gaping. I thought she would scream again; but now at last came the words.

'In Athens it began, he started then to come after me, but he said it was to cure my head, in Athens I didn't know. It was here he told me, here in Troizen; I have been almost dead with fear. I dared not tell you, how could I tell you of your son, what he was, what he meant? He wanted me, oh yes! But it was more, it was more. This is the truth, Theseus. He has taken a vow to the Goddess, to bring back her rule again.'

We were alone in the grove, beside the ancient altar. The men I had sent away had followed after the chase. Great hands seemed to press my head, crushing it down into the earth.

'He said he had omens, that he must marry Minos' daughter and make her Goddess-on-Earth. Then the power would return and we should rule the world. I swear it, Theseus, I swear by this holy stone.' A great shiver shook her body. '"Let me reign with you," he said, "and love you; and when She calls me, it will be nothing for me to die. For we shall be as gods, remembered for ever." That is what he said.'

The sounds of pursuit had sunk. The crowd was coming back towards the grove. He must have stopped to wait for them. 'Not yet!' I thought. 'Can't they give me time?' My brow felt bursting. I longed to be alone as a wounded man wants water. But her voice rushed on.

'I said to him, "Oh, how can you say so when your father lives?" and he answered, "He is under Her curse and the land is sick with it. She calls men and sets them by, and he has had his time."'

Through the beating in my head I heard men's low muttering voices, broken with their heavy breathing from the run. He was walking among them, free, looking straight before him, like a man led to his death.

The women had come up from the Palace. They hovered among the trees, like scared birds, flustered and twittering, each urging another forward, exclaiming in whispers at her bruises and torn clothes. Suddenly she grabbed my arm again. 'Don't kill him, Theseus, don't kill him! He could not help it, he was mad as the maenads are.'

I thought of Naxos; of the bloody hands, torn flesh; the sleeping girl draggled with blood and wine. Blood seemed everywhere; it was the colour of the buzzing sky. 'It is like the earthquake warning,' I thought, and then the thought passed by. Her hands on my arm were like her sister's hands. I pulled them off, and signed for the women. The squat old altar looked at me, each crack in the stone a grinning mouth and every hole an eye.

They were here. He stood before me. His hair was all dishevelled; there was a bleeding place, where it had been torn. His tunic was split along the shoulder. His eyes met mine. So a stag will stand when you have it run down and it can go no longer, looking at you as if it saw some vision, waiting for the spear.

The women crept up to Phaedra; one wrapped her in a cloak, another held a flask to her lips; they waited my leave to take her away. Her bruises were darkening; she might have been a beaten slave. The sickness, the noises in my head, were making me almost mad; I found my hand on my dagger. There was a scream of birds, above the birdlike cries of the women, a lowing of cattle from the byres, a dog's longdrawn howl. They were the sounds of earth; all this was true. I pointed to my wife, huddled shivering into the cloak, and said to my son, 'Did you do this?'

He did not speak. But he turned his eyes to her. It was a long, dark look. She covered her face and broke into wailing, muffled by the cloth. I signed to the women; they led her off, murmuring, through the trees.

His eyes met mine; and at that his face closed up, his mouth set like a seal. All this while, as the horror in me mounted and turned to rage, some hope had held out, like the watchman of a

doomed city alone upon the wall. No signal came; there would be
no message. Now all my life's enemies met in him.

I spoke. But the words have gone from me. Not long after, I
was taken sick; and when I came to myself, the words had gone.
Yet sometimes I wake, with the sound just fading. Somewhere
within me are the words; and I have a fear to sleep, lest my sleep
release them.

So clear seemed his guilt, like far hills before the storm: how he
had watched at the shrine, and told me of an omen; had taken
Akamas to Troizen, to make her follow; given me a woman, to
keep me from her; and fled my presence day after day, lest I should
read his thoughts. He had wept, to hear she was going. Today had
been his last chance. It seemed as clear as if a god had shouted it
in my ear. Indeed my ears were ringing.

As I spoke these words I have forgotten, the men about him all
drew aside. He was not King of Troizen yet, and now would never
be. He had broken the sacred hearth-laws; ravished his father's wife;
and I was not his father only, nor his guest, but High King of Attica,
Megara, and Eleusis, guardian of Thebes and Lord of Crete. How
could they dare to choose my enemy?

He stood and heard me. Not once did he part his lips to answer.
But near the end, I saw his hands clench at his sides, his nostrils
widen, his eyes stare as one sees them in battle above a shield. He
took one step forward, and set his teeth, and stepped back again;
and I read in his face, as clear as words on marble, 'Some god hold
me back, before I take this little man and break him between my
hands.' Then, if I could, I would have struck him dead.

The anger that rose in me seemed the wrath of the earth itself.
It flowed up through my feet, as the earthfire rises in some burning
mountain before it destroys the land. And then, as if my mind had
been lit with flame, I knew that it was true. It was not my anger
only. The dog had howled and the birds had cried, and my head
had tightened; yet I had not felt Poseidon's warning, because my
anger had risen in time with his. Now I felt it, and felt it soon to fall;
the god my father standing by me, to avenge my bitter wrong.

It was like a thunderbolt in my hand. They were all looking at
me in fear, as if at something more than mortal; yes, he also. And in

the strength of the god I stuck my foot upon the earth, crying, 'Go out of my lands and from my sight for ever. Go with my curse, and the curse of Earth-Shaking Poseidon; and beware of his wrath, for it will be soon!'

One moment he was there, white-faced, standing like stone; the next there was an empty place, and the people staring after him. They stood and gazed; but no one followed, as they would have followed some other man, to stone him out of the land. They had loved him; I suppose it seemed to them his madness and his doom were sent from heaven, and they had best leave him to the gods. He was gone; and as rage like a fever started to cool in me, I felt the earthquake sickness, just as it had always been.

I closed my aching eyes. A picture flashed behind them, as if it had been waiting there; the groves of Epidauros, drenched with peace and rain. Then I, being priest as well as king, remembered how all my life, since I was a child at Poseidon's sanctuary, I had held his warning as a trust to save the people, and never used it for a curse.

I woke to myself, and looked about me, and said to the folk of Troizen, 'I have had the sign of Poseidon. He will shake the earth, and soon. Warn them in all the houses, to come out of doors. Send word to the Palace.'

They groaned with awe, and started to run off; soon I heard heralds' horns. Then no one was left about me, but men of my own from Athens, standing uncertainly a little way off, fearing to come or go. I was alone, hearing the noise of the alarm spreading all the way down to Troizen from the Citadel; and with it another sound, the triple hoof-beat of a chariot team on the road below. It made me shudder, with the wrath of the god so near. That was how I heard it first, a wicked beating upon the earth, going through my head. Then I remembered. I had given out my warning to every soul in Troizen. Only for him I had wrapped it up in darkness, that hearing he might not understand.

I stood on the prickling earth, my heart still pounding from my own anger and the god's. The Palace was like a skep of bees when a horse has kicked it; women running out with babies, pots and bundles, and stewards with precious things. There was a stir in the great doors; they were bringing out old Pittheus in a curtained litter. I looked beyond. Far down the road, the bright head vanished in the footslopes towards the Psiphian shore. The fastest team in Troizen, following, would not overtake him now.

The fear of the earthquake was working in me, cold and sinking, as I had known it since a child, overshadowing all the rest; man's greatest wrath is like the stamp of a child's foot, beside the gods'. Old habit gave me the feel of it; not so bad as some that I had known, at least, not here; for it seemed this was the fringe of it, the centre further off. Turning about, as a dog does for the scent, I felt my neck-hairs rise when I faced the sea.

The waters of the straits were as still as molten lead. On the windless air, I heard horses screaming and whinnying, as the grooms led them from the stables into the field. Then through their noise I heard a voice quite near me, labouring and hoarse, say, 'King Theseus! Sir!'

A big warrior, the Palace wrestler who taught the youths, was ploughing up through the grove towards me, with a burden in his arms. When I turned, he laid it down upon the ground. It was Akamas. He thrust off the man, who was trying to prop his head, and leaned back on his elbows, fighting for breath, his body arched like a bow, jerking and gasping. The man said to me, 'He would come, sir. I found him down there; he had been trying to run and fallen. Sir, he keeps saying he must see you before he dies.'

The boy rose on one hand, and stretched the other out to me, beckoning me near. His face was white about the mouth, which was almost blue. On a great hiss of breath he said, '*Father*!' and clutched his chest with both hands, as if he would tear it open to let in air. His eyes were fixed on mine; charged not with terror, but with speech.

I went and bent over him, the son that I had left. 'Can it be,' I thought, 'that the god's sign has come down to him, and he lacks the strength to bear it? Yet it proves him my true son, this one at least.' I said to him, 'Hold on, lad, it will be over before long, and the fear will pass.'

He shook his head, and made a harsh sound in his throat, cut off by choking. His face filled with blood, like a hanged man's; then he snatched at a breath, and cried out his brother's name.

'No more!' I said. 'You are sick, and you know nothing. Rest, and be silent.' His chest worked up and down, labouring with words. 'Be still. Later you will understand.' Tears of pain and struggle had filled his eyes; half out of my mind as I was, I pitied him. 'Hush!' I said. 'He has gone away.'

Such a spasm seized him, that it took my mind from the earthquake; it seemed he would never breathe again. He was almost black, when he hurled from his knees up to his feet, and flung his arms at the sky. His breath crowed in his throat and he cried aloud, 'Paian Apollo!' He stood there, swaying; then turned to the man who had carried him, and said hoarsely but quite steadily, 'Thank you, Sirios. You can go.'

The man looked at me, and at my nod went off. I helped the boy down again and knelt beside him. Before ever he spoke, some shadow brushed me with cold. But I said to myself it was the coming earthquake.

'Now quiet,' I said. 'Or it will start again.'

'I can die. I was afraid before.' He nursed this rough flat voice, easing it along like a dead-beat horse. He was very weak. 'I can die if I tell you first. Hippolytos . . . what you cursed him for . . . it isn't true.'

'Hush, that is finished. It is for the gods to judge.'

'Let them hear me! Let them choke me if I lie!' His eyes opened and he caught his breath; then he drew it clear. But he whispered after, to save his strength. So robbers must look, white-faced and whispering, who creep into a royal tomb. 'He said no. *She* asked him, *she* . . .' His working fingers dug into the ground. '. . . in Athens,' he said. 'I *heard*.'

I stared before me, knowing the wound was mortal; soon I would begin bleeding, soon would come the pain. The boy reached for my hand, and took it, though it was little thought I had for him. Only a god can guess what he must have suffered; and he a Cretan, for whom the mother is god on earth.

His hushed, thief's voice ran on. 'I nearly died then. I hated him too, because of what he called her. But he said to me after, "I was wrong to be angry. She trusted me." He came to me the next day, when I was sick, to say that he was sorry. "Don't be afraid, Akamas," he said. "I won't tell Father, or anyone else on earth. I'd swear it to you, but an oath to a god is greater. I gave her the pledge of Asklepios, which binds a man till death."'

I lacked even the strength to say to him, 'It is enough.'

'You see,' he said, 'it was the secret of her sickness. So he had to keep it.'

The sight of the woman rose before me. Bruised like a slave; a slave's terror too, and a slave's lies. If her tale had been true, she would have scratched his face, or bitten him. His torn tunic and dragged-out hair – he had been pulled at, not thrust away. Those weals upon her shoulders and her throat were the marks not of his lust, but of his anger, the rage of the lion who sees the bars of the trap on every side. When she screamed, he had shaken her in blind fury, forgetting his own strength. I out of all men, how could I not have known?

'He said to me' – the boy's voice was getting stronger – '"We will go together, and be the guests of Apollo. All evil is a sickness, and his music heals it. At Epidauros, everything will be well."'

I stood up. My brows were dizzy, my feet were tingling. The flat oily sea made me sicker than any storm. I looked along the road to Epidauros, the road that ran by the shore.

'Father, it is true, I swear, I swear! If I lie may Apollo shoot me dead! It is true! Quick, Father, and stop the earthquake!'

Horror crept over me. I cried aloud to him, 'I am not a god!' but his dark eyes, fixed on mine, seemed more than his own. He had challenged death, offering his fear in sacrifice; and the holiness had not brushed off him yet. The god in him had cried to the god in me; but there was no god to answer, only the feel of a sickness in the ground.

I said, 'Stay here, where you are. I will go and find him.'

I ran off down the olive-slope, calling to my men, who came pounding after, grim-faced with fright. Over my shoulder, I saw the old wrestler plodding back to the boy. He was sitting quietly. What inward fetter broke in him that day I do not know; but from that time on the fits grew short and mild, and now he has reached manhood, they are gone.

Down on the horse-field they had picketed the chariot-teams, lest they should bolt when the earth shook. Most of them were squealing and plunging on their hobbles; I picked out a quiet pair, and shouted for a racing chariot. It was the first time I had raised my voice with an earthquake coming, since I was a child.

As I urged them down to the shore, I felt neither fear nor awe, only a strangeness, like high fever. The horses felt it in me; they dashed along hardly needing the whip, as if they wanted to get away from the man behind them. So too did I.

There is time, I thought, there is still time. He had been gone, how long? As long as it takes to string a lyre and tune it; to row a ship out of harbour; to drive a few turns round the track? And then I thought, 'How soon?'

As I laboured over the soggy mudflats, I thought of the slave-girl he had sent me, lest quarrelling with Phaedra I might learn the truth. He had feared for me, and for his brother; the truth of his own danger he had only seen too late. He had not the mind that foreknows such things.

The road climbed again; far off between two cypress-clumps I glimpsed his chariot. As I looked, it slowed to a walk. He has seen me, I thought; he is waiting; all is saved. I waved, to catch his eye. But he had only paused to breathe his team; he was off again. He had all three of his horses; after all, he was going away for good. As they started up, I saw they were getting restive. Next moment he was out of sight.

The road was good; it had not rained for three days. I whipped up my team; but there was a change. Though they had not felt it in the horse-field, they felt it now. They checked and plunged; one reared up screaming; I had all I could do to hold them. As I stood leaning back against the reins, over the tossing heads I saw the bay below. And it had moved away. Even as I watched, the waters crept out further, showing the sea-floor no living man has seen, all weed and rotting boat-hulls. And still they sank, as if some great mouth below were swallowing them in.

I knew what the horses knew. The chariot turned, a beast with three heads filled with one fear. We charged off the road and up into the farmland, ploughing across the new-sown fields, breaking the water-channels, crashing through young vines. The farmer's wife and all his children, hearing the din, ran shouting out of doors. The god was their friend. He sent them me for a blessing. Who can trace the pathways of the Immortals?

The horses bolted on, past the vines into untilled scrub; the wheels leaped and lurched over clods and stones. I had hitched the reins about me, but only with one turn, for fear of something like this. As the brush slowed them, I loosed myself and jumped clear. I fell and rolled, and got up shaken and bruised, shuddering from the touch of earth. All the cattle in the byres were lowing and bawling. A he-goat with wicked eyes opened his mouth in a wild cry. And with that came the earthquake.

The ground jolted and jarred; there was a rumble of stones as the farm fell down in rubble. I heard the wife wail, the man shout out to her, hoarse with terror, from the fields. The children began to scream and the dogs to howl. The earthquake sickness cleared from my head and belly. 'It is over,' I thought. 'Then why do I feel this fear?'

A hare raced past me, almost brushing my leg, taking great bounds uphill. And then I saw the water coming.

The bay was filling again; not slyly, as it had emptied, but in a great rushing wave, climbing the shores. It washed right over the Psiphia mole, lifting the fishing-boats upon it like toys on a child's string. Right over the chariot-road below me ran the salt sea, and climbed the ploughland; spent itself, and paused, and went sucking back from the scoured land. There was a hush like death; and in this quiet, before all the outcries began again, I heard from northward along the road the squeal of furious horses, mixed with the great bellow of a bull.

I did not ask, 'What is it?' It was the voice of my fear.

Rising above the din, like the war-cry of a king above the battle, I heard a shout I would have known among the shouts of a thousand men. It ceased, broken half-way. The wild neighing rose, and stopped, and rose again. My own pair, caught in the traces round the foundered chariot, whinnied in dread.

I ran to them, dragging at the milling tangle, shouting for someone to give a hand. The farm people went on scrabbling in their ruins; after the god's passing, they had no ear for kings. I cut loose with my dagger the horse that was not lame, and knotted the reins together. He could carry my weight that far.

There was nothing left you could call a road. It was all slime and flotsam, channels and slides of stones. The horse had been broke to draw; he slithered and pecked and stumbled, and I dared not press him. I myself could have run faster, a few years ago.

The mud had dying fish in it, flapping and squirming. There was a hissing by the road; the horse shied, and nearly threw me; a great dolphin, whistling through his blowhole, was trying to thrash towards the sea. The road climbed, for the slope grows steep there; it would soon be above the flood-line; yet still I heard horses crying, from where they had cried before, pausing sometimes as a trapped beast will pause from weariness, before it begins again. The bull bellowed once more, a sound of rage, or anguish. Struggling with my mount, which was getting scared again, I listened for another voice. But no voice called.

At the top of the rise, the road bent round. Then I saw, and got off the horse and ran.

Less than a bowshot off, on the shore below the road, a bloody mass of snared beasts struggled and heaved; three mangled horses, lashing and lunging. Above, blocking the road they had crashed down from, stood a bull, head down. He bellowed with fear and anger, and lurched, trying to paw the ground; lamed in a foreleg by the floodwave that had swept him from his broken pen. Here he had struggled back to land, coated with weed and slime; a black bull of Poseidon, a bull from the sea.

There were men down there. As I ran, they were among the horses, killing them with cleavers. One after another gave a last choked scream. Scarlet blood drenched everything; the struggling ceased. The men clustered, bending, over something beyond.

They had cut him loose from the reins, when I got down there, and were pulling out the splinters of the chariot that had gone through his flesh like spears. He lay in ruin, like the horses; a splendid creature broken everywhere, torn and muddied, flayed on the rocks and sand. But the beasts were quiet; dead meat, out of their pain; while he groaned and moved. In his blood-wet face his eyes were open, and looked in mine.

The men called out to me, telling me who he was. They took me for some passing wayfarer, seeing me on foot, miry and bruised; and shouted the news at me altogether, as shocked men do. They had been working in the fields above; their farm had stood through the shock, and they had watched it all. They told how his horses had bolted at the earthquake, yet somehow he had got them in hand. But the water had come up, with the bull upon it, floundering out clear in the way. And then . . . they pointed to the hacked off reins, still lashed round his middle in the double-hitch of the charioteer.

He put one hand to the ground, and tried to lift himself, and sank back with a cry; his back was broken. Someone said, 'He is gone'; but his eyes opened again. Two of the men were arguing what farm the bull had come from, and who had the right to keep it now; another said it should be offered to Poseidon, or he would be angry and strike again. But the man who had cut the reins away said to me, 'Look, friend; bad news is always best brought by a stranger. Will you go up to Troizen, and tell the King?'

I said, 'I am Theseus. I am his father.'

They stared gaping, and knuckling their brows; they could not keep their eyes from running over me, a dirty unkempt man, haggard and stammering, whose face they had scarcely glanced at, one of themselves. I sent them to fetch a hurdle; one offered me his garment to stop the blood with; then we two were alone.

He was bleeding from a dozen wounds, and from within. I knew he was past all help; yet I would not know it, and bent above him doing useless things. As I worked I spoke, telling him I knew everything, begging him for a sign. His eyes were empty. But after a while they changed; and his lips moved. He spoke to me. He did not know me; but dying men are glad of company. He said, 'Not even the gods are just!'

He was quiet a long time then. I laid my hand on his head, and kissed him, and tried again to be understood. I could not tell if he heard. For a moment his eyes half-wakened; they stared straight upward, in a bitter loneliness; then they grew blank again. His blood soaked through the rags and his face grew whiter. At last came the men with the hurdle. As we shifted him on to it he cried aloud; but there was no telling if his mind was clear. I helped them carry him till two more men came; they had been killing the bull, since they could not move it. We got him up to the road, and the men said, 'Shall we take him to the house, sir? Or on to Troizen?'

I heard a breath from him. His hand moved. I touched it and said, 'No. To Epidauros.' Then his fingers closed on mine.

The clouds had parted. Over the sea they still looked dark; but there was a patch of blue above the mountain. All the birds were singing, loudly, as they do after an earthquake, claiming their boundaries, or glad to be alive. Someone had gone ahead to get more bearers; he was too heavy for one set to carry far. He was still, and I hoped that he felt nothing; but when the litter jolted once, I saw his teeth clench with pain.

The men were tired, and the others had not come yet. There was a clump of plane-trees by the road, and a trickle of water, a little winter stream. The ground was flat there; and I said to the bearers, 'Rest awhile.'

One of them had his bronze cup tied in his belt; he filled it from the stream, and I moistened the boy's mouth, for his lips were dry. His eyes had been shut; but now he opened them and looked upward, where the branches stood against the blue, with a few golden leaves. His hand touched my wrist and he whispered, 'Listen!'

There was a lark above. A little tinkle came from the stream. And up the hill was a herd-boy piping, who, when the earthquake struck, had had no more to lose than the birds.

'Listen,' he murmured, smiling. 'Epidauros!'

I looked at him. It was clear by now he would never get there alive; so I answered, 'Yes.'

He shut his eyes again. His breathing was so quiet that I could not hear it, and thought it was the end. The men withdrew a little way; and I knelt beside him, covering my face. Then he said, 'Father.'

'Yes?' I leaned down; I could tell, from the way he forced it out, he knew that he was going. 'Forgive me your blood,'

I said. 'Though the gods will not, nor I myself, yet do you forgive it.'

'Father,' he murmured, 'I am sorry I was angry. All this had to be. Because . . .' He looked at me, to say he had not the strength to finish, begging my pardon. I saw that his eyes were going blind. His head rolled back, facing the blue sky; like the sky it grew calm and clear. 'I have had a true dream,' he said. 'I shall die a well man now.' His fingers pressed my hand; so cold, it was as if he spoke to me from beyond the River. 'Father . . . offer Asklepios a cock for me . . . do not forget.'

I said, 'I will remember. Is there anything else?'

He made no answer. Soon his lips parted; his soul went forth in a sigh, and I closed his eyes.

Presently came some of the doctor-priests from Epidauros, who had heard the news. They brought on his body to the sanctuary, though, as everyone knows, it is unlawful for a corpse to lie there. They said they could not be sure that he was dead; talking across me with their eyes, as doctors do. He was very dear to them. Even when his corpse was growing cold, they warmed him and would not own it; and I have been told that, all their arts having failed, they turned to some old magic of the Shore Folk, which their law forbade them, and which had not been practised for a hundred years. The Priest-King died soon after, suddenly, struck down as he worked, the swift death of Apollo; and it was said that the god was angry with him, for trying to raise the dead.

I cannot tell; for I went away leaving the body with them. I knew that he was dead, and no god would raise him. For me there was work in Troizen waiting.

The wailing of women met me; by this time, the news had been pieced together, and all was known. My mother was leading them, weeping out his praises as the words came to her, which later she would shape into the funeral chant. She broke off her crying to come and meet me. The rest all covered their eyes with their hair.

She had nothing to say, having foreseen the curse so long before; so she embraced me with the common words of any mother. I kissed her – for he had been like her youngest son – and said we would talk later. Then I asked for my wife.

'The women were angry,' my mother answered. 'I warned her of it; not for her sake, but for fear of something unseemly. I suppose she is in her room.'

I went up through the empty Palace. Those who saw me far off turned quickly out of my way; but there were few to see. An old servant, whom I ran into at a corner, told me that King Pittheus was sleeping; no one had dared yet to bring him the news. I paused for a moment; but I had already enough to do. Better he had died yesterday. But they say that the end of man's life is sorrow.

As I climbed the stairs, I thought of the tale I had heard from Phaedra, how Hippolytos had sworn to bring back the Old Religion, what he had said. A long tale, for a woman to remember who has just been ravished in the fields. And yet, a long one to make up in a moment, even under the spur of fear. I saw it now. Well she might remember, every word! Many a night she must have lain with these words in mind, trying them this way and that, getting them perfect, as harpers do; getting them ready. They had been her words to him.

I came to her room, and knocked at the outer door. None answered. I went into mine, and tried the door between. That was locked too. I called to her to open; silence still. I listened, and felt that the silence breathed. The outer door was strong, but this one was light. It did not take long to force it.

The room was empty. Then I looked again, and saw a shudder in a press of clothes. I dragged at them, and pulled her out. She cringed and crawled about me, clasping my knees, snivelling and praying. Like a slave, I thought; like a lying slave; the daughter of a thousand years of kings. Her throat was still marked from his fingers. I took her by it, to push her off me. Till I saw her eyes, and their expectation, I don't think I knew what I meant to do. But she showed me her own deserving.

She died hard. When I thought it was long over, and let her go, she started to move again. At last I let her fall; she lay still then, one bundle more in the tumble of clothes from the press, which smelt of Crete.

And then I thought, 'Will her lies live after her? There are always men glad to think the worst of the best. She should have been made to bear witness first before the people. I have failed him once again.'

Then I said aloud, 'By Zeus, she shall speak for him, even now! She shall make good my son's honour, living or dead.'

There was ink and paper in the room. I can write the Cretan hand; I wrote it small, like a woman. Here in Troizen, that would be enough.

'I slandered Hippolytos, to cover my own shame. I asked and he refused. I can bear my life no longer.'

This letter I bound into her hand, with a ribbon from among the clothes. As I did it, I saw that the inner curve of her arm was white and tender, her breast round, firm and fair. I remembered his heavy eyes at morning, his day-long wanderings, coming home dead tired. Had he been tempted? What if he had; it is the hard fight earns the garland. Well, he was avenged.

I made a noose from a girdle, and tied it to a sheet knotted round a beam. When she was hanging, I overturned the chair that I had stood on, under her feet. Then I went down, to show the broken door and what I had found behind it.

All over Troizen, his name is held in honour. It is growing holy; each year the maidens offer at his tomb, and clip their hair. I did for him what I could. Maybe it was not what he would have asked for, if he could have spoken. But a man can only give what he has, being what he is.

22

These things all stand as clear in my mind as yesterday. It is yesterday that I forget.

Was it after one summer, or two, or three, that the god's hand struck me? I know I was at sea with Pirithoos (for a man must be somewhere, while he walks under the sun) and seeing Melian pirates sailing hull-down with loot, we bore down on them to take the prize. I remember, I think, the sight of them nearing. Then I felt giddy, and my eyes went black; and when I opened them, it was night. I was on a pallet, in a peasant's house; there were women chattering, and two of my men leaning over me, calling the rest to witness that they had said I was alive, and look! my eyes were open.

They all asked me how I did. But when I tried to answer, the half of my mouth felt numb, and my speech slurred like a drunkard's; and when I moved, only my right hand answered me. I reached the right hand over, to feel the left; the right seemed to touch the hand of a corpse, and the left felt nothing.

My men told me that before the ships engaged, as I gave the war-cry, I had fallen down like the dead. It was too late to avoid the battle. It had been bitter, with so many killed that in the end neither had claimed the victory, but the ships that were left had limped away. When I asked after Pirithoos, they said his ship had been rammed, and sunk with all hands. This I heard, as one hears things without meaning.

All that were left of my crew were here in the hut with me, a scant dozen. The rest were killed or drowned. They had been laying my body out, to wrap it up and bring it home for burial, and had begun to fold the sail about me, when they saw I was still alive. When they sought for my wound they could find nothing; I had fallen, they said, before the weapons began to fly.

The peasant women spooned milk into my mouth and wiped my face. Then I told them all to go, and lay for a long while, thinking.

Perhaps it was the Mother who had struck me down. I had stolen two of her daughters out of her shrines, and tamed her worship at Eleusis. All those who follow the Old Religion, or fear it still, say that it was the Mother. Or it may have been Apollo; for I was struck without pain, as men are killed by his gentle arrows; and as I was only half to blame for his good servant's death, he left me half alive. But I have come to think it was Poseidon Earth-Shaker, because I turned his blessing into a curse. I think so; and I have good cause.

I felt no pain in my body, and little yet in my mind. At first, I scarcely reproached the gods that I was not dead. Yet I, who had forgotten, or ceased to care, that I was a man no longer, remembered I was a king. Often I had said to myself that I ought not to die before my heir reached manhood. I had gone roving just the same, saying, 'If it is fated, it will come.' Yet I had never thought to be dead and living.

When one of my men came back, I asked him if the people here knew who I was. He said no, only that I was the captain; they were ignorant folk, having only the Shore Folk speech, and that uncouthly. I told him to leave it so.

There is a little isle of mine, northward of Crete, with open sea around it. Pirithoos and I used to put in there, to mend our ships and get water, and sometimes to hide our loot till we could bring it home. We had a little stronghold and a house within it, looked after by one or two old girls of ours we still had a kindness for, though they were getting on.

Here, when I could be moved, I bade them bring me; and here I lay all day, or sat in the chair that I was carried to, looking at a little wall with a fig-tree in it, and a gateway, and a square of sea. The women fed me, and kept me clean, and tended me like a baby. Hour after hour I sat, watching a bird pecking a fig, or a passing sail, and thinking how I could keep my enemies in fear of me till the time was ripe to die. Yes; while the child waited for his nurse to bring the posset or the sponge, the king still thought. Him the god's stroke did not destroy. The warrior, the lover, the wrestler, the singer, he has outlived them all. He is Theseus, it seems.

There was gold on the island, as I have said, and a boat that the men could handle. I sent them out for stores, and wondered if I would ever see them more; why should men stand by me, whom the gods had all forsaken? But they came back, stocked up for winter. For four long years, my life has been in their hands. There was one, I am told, who said among his friends, 'Let us take the gold, and ask him where the rest is; it is easy to make a sick man talk. Then we can kill him, and sell the news to Idomeneus, in Crete.' I learned this from them, when they got tired at last of hearing me ask where the man had got to. Later they showed me his grave.

When I had thought what best to do, I sent the chanty-man, who was a good harper and quick-thinking, back to Athens with a letter from me, sealed with my seal. It said I had had omens, and an oracle, to go down into a secret shrine below the earth, and be purified by Mother Dia, whom I had offended. I would come back full of luck, and destroy my enemies; meantime my council must govern and uphold the laws, and have a good account to render me after. I told the man to go a long way round, changing ships often, and coming to Athens from the north. He was not to know the shrine where I was being purified, because I had parted from him on the way; if they pressed him, he had last seen me in Epiros. There are many caves in the mountains there, which are said to go down into the land of Hades. So he went off; he did his work well, and I made it good to him. None of those eleven men need ever want, nor their sons' sons.

It was no matter, I thought, whether the Athenians swallowed my tale whole. If they thought I had gone off for my own reasons, and would come back in my own time, it was enough.

The girls nursed me kindly. They had good hearts, as I had known when I gave them this quiet harbour to grow old in, not thinking I would need it too. They fetched the ancient wise-woman of the island, who came every day to rub my deadened side with oil and wine, saying the flesh would mortify without it. She knew the tales of the Shore Folk, going back to the time of the Titans, and the beginnings of men on earth; and like a child I would never let her go without a story. I had not been used to sit still, except while I thought what to do next. Sometimes it seemed the days would never end; and when night came, I would lie watching the stars, to count the hours till morning.

I thought of my life, the good and the evil days; of the gods, and fate; how much of a man's life and of his soul they make for him, how much he makes for himself. What if Pirithoos had not come for me, when I was setting out for Crete? What man would I have become? What Cretan son had gone unborn, in the years that made Hippolytos? Or what if Phaedra had cried 'Rape!' another day, when the earthquake sickness was not on me? Yet I had made already the man who heard that cry. Fate and will, will and fate, like earth and sky bringing forth the grain together; and which the bread tastes of, no man knows.

One morning when I had been there a month, or perhaps a season, I lay awake as the day was breaking. The cocks had crowed, and I could see the dark sea-margin against a glimmering sky. My thoughts were far off, at the Bull Dance, or some old war; when the floor shook beneath my bed, and my cup fell from the stand beside me. Voices of folk just wakened filled the house, calling on Earth-Shaker Poseidon. The cocks crowed again; I remembered how noisy they had been before, crying all together. To them the god had sent his warning; but none to me.

So I knew who had struck me, and why. The Immortals are just; one cannot mock them. He had cast off his son, as I had cast off mine.

One of the women came to see I had taken no harm, and picked up the fallen cup, and went away. When all was quiet again, I pulled myself up a little on my good arm, and looked at the table across the room. The knife was there, which they had cut my food with. If I roll from the bed, I thought, and along the floor, surely my arm will reach it. The earth grows weary of my weight, and has carried it long enough.

To edge myself over, I lifted my left arm with the other, to shift its weight. And as I looked at the hand, I saw the fingers moving, grasp for grasp. Only a little way; but at my will they straightened, and curved again. I touched them; the sense was dull, but it was there. The life was coming back to them.

The sun was rising. I thought of Athens, and all that I had built there. And even though the god's sign had left me, yet all that I was said, 'Mine!' So I lived, and waited.

The seasons passed. Slowly, month by month, the life crept back into the dead limbs like sap into a withered tree. After the movement and the feeling, it was as long again till some strength returned. I stood against two men's shoulders; then with one man; then holding by the chair; but it was another year before I could walk alone. And then I dragged one foot, as I do a little still.

On a day in spring, I called the women to trim my hair and beard, and asked for a mirror. I looked ten years older; my hair was almost white; the left-hand corner of my mouth and eye still had a downward turn, and that side of my face looked always sour. But it seemed men would still know me. When I was ready, I picked up my staff and walked by myself into the sunshine. My men saw me, and cheered.

That evening I sent for my steersman Idaios, and said to him, 'Soon we sail home.' He answered, 'Sir, I think it is time.'

I asked him what he meant; he said he had heard there was trouble in Athens, or some disorders, but the men he had it from were ignorant islanders, and knew no more.

When my men came and went, they had wisely kept as near the truth as they could; saying they were seamen of mine I had left upon the island to keep a base for my ships. People do not meddle with a pirate hold. With this tale, they would ask for news of me, and learn what was being said.

Idaios had made out he was telling me everything; but now he owned he had been hearing rumours about Athens for a year. 'My lord, I know you. One way or another, from doing too little or too much, you'd have come by your death. Well, I must answer for it. I did what seemed the best.'

It was a good while since others had decided what was best for me. But I owed him too much to be angry. By his lights he was right; and I am still glad we parted friends.

And yet, when I got to Athens, I wished many times I had died upon the island, suddenly, at the hand of the god; they say the second time ends a man without pain. While I was there, sitting in the little window, watching a locust nibble at a leaf, or a lizard catching flies, I thought myself unhappy; yet in my mind I still possessed the fruits of all my lifework, standing for men to see in the time to come. I was rich, if I had known.

What is this man, Menestheus? Hippolytos once asked me that; he saw further into him than I, but still not far. His own mind was too single, seeing in other men not his own image, but a god's child crying to be set free. He could never have followed to its heart that twisting labyrinth, nor seen with that squinting eye, nor read desires that did not know even themselves – he who had lent all his will to the gods of light. No; even he, if he had been King, would not have seen what he had to deal with. But maybe some god who loved him might have fought for him. None did for me.

A conqueror, a rival, I could have understood. He would have seized what I had made, and boasted of it. His bards would make songs about the great realm he had taken from King Theseus, for himself and his sons' sons. Such a man would never have left me living. But he would have left what I built to stand.

But Menestheus . . . he is like a doctor who weeps over the sick, and gives them poison, persuading himself it will do them good. He has another man within him, whom he obeys, but whose face he has never seen.

Little by little, while I was gone, the power came into his hands. But I am not even sure he plotted for it; that is, the Menestheus whom Menestheus knew. He would say of himself that he taught men to be free, to trust in themselves, to hold up their heads before men and gods, to bear no wrongs. It may be he would truly have taught these things, if the whole man had desired them.

Did he want the people to love him? Yet he himself loved no man, for what in himself he was; a man was dead to Menestheus, unless he was a cause to fight for. But when at Menestheus' urging he had embroiled himself with powerful enemies, where

Menestheus had not strength to back him, and had increased his own wrongs sixfold, then he must hate six men where he had hated one before; so much the more would Menestheus love him, and take credit for having been his friend. In my own time, when I had a wild beast like Prokrustes to put down, I never moved till I could crush him quickly, and set his prisoners free. But Menestheus, if someone was oppressive, would threaten and bluster long before he could perform, so as to be praised for hating evil; then the man grew angry, and hurt all those in his power to hurt; and Menestheus had more wrongs to shout about. Men who did good in quiet, without anger, he thought were spiritless, or corrupt. Anger he understood; but he had no kindness for men before the wrong was done, which would have kept it undone.

All custom he hated, whether it had outlived its use or not. He hated all obedience, whether to good law or bad. He would root out all honour and reverence from the earth, to keep one man from getting a scruple more than his due. Maybe there was only hatred at his core, and whatever he had found around him, that he would have destroyed. For surely if it had been men that he loved, or justice, he could have built something on the ruins that he made?

Before, when I have tried to understand my enemies, it has been to plan against them. Why try now when it is finished, why not be content to curse? But while man is man he must look and think; if not forward, back. We are born asking why, and so we end. So the gods made us.

Would he have had me poisoned or stabbed in Athens, if he had dared? The Palace people showed they loved me still; he might not have lived long after. Was it cunning, or some flaw of will, or the wish to think well of himself, that made him leave me alive to struggle with the chaos of the broken kingdoms, worse by far than they were in my father's day? When I banished him for his bad stewardship, he even went, but not very far. You need not go far now, to leave the Attic kingdom.

Crete broke away two years ago and more; Idomeneus is King there. While I was sick, every man on the island knew that but I. Megara has found a prince of its ancient kindred; and they say that now when you cross the Isthmus, once more you need a Guard of seventy spears. Only Eleusis keeps its Mystery, unchanged since Orpheus shaped it. A life is there that has grown beyond his or mine. It will take more than Menestheus, to put that out. More than darkness; a greater light.

The secrecy of my sickness has fought against me. A few of the Shore Folk heard something, wild ignorant folk who did not know where to sell it, but let it blow here and there like thistle seed. Perhaps the old wise-woman spun it into one of her tales. The truth has mixed with the lie I put about; they are saying I went down into the earth to ravish a sacred priestess, and was cursed by the Goddess, and spent four years there in a magic chair my limbs had grown to; that my legs are wasted, and my left foot limps, because when at last I was pulled free the flesh was torn away. From all this they argue that the gods are no longer with me, and my luck is out. Even missing the sea-marks, one can still make port.

I saw young Akamas, whom I left in Euboia with a chief I trust. He will be safe enough there. The people of Athens do not hate him, but think him too much a Cretan, while Menestheus is of the ancient kin. I can hardly blame him for not having stopped Menestheus, who started his work when the lad was barely fifteen. He was so shocked by the change in me, that trying to hide it took up all his mind, and it was hard to find out what he thought. But he seems not to hate Menestheus, even to think of him as a man who has done his best. Year by year, as he has been growing up, his heritage has been shrinking; it seems his ambition too has been growing backwards. Of his mother, we did not speak.

He is happiest among the other lads in Euboia, dancing and riding and making love (he does not care for girls) and being as like as he can to all the rest. I can see a day when Menestheus leads forth the men of Athens to some foreign war he should have kept them clear of, with Akamas carrying a shield under his command; if he wins honour among his comrades, he will ask no more. Yet he is my son; and, as I have seen, a god has touched him. Some day, I believe, in Athens' hour of need, the god will speak again, and give her back a King.

As for me, I cannot stand steady in a chariot now, nor grasp a shield; my left-hand fingers have never got back their grip. And I, who stood on the Rock of Athens and broke the northern hordes; who cleansed the Isthmus, and changed the customs of Eleusis; who killed Asterion Minotaur in the throne room of the Labyrinth, and carried the bounds of Attica as far as the Isle of Pelops: I will not sit down in the house of my fathers to hear young children say, 'Was that Theseus once?'

Menestheus has sowed; let him do the reaping. Yet these are my people; and I tried to warn them, before I went away. Age after age, the tides have risen in the northland. They rose in my day; they will rise again. I know that they will rise. But my face has changed, and my voice; the people thought I was calling this evil down, as a curse upon the City. And thus I parted from Athens. Maybe the gods are just; but the man is gone who could have shown it me.

It was for Crete that I set sail. Idomeneus is a man I can understand. Being once secure in power, he will be noble; and I have never wronged him, for that to make me ashamed. If I had gone to my old Palace in the south, to end my days there, he would have been courteous and free, offering me the show of kingship as I did to his father once. To sit on a Cretan terrace, watching the darkening of the grapes; a man might do worse, who can do nothing better.

So I set out from Euboia. But a wind of fate blew me to Skyros.

It is a windy island, shaped like a bull's brow; on one horn hangs the Citadel with a tall cliff under, for fear of such pirates as I have been. Not that Skyros has been the worse for me; it has a name for stony fields and half-filled grain jars, and I have never robbed the poor. King Lykomedes made me as welcome as if it were ten years back. As we sat over our wine, he told me he often puts out to sea himself upon adventure, when the last harvest has been poor. I had heard so, though our paths have never crossed. He is a man of the Shore Folk, dark-bearded, with shadowy eyes, one who does not tell all his mind. It is said of him that he was reared in the shrine at Naxos, and is the son of a priestess by the god.

Of this we did not speak. We swapped old sea-tales; and he told me he, like Pirithoos, was sent in his boyhood to the Kentaur hills. Old Handy, he says, is still alive in some high cave on Pelion; his people are fewer, but his school goes on. One of his boys, the King of Phlia's heir, is a guest here now on Skyros; hidden to avoid some fate of an early death, which his priestess mother saw in omens. They chose an island to stop him from running away; for the death-fate carried an everlasting fame along with it, and the boy would have gone consenting.

As we sat in the window, Lykomedes showed him to me, climbing up the long stairs of the rock. Up he came, out of the evening shadow into the last kiss of the sun, as springy and brisk as noonday, his arm around a dark-haired friend. The god who sent him that blazing pride should not have added love to be burned upon it. His mother will lose her pains, for he carries his doom within him. He did not see me; and yet his eyes spoke to mine.

King Lykomedes, standing at my shoulder, said, 'He was off somewhere, when your ship came in. He will think this the great day of his life, when he learns who is here. Whenever, for his father's sake, I try to keep him back from some reckless dare or other, he always tells me "Theseus would have done it". That is his touchstone for a man.'

He beckoned up his servant, saying, 'Go tell Prince Achilles to wash and put on his best, and come up here.'

I said it had been a long day and a rough crossing, and I would rather see the boy tomorrow. He called the man back and said no more of it, but led me to my room. It is near the crest of the crag; for the Palace is built into it like a swallow's nest. In the glow of the sunken sun one could see all over the island, and, beyond, great sweeps of sea.

'In clear weather,' he said, 'one sees Euboia. Yes, that point of light must be a watch-fire there. But you are used to an eagle's perch; I think your Rock is higher?'

'No,' I answered. 'Yours has a hill below it, and mine a plain. This stands higher by far. But if you take cliff for cliff, just the sheer drop, I daresay there is not much in it.'

'If my house speaks of home to you,' he said, 'so use it, and I am content.'

I lay down, being tired, and sent off my servants. I was thinking, before I fell asleep, of the flashing light-footed boy, awaiting tomorrow. It would be good to spare him that. Let him keep this Theseus who speaks for the god within him. Why change a god for a lame old man with a twisted mouth? I could warn him of what he is; but it would not alter him. Man born of woman cannot outrun his fate. What need, then, to trouble his short morning with the griefs of time? He will never live to know them.

So I was thinking, when weariness closed my eyes. I slept; and I dreamed of Marathon.

It seemed I was wakened by a great din of battle. I leaped from my naked bed; I was in old Hekaline's cottage, young again, with my arms beside me. I snatched them and ran outside. The sun shone brightly; beached along the strand was a great fleet of warships, full of outlandish warriors scrambling ashore. They were too many for pirates; it was war, and a great one; for all the men of Athens were there, drawn up to defend their fields. As one finds in dreams, there was something quaint about them; they had helms of bronze, with curving crests like the hoopoe's, and little round shields painted with beasts and birds. But I knew them for my people; and few enough they looked, facing that horde, as we were when the Scythians came. I thought of the City, the women and children waiting; and I forgot I had ever suffered wrong from Athens. Once more I was the King.

It was all foot-fighting; I don't know where the chariots were. Just then some chief started the paean, and they gave the war-yell, charging at a run. I thought, 'They know I am with them! Marathon always brought me luck, and I am the luck of Marathon.' My feet were light as I raced up through the press into the vanguard; and when I reached the line of the barbarians, in my hands was the sacred axe of Crete, that I used to kill the Minotaur. I swung it about my head; the outlanders gave backward; then the men of Athens knew me, and started to cry my name. The enemy were on the run for their ships, clambering and falling and drowning; it was victory, clear and sure. We gave a great yell of triumph; and my own noise woke me. I was lying with the moon upon my face, by the window that looked down at the crags of Skyros.

Sound travels far on a quiet night; even so high, I heard the sound of the sea.

The dream is gone; why has it left no grief of loss behind it? Hope comes in these waves, like water filling a dried-up pool. Here from the window, I see the sea smooth as a mirror spread with moonlight; yet the sound grows. Is it true, then, as Oedipus said to me at Kolonos, that the Power returns? The gods sent me as a guide to him; have they sent Lykomedes now to me? 'If my house speaks of home to you, so use it.'

Yes; it is rising. Not high and exultant, as it was upon the Pnyx; but steady, sure and strong. Bitterness scours away in it. I will not offer my death to strangers, like Oedipus of Thebes. Let Father Poseidon have it, to keep against my people's need. There will be a time, as my dream foretold. In the dream they had no king with them; maybe he would not make the offering. They knew me, and cried my name. Some harper had brought it down to them. While the bard sings and the child remembers, I shall not perish from off the Rock.

This balcony clings to the living cliff. I see a walk beyond it, threading the crag. That will do well. If I go from here, it might be said that Lykomedes murdered me. It would be discourteous to shame my host. But there is only Akamas left to ask my blood-price; and he, though he is half Cretan, knows well enough how the Erechthids die.

Surely goats made this track. That boy, Achilles, might scramble here for a dare. No place, this, for a dragging foot; but all the better. It will seem like mischance, except to those who know.

The tide comes in. A swelling sea, calm, strong and shining. To swim under the moon, onward and onward, plunging with the dolphins, singing . . . To leap with the wind in my hair . . .

Author's Note

The legend of Theseus, as it came down to the Greeks of the classical period, is briefly summarised at the end of this Note. It may be in place here, however, to explain how I interpreted the story of his youth up to his return from Crete in an earlier book, *The King Must Die*.

It is assumed there that two forms of divine kingship co-existed in Mycenaean Greece. The Pelasgians, or Shore Folk, and the Minoans, worshipped the Earth Mother, whose king consort was an inferior, expendable figure, sacrificed after each cycle of the crops so that his youth and potency could be forever renewed. Though in Crete a Greek conquest had brought hereditary kingship, parts of the old cult remained. Ariadne was its High Priestess by right of birth.

But Theseus' forebears, patriarchal invaders from the north, saw their kings as direct intermediaries between the people and the sky gods on whose life-giving rain the crops depended. On the King, therefore, devolved the noble responsibility of offering his own life as supreme sacrifice when, in times of great crisis, the auguries demanded it. Theseus, whose whole life-story implies a tension and conflict between these two principles, is supposed to have been reared in Troizen with a sense of his royal destiny, to have imposed the Olympian cult at Eleusis after a ritual king-killing, and presented himself to his father in Athens after putting down the bandits of the Isthmus in a victorious military operation. Having been recognised as King Aigeus' heir, he offered himself as a voluntary sacrifice when the Cretan tribute of youths and girls fell due.

The doom of these young people, as most scholars agree, must have been to take part in the dangerous sport of bull-leaping so often depicted in Minoan art; and I represented the Minotaur as the human son of Queen Pasiphae's adultery, plotting to destroy the dying King Minos and usurp the throne. Theseus, by his skill and leadership in the Bull Dance, kept his team of Athenians alive till in the confusion following one of the great Cretan earthquakes (of whose approach he had an inherited premonition) he led the oppressed native serfs and the captive bull-dancers in a successful revolt. Ariadne, who had fallen in love with him for his prowess in the ring and helped in his conspiracy, sailed with him for Athens. But when the ship put in at Naxos, he found to his horror that, reverting to the most savage rites of the ancient religion, she joined the maenads in the yearly Dionysiac orgy, and helped them tear their young King to pieces, like Agave in the *Bacchae* of Euripides. Abandoning her in her exhausted sleep, he went home alone. It is here that *The Bull From The Sea* takes up the story.

The Amazons of classical legend seem to be a product of two fused traditions. I see no need to doubt, though I have not adopted it, Herodotus' account of a tribe whose women, after the slaughter of all their men, preferred to form their own fighting community rather than endure the miseries of an alien bondage, so movingly described by Homer's Hector, and so little changed even in historic times. I have preferred, however, partly because it accounts so much better for the role of the Amazons in the great invasion, to make them warrior priestesses of Artemis, such as those who, Pausanias said, used to guard her sanctuary at Ephesos. Many races and religions show vestiges of such corps, sometimes surviving as the bodyguards of sacred kings. Megathenes found them in the Aryan kingdoms of North India in 300 B.C., as did Sir Richard Burton two thousand years later, though then reduced to a purely decorative function.

The Amazons of Pontos belonged traditionally to the race of the White Scythians, hence their silver hair; the single plait occurs in Anatolian figurines of girls or goddesses across several millennia. The Ephesian Amazons are said to have danced with cymbals and sistra; but the weapon-dance is derived from one that I myself have witnessed, though done by men and boys – the Moslem 'Khalifa'. It is a strange, impressive, and undoubtedly true performance; the sharp points and edges are offered to the watchers to test before, at the climax of the music, the flesh is pierced and does not bleed.

Though the later legend makes Theseus marry Phaedra only after Hippolyta's death in battle, or after a faithless rejection which caused her to declare war in revenge (but Plutarch rejects this version as corrupt), marriage to the Cretan princess was a dynastic necessity so obvious that it, or at least a betrothal, would have had to take place soon after his conquest of the island. The legend gives her more than one child by him, but says little of Akamas. After a time of refuge in Euboia, where he was reared as a private gentleman, he went, it seems still with the same status, to the Trojan War. There he proved brave and trustworthy enough to be picked for the forlorn hope in the Wooden Horse; yet nothing is said of any quarrel with Menestheus, who led the Athenians as King. Some say Menestheus was killed, others that he died, others again that he was deposed by the Athenians. In any case, Akamas succeeded to the throne, in what circumstances is not related.

His role in revealing the guilt of Phaedra is my own device. Theseus learned the truth; each teller of the tale has supplied a different mouthpiece, human or divine. The constant elements are the attempted seduction, the young man's silence under the woman's slander, Theseus' invocation of Poseidon, and the wave-borne sea bull. Since Theseus' career was not that of a stupid man, it must have needed more than a sudden wild accusation to persuade him that his son had so belied his nature. Euripides makes Phaedra hang herself, leaving a written charge against Hippolytos; a gesture persuasive enough, but rather large for so mean a purpose. I have borrowed on purpose the young man's dying words; it seems to me a possibility well worth considering, that Socrates, who faced his death with such unswerving constancy, made his offering in thanks for a revealing dream.

The dead youth vanishes in mystery. Some say the Troizenians knew his tomb, but would not show it to strangers; some that Artemis carried him to Epidauros, where Asklepios raised him from the dead, but was struck down by Zeus for this presumption. The youth was then conveyed by the goddess to Italy, where he haunts the sacred wood of Virbius disguised as an ancient man. I was once told by a witch-doctor a curious African folk tale with a rather similar ending, about an English Queen Johanna who, after founding the city of Johannesburg, was murdered by the Boers. Her son, though hidden from them till his adolescence, was murdered in his turn. They buried him in Pretoria but, to conceal the crime, put over the grave the likeness of an old man, which I identified as the Kruger Memorial. If you stand close by the statue, my informant said, sometimes you hear a little, little voice; but if the police see you listening, they move you on.

The remarkably widespread forays of Theseus in pursuit of various women have often been remarked on, and explained away in religious terms as the suppression of goddesses' shrines. But it seems to me that the ancient and aristocratic pursuit of piracy accounts for all these episodes with much less trouble.

In 490 B.C. the Persians landed at Marathon, and were thrown back by the Athenians against overwhelming odds. Afterwards the victors reported that Theseus had appeared on the field in arms to lead them, like the fighting angels of Mons. This gave great impetus to his hero-cult in Athens; and in 475 his alleged bones were brought back by Kimon from Skyros, after a campaign for which the story of Lykomedes' guest-murder must have made good propaganda. Legend says nothing of any such belief by Theseus' own heirs; and an alternative version, in which Theseus fell from the cliff by a slip of the foot, continued to survive. The likeness of his death to his father's is very striking.

His epitaph may best be left to Plutarch. 'His tomb is a sanctuary and refuge for runaway slaves, and all men of low estate who fear the mighty; in memory that Theseus while he lived defended the oppressed, and heard the suppliant's prayer with kindness.'

The Legend of Theseus as told in Classical Greece

King Aigeus of Athens, dogged by misfortune and childless through the enmity of Aphrodite, established her worship in Athens and went to consult the Delphic Oracle. It enjoined him not to untie his wine-skin till he reached home again, or he would die one day of grief. On his way back through Troizen he told his story to King Pittheus, who, guessing that some notable birth was portended, led Aigeus while drunk to the bed of his daughter Aithra. Later in the same night, she was commanded in a dream to wade over to the island shrine of Athene, where Poseidon also lay with her. When Aigeus awoke he left his sword and sandals under an altar of Zeus, telling Aithra, if a son was born, to send him to Athens as soon as he could lift the stone. This feat Theseus achieved when only sixteen; he was then already a youth of heroic size and strength, skilled with the lyre, and the inventor of scientific wrestling.

Choosing to travel to Athens by the Isthmus road, in order to prove himself against its dangers, he overthrew in single combat all the monsters and tyrants who made its travellers their prey. In Megara he killed the giant sow Phaia, and in Eleusis slew King Kerkyon, who slaughtered wayfarers by forcing them to wrestle to the death.

When he reached Athens, the witch Medea, his father's mistress, divined his parentage, and to secure her own son's succession persuaded Aigeus that this formidable youth was a threat to his throne. Aigeus prepared a poisoned cup to give him at a public feast; but Theseus displayed the sword in the nick of time. Aigeus dashed the cup from his lips and joyfully embraced him; the witch escaped in her chariot drawn by winged dragons.

Aigeus adopted Theseus as his heir amid public rejoicing; Pallas, the former heir, and his fifty sons, were killed by the young prince or driven into exile. Theseus won further honour by taming a wild bull which was ravaging the Marathon plain. Soon after, however, the City was plunged in mourning by the arrival of the Cretan tribute-vessel, with a demand for the boys and girls regularly sent off to be devoured by the Minotaur.

King Minos of Crete had been provided by Poseidon, in answer to a vow, with a magnificent bull for sacrifice, but had kept it for himself. As a punishment Aphrodite visited his queen, Pasiphae, with a monstrous passion for it, which she consummated within a hollow cow made for her by Daidalos the master-craftsman. Their offspring was the Minotaur, a being with a man's body and bull's head, who fed on human flesh. To conceal his shame, Minos had an impenetrable Labyrinth made by Daidalos, where he withdrew from the world, and in the heart of the maze concealed the Minotaur, introducing a supply of human victims into his den.

The quota from Athens was seven youths and seven maidens. Among these went Theseus; according to most versions, by his own choice, though others say by lot. At his departure, his father charged him to change the black sail of the sacrificial ship to a white one, should he return alive.

On his arrival at Crete, Minos mocked his claim to be the son of Poseidon, and challenged him to retrieve a ring thrown in the sea. Theseus received from the sea-nymphs not only the ring, but the golden crown of Thetis. His exploit caused Minos' daughter, Ariadne, to fall in love with him; she gave him in secret a ball of thread with which to retrace his steps through the Labyrinth, and a sword to kill the Minotaur.

This deed accomplished, Theseus gathered the Athenian youths; but the girls were imprisoned apart. Theseus had prepared for this in Athens by training two brave but effeminate-looking boys to take the place of two girl victims. These unbarred the women's quarters, and all the victims escaped to Athens, taking with them Ariadne, whom, however, Theseus abandoned on the island of Naxos. Dionysos, finding her there, became enamoured of her and made her the chief of his maenad train. Coming in sight of Athens, Theseus forgot to change the mourning sail for a white one, with the result that Aigeus in grief leaped off the

Acropolis, or off a high rock into the sea. Theseus thus succeeded to the throne.

During his reign he is said to have unified Attica and given laws to its three estates of landowner, farmer and craftsman. He was famed for his protection of ill-used servants and slaves, for whom his shrine remained a sanctuary down to historic times. Pirithoos, King of the Lapiths, raided his cattle as a challenge; but the young warriors took to each other in the field and swore eternal friendship. Theseus took part in the Kaledonian Boar-Hunt and the battle of the Lapiths and Kentaurs, and is said to have emulated the feats of Herakles. In a foray against the Amazons he carried off their queen Hippolyta. Later her people in revenge invaded Attica; but Hippolyta took the field at Theseus' side, where an arrow killed her. Before this however she had borne him a son, Hippolytos.

After her death, Theseus sent for and married Phaedra, King Minos' youngest daughter. Hippolytos was now a strong and beautiful youth, devoted to horsemanship and to the chaste cult of Artemis, his mother's tutelary deity. Soon Phaedra was seized with a consuming passion for him, and begged her old nurse to plead her cause. Upon his shocked refusal she hanged herself, leaving a letter which accused him of her rape. Theseus, convinced by the fact of her death, drove out his son, and invoked the death-curse entrusted to him by his father Poseidon. As Hippolytos drove his chariot along the rocky coastal road, the god sent a huge wave, bearing on its crest a sea bull, which stampeded his horses. His battered corpse was brought back to Theseus, who had learned the truth too late.

Thereafter, Theseus' luck forsook him. While helping in Pirithoos' attempt to abduct Persephone, he was confined in the underworld in torment for four years, till Herakles released him. On his return he found Athens sunk into lawlessness and sedition. Failing to restore the rule of law, he cursed the City and set sail for Crete. On the way he stopped at Skyros, where through his host's treachery he fell off a high rock into the sea.

Select Bibliography

PLUTARCH. *Life of Theseus*

M. VENTRIS AND J. CHADWICK. *Documents in Mycenaean Greek*

L. R. PALMER *Mycenaean Greek Texts from Pylos, Achaeans and Indo-Europeans*

J. CHADWICK. *The Earliest Greeks*

A. J. B. WACE. *Mycenae; the Mycenae Tablets*

J. D. S. PENDLEBURY. *The Palace of Minos, Knossos*

C. ZERVOS. *L'Art de la Crète, Néolithique et Minoenne*

I. THALLON HILL. *The Ancient City of Athens*

The Principal Upanishads, ed. S. RADHAKRISHNAN

R. GRAVES. *The Greek Myths*

ERANOS YEAR BOOKS 2. *The Mysteries*

W. F. OTTO. *The Homeric Gods*

G. GLOTZ. *Ancient Greece at Work*

M. I. FINLAY. *The World of Odysseus*

L. COTTRELL. *The Bull of Minos*

HERODOTUS. *History*

C. KERENYI. *The Gods of the Greeks*
     The Heroes of the Greeks

H. L. LORIMER. *Homer and the Monuments*

BOTHMER. *Amazons in Greek Art*

G. C. ROTHERY. *The Amazons in Antiquity and Modern Times*

L. CASSON. *The Ancient Mariners*

E. O. JAMES. *The Cult of the Mother Goddess*

S. MARINATOS. *Crete and Mycenae*

Also by Mary Renault in Arrow:
The Alexander Trilogy

Fire From Heaven

The boy Alexander, and his rise to power

At twenty, when his reign began, Alexander The Great was already a seasoned soldier and a complex, passionate man. *Fire From Heaven* tells the story of the boy Alexander, and the years that shaped him. Resolute, fearless, inheriting a striking beauty, Alexander still needed much to make him The Great. He must survive, though with lifelong scars, the dark furies of his Dionysiac mother, who kept him uncertain even of his own paternity; respect his father's talent for war and kingcraft, though sickened by his sexual grossness; and come to terms with his heritage from both.

The Persian Boy

Alexander The Great through the eyes of his lover and servant

The Persian Boy tells the story of the climactic last seven years of Alexander The Great's life through the eyes of his lover, Bagoas. Abducted and gelded as a boy, Bagoas was sold as a courtesan to King Darius of Persia, but found freedom with Alexander after the Macedon army conquered his homeland. Taken as an attendant into Alexander's household, the beautiful young eunuch becomes the great general's lover and their relationship sustains Alexander as he survives assassination plots, the demands of two foreign wives, a mutinous army, and his own ferocious temper.

Funeral Games

The death of Alexander The Great

As *Funeral Games* opens, Alexander The Great lies dying. Around his body gather the generals, the provincial satraps and the royal wives, already competing for the prizes of power and land. Only Bagoas, the Persian boy mourning in the shadows, wants nothing. Tracing the events of the fifteen years following Alexander's death, *Funeral Games* sees his mighty empire disintegrate, and brings Mary Renault's Alexander trilogy to a dramatic close.

arrow books